HIGH
RISK

VIVIAN AREND

BERKLEY BOOKS, NEW YORK

THE BERKLEY PUBLISHING GROUP
Published by the Penguin Group
Penguin Group (USA) Inc.
375 Hudson Street, New York, New York 10014, USA

USA / Canada / UK / Ireland / Australia / New Zealand / India / South Africa / China

Penguin Books Ltd., Registered Offices: 80 Strand, London WC2R 0RL, England
For more information about the Penguin Group, visit penguin.com.

HIGH RISK

A Berkley Book / published by arrangement with the author

For information, address: The Berkley Publishing Group,
a division of Penguin Group (USA) Inc.,
375 Hudson Street, New York, New York 10014.

ISBN: 978-0-425-26333-4

PUBLISHING HISTORY
Berkley mass-market edition / March 2013

PRINTED IN THE UNITED STATES OF AMERICA

10 9 8 7 6 5 4 3 2 1

Cover art by Gene Mollica. Cover design by Lesley Worrell.
Interior text design by Laura K. Corless.

ALWAYS LEARNING   PEARSON

ACKNOWLEDGMENTS

Wonderful people have encouraged me at every step of this adventure. Anne Scott brought me into the publishing world and guided me through everything from track changes to how to fill plot holes. Bree Bridges and Donna Herren have been my sounding board (or two by four) as needed. Maya Banks's encouragement to try something new came at just the right time. My agent, Kim Whalen, is a rock star in her own right, not even blinking when I submitted a "so, I kind of have an idea, what do you think?" proposal. And now the team at Berkley lifts me to new heights: Cindy Hwang is every bit as amazing as I'd heard. The art department has brought Marcus and Becki to life.

To every one of you: Thanks for sharing your skills and cheering me on.

PROLOGUE
||||||||||||||||||||||||||

September
Grand Teton, Wyoming

Thick fog enveloped her, fading the brilliant green needles of the nearby spruce to a nondescript grey. Becki adjusted her grasp on the climbing rope, reset her feet. Worked to steady the rolling in her gut.

"You ready? Sometime today would be great." Dane's teasing tones removed the sting from his words.

"Bastard," Becki muttered as she peered over her shoulder in yet another futile attempt to find a safe path off the mountainside. What she needed was for the dense cloud cover that had rolled in out of season and out of nowhere to vanish.

"I heard that."

She snorted in spite of the fear tangoing in her veins. "Bastard with Superman hearing. Good for you." She squinted, then opened her eyes as wide as possible. It was no use. "Dane, I can't see a bloody thing. I could be on route, or hanging over a thousand-foot free fall for all I know."

"You want me to go first?"

Now he offered. "You couldn't have said something fifteen minutes ago? Jerk."

He laughed. The familiar sound warmed her in spite of the tension there'd been between them the entire weekend. She and Dane had been climbing partners and lovers for long enough to forgive a few strained conversations.

"Yeah, but I'm *your* jerk, right?"

Becki sighed. Even with his moments of childishness, and the peculiar way he'd been acting the past couple of weeks, she did care for him as much as she cared for anyone. "Yes, Dane, you're my jerk."

"Bec? Love you."

She leaned back, staring up the hillside. Maybe a glimpse of his face would explain the uncharacteristic quiver in his voice. "Dane?"

All hell broke loose.

The rock wall to her left gave way, an entire slab of granite dropping in one chunk. A splash of red flashed past as Dane shrieked. Becki's heart pounded, the echo of her own scream loud in her ears. Then her rope harness jerked, dragging her upward, slamming her against the mountainside as she lost her footing.

As Dane fell, the rope connection between them dragged her in the opposite direction toward their safety anchor. She twisted, tucking in her legs, using her elbows and upper arms to attempt to belay their motion. Scrambling for a firm hold, palms ripping against small rocks.

As quickly as it began, Becki jolted to a stop.

Knuckles throbbing with pain, breath ragged, she grabbed blindly for where the rope attached to her climbing belt. She slid her aching hands upward, following the thick cord to discover the coarse bark of a stump, the twisted fibers tangled around the jagged protrusion.

She hauled herself higher using small footholds, clinging to the mountain until she could add additional loops to make the accidental anchor more secure.

She screamed into the misty abyss. "Dane."

No answer.

Becki alternated between glancing down for a sign of her partner and peering upward, trying to calculate how far from the top she was.

The eerie silence from below caused her hands to shake. Her limbs jerked as she climbed, adjusting ropes, anchoring herself and keeping Dane's lifeline in control.

A soft breeze pushed the clouds against her, soaking her to the skin, but increasing her hopes. If the wind picked up and blew away the mist, she'd be able to see Dane easier.

"Dane."

Still no answer as she scrambled to set additional anchors.

Another moment passed before she managed to pull herself over the lip, now farther to the right than she'd been when they first reached the edge to rappel down. The sight of the raw new surface where the mountain had given way made bile rise. She shoved away the fear—she'd have time to freak out after her partner was safe.

"Dane. Answer me, dammit. Whistle."

The rope was heavy with his weight, so she had to assume he was unconscious. Becki calmed her breathing and centered herself, methodically grabbing the equipment she needed to belay him.

The wind increased as she worked, flapping the edges of her hood as if ghostly fingers were playing with her. Visibility improved as she maneuvered into position, each move careful yet as rapid as possible.

"I got you, Dane. Hang in there, okay? Everything's going to be fine."

She wrapped her fingers around the cord to haul him to safety.

The mountain shifted again.

The secondary rope she'd anchored to a sturdy tree snagged tight before she'd fallen more than a couple of meters. The backup system locked her in position as the main rope, the one leading to Dane, jerked erratically. Becki skidded on the moving rocks, scrambling to find a place to stand. She twisted, planting her feet into a wide stance to stop from spinning. It worked enough to put her facing the wall, a shower of stones descending from above and crashing into her shoulders. Instinctively she ensured the safety lock on Dane's lifeline was engaged, her fingers moving rapidly even as something heavy struck her helmet, and the world went black.

CHAPTER 1
''''''''''''''''''''''''''''''

May
Banff National Park

"I'd like to fire their asses. Every damn one of them." Marcus stared out his office window at the clouds wafting past Mount Rundle. The peaceful serenity of the Banff panorama didn't match his internal turmoil.

"You'd regret it when you get a call and need a full crew to go save a Boy Scout troop in trouble." David gestured for him to sit. "Stop pacing. Your team made a mistake. They screwed up. Look on the good side. It was a training exercise, and no one died."

If they'd still been teens, Marcus would have thrown a fist in David's direction. "Look on the good side? Since when did you become Suzy fucking Sunshine? You ripped the ears off one of your first-year students last month for messing up. I hold my team to a higher standard than a bunch of rescue wannabes."

"My student? Oh, come on. That's different." David snapped his mouth shut, probably annoyed that his rare outburst had been carried on the grapevine.

Marcus dropped into his desk chair, pleased to witness

his brother's guilty expression. Being fuming mad didn't mean he couldn't enjoy taking a dig or two. He was glad they didn't work together, though. Years ago David had taken his backcountry skills in a different direction, choosing to pass on his expertise to the next generation. He'd established one of the highest-ranked training centres in North America. Graduates from David's institute were currently employed across the United States and Canada, hauling people out of life-and-death situations in the mountains and rivers of national parks and other wilderness settings.

Teaching had never been on Marcus's agenda. Instead, he'd been busy saving the bloody world. Using his abilities in one or another of the hot zones where getting caught was less a matter of apologizing and offering restitution, and more about picking up as many pieces as you could find and shoving them into a bag to take home.

Now, years later, Banff had become a safe place where when things got tough, there was someone who cared unconditionally. Because he was the first to admit there were times he was less than easy to get along with.

David nabbed a magazine off the side table and shook it at him. "This conversation isn't about my school, or my students. If your squad blew it, deal with it. They need a bit of boot camp. They're spoiled. Being named 'the best of the best' has gone to their heads. Plus, they're spending more time in the bar enjoying people fawning over them than they are training—it adds up, bro. Mistakes were bound to happen."

Excuses weren't acceptable. Marcus shook his head. "Not on my watch. That's not what getting selected to work for Lifeline is about. I expect them to be on all the time, David."

"I know, I know. When you organized your squad, you said you were going to keep it tight and make it special. Three years—God, I can't believe it's been such a short time. You've done amazing things with them, but maybe you need to regroup."

Marcus dragged his hand through his hair and consciously released a slow breath. Regrouping was what he was doing, but pouring a tall glass of something strong and forgetting everything for a while was tempting.

Three years didn't seem like long enough to have changed his entire direction in life. Globe-trotting and working undercover—he hadn't expected the secretive recovery operations he'd been involved with to last forever, but he'd never thought his career would vanish with one bad decision.

On someone else's part.

He glanced involuntarily at the stump of his left arm. On a side table just beyond his line of sight lay his modified prosthetic, the one he wore only when absolutely necessary. Physically he'd healed and moved on. Mentally—there were still days when cursing wasn't enough.

Still, returning to Banff after he'd been discharged from the hospital had been a no-brainer. Setting up a private rescue company had always been the fallback plan for when he decided to get out of working for others. He'd recruited the best, trained them hard, and now they were the go-to squad called in for high-risk and impossible rescues.

The sight of one of that elite team Z-clipping during a routine training exercise and potentially killing more than the rescue attempt flashed into his brain again, and he growled in frustration. "If this is what becoming famous does, I'm keeping my squad in the dark from here on. I should have told that reporter to take his damn camera and shove it up his ass."

"Don't blame Nathan for writing the article. Blame *Sports Illustrated* for publishing it and making the theme for the entire magazine a salute to your 'death-defying gods and goddesses of the wilderness.'"

"Stow it. We've established what caused the problem. My team has gotten fat and lazy sitting on their laurels."

"So, increase their regular training. We're between skiing and hiking season. With the school on semester break until June first, you're welcome to access any of the equipment. Perfect time for some intense workouts to get their act together." David sneered. "Maybe you should consider joining them instead of teaching from the sidelines."

Bastard. David was the only one brave enough to taunt him. "You implying I'm out of shape?"

"If the tire fits—"

Marcus threw a pen across the room, his brother deflecting it easily. "I've been coordinating, not flying rescues. Plus dealing with office work. I'm still in shape—I'm not too weak to beat your ass."

"Fine, you're in decent physical shape, but you're nowhere near as technically qualified as before." David lifted his chin in challenge. "And don't give me the excuse you only have one arm, because you told me from day one you'd never let that hold you back."

"Goddammit, you are a son of a bitch sometimes, aren't you?"

His brother grinned. "I know very well that you were the inspiration behind a lot of those kids wanting to sign on with Lifeline. If the legend can let himself go soft . . . Think about it."

He had been. Marcus pulled out a file folder and tossed it across his desk. "Fine. You win. ASAP the team is back in basic training."

It only took a few minutes for David to flip through the pages, swearing softly. He dropped the file to the floor, one page clutched in his hand. "You tricky bastard, you already had a plan organized even while you were bitching at me. When did you get this in place?"

Pulling a fast one on his brother felt damn good. "Your school secretary has been amazing. I'm thinking of stealing her away."

"You can't afford her." The single page David had pulled was shaken in his direction. "You don't have anyone listed for rope training."

Marcus shook his head. "Your lead instructor said he's got plans for the semester break. You have any other ideas?"

A grin broke across David's face so quickly it was frightening. "It's funny you ask. I just brought in an expert to plan some specialized classes. She's going to join the school next semester as a general instructor and overseer."

"She?"

"Rebecca James."

His brother said her name so casually. As if she weren't the one woman everyone in the mountain community knew. David must have been itching to share his good fortune in nabbing her for a job.

A shot of adrenaline flared through Marcus's body in direct opposition to what David was probably expecting. *Holy shit.* Holy fucking shit.

Becki James.

He determinedly copied David's nonchalance. "She's going into teaching?"

David nodded slowly. "Her contract with the U.S. Parks Department in Yellowstone was up anyway, and she said she wanted to take a little time off, so I issued an invitation."

For one brief second a kind of panic hit as Marcus wondered if this was a setup, if his brother had arranged this to jerk him out of his gloom. The sensation faded as rapidly as it arrived. As far as he knew, the long-ago sexual escapade between him and Becki was still a complete secret. The chances that David would remember he'd visited the school while she was a student were slim. If he was going to keep it that way, he needed his alarm to remain hidden.

"You have a funny idea of time off if you asked her to come teach. Wasn't it you who suggested I go somewhere like a deserted island for my next holiday so I didn't feel the need to keep rescuing people?"

"Face it, bro, you're just a big old Saint Bernard."

Right. "Tell that to the team who fucked up their rope climb yesterday. I doubt they were calling me a Saint Bernard last night. Pit bull, asshole, scary son of a bitch—those were more likely the names crossing their lips."

David grinned. "Gee, I wonder why. . . ."

Marcus stopped for a moment and considered. He might have an ulterior motive in asking the question, but it was a legitimate one. "Is Rebecca any good as a teacher? I mean, we got the media reports last September, and that's it. She may have been involved in a high-profile rescue, but field-work isn't teaching. You know that."

"One of the best. She trained here, you know."

"Really? Why didn't you mention that sooner?" This conversation was going nowhere fast. David seemed pleased to have scored such a high-ranked instructor.

Marcus changed mental tracks. Would having her around be an issue? So what if he and Becki had a slight sexual history?

Although calling it *slight* turned it into the biggest bullshit of the day yet.

"She's a BSR grad, and she's in town?"

David nodded. "Staying in the school dorms. I offered her a hotel room until the teachers' apartments are done being renovated, but she said she was happy to use a student space while the kids are on break for the next three weeks. Why don't you go see her? Take her out for lunch."

A sneaky suspicion stole over Marcus. "Why?"

David blinked. "What do you mean? So you can ask her to train your squad."

"Maybe we should let her settle in. Enjoy the break before semester begins."

"Look, if you don't want the best for your team, that's fine. I'm not telling you to fuck her. Just be nice to her. Make her feel welcome."

Marcus choked on hearing *fuck her.*

David must have thought his reaction meant something else. He glared across the room. "Goddamn, Marcus. If *Sports Illustrated* had heard about her before Lifeline, they'd have forgotten you completely."

"Fine. What room is she in?"

David flipped him off. "So glad you're willing to make the sacrifice. Three-oh-five. I know she arrived this morn-ing, but I can't guarantee she's there. And she said she needed to pick up a new cell phone today rather than use her U.S. one, so I don't even have a number for you to call."

Marcus waved it off. "Details. I can track her down."

"Hey." David gave him a dirty look, and suddenly it was twenty years earlier, and Marcus was being warned by his more cautious sibling. "Don't be an ass to her. I want her to stay, and I don't need you mucking around."

Oh, Jesus. Mucking around was totally off the agenda for so damn many reasons. "When am I an ass?"

"Lately? Most of the time." David reassembled the file and returned it to the desk. "You are the best at what you do. I mean it, Marcus. But you've also gotten cold over the past year. Try to lighten up, okay? I know we're in a tough business, and there are moments we've got to be serious, but you're not the same guy you used to be. I kind of miss him."

Marcus thumped his brother on the back and walked him to the door. "Hopefully he's still around. Maybe I'll find him as I polish up my technical skills."

And maybe pigs would fly.

He didn't need to be all light and sparkly to be good at what he did, but there was no reason to argue that point right now. And walking back into Becki's life after seven years— hell of a way to try to lighten up.

Becki closed the closet, a sense of déjà vu hitting as her clothing vanished behind the familiar wooden doors. Even though the fabric on the other side of the door was a lot more expensive than when she'd first walked into the school, the garments were pretty much the same. Comfortable, easy to wear. Except for the single fancy dress she'd brought along on a whim, Mountain Equipment Co-op was still her designer of choice.

She strolled to the window to reacquaint herself with the surroundings. Set on the hillside, the dorms had the most spectacular view of Mount Rundle, its distinctive jagged top cutting an angled line against the pastel-blue Alberta sky. Small, pale-green buds trembled in the light breeze. The trees were slower to leaf out here than in nearby Calgary, the higher elevation and cooler nights of the mountains holding back the spring.

The window was already open. Fresh air flooded the room and swirled over the queen-size bed. Beyond the increased size of sleeping arrangements, not much else had changed from when she'd been a student. A desk. A bulletin board on the wall with a single motivating quote painted across the top: *I am the captain of my soul.*

It was like going back in time, and a shiver raced up her spine.

She'd agreed quickly enough when David Landers asked her to accept a teaching position, then gotten to ponder the why of her rapid decision at leisure the entire trip from Jackson, Wyoming, to Banff. She wasn't twenty-three anymore. She wasn't the headstrong, dynamic leader admired and hated in turns by her classmates.

Only she wasn't really sure who she was instead. Somewhere along the way, she'd lost track.

And when you got lost, you went back to the beginning and started again.

On an impulse, Becki slid open the desk drawer. She pulled out the set of coloured markers she suspected she'd find there. A sheet of paper joined the markers on the desktop, and without any further consideration she wrote in block letters.

BEGINS WITH A SINGLE STEP

She tacked the bold statement in the middle of the bulletin board before stepping away to examine it. As a motivation, that was all she needed. She didn't have to solve all the problems of who she was right now, who she'd be in the future. One step at a time, she'd find out.

The sunshine beckoned, so she exchanged her travel clothes for running pants, adding a water bottle holder. She was debating gloves or no gloves—temperatures were still nippy—when there was a knock on the door.

She peered out the security peephole and nearly died.

Marcus.

His face had matured. She'd thought him handsome before, all those years ago, but at thirty he'd still been young. Not *babyish*—that word would never have crossed anyone's mind in describing Marcus—but more like *unrealized potential*. Now? His cheeks and jaw were firmer, his blue eyes just as alert. Small character lines extended from the corners, and she wanted to touch them. To smooth away the crease marks between his brows.

His shoulders were as wide as she remembered, his open jacket stretched over a firm chest. Her mouth went dry recalling exactly how firm his body had been. Was.

He knocked again and she jerked into action, even as memories tumbled in her brain.

As the door opened, Marcus dragged on his best manners. *See, David, I can be something better than an asshole when I want to be.*

He pinned his smile in place as he spoke to the woman slowly coming into view. "Rebecca James? I don't know if you remember me. . . ."

A rock slide couldn't have hit with more impact. Even knowing she was going to be there didn't reduce the shock. The face before him wasn't only pretty, it was familiar. Very familiar. He hadn't seen it in real life for years, but he'd seen it plenty in his mind.

Her eyes lit for a split second before her smile faded, as if she weren't sure what to do next.

He sure the hell didn't.

"Hi, Marcus. Nice to see you again." She straightened, clutching the front of her water bottle holder. "Are you visiting David?"

"I live here."

"In Banff? Since when?"

"For the past four years." He gestured into the room, still reeling from the shock. "And you've gone back to your student days."

Suddenly that was the worst possible thing he could have said, because all he could picture was her naked and spread before him—on the bed, in the giant tub at the Banff Springs Hotel. Up against the wall, her skin slick with moisture as he pinned her in place and rocked his cock into her willing body again and again.

One wicked weekend. Taking him and breaking him apart with her sensuality.

He was staring—he knew he was. But her lips were still firm, that hint of mischief there as she smiled. While her dark brown hair was pulled back into a tidy ponytail, his mental images were of it tousled around her head as he held himself over her, intimately connected. The curves of her body were clearly visible under her tight running outfit, and he had the urge to strip her and see exactly how well his memories lined up with the new reality.

The door shifted position and Marcus snapped his gaze off her hips, where he'd been momentarily trapped.

Her smile had gotten bigger. "Seems you haven't changed much."

Her teasing tone saved his butt. She wasn't pissed off; that was good. He leaned against the door frame, and this time it was his turn to have her touch him with her gaze, assessing, weighing.

He saw it on her face, the moment she spotted his arm. Or more accurately, where his arm wasn't. The empty lower sleeve on his left was pinned up so it wouldn't flap. It was a simple enough solution that at a glance left tourists in town completely oblivious.

"Oh, damn. Marcus? When . . . ? I'm so sorry."

The sexual buzz died in a flash as he prepared to reassure her, and be all understanding and shit. The usual hassle he went through when dealing with someone about to freak over his missing limb.

He expected her to flee into her room in disgust, or stand frozen uncertain what to do—the two most common responses to his amputation. It shocked the hell out of him when she moved forward instead and planted her hand on his shoulder. He was the one rendered speechless as she lightly squeezed lower and lower until she found the end of the stump, just past his elbow.

She nodded briefly a second before deep crimson flushed her face. "Oh, dear. That was really, really rude. I'm sorry."

He caught her with his right hand before she could step

back. "No worries. Refreshing response, actually. It's nice to see you're not going to run screaming in terror."

Her jaw dropped. "No. Way. You're telling me that—no, later. First, how long ago?"

"Four years."

Understanding lit her eyes. "Way to be welcomed home. I am sorry. You mind talking about it?"

He released his grip on her upper arm, letting his fingers slip over the soft fabric of her running shirt like a caress. There was more to the woman now than when she'd been a hotshot rock star on the climbing wall. Getting her to help train his crew was no longer the only thing on his agenda.

"I don't mind telling the story, but I'm interrupting your run. Shall I come back later? Can I take you out for lunch? I'd like to talk to you about a few things."

More than a few things.

She didn't hesitate. "You want to run with me? I can wait until you get changed."

Oh God. He hadn't lied to David when he said he'd been keeping in shape the best he could, but if Becki was anything now like she'd been years ago, he didn't expect a run with her to be a light stroll through the park. Becki always had been all about the challenges.

What the hell. He'd never stepped back from a challenge before. "I have workout gear in the staff room. Meet me by the gym doors?"

Becki nodded as her thorough examination of him resumed. Marcus forced his thoughts to icebergs and math equations to keep his body from responding to the heat in her eyes. Running was going to be bad enough without his dick being hard.

She was finally done, the seductive smile that had first caught his attention so long ago firmly back in place. "Then I'll finish getting ready and see you there."

He was still staring at her ass when she closed the door on him.

CHAPTER 2

''''''''''''''''''''''''''''''''

She set one foot on the railing and stretched as she waited, wondering again if her instinctive urge to blurt the first thing she thought of would ever lessen.

Asking Marcus to join her? Fine—they had years to catch up on. They hadn't had much of a relationship before he'd disappeared, and even casual acquaintances could enjoy a spur-of-the-moment workout. A *get to know you better* outing.

But join her on a *run*?

She'd have to stop the post-training images from distracting her. The ones where he stripped off his shirt as they stretched, the slick of sweat on his skin highlighting his muscles. He had aged well. She wanted to know if his abdomen was still rock solid, and if when he pressed his body over hers if he'd be able to hold her trapped with one hand—

And that was exactly where this wasn't supposed to go.

She sighed. Taking control of her rampaging thoughts, she leaned against the side of the building and stared into the forest, skimming her gaze over the bits and pieces of the city visible in the distance. As if someone had taken a snapshot of her years ago, and she'd stepped back in time. It was familiar, and yet she wasn't the same person. This wasn't about going home, not really. It was a new beginning.

The door beside her opened and Marcus walked out, his head snapping toward her as a sexy melt-her-panties smile lit his face.

Starting new? They'd had only one weekend. Who was to say they couldn't simply have another sometime?

He held out water, condensation glistening on the surface of the plastic. "I grabbed you a cold one from the staff fridge."

Becki accepted it happily, pouring the icy water into the bottle that fit in her belt holder. Marcus threw the empty into the gym and tugged the door shut behind him.

"How long and how hard?" she asked. The question escaped before she could consider the innuendo. Her face must have been beet red.

His grin widened. "An hour, and I'm game for hill repeats, if you are."

The old training routes around the school were still etched into her mind. "Heartbreak Hill?"

He nodded, and they moved in unison to the relatively level warm-up path. The wide trail wove through the forested area, small rises and dips, nothing too imposing.

The temporary silence between them felt easy, but her curiosity needed to be answered. "You returned four years ago? So that means you got back a year after I left."

Marcus dodged a fallen branch. "I needed a home base. David was still happy here in Banff, and I figured, why not?"

"Are you teaching, then?"

"No, I organized a private search-and-rescue company. The federal government can't keep up with the demand to haul people's butts out of trouble, so I stepped in."

Becki nodded. It was exactly the kind of job she'd expected him to be involved in. "I hear you. I've been doing something similar in Yellowstone for the past couple of years."

They fell silent as the incline increased. Marcus enjoyed the pump of blood through his limbs, the sense of energy he always got when pushing his body. Becki ran with an effortless gait, her muscles firm as they flexed and extended in rhythmic rotations.

"Five repeats?" she asked, and Marcus swore.

"Glutton for punishment?"

Becki jogged on the spot as they eyed the steep slope of the hill before them. "Preventive maintenance. It's been years since I set foot in the candy shop, and I'd far prefer to pay for my overindulgence prior to devouring the fudge than after."

Flashbacks to drizzling chocolate sauce over her skin and licking her clean weren't going to help him finish this workout. "Fine. Set number one."

He took off immediately, thinking to get the jump on her, but she'd turned as he'd spoken, and he found himself staring eye level at her ass. The curve of where her long legs met her gently rounded cheeks flexed right there in front of him.

His goddamn dick got hard.

Fortunately the incline they headed up was enough that the pain setting into his muscles offered distraction. It was a near-vertical sprint, like racing a set of stairs in the fire hall, although without the hose over his shoulder. Together they dodged the rough footing, the massive exposed rocks creating a maze to weave between. They crested the summit of the hill and slowed. Breathing heavily, chests rising and falling, they sucked for oxygen and jogged the cutline back to the base for round two.

"You're in good shape," he managed, without sounding too much like a pack-a-day smoker.

Becki gave him a grin. "One of the rules you taught me. Give one hundred percent."

"Ha, you remember those lessons?" A flush of desire

swept him. What was he saying? He remembered in freak-ish detail everything she'd taught *him* that weekend.

They were at the bottom of the hill, and Becki turned toward him. Her chin went down slightly, and she stared from under her lashes. "Those lessons were very memo-rable."

Goddamn fucking yes. He wasn't sure whether he should smile or run like a scared little girl as her expression grew more sultry by the second.

Did he want a repeat of their wild fling? Hell, yeah, but he wasn't sure of the big picture right now, and if she was going to talk about rules, then he was going to go back to the first one he'd insisted on teaching her so long ago.

Be patient.

They were here now, and adults—they had more to explore than simply the brain-melting physical attraction they'd shared. If things worked out, the sex would come later. He wanted to know more about where she'd been, and what she was doing now. Since David had persuaded her to join the school, she'd be around for at least a year. Time enough to reignite the sheets.

So he took the easy out.

"Round two?"

She was gone without a word, and once again he faced the torment of staring at her ass the entire sprint up the hillside.

The gym had been renovated since the last time she was there. The mats were sparkling new, super-cushiony, and an incredible selection of auto-belayers lined the south wall. The entire face of the east wall was also covered from floor to ceiling in climbing holds, including a lovely overhang section that made her fingers itch to test them.

She finished admiring the renovations from her relaxed position flat on her back. With one leg raised to the ceiling, she flexed her ankle, pulling the limb closer and groaning at how good it felt to stretch the tight muscles.

Stony silence greeted her from her left.

"Did I wear you out?" she asked, hiding her amusement. Marcus had been less talkative the second half of their run, and she didn't think it was because he was exhausted.

The mats squeaked as he rolled farther away from her, rising to face the wall as he stretched his hamstrings. "A little."

Liar. Every move he made screamed she was driving him crazy. She'd been the center of focused attention before, his and other men's. She knew when someone was checking her out, and the tingle inside was no less inspiring than it had been years ago.

"I'm impressed with what David has done to the place. You ever stop in and help with the classes anymore?"

This time he turned to face her, and the heat in his eyes was enough to send a streak of fire through her core. Oh God, she was going to melt right there on the crash mat. She debated squeezing her legs together to ease a little of the throbbing in her clit, but that would be as obvious as rubbing a hand over herself.

He cleared his throat and glanced away. "I'm usually too busy to come and deal with the students. I've got my team in place—don't need anyone new right now."

The steam building between them was borderline tangible. Touchable, boiling-point hot, making her needy and aching all at the same time. The weariness in her limbs had been replaced by another sensation altogether, and if she wasn't careful, she'd be jumping him right here and now.

She took pity on him, and herself, and rocked to a sitting position. His stare remained locked on a spot a few feet from her body, and she had to assume it was so he'd stop stripping her in his mind.

Too bad.

Good lord, she was pathetic. This wasn't the way to make an impression. Not to mention she would be working for his brother—this wasn't the time to do anything stupid. She had to slow down, at least a little.

She casually pulled on her jacket and switched positions

to a less provocative stance, even as she continued stretching. "Tell me about your team. You said you have six on the squad?"

Marcus nodded. "Pilot, winch man, paramedic, and the rest on ropes or whatever else it takes to get to the emergency. I work the call centre, or there's a trained EMT who assists. Couple of them are water experts, with scuba skills and such, but we don't get many of those calls—it's mainly winter avalanche or rock disasters outside the Forestry and RCMP abilities."

She would have died to get onto a team like that out of school. "Incredible. Where were you when I was first looking for work?"

He hesitated. "Probably getting in trouble overseas."

Shit. A wash of sympathy and dismay struck. How stupid of her to not have realized. "Oh, Marcus, I'm sorry. I didn't mean—"

He gave her a wry grin. "Forget it. It was a joke, but obviously a poor one. You would have enjoyed the first team I assembled—you would have been the only woman."

She followed his lead and ignored her blunder, partly because she was shocked at his admission. "You don't hire women? I'm surprised."

He shrugged. "I hire the best. That year, none of the successful candidates were female. There's been a little turnover, and now I've got two ladies on the squad. You'll like my lead rope hand—she's as cocky on the wall as you were."

Their eyes locked again— and memories of how her brash attitude had brought them together for the brief fling surged up like some pornographic lust track.

His dark head between her legs, tongue doing indescribably wonderful things. She buried her fingers in his hair and tugged until he was in the perfect position. Tension building, her limbs shaking . . .

Becki tore her gaze away and contemplated upending her water bottle over her head. Sweet lord, it was hotter in the gym than she remembered. She scrambled for something to say. Anything, now desperate to switch her mental track to safer topics. What had they been talking about?

The team. His team. *Right*.

"Your squad is based here in Banff?—Hang on, I *have* heard of you." There'd been a news article she'd read in the past couple of months. "Didn't you recently win some kind of award?"

A long, weary sigh escaped him.

Not the reaction she'd expected. She lifted a brow.

He nodded. "Sort of. Media attention's been a pain in the ass."

Becki snorted. "Actually, I know a little about that. Getting lots of notice for doing my job? No thanks. Dodging newshounds got really old, really fast."

Evading the reporters who'd incessantly hounded her for information regarding her rescue of the girls had been bad enough. Worse were the horrid, unanswerable demands for more details of what happened to Dane. A shiver went over her skin, and suddenly she felt a little dirty for flirting with Marcus. It had been barely eight months since her lover died. Why was she acting like a groupie with a feverish crush?

Because you're not the one who died, her mind taunted.

She scrambled to her feet and covered her unease with a long drink from her water bottle. She lowered it to find Marcus focused on her.

"And that brings me back to you. David said you're joining his teaching pool—starting the summer semester."

"June fourth is my first class."

He was still staring, but now there was a calculated twist to his expression. "I'm running my crew through boot camp for the next three weeks. Need a rope trainer. David says you're the best. You interested in a temporary job?"

Already? Teaching was what she'd come here to do, but she thought she'd have a couple of weeks to brace up her defenses before actually beginning. "David thinks I'm the best—that's good to hear. What's your opinion?"

"I haven't seen you climb in a long time, but you always had the potential."

"You want me to take a test? Submit a training program? Anything like that before you offer me a position?"

Marcus smirked. "Nope. Rule three."

It was the last thing she'd expected him to toss her way. Instant heat flushed her. His words took her back to their weekend fling. To the rules that were burned into her flesh as deeply as they were etched into her brain. "*Trust your team*? How does that fit into this situation?"

"My brother says you're the best. He enticed you to join him, and if that picky son of a gun wants you, then I want you, too."

Oh, the places she could take that comment.

She gathered her things together as she thought it through. "Full squad?"

"Yes. Pilot for basic refresher only—she doesn't need a full workup on ropes, but she needs to remember people are working like hell on the other end when she's in the air swinging them."

Okay, that was impressive. "She? Your pilot is a woman?"

He pushed open the gym door and held it for her, his grin firmly back in place. "Erin's the best."

She blinked as she stepped into the sunshine. Deep breaths filled her lungs with more than the crisp mountain air. Filled her soul with a familiar peace she'd been missing ever since the accident.

"Booki?"

His tone had dropped a notch, and she turned to face him.

"I didn't mean to rush you. I know it's something you probably need to think about, but the offer is there."

"I wasn't expecting work right away, but I'll seriously consider it."

He nodded. "Great."

They were already halfway back to the dorms, her footsteps following the familiar path from so long ago. "You live right in town, then?"

"Found a great place. Big backyard that's nice and private. Wide-open deck with a hot tub . . ."

His voice died away, and suddenly her sticky sweaty self

was back on the *sweating for a different reason* track. Thoughts of hot tubs and Marcus were not on the current agenda.

He cleared his throat again. "I've got an idea. Come out tonight and meet the team. No pressure in terms of the training, but since you've moved back to Banff, they're a great group of people to spend some time with."

She snatched greedily at the change of topic. "That sounds fun. Anywhere in particular?"

"You know our usual stomping grounds." He chuckled. "I think you were the one who started the tradition."

No. Way. "Rose and Crown? The pub is still around?"

"Yeah, and they continue to throw out David's students on a regular basis, but if you promise to behave maybe you can get away without being arrested this time."

Drat, it seemed her school–days sins were far too well known. There was no use in wallowing in doubt, though. "I'd love to, only I'll warn you, I'm not as big on the jalapeño-eating contests as I was back then."

"Oh God, no. We'll stick to wings and chips."

She groaned, her mouth instantly watering like some damn Pavlovian dog. "We should have done ten hill repeats if we're going to eat that crap."

He stepped back, full grin in place. "Meet you at six?"

"Perfect."

Marcus was gone before she'd made it through the dormitory doors. Her body screamed for a shower and a rest, her mind filled with a morass of questions and scattered images of the time she'd spent in the school in her past.

Including shockingly detailed memories of the most intense sexual experience she'd ever had in her life.

Returning to Banff was turning out to be far more complicated, and far more interesting, than she ever expected.

She was removing her bottle holder before she realized that other than when he'd attempted to joke about it, she'd never once thought of Marcus's missing limb.

CHAPTER 3
''''''''''''''''''''''''''''''

The music volume as she pushed open the bar doors at the Rose and Crown was perfect—loud enough the intoxicating rhythm pulsed in her veins, low enough voices were clearly audible without shouting. Becki took the long staircase two steps at a time, pausing on the second-floor landing to look around, pleased to recognize familiar decor. The dartboard still hung in the same place, there were comfortable chairs gathered in groups, and the scent of smoky barbecue and dark ale filled the air.

The sensation of coming home grew stronger.

Across the room Marcus rose to his feet and waved, and another shot of high-test lust drilled through her. The faded blue cotton shirt that stretched over his broad chest looked soft. Dark hair that was longer than in her memories framed his strong features, while the slight wave still made her itch to drive her fingers into the thick mass and drag their mouths together.

Oh boy.

She reined in her libido and turned her attention to the

group sprawled in the overstuffed chairs. She guessed their ages anywhere between twenty-five and forty. Two women and three men not counting Marcus. They looked so completely at ease with each other, they had to be part of his team.

The young blond man taking up an entire loveseat by himself leapt to his feet and scrambled forward, thrusting out his hand. "I didn't believe Marcus when he said *the* Rebecca James was in town. I am so fucking excited to meet you—"

"Good grief, Devon. Can you not go ten seconds without putting your foot in your mouth?" The petite woman seated beside Marcus rolled her eyes. "Hi, Rebecca. I'm Alisha. Excuse the puppy, he's not housebroken yet."

Becki grinned at the pretty blonde. "Hi, Alisha." She wrapped her fingers around Devon's and returned his sturdy handshake. "Devon, nice to meet you, too, only please, call me Becki."

He winked cheekily, then tugged her toward the loveseat, giving her room to join him. "That is the more familiar name. The one we've seen plastered all over the record boards at school. At least until they had to take them down to put up mine."

Across the table Alisha groaned loudly. "You did not just say that. Someone tell me he didn't say that."

Devon shrugged. "It's true. Well, only the swimming records. Your name is still listed for a few things."

He twisted to grin at Becki, one hundred percent cocky attitude and self-importance, and she had to fight from laughing out loud.

She could see her younger self so clearly in the young man it was scary.

"You're such an ass, Devon." Alisha leaned back in her chair and crossed her arms.

He tossed a snarky comment in her direction. Becki ignored their continuing banter to answer the touch on her arm on the other side.

A muscular, dark-haired man offered his hand. "Welcome to the madhouse. Name's Tripp."

"One of the Lifeline team?"

"Since day one. Ropes and avalanche are my specialties. If you're going to be in town for a while, I'd love to do a climb with you." He pointed across the table. "In the meantime, I'll introduce the rest of the motley crew. Erin Tate flies the bird. Anders there beside Marcus is our winch man."

Anders waved. Erin raised her glass in the air. "Let us know your poison. We already ordered wings, so they should be here shortly."

Becki was impressed all over again. The dark-skinned woman who'd greeted her seemed far too young to be the pilot. The woman had to be a rock star.

A quick head count proved the numbers didn't add up. "Is one of the team missing?" Becki asked.

"Xavier. I'm sure you'll meet him soon enough. He's easily recognizable—picture Spider-Man on Red Bull. By the way, don't mind Devon," Tripp confided in a softer tone. "He's been vibrating with excitement since he heard you were going to show up tonight. The bragging is just his nerves talking."

Becki couldn't help but laugh this time. "I'm not offended. I'm surprised any of my records stand after this long."

Tripp pointed to the young woman across the table still in heated debate with Devon. "Alisha's lead on ropes for Lifeline—she managed to beat your freestyle climbing time her final year in the school. She and Devon are the only ones who were trained here in Banff. The rest of us worked around the country before Marcus hired us."

The mention of his name made her glance up to discover Marcus staring intently at her with something dangerous and wild showing in the depths of his eyes. Her nipples tightened, and she was damn glad she was wearing both a dark shirt and a bra with enough material to it that her involuntary reaction wouldn't be noticeable.

She covered the rest of her response by putting in her drink order before turning to pull Devon from his teasing into a rational discussion.

Over the next three hours she consumed more teriyaki

and buffalo wings than were strictly necessary, laughter and conversation flowing around her. People changed position to chat with others, but it wasn't until nine that she finally ended up with Marcus at her side.

It wasn't as if she'd been avoiding him—not really—but it was easier to sneak glances at him when he was directly across from her.

He offered her another serving of wings. "You enjoying yourself?"

"Yes, but, oh God, take that plate away. I'm going to explode if I eat any more."

He chuckled as he put the platter back on the table, where Tripp and Devon instantly claimed the remaining contents. "Just so you know, we don't do this every day. More often we go for something moderately healthy, or do a potluck at someone's house."

"A little excess once in a while is fine."

"Agreed." He leaned back, which put his body close enough that heat caressed her. "What do you think? Could you handle spending a few weeks helping work them over? Devon especially?"

She laughed. "I like him. I like them all. You've got a good group here, Marcus. You should be proud."

He twisted and moved in closer until his mouth hovered over her ear. He lowered his volume, keeping the conversation private. "I am—but I also know they need a kick in the ass right now. Someone like you setting them on their toes will help them hit the spring and summer season in the right frame of mind. Sharp—ready for whatever gets thrown at them."

The words he shared were logical, but she was having the toughest time concentrating on anything but the warm caress of air escaping his lips and tickling along her neckline. A shiver rushed her, and it took everything in her to stay vertical. To resist pressing against his torso and allowing their innocent intimacy to become something far from chaste.

"Becki?" Marcus dropped his hand onto her thigh and squeezed lightly. "You okay?"

She lifted her chin to meet his gaze, tossing off the buzz of desire that was turning her mind to mush. "Sorry. I'm drifting. It's been a long day, and while I'll admit I'm extremely interested, I need some time to consider."

"No problem." He nodded. Paused. "Can I give you a ride back to your room?"

Oh God. There was that darkness in his gaze—nothing frightening except in how much it made her ache. Made her need. Whether he intended it to right now or not, because he didn't seem to be trying to seduce her.

He was simply a big old bag of catnip, and she a very fascinated cat.

Becki made herself do the right thing. "Thanks, no ride needed. I've got my car just outside. Can you give me your contact information? I'll call you in the morning."

They stood, and she gave her farewells to the group. Alisha rose as well, pulling on her jacket. "If you're headed uphill, can I grab a lift?"

"Of course." Becki turned to Marcus, accepting his business card, ignoring the warmth of his fingers as they brushed together. "I'll be in touch."

The cool night air was a needed balm, whooshing over her face and cooling her heated cheeks. She smiled at the younger woman and tilted her head to the right. "Down the street and around the corner one block."

Alisha nodded. "Thanks for this. I live not far from the dorms. I have a vehicle, but I walked to the pub."

"You have a place to yourself?" Becki remembered how tough it could be to find accommodations in Banff.

"I do—an attic suite. It's a little on the small side, but the bonus is there's no one above me to make noise and wake me. And my landlords are pretty quiet. They don't mind me taking off at all hours, either, when I get a call."

They crawled into Becki's car, and she had to concentrate on dealing with the traffic for a few minutes. "I don't remember seeing this many people on the road before. Friday night rush?"

"Something like that. It'll get busier as the summer tourist season rolls in, but you know that from working in Yellowstone. I imagine it's the same there." Alisha peered out the window and pointed to the side. "Second turn on the right, and my house is the last one on the block."

Becki drove in silence for a moment. Yellowstone seemed so far away, and yet it wasn't. The national park had been a part of her life for many years, and even the thought of the place brought a longing. "Summer rush, ski season—there's always something to get people into trouble."

"You miss it?" Alisha asked.

Straight honest truth poured out before she could think it through. "I do. Yellowstone was home. I love the mountains here as well, but something there calls to me."

"Are you planning on going back?"

Becki marvelled that the seemingly innocuous questions managed to hit nerves so raw and fragile. "Not yet. Maybe someday."

She pulled in front of the indicated driveway and waited as the woman got out.

"Are you going to be around for a while?" Alisha asked, sticking her head back into the vehicle as she leaned on the open door frame. "Because, well, it's forward of me, but I would love to have you join me for a climb. Teach me a few things."

Becki smiled across the car at her. Alisha's enthusiasm was contagious. Spending time with the Lifeline team wouldn't be a chore. "From what I hear, you're a pretty incredible climber yourself. Maybe you can teach me some new tricks."

Alisha grinned. "That means you're staying?"

"You might be sick of me before you know it," Becki warned.

"I doubt it. Will you be around the school tomorrow? Can I catch you there?"

"You're serious? Saturday and you want to hit the gym?" Alisha gave her a look, and Becki laughed. "Okay, yes, I planned to work out tomorrow as well. I wanted to check out the new climbing wall. Want to join me around ten?"

Instant delight filled the other woman's face. "That would be awesome. I'll bring lunch for after we're done."

It took only five minutes after leaving Alisha for Becki to complete the drive to her parking lot and make her way toward her dorm room. The place was deserted between semesters, and the peace and quiet was exactly what she needed.

Becki paused outside the doors, then scrambled onto a massive boulder arranged in the middle of a garden area. Stars were beginning to show through the wisps of clouds overhead, and she got herself into a more comfortable position to sit and admire them for a while.

There was no reason she couldn't take on the training Marcus had requested of her. She'd enjoyed the evening immensely. Search-and-rescue people were a rather obsessed lot. Being around a group of individuals who all had the same focus, the same goals she did—it was refreshing and motivating all at the same time.

Her uncontrollable urge to strip the man himself and ride him until they were both screaming was a separate issue. Something she'd have to deal with, but right now she needed to decide if she was going to take on the teaching challenge. She wanted to. That was the truth.

Only there was no way she could accept the position without letting Marcus know a few important details. Information she'd managed to keep from the media. Let him choose if he still wanted her around his team after he knew the full story.

Staring at the stars and the clouds drifting past was much simpler than figuring out how to explain that although she remembered every second of her and Marcus's time together in minute sexual detail, she had no memories whatsoever of the accident eight months earlier that had killed her partner.

Marcus tossed his coat on the hook beside the door, kicked off his shoes, and headed directly for the bathroom. He dropped his clothes on the counter, cranked on the water, and stepped in before there was a chance of heat.

The icy cold spray did nothing to ease the aching hardness in his cock.

Fuck it all, the entire day had been an exercise in torture. From the moment he'd laid eyes on Becki, there'd been no stopping the vivid images assaulting him. Memories like her naked and spread-eagle, her fingers dipping into her wet cunt before moving in circles until orgasm shook her entire body.

Or Becki grinning as he tossed her onto the bed and crawled after her, pinning her in place with his body as he kissed the living daylights out of her.

The water warmed, slipping over his skin, chasing away the slight chill in the room but intensifying his need. He grabbed the soap, scrubbing hard in a feeble attempt to distract himself. This wasn't only about sex. About his attraction to her. Yes, they had a past—but it had been so brief. Fleeting. No matter how impressive the details were of the weekend they'd shared, he wanted her around for more than just another fling.

But goddamn if he didn't just *want*.

Another memory assaulted him—Becki on her knees, taking delight in lapping and licking his cock until he'd captured her head in his hands and held her in place. She'd stared at him and opened wide to suck him deep.

It was no bloody use. Marcus gave up and wrapped his fingers around his dick.

Her mouth had been softer than his grip. Wetter—slick with saliva . . .

He rested his cock on her bottom lip and slid in slowly, relishing the heat, the way she rolled her tongue along the sensitive ridge.

"Suck hard," he commanded, and she pursed her lips, drawing tight around him as he withdrew nearly all the way. His cock glistened in the dim moonlight shining in the window, moisture painting him. "Oh, yeah. That's it. So sweet. So good."

He pressed in again, controlling her position, maintaining a smooth rhythm. Only feeding her a portion of his length as he delighted in the intoxicating draw of pressure.

Becki dropped her hands between her legs, fingers moving steadily, little gasps escaping her as she played with her clit.

"You want to come?" he asked.

Her green eyes opened wide, answering without words. But she also tilted her head slightly and relaxed her neck, allowing him to press forward and bury his cock so deep the crown bumped her throat.

"Fuck, yeah. That's it. Take it all. I'm going to come, and you're going to swallow everything. Every drop, understand?"

Becki nodded as much as she could, her half-lidded gaze focused on him, her face flushed with passion. Her nostrils flared as she breathed slowly and accepted his increasingly erratic thrusts.

Her body shook.

"So close. God, I love watching you come. You are so beautiful. So fucking beautiful."

Becki squeezed her eyes closed and shuddered hard, the hand between her legs slowing, the other gripping his hip with bruising pressure as she wavered, fighting to keep her balance.

All through her orgasm he supported her. Watched her. Held on to his control by sheer willpower until she was done.

Then he went wild.

He pulsed forward. Again. Again. Balls tight, pressure building until he buried his cock as deep as he could and his climax tore from him. Pulse after pulse filled her throat and he drew back, his cock still jerking, seed escaping to splay over her lips.

His balls were empty, his cock spent, and Marcus leaned his forehead against the wall of the shower stall and tried to calm his breathing. Holy fucking *shit*—he hadn't had that violent an orgasm since . . .

Yeah. Pretty much since the last time he'd imagined Becki was sucking him off. Or under him as he fucked her hard. Or otherwise being submissive to his sexual commands.

He twisted, leaning his shoulders on the wall as he stared into the steam. He was old enough to keep work and pleasure separate if necessary, but damn if he wanted to this time. If Becki agreed to help train the team, great. But one way or another he wasn't going to stop pursuing her.

He wanted her. He was pretty sure she wanted him, too. And if there was one thing he hadn't lost, it was the ability to pursue a goal. Becki James had briefly, yet powerfully, impacted his past.

Rebecca James? She was going to be a very pleasurable part of his future, and he'd make damn sure it was more than pleasurable for her as well.

CHAPTER 4

ꞏꞏꞏꞏꞏꞏꞏꞏꞏꞏꞏꞏꞏꞏꞏꞏꞏꞏꞏꞏꞏꞏꞏꞏꞏꞏꞏꞏ

She was awake far too early. By eight A.M. Becki had already stretched, showered, and tossed together a few notes regarding training ideas for Lifeline.

Considering she'd already been preparing a course syllabus for the upcoming semester for David, the idea of working with an elite squad for the short term was a great opportunity. They'd be able to take her lessons and provide feedback during recap.

Her fingers cramped on the pencil, and she shook them. Crazy to think she had lost that much strength. Since the accident she'd been running and swimming, but she hadn't climbed.

Something held her back. The psychologist who'd worked with her had told her to listen to herself. Not to push it. That her body and mind would know when it was time.

Her thoughts returned to the climbing wall in the gym, and her anticipation rose. Yeah, it was time.

As long as she had a job when this was all over.

She picked up the phone. His line was ringing before she

realized it might be too early to call Marcus. Hanging up or waiting it out—which was better?

He answered on the second ring and stole her choices. "Good morning, Becki."

"Umm, morning." Right away flustered and on edge. Not to mention instantly battling the shiver that had raced along her spine at the sound of his voice. "Neat trick. How did you know it was me?"

"Call display says Banff Search and Rescue Dorms. You're the only one there right now."

"Gotcha. Hey, sorry for calling so early."

He chuckled, and the skin on her forearms stood on edge. "Trust me, you didn't wake me. What's on your mind?"

"Could we meet for breakfast? I'd like to talk to you a little more." *I need to confess something before I get my hopes up.*

"What about lunch?" he asked.

Shoot. "I promised to meet Alisha at the gym at ten o'clock. We were going to climb, then have lunch together. I don't know how to get hold of her to change that."

"No worries. Breakfast it is. I'll come get you."

She stared at the phone after he hung up like it was haunted, the echo of his click carrying through the dorm room and fading into an eerie silence. It was crazy how listening to him brought back such an intense rush of emotion. Of physical longing.

This had to stop if she was going to work with the man. So she'd just haul out the lessons and force them to work for her this time, in this situation.

Lesson number two—*move decisively*. In this case, she was going to make it all about work. That was how she'd talk, how she'd act. And most definitely how she'd think. No more wondering how Marcus looked stripped to nothing.

She could control herself. She'd had years of training.

Walking to the parking lot to meet him, though, gave her enough time to regret having to put her thoughts on hold, because *damn*, the dreams she'd had the previous night had been lovely.

A bright red truck was already waiting at the curb. She peered in the passenger-side window cautiously. Marcus waved at her and she hopped in, the smooth leather of the seats warm under her fingers.

"That didn't take long."

"I was in the area." He smiled, and the dark stubble along his jaw did its best to break her mental resolve to stop objectifying him. His hair was wilder than last night, and she busied herself clicking the seat belt closed before she did something stupid like reaching out to straighten the unruly strands.

Decisive, remember? She firmly kicked her imagination in the butt. "Just a coffee shop is fine with me. If I'm climbing in a little over an hour I don't need anything big."

"Bagels okay?"

He signalled a turn at her affirmation, taking them down the hill and back toward the city centre. Becki watched as he drove, his right hand firmly holding the wheel, his shorter limb on the left resting briefly against an extended shaft attached to the turn signal. Marcus wore a long-sleeved jacket, and if she hadn't known his left hand was missing, she never would have suspected.

"Driving is simple," Marcus said.

She blinked, trying to figure out where his comment came from. "Pardon me?"

"You're checking to see how I drive with one hand. Driving is easy—try it sometime. I bet you use mainly one hand on the wheel. If you drive an automatic, most people take all kinds of liberties after they get comfortable. Maybe if my limb were completely gone it would be different, but with as much forearm as I still have, there's not much change in my technique."

He pulled in front of a shop and parked, shut off the vehicle, and turned toward her.

Oh God. "I'm sorry. That was rude."

Marcus shook his head. "No, I think we established what you're doing isn't rude. You're curious. I get that."

Becki dragged her fingers through her hair, pulling

strands off her face. "But I'm not a five-year-old who doesn't know curiosity can still become inappropriate."

He raised a brow at her, the smooth arc combining with his wry grin and turning his face into mesmerizing art. "Frankly I'd far prefer to have you asking questions than staring at me on the sly. Gets so damn old so fast."

She nodded, following his lead when he exited the truck. He pulled open the shop door, and a rush of heated air hit her, the aroma of fresh baked goods washing them both with sweetness.

"You are evil, Marcus Landers."

He pointed to a table in the corner that was free. "Evil?"

Becki slipped onto the padded cushion of the booth and took another deep breath. "I swear I'm going to put on weight just living in Banff. I might be back at school, but I don't need a freshman fifteen, thank you. Cinnamon buns?" She moaned in mock ecstasy.

He laughed. "Tell me what you want, and I'll put in our order."

"I suppose if I said all I wanted was a coffee and a plain bagel, you'd know I was lying."

Marcus shrugged. "Lying, but understandable. Maybe we can split a cinnamon bun between the two of us later if we're good."

He strode to the counter and spoke with the attendant. Becki stared at his profile, his dark hair long enough it was curling at the back of his neck. The edges of his lips lifted in a smile as he finished, and the girl across from him turned pink-cheeked as she rushed to fill his order. Becki removed her coat and hid her own grin. Marcus definitely knew how to charm them.

She glanced up from slinging her coat over the back of the booth to find him settled in the opposite booth. He'd opened his jacket and leaned back comfortably, his sharp gaze taking her in. He kept his left arm tucked against his side, casual, yet somewhat hiding his missing limb.

She was pretty sure that was for other people's sake more than his own.

Marcus, through and through. The qualities that had attracted her to him in the first place had been long, even if lust appeal had been the strongest. Putting aside the weekend they'd spent together, she concentrated on the other things she remembered about him. His confidence, his wisdom.

She leaned forward and pulled in her courage. If she had to spill the beans, this was the man she wanted to share them with.

"I've been considering your offer."

His chin dropped slightly as he waited.

"Last night was wonderful. You've got an amazing team, and I would be honoured to spend time with them. Working with you."

Marcus's gaze lowered to her fingers. She consciously unclenched them from where she'd grabbed hold of the table edge.

"Why do I hear an unspoken 'but . . .' in your words?" he asked.

Becki took a deep breath. "Because before you hire me you need to know that the accident last year? When Dane died?" She swallowed hard and forced herself forward. "I remember going climbing. I remember camping that night, and the next memory I have is of walking the final stages of the trail with the governor's daughter and her friend in tow. Nothing else."

All his casual relaxation vanished. Marcus leaned forward, elbows resting on the table as his concerned gaze took her in. "Nothing?"

She sighed. "I figure there's about a twelve-hour gap, maybe fourteen. We bivouacked on a spur when the weather turned on us. I remember setting up camp and crawling into my sleeping bag. I don't remember packing in the morning, even though we had to—I was still carrying most of my gear when I met the rescue crews at the base of the mountain."

"Why didn't anyone—oh hell, okay. Dane." He nodded slowly. "You can't remember the accident."

"No. And it's . . ." Shoot, she refused to break down

again. Becki took a quick breath, the sticky sweetness in the air soured now by having to share this. She fought for control. "I was cleared of negligence. The reports the girls gave confirmed that while I was competent enough to get them out of the mess they were in, I didn't talk to them normally. I rescued them like I was on autopilot. That was their term for it."

Marcus leaned back and made room for the plates being lowered in front of them. Coffee, bagels. He stirred sugar into her cup and pushed it across the table. She snatched it up, the heat of the mug warming her cold fingers. She'd already taken a swallow before she realized he'd remembered how she drank her coffee.

"Why do I need to know this before I hire you? Does David know?"

Becki paused. "David doesn't know yet. I was planning on telling him, but to be honest? The position he hired me for requires no direct contact with the students. I'd be working through the instructors. If there were any questions of my abilities, having that—"

"Good God, you think anyone is going to question your competence?" Marcus snapped. "If anything, this proves your skills are impeccable. Even half out of your mind, you still rescued the girls."

She snorted. "Half out of my mind is the problem, Marcus. I don't know what happened, and it's more than a frustration. I'm serious. Maybe I am strong enough at what I do to kick into automatic when presented with an emergency situation. Just because it happened once, I don't dare trust it will automatically happen again. You need to know."

"Because you'll be dealing directly with the team?"

"Yes." She lifted her cup and drank deeply, hiding behind the fragile ceramic. Funny how much she suddenly wanted this job. Wanted to be able to work with the crew. "What happens if I'm on the end of a rope belaying Alisha and something goes wrong?"

"But you were planning on climbing with her today. . . ."

Implying she'd already made one bad decision? Becki searched Marcus's face, but he was doing his imitation of a stone wall. Impossible to tell what he was thinking.

"Yes. Because the room is full of auto-belayers. I thought I could easily get around having to rope up with her."

He took another bite of his bagel, pointing toward her breakfast. "Eat."

Damn man. She added jam and ignored him for a minute. Maybe he needed time to process what she'd shared. Heaven knew she'd have to think for a bit in his circumstance.

They finished their food quickly, the last dredges of her coffee cold as she swallowed the crumbs. Still waiting for him to talk.

She wasn't expecting him to reach over the table and catch hold of her hand.

"I have no problem with you working the team. It's your expertise and experience they look up to. And your situation, if you're willing to share, can be both a warning and an inspiration."

He was right—she had to tell the team so they knew the risks as well. "I kept it out of the media. Secrecy was a hard slog to achieve, but if you think I can trust your team, I'm willing."

Even saying the words had tension filling her belly. The climbing community was like family. Which meant for every person who would support and be there for her, another would step forward and willingly rake her over the coals. Revile her, because the assumption had to be that she killed her partner.

No one knew how to hurt quite like family did.

He was still holding her hand, his fingers curled protectively around hers. "You can trust them. You can trust me."

Becki nodded.

He squeezed tighter before releasing her, shifting back in his seat. The unreadable expression was gone, revealing something close to embarrassment. "I have a favour to ask."

This time she waited.

He twisted a grin at her. "I want to train with you as well."
Oh really. "With the team?"

Marcus coughed into his fist and gazed at the ceiling for a moment. *God*, was this stupidly awkward. "No. Yes, maybe later." He shook his head and laughed, an ironic deprecating laugh. "I climbed after the accident. Got a couple attachments adapted for the prosthetic, but I've gotten out of the habit."

Her eyes went wide for a moment before she nodded. "Okay. We can do some time together. If you're sure—"

"Stop it already with the warning. I'm not deaf, and you're not dangerous."

"Denying the possibility is irresponsible," she snapped, "but that wasn't what I was going to say."

Her indignation made her face brighten with heat. He liked how she looked all riled up. "Sorry. Go on."

Becki grabbed her coat from behind her as she rose to her feet. "Just wanted to warn you that I won't go easy on you. You sure you can handle it?"

Nice. The images of handling Becki probably weren't the ones she was thinking of, but they'd get there eventually. His goal of getting her back into his bed had to start somewhere, and having ropes involved?

He was totally okay with that.

They were at the door of the shop, where she'd managed to nab the door ahead of him, pulling it open and standing waiting for him to pass through. He paused as he stepped next to her, close enough he didn't have to speak loudly to respond.

"I look forward to handling anything you want to send my way."

Her cheeks were already flushing before he turned and headed to the truck.

She didn't say anything when she joined him, just made a show of examining the shops along Banff Avenue before he turned up the hill to head to the school. Hiding her face from him.

Marcus bit back his grin and whistled all the way to the gym.

She grabbed her bag from the backseat. "Thanks for breakfast. When do you want to get together to discuss things in more detail?"

"Tonight?"

Becki bit her bottom lip briefly. "What about this afternoon?"

He shrugged, getting out and heading around to her side of the vehicle. "Either is fine."

She frowned as he stood waiting for her. "What are you doing?"

"You're meeting Alisha, right? At ten?"

She nodded.

"I still have time, then. Come on."

Her hesitation to enter the gym made him wonder what exactly she thought they were going to do.

"Holy cow."

Marcus pulled the door shut and pulled the bag he'd brought along with him from under his arm. "Okay guys, you can stop."

CHAPTER 5

''''''''''''''''''''''''''''''

Six sweaty faces turned toward them. Becki glanced around the space, quickly identifying the entire Lifeline team.

Erin sat on a bench, a pair of dumbbells resting on her thighs. Anders uncurled himself from the sit-up bench beside her. Tripp leaned on a wall, his chest rocking as he breathed heavily. Devon rolled over and pushed himself to vertical, his shirtless chest shining with a slick of sweat. "So nice of you to return, oh mighty overlord."

A loud buzzer went off, and Alisha stomped over the floor to hit a switch on the wall. She sagged cross-legged to the floor. "I don't know, Devon, that wasn't so bad."

The way she allowed herself to collapse to her back in a messy heap made the words an obvious lie.

"You'll live. I brought cinnamon rolls. Who wants one?"

Marcus held up an oversized bag that Becki hadn't noticed before, too caught up in trying to keep the words he'd tossed at her in the door of the shop from filling her brain with sexual ideas.

Damn the man anyway.

"When did your team get here?" she asked.

"Yeah, Marcus, what time did you get us up? Bet you'll never confess what a truly evil, creative person you are." A new man, thinner but wiry with muscle, made his way forward to hold out a hand to her. "Oops. Hang on." He wiped his fingers on his towel before starting over. "Xavier. Welcome to hell."

She shook his hand, still trying to figure out what was going on. "You guys were working out while we were having breakfast?"

Loud groans echoed back.

Marcus scratched his neck. "You had to mention that out loud?"

Tripp had taken possession of the paper bag. "Oh, we figured you were lazing somewhere. One phone call, and we're doing endless loops in the gym while you're taking it easy and sucking back coffee. Nice. About what we expected."

"You look like zombies," Marcus offered. He paced over to where Alisha still lay on the floor. He leaned over her, head tilting to the side as he examined her. "Shall I bury you?"

"Please. Somewhere cool."

He laughed and held out his hand. Dragged her to her feet and patted her on the back, sending her toward where the others were gathering.

The smell in the air was now something between sweat and cinnamon. Becki grinned as the group took over the bag and demolished the contents in short order. She sat next to Alisha and watched as the young woman licked her fingers clean.

"I'm not even going to apologize for scarfing that down like an animal," Alisha said.

"Hey, no apologies needed. I know what it's like. I trained here as well, and while it looks as if Marcus is a little more . . . creative than some of my instructors, I know what it's like to be ravenous after a workout."

"Creative?" Erin gasped. "That's too mild. Try bloody possessed."

Becki checked out the pilot, surprised at the passion behind the words but not willing to make a scene.

Marcus laid a hand on Erin's shoulder. "You needed a little unsettling. Think it worked?"

"Bastard."

He laughed. "There, there, you can go home and sleep. After you finish the problems I've left you."

Erin's curses trailed from her lips the entire time she stomped across the floor toward where a small desk waited.

Marcus turned to Becki. "Fuel calculations for a dozen different scenarios. Estimating flight time and air capabilities."

Sound logic. Making the pilot have to complete the challenge after a hard workout proved to both of them she could do the same in tough conditions. Becki approved, even though it was a harsh training technique.

She turned to Alisha. "What time did you get here?"

Alisha had her eyes closed as she leaned over her outstretched legs. "Get here to the gym, or what time did Mr. Diabolical get us out of bed? Because the phone rang at oh three hundred."

Oh God. "Really?" Becki looked around at the group with a lot more understanding. "You've been up since three A.M.?"

Devon flashed her a tired grin. "Never went to bed. Tripp and I were still at the bar."

Becki caught Marcus's expression before he managed to get it under control. She stepped to his side and spoke quietly. "You *are* evil, aren't you?"

He shrugged. "They're getting paid to stay sharp. Sometimes it hurts when you put steel to the iron to sharpen it."

He clapped his hands together. "Okay, break's over. One last task for each of you, then you're free until tomorrow."

"What time?" Xavier asked. "Not that I'm suspicious now, or anything."

"Seven A.M. for you, Tripp, Devon, and Alisha. Anders and Erin will be working at the field all day."

Xavier nodded wearily. "What's our final portion of poison?"

"Hit the pool," Marcus ordered. "Sixteen hundred meters free, then eight hundred of your most hated—kick or pull. And stretch after."

Devon smacked Xavier on the shoulder, and together with Tripp they headed toward the men's change room, grumbling good-naturedly between themselves.

Alisha stood before them, clutching the towel draped around her neck. "Marcus—permission to do wall repeats instead? I'd like to make the upper body work as specific as possible."

Marcus considered for a moment. "Fine. Use the autobelayer. Down climb as well as up, got it?"

She nodded, twisting her face into a grimace. "Umm, Becki? You mind if I take a rain check on that climb together? I have a feeling I'll have noodle arms before this is over."

"No problem. There's plenty of time."

Marcus stepped closer as Alisha buckled on her climbing harness. "Becki is going to give you guys some training over the next while. What do you think?"

The young woman's face lit up. "Really? Oh God, that is awesome. That makes up for having to ride in the back of an open pickup this morning."

Becki couldn't stop a burst of laughter from escaping. "What?"

Alisha stepped to the wall. "Didn't he tell you? Calls at three, picks us up ten minutes later to take us to pack gear. Only he didn't take us straight there, he drove us down the TransCanada for an hour before pulling into the hangar and making us prep in the dark."

Becki stared at Marcus, not sure if she was ready for his methods.

"Don't look at me like that. It can be cold in the back of the chopper flying to a drop site. They need to be ready."

She couldn't argue. "You are inspired, they've got to give you that much."

Alisha tightened the locking carabiner on the rope. "He'd better not let any of us buy him coffee for a few days, because he's not the only inspired one in the lot."

Marcus snorted.

She placed her hands on the wall. "Ready, boss."

"Get going."

Becki straightened her spine as all his attention turned her way. She had to concentrate on the job, which meant tearing her gaze off Marcus and putting it back on the woman slipping smoothly up the wall. Becki analyzed Alisha's choice of handholds, looking for areas to improve.

Alisha was damn good. It was still a training exercise, so she didn't take the easiest path, yet she didn't waver in her selections, either. Steady. Sure. Reach, weight transfer. Reach, extension. After five minutes it was pretty clear there was a reason this woman was Marcus's lead hand.

"I'm going to be hard-pressed to improve her skills." Becki spoke quietly, but she knew Marcus heard. He was right there, analyzing alongside her. The heat of his body brushing hers.

"I told you, I hire the best." He laid his hand on her shoulder. The weight of it made something inside her tremble. She locked her legs tight to stop the instant impulse to go to her knees.

"Take my cock out and suck me." He slipped his hand off, threading his fingers through her hair and tugging lightly. "I want to feel your lips around me. Want to see you open that sweet mouth and surround me until I can't take another second. Blow my mind, Becki. Show me what you can do."

She swallowed hard, lifting her arms to fold them in front of her. Defense against her urges, a way to hide how quickly her body reacted to the merest whisper of a memory.

"Why don't you belt up? I'll belay you," Marcus offered.

Becki cleared her throat, keeping her gaze on Alisha's careful descent. "If you want, I can belay you."

"Didn't bring the right attachment." Marcus stepped to the side, his hand casually stroking her arm and causing more knee-jerk reactions in her core. "I have the claw. I can belay."

Anything to get her blood pumping for some reason other than standing too close to him. She nodded and went for her gym bag. By the time she was hooked up, Marcus had returned, his prosthesis strapped in place.

Remembering his words from earlier—that it was better to simply look than steal peeks—she walked right up, stopping in front of him.

"You want to show me how that works?"

"Like an arm."

Jeez. Fine, if he wanted to be like that. "Yeah, because I have metal pinchers at the ends of both my limbs. Come on, Marcus."

He laughed and lifted his elbow in front of her, forearm held parallel to her face. She caught hold of his bicep and followed the strapping that looped over his shoulder with her fingers. "High-tensile webbing?"

"Strong as what you've got in your harness. Double loop system, so if one fails there's time to bail before the second gives. Bar a freak accident where both straps get cut simultaneously, the system is bombproof."

She'd reversed her exploration already, passing over his elbow and examining the actual prosthesis. "Does it hurt? When you use the—what did you call it? Claw?"

"Sometimes there's a kind of achy pressure. Phantom pain gets me more often, or plain old soreness from the stump in the socket. I fell once and bruised it hard, but no worse than any fall I'd taken previously. Like spraining a wrist or bruising the ball of your palm—hurts like a bitch." Marcus pulled his arm back slightly before closing the dual metal fingers at the end around her wrist. "It took time to learn control, but I can handle rope. If you want, we can double-rope you, put you on a backup—"

"Don't be stupid." It was her turn to be indignant. "You said I was nuts to think I'd lost skills. If you say you're competent, I trust you."

She grabbed a top rope, tossing one end at him, and focused on getting her figure-eight knot completed.

Alisha hit the ground, ten feet down the wall from them. Her ponytail had worked loose, strands of hair hanging in front of her eyes. "Done."

"Five more," Marcus ordered.

"Oh God, really?"

"Should have taken the pool option if you want to argue."

Alisha flashed him her middle finger but started up again. Her forearms trembled as she moved slower than before.

Becki waited until Alisha was out of earshot. "The team will do anything for you."

"And I will do anything to keep them at the top of their game. It's people's lives at stake, Becki. You know it."

His soft-spoken words seemed such a contrast to the firm persona he'd shown the others that she had to turn to see what had caused the change.

He raised a brow. "What?"

Oblivious. Fine, she wouldn't bother now, but if he wanted to train with her? There might be more lessons coming than he expected.

Becki crackled her knuckles, shook out her fingers, and put her hands to the wall. "On belay?"

"Belay on."

She placed a toe on a tiny sloper and took a step. Fingers tight around one hold, torso stretching as she reached upward. Behind her Marcus handled the ropes smoothly, no pressure tugging at her waist belt. Climbing with a competent partner was always so much more enjoyable.

She tilted her head back to examine the route . . .

The wind whipped around her, batting the hoodie against her head, pounding the light rain and the cloud cover into her until she was soaking wet. She hung, swinging lightly, something icy cold pressing her back. Becki blinked, squinted to focus, but nothing helped. Visibility remained at zero. She turned to face the wall and planted her feet, a sense of powerlessness rolling over her.

"You ready? Sometime today would be great."

Dane's sense of timing was lousy. Not to mention, his sense of humour needed an overhaul. "Bastard," *she muttered.*

"I heard that."

Of course he had. "Bastard with Superman hearing. Good for you." *Her frustration grew. This was why she hadn't wanted to head in this direction for their descent, only he'd insisted. Now she was caught between one bad situation and another.* "Dane, I can't see a bloody thing. I could be exactly on route, or hanging over a thousand-foot free fall for all I know."

Dane hesitated, then grudgingly asked, "You want me to go first?"

Yes, as a matter of fact. And I as much as told you that before stepping over the ledge. "You couldn't have said something fifteen minutes ago? Jerk."

"Yeah, but I'm your jerk, right?"

He laughed. The sound echoed off the rocks, and she instinctively tightened her grip on the rope. His amusement at her expense wasn't welcome right now, not after the weekend they'd spent together. The weekend that had fit in perfectly with the painfully selfish way he'd been acting over the past weeks.

Something had changed, and she wasn't sure she liked where their relationship seemed headed. Still, she pulled herself together and responded as plainly as possible. "Yes, Dane, you're my jerk."

Because saying anything else at this moment would be monumentally stupid.

"Bec? Love you."

She leaned back, staring up the hillside. What was going on? That confession was the last thing she expected to hear. "Dane?"

All hell broke loose . . .

CHAPTER 6

||||||||||||||||||||||||||||||

"Becki."

She was more than halfway up the wall, climbing well, when she froze. Both hands in position, feet squarely set. Marcus waited for the next move.

It never came. She just . . . stopped.

"Becki." He took up the extra slack, pulling her slightly as the rope he had locked in place passed over the anchor at the roofline and descended to her waist belt. If he wanted to, he could pry her free by dragging her upward, but that was a last-ditch rescue move.

If he could get her to move, he could avoid jerking her free and risk smashing her into the wall.

He shouted again, and when there was no response, he shifted to plan B.

"Alisha. Drop."

"Dropping." She had already let go of the wall, the self-belayer jerking into action like a modified seat belt security strap. The attachment connected to her belt lowered her slowly to the floor. She was in position, the second anchor

rope loose, the fastener held in her fingers toward the wall.
The instant the hook came within reach, she slammed the
metal buckle of the carabiner through the cam, grabbed
the vertical rope, and gave herself enough slack to remove
the clip from her harness.

The line snapped tight to the wall as she released it to
race to his side. "What do you need?"

No questions. No hesitation. Becki had been right, his
team was good. "Take over belaying. I'm going to go
secure her."

Alisha nodded. "Hold the ropes tight." She waited until
he proved he had a solid grasp. She caught hold of the carabiner attached to his harness, twirled the lock open, then
transferred the hook to her own belt. One more move and
she'd snagged above where he had the rope in a death grip.
"On belay. You climb."

He allowed her to pull the weight from his grasp, not
trusting until she actually took it from him.

Alisha twirled a foot into the loose rope on the floor,
turning her body into a backup anchor. He didn't have time
to rope up himself. Didn't have time for anything but to step
to the wall and climb.

God, he should have done more of this over the past year.
Not only his lack of training frustrated him as he climbed,
but the mostly useless claw tool also hindered him. Only
the portion directly at the base functioned as a small hook.
Didn't matter. He'd do what he had to.

"To your right, and up about three inches. Nice big jug
for your foot. Good. Now the blue ribbon on the left, there's
enough ledge for your forearm." Alisha continued to talk
him through the ascent as he scrambled mostly one-handed
up the wall. He crawled over Becki, guarding her with his
body, planting his feet solidly, his torso leaning against her
as he caught hold of the safety rope with his right hand.

Only then did he slip his left arm around her waist and
pull her to him. "I got you, Becki. You're okay."

Alisha called from below. "Got you both. Ready for
lower?"

"One second." He squeezed Becki. "Come on, you with me?"

A slow stuttering gasp escaped her.

Good, someone was still home. "Becki, I need you to let go of the wall. I'm right here, and I've got you, but we want Alisha to lower us. You ready for that?"

She didn't move. Her fingers were still white-knuckling the holds. *Dammit.*

He tucked his face right beside hers and nudged her cheek with his.

Her body went slack, her weight increasing.

"Alisha, hold tight." Becki's collapse put two full body weights on the rope, and his belayer was totally fatigued. This could be a quick trip down.

He should have let Alisha climb, but logic hadn't been a part of his thought process. It was Becki in trouble, dammit. He took a deep breath and braced himself.

"I'm going to peel her off the wall. She's passed out. You ready?"

He felt it, the slight change of pressure as Alisha managed to lift their weight an inch or so. "No problem. Pull her off. I've got you solid."

"Come on, Becki, I've got you. Trust me, okay?" The words were unneeded, at least for her sake, but he had to say it. Had to reassure himself as he leaned back and took her with him. He settled her into his lap, his arm around her an iron bar securing her in place. If Alisha did lose control of the ropes, they'd hit the crash mats, not the floor. He'd protect Becki from being slammed too hard with his body.

Still wasn't his idea of a good time, crashing.

The instant Becki was clear from the wall, he snapped out his order. "Lower."

"Lowering. Walk your way to the left a little, if possible."

Alisha released the line smoothly, and Marcus breathed a sigh of relief as they passed the fifteen-foot marker. The ten. When they reached the floor, his ass coming to a nice easy landing, he glanced to the side to discover why Alisha had issued her strange warning to move to the left. She lay flat on her back, butt to the wall and legs extended toward the ceiling. She'd jammed her feet against a couple of larger holds and slipped the rope under her body to get enough leverage to counter the double weight.

He'd praise her ingenuity later. Now his attention was on the woman in his arms.

"Becki, we're down. Come on."

He was ready to lay her out and check her over when she sat up and blinked in confusion. "Marcus?"

"Yeah."

She frowned, a crease appearing between her brows as she looked around them, at the tangle of ropes, their positioning on the mat. She glanced at the wall, then back at him.

"Why are you—?" Her eyes widened in panic. "Oh, no."

Her struggles to stand were hindered by the ropes still connecting them. "It's okay. You're fine. No one got hurt."

Her lips pressed into a thin line as she scrambled at the knot securing the rope to her waist belt.

Alisha stepped over, helping to straighten the tangled mess. "You want a hand with the knot, Marcus?"

"No, but thank you." He tapped her on the shoulder. "Get yourself a massage at the hot springs if you want one. On my tab."

Her face lit up. "Deal." She glanced at the other woman, her concern clear. "Becki, you need anything?"

"She'll be okay," Marcus cut in. "Grab your stuff, and you're free to go."

Alisha slid her gaze off Becki as she nodded. "See you tomorrow at seven. Becki, I'll call."

The young woman fled the gym, pretty much as Marcus hoped she would. This next part would be better done without any witnesses. He covered Becki's fingers and stilled her attempt at the rope. "Slow down. We need to talk."

"No, I need to get the hell out of here."

"Because you had a panic attack?" Marcus circled her wrists with his fingers and pinned her in position. "Nothing happened. It worked out fine."

"Nothing happened?" she shouted. Becki jerked her

hands back, but he refused to release her. She set her jaw and glared. "I don't *know* what happened, Marcus, that's the trouble. My God, I did it again. I blacked out. What—"

She closed her eyes and stiffened, trembling shaking her limbs. Marcus loosened his grip, instead stepping in closer to catch hold of her neck and pull her tight against his body. She stood stiffly, her head tucked under his chin, arms rigid at her sides. At least until he'd held her for a couple of minutes, breathing slowly, willing her to relax. Willing her to put it behind her.

When she snuck her arms around him and squeezed him tight, it was his turn to finally take a real breath.

Becki lifted her hands to his chest and pushed them apart. "I'm sorry. Panic doesn't help. Neither does shouting. Thank you. I assume you had to rescue my ass."

He nodded. "Alisha helped. You'll want to thank her as well."

"Great, there goes my hero status." Becki shook her head. "Well, I wasn't that keen on being the climbing goddess anyway."

She pulled the rope end from the figure eight and loosened herself in short order now that she wasn't shaking.

"You've still got a lot to offer the team. This doesn't change anything."

Becki looked at him like he'd grown another head. "It changes everything. You can't be serious. You're not still thinking about trusting me with your team?"

"You thinking of giving up? Quitting completely and finding a new job?"

Her head dropped, but only for a second. Then she stared at him intently. "Never. I will get over this. I don't know when—"

"And if I offer to train you, like you offered me, you think you can find anyone or any place better to help you take those steps? Or a better time than right now to start?"

Becki undid the waist belt connections, letting the heavy harness fall to the floor with a sudden crash. "No. No, and no. Damn you, Marcus, you're turning this into another training session, and I was supposed to be all grown up and doing the teaching this time."

"Can I help it if you forgot a few of the lessons I taught you? I'm offering a refresher."

He shouldn't have taken it there. Not now, not when she was still freshly terrified. But hell if he was going to let her run away. Or even walk—this was too important.

Something about seeing her freeze had changed everything. It was no longer just sexual interest he felt, the lingering desire to get physical. Her panic had triggered an emotion he hadn't experienced in what seemed to be forever. The need to get emotionally involved—to make a difference. This time on a personal level, not something worthwhile but generic like the distraction of his rescue squad.

It was as if embers had been stirred under him, cracking the icy core inside him. The desire to focus on something other than the misery he spent so much energy hiding from the team. His personal ghosts had haunted him for far too long, and by now he never expected them to go away. He'd accepted his occasional nightmares as unavoidable, but allowing her to suffer if there was any way to help was unacceptable.

Making sure that Becki didn't have to deal with unanswered questions for the next four years of her life—it was a good goal to which to turn his considerable attention. If he had to smack her with the one common denominator they'd had all those years ago—sex—he'd damn well take advantage of it.

Her expression changed from indignation to passion before she snapped a lid on her control.

Marcus didn't let up. "Together we'll train the team. Outside of that time, you will train me and help me figure out how to use this arm as well as I used to. In exchange, I will train you, and we'll get to the bottom of whatever the hell happened to you."

"What if it never comes? What if everything stays a mystery?" she demanded.

"Then we concentrate on getting you back to climbing."

He broke eye contact, focusing instead on freeing his own rope. "The mind is a curious thing, Becki. Maybe you won't ever know exactly what happened during the accident. Doesn't mean you can't learn to climb and not have to worry about freezing."

She blew out a long, unsteady breath. "So that's what happened?"

"Yeah." He was finally loose, straightening the rope and allowing it to fall smoothly into place against the wall. "Wait. That's another thing on the list."

"There's a list?"

He glanced up, pleased to see she was smiling a little. "There's always a list with me."

Oh yeah. Her eyes heated. "What did I miss this time?"

"You will not apologize if—and that's *if*, not when—you need to be saved again."

Becki stared at the wall. "Bloody sadist."

"Not at all. I won't enjoy a minute of it if you don't want me to."

She snorted, then gathered her things. "Why do I feel as if I signed up for something way worse than what you put your team through? And by the way, even if you're not a sadist, you're a mean son of a bitch. You called them out of bed after taking them for wings and drinks last night?"

"Also made them do repeats while we had breakfast. Don't forget that part."

An aura of sadness and fear still clung to her, but she seemed far more willing to keep moving forward with him than a few minutes before. Becki lifted her gym bag straps over her shoulder, settling the bag against her hip. She glanced around at the gym and shook her head. "Never thought this place would end up breaking me."

"It's not going to. You're going to come out on top."

She raised a brow and nodded curtly. "I am. I will."

The determined line of her jaw said it louder than her words.

CHAPTER 7

'''''''''''''''''''''''''''''''

She was out the door and headed for the dorms, frustrated energy making her stride quick and wide. Her mind was stuffed full and yet empty—everything as tangled together as the ropes had been: Unusable. Impossible.

The first holds had been perfect. The sensation of her body obeying her commands a thrill as always. She'd planned on testing her limits to see what she had to regain.

It seemed a whole hell of a lot. Everything that had defined her now lay in a mess, her identity tangled and tattered.

She hadn't realized how much it would hurt to have her abilities questioned all over again, and it didn't matter that Marcus said he didn't doubt her. She doubted herself, and that meant she was back to square one.

A rock kicked up beside her and she startled to discover Marcus pacing at her side. "Shit. Have you been there the entire time?"

"We need to talk." He adjusted the bag he carried.

"About the team's schedule. Right. This afternoon."

"Well, there's also the issue of our training, details of which we can add to the official meeting. In the meantime, I need a workout. Want to join me?"

A workout was exactly what she needed. Sweaty, mindless, physically demanding activity to wipe away her need to analyze and reanalyze every second of what went wrong this morning. "Another run?"

He shook his head. "A swim."

They were at the doors to the dorms. "Deal. Where?"

"Back at the school?" Marcus stood and waited, his strong body at ease like some kind of hunting cat waiting for the exact right moment to pounce. "Or the Banff Centre, or the rec centre. Your choice."

She wasn't going willingly back into the school, not today. No matter what she'd said about not letting the place beat her, she needed a breather. "Rec centre. We can do a few weights as well."

"Deal. I'll meet you there in twenty minutes."

He walked the slight hill to where his truck was parked, and she couldn't turn away. His broad shoulders, the flex of his ass under his pants. She'd spent a month studying him on the sly when they'd first met, and the same magnetism that had pulled her in back then was still there. Still had her staring long after she should have gone to grab her swim things.

What was it about Marcus? What made her lose all common sense and want to flirt and carry on like some infatuated teenager? Even shaken from the experience on the wall, he caught her attention and made everything else she should be concentrating on slip away.

She had to rush to make it in time.

Stepping to the exterior doors of the rec centre pulled an involuntary smile to her lips. The stonework and glass made the huge building nestle into the trees as if it had grown there. The rustic construction style was shared by many businesses and homes in the Banff area. Like the mountains rising around them, the human-made structure became a fitting part of the whole. The log features carried the taste of nature inside as well. Becki took a deep, satisfied breath as she stopped at the desk to pay.

A sense of the familiar, the . . . rightness. This was exactly what she needed to counter her chaotic soul.

The girl behind the desk smiled at her. "Becki James?"

Becki hesitated, trying to place the face. "Yes?"

"You're already paid for. You can stop by any time and get your picture done for the pass. For now, let me put this on you." The girl held out a brightly coloured wristband.

Obviously Marcus had beat her to the centre. "Are there any pool restrictions today? Or in the gym?"

The girl shook her head. "Nothing booked in the gym until after supper. In the pool, there's an aquasize class in about thirty minutes, but the deep tank will be free, and there's always at least one lane kept open for laps."

"Thanks."

Becki changed before stopping by the floor-to-ceiling windows to check the aquatic centre. The sunshine had faded to grey as clouds moved in, but in the pool area an oasis of light and heat remained.

"Weights first?"

She twirled to discover Marcus standing directly behind her. He'd changed as well into casual running shorts and a well-worn T-shirt with the logo of one of the local restaurants emblazoned across the front. A neoprene sleeve covered his stump and wrapped over his elbow—probably both for protection and to provide a better grip. "You move very quietly for a big man."

"Helps me sneak up on all those innocent deer in the parking lot. Come on."

He held open the door to the weight room and she stepped in, the cool of the air-conditioning brushing the bare skin of her arms and legs like a caress. A few others were in the room, doing bicep curls or using the machines. Rock music from the local station played softly in the background, a fitting counter to the low-pitched hum of the treadmills.

"General arms, legs? What are you thinking?" she asked.

"Up to you. I'm game for more lower-body work in here—the swim later will be enough upper body to finish."

Perfect. She pointed to a couple of steppers that faced the exterior windows, and soon they were both moving. Outside the grey skies had gone nearly white, the brown grass making everything almost monochromatic. The mountaintops were dusted with fresh snow—the rain earlier in the week freezing at the higher elevations. Spring in Alberta—there was still a long way to go to get to the lush green that would take over the place in the summer.

The conversation as they warmed up stayed generic. Comfortable. Fifteen minutes passed quickly as Marcus led the discussion of nothing important. Becki was grateful, even as she cursed herself for spending more time looking at his reflection in the mirrorlike glass than staring through it at the gorgeous mountains surrounding them.

They moved to the weights, and she took charge. "Squats. We'll use the power rack, if you don't mind."

"Not at all. Load your starting weight—I'll follow after. I don't need to try to impress you, do I? Loading three times as much weight on seems like a useless venture."

She snorted. "Trust me, being impressive in the workout room isn't. I've spent too much time around people who easily outpressed me, yet couldn't transfer that into any kind of strength when they needed it most."

Becki stepped under the bar, resting it on her shoulders as comfortably as possible, which meant not very. She stood the final two inches it took to release the security clasps, twisting the metal bar to flip the hooks out of the way.

She focused on her reflection in the mirror. Legs spread shoulder width apart, toes facing forward, she bent her knees and lowered the weight until she was in a sitting position. Reversing direction made all the muscles in the front of her thighs engage, the thicker bands in her butt having to work to bring her back to vertical.

"One. Nice form. You keep that up, and I'm going to feel like a wimp when it's my turn," Marcus teased.

"You'll have as good form or better—remember, you

asked me to train you. I don't let my partners muck around."
Becki continued on as she spoke, the blood moving into her
legs warming her. Her heart rate steadied, and she concentrated to keep her breathing smooth.

All the different components of training were a balancing
act she loved. Part of using her body as the tool, making it
fit, keeping it strong. Making demands now so that in the
field she would go on autopilot and do what needed to be
done.

Marcus kept his count going, walking behind her to rest
his hand on the metal bar between where it rested on her
shoulder and the palm of her right hand.

"I hope you don't expect me to flake out this soon," Becki
said. "It's going to be a damn short workout if you're spotting me already."

He chuckled. "Don't be offended. I'm sure you can easily finish this set."

She completed two more squats, only now? She wasn't
focusing on her core body. On watching her legs to make
sure she powered up using her thighs.

No, a lot more of her attention was struck by the distance
he stood behind her. How the heat from his torso crossed
the narrow gap between them, and how when she did complete the set and twisted the bar to engage the security
hooks, he slipped his hand to her shoulder and trailed his
fingers down her back.

"Good start." Marcus switched positions with her. He
had to bend lower to get under the bar, and she was way too
aware of his glute muscles rubbing past her thigh.

Becki stepped back to a nice safe distance.

His gaze in the mirror as he began his set? Mocked her.
He knew why she'd moved away.

Oh God.

Becki took a drink from her water bottle and reconsidered her entire game plan. Working out with Marcus wasn't
supposed to be some kind of long, extended session of
foreplay.

"You going to count for me? That was three." His wink

only made her more aware of him. Of his dark colouring reflected in the mirror. Of the way his shoulder muscles bunched against the fabric of his shirt as he had his arms raised to support the bar.

"Four." She had to think of other things. "Adjust your right foot. Your hip is out of line at the bottom of the squat." He followed her directions, but on the next repeat he still was wrong. "More."

"More what?" Marcus hooked the bar into position and stepped from under it. "Show me when I'm not holding the weight."

Becki nodded. "Face the mirror."

He turned. Lowered himself. She stepped behind him and leaned in. "Here, you're pressing your hip back at the three-quarter point."

"Like this?"

Marcus adjusted, but it wasn't enough. She placed her hand to the outside of his knee, but he was still out of line. She pressed her hip against his butt as well to get him to move the way she wanted. "There. Do you feel that?"

His voice was lower when he spoke. "I feel it."

Becki snapped her head up to find his face only inches away from hers. She was pressed tight to his torso, her left breast against his arm as she reached her right hand forward. Basically, she'd wrapped herself around him.

She scurried back to safety. "You're a terrible person, Marcus Landers."

"I think we established that fact a long time ago."

He got under the weight and proceeded to do five more squats, all with impeccable positioning. His heated expression taunted her because she had lost the ability to tell him to cut it out.

The entire damn training session turned into a twisted form of sexual torment.

Marcus stood beside her to spot her. Always in a way that was logical, but a little too close. He didn't take the weights from her when they switched position; he laid his hand on her and touched lightly. Her forearm. Her waist. The swoop of her lower back right over her ass. All the while watching her with his dark eyes, the trace of a smile on his lips.

She could have said no. Should have said no, but after the morning's stress—

No, there was no excuse other than she wanted it. Accepted it. Wanted to revel in the fact that this man made her feel completely and utterly alive.

He caught hold of her towel as she stood after completing the final machine. His fingers wrapped slowly around the fabric and pulled her closer. They'd both worked hard enough she was sweaty, a sheen of moisture covering her bare arms.

The desire to rub all over him like she was marking territory wasn't good, but she'd given up telling herself that thirty minutes earlier.

He looked at her, his gaze fixed on her lips. Instinctively, she licked them.

His eyes closed briefly, mouth closing tight over a groan. When he did speak, it was soft—for her ears only. "I don't know if I should compliment you on your workout ethics or assume I'm the only one feeling the heat."

She hesitated. Lying was no use, but the urge to take out a few of her own frustrations on him made her reckless. "We said we'd work out together, not fuck each other's brains out."

The answering flash in his eyes said she might have made a mistake poking the beast.

So when he simply stepped back she was a little disappointed, and how twisted was that?

He nodded slowly. Let loose his grip on her towel.

"Right. Good point." He trailed his fingers the length of material where it hung between her breasts, his knuckles skimming the side of one curve. Her breath caught in her throat. The way his smile grew darker made it clear he'd caught her reaction.

Fake it. It was her only defense left. "See you in the pool?"

He nodded, moving away from where he'd had her trapped by his body. She slid past, ignoring the brush of their torsos as much as possible.

Just before she'd completely made it to freedom, he spoke.

"Becki?"

She turned to face him. "Yeah?"

He full-out grinned, and her knees trembled. "About working out together? You let me know when you want to make some additions to the list."

Becki fled, hoping there would be a power shortage and the pool would be icy cold.

She was in so much trouble.

CHAPTER 8
''''''''''''''''''''''''''''''''

Marcus passed the pile of paperwork across the table to David. "Thanks for bringing all that over."

"No problem. No use both of us fussing with a trip to the accountant." David slipped the files back into his briefcase and tossed it aside before staring out the window. "Slow spring. Weather reports are calling for more snow later this week."

"Trails are going to be a mess for a long time still." Marcus looked his brother over with amusement. "And now that you've done me a favour and made some prerequisite small talk, what do you want?"

"What? I can't drop in for a visit? I'm crushed."

"Right. When you stop in for a visit you head to the fridge and drink my beer." Marcus leaned on the glass of the French doors leading onto the deck. "Spit it out."

David's mouth twisted into a wry grin. "Fine. Fund-raiser for the school."

"What about it?" Marcus eyed the calendar on the wall. "It's in two weeks. You have troubles with the booking?"

"Of course not. Everything's been organized since last year. Ballroom at the Banff Springs, cocktails, dancing. A little motivation speech or two from some local celebrities . . ." David trailed off. "You know, staring at a person with that expression doesn't encourage communication."

"I figure my expression should match what I'm thinking. Explain why you looked at me when you said *local celebrities.*"

His brother shrugged. "I'm listed as the MC as usual. But having you and the Lifeline team show up—"

"Oh, no. Asking the team is one thing—most of them love doing the dog-and-pony routine for you. But you promised you'd never again suggest I put on a monkey suit and parade around for people to throw peanuts at. I won't do it, David. It's not worth it."

"Yeah, well, last year Lifeline hadn't recently gained any major acclaim, and having the team there in their monkey suits still brought in enough to help put a couple of kids through on a scholarship and equip the weight room."

Marcus sighed. "You had to mention that damn article again."

"They'll be running snippets all week leading up to the event." David raised his hands in defense as Marcus stepped toward him. "Not my idea, by the way. Paper told me what they had planned. Face facts—you're big news."

"Because there's nothing happening—that's the only reason it's still news." He had good reasons for his animosity toward gala events, but David was right. The fund-raiser brought in the money and made a great evening for locals and tourists alike. "I'll mention it to the team. You'll probably get at least half of them. Alisha and Devon for sure. They'd be great reps as alumni and all that crap."

"That's what the board wants—they want to play up having the team around as a draw for the event."

"Just to be clear, I'm not speaking," Marcus growled. "I'm not crawling behind any microphone and waxing poetic about how saving lives saved my life."

"Got it. I know that. Wouldn't dream of pushing you into anything you're not comfortable with."

All of Marcus's bullshit monitors went off at the same time. He glanced over at David, who squirmed under his scrutiny. "Who do they really want to speak? Because I can tell from the way you're twitching you think I won't like it."

David cleared his throat. "The board wants me to ask Becki."

"Goddamn, no." Marcus shook his head.

"She'd be great," David insisted. "If she's anywhere near as good a public speaker as she was during her school days, it'll be a huge success. Man, she could talk her way out of anything back then—she'll charm the money from their pockets."

"You'd really put her into that position now? I told you what happened when she climbed. Give her time, idiot."

David rolled his eyes. "I don't expect her to scale the interior of the hotel and belay to the podium, Marcus. She'll say a few words about the school and how great it is to be back. That's it."

"If that's it, why are you looking at me for permission before seeing if she's interested?"

David smiled sheepishly. "If you ask her, she'll do it."

"What?"

"Oh hell, you think I haven't already spotted you've marked territory on her? You as good as pissed on the corner of the dorm house when you were talking about her yesterday."

Marcus shook his head and went for the fridge. "You're fucking nuts."

His brother leaned back in his chair and crossed his arms. "Don't even try the innocent act. I know you too well, and you've got her labeled as yours already. Or are you saying I can ask her to come with me to the food and wine festival next week? I haven't got a date, and it would be good for her to get out. Meet a few more people than just the team. Or I could take her dancing."

"She'll be working for you. You don't date employees." Marcus kept his expression as blank as possible.

David hummed. "Well, this is a different situation, don't you think? She's more like my equal than a direct employee. I doubt it's a problem. And with her being around all the time now?" He stood and considered. "You know, I was pulling your leg, but if you're serious about not being interested, then damn, maybe I *will* give her a little more attention."

Marcus deliberately unclenched his fingers and spread them casually on the island countertop. "Whatever. Just don't think you should ask her to speak yet."

"You're right. I'll give the lecture as planned if I have to. That's not an issue." David stared at the ceiling. "I bet she looks great in a dress. She kicks butt in climbing gear. Your guys are working with her this afternoon? Maybe I'll come by and watch for a while."

"Maybe you should find something else to do."

"No, I think I need to roll with this. I'll come by to make sure she's settling in comfortably." David stepped forward to slap Marcus on the shoulder. "You know, this is awesome. I haven't felt this interested in anyone in a while. Of course, it's partly the way she moves, combined with knowing how strong she is. Damn, can't you imagine her using her climbing grip on your dick? Or her thighs—I bet she could crawl up a guy and—"

Red-hot anger rolled through him, and Marcus blinked in surprise to find he'd grabbed his brother by the shirtfront.

David didn't so much as twitch. Just stood his ground and smirked.

"Fuck. You," Marcus growled, releasing his grip and stepping away in disgust. He had the control of a two-year-old when it came to Becki.

"Lying to me never works. You should know that by now," David drawled. "Besides, what's the point? There's nothing wrong with you being hot for her."

Nothing and everything. "Stay out of it, David."

"Over and out. Except . . ." David tapped the countertop. "If you won't ask if she'd like to be the keynote, I'm going to. She deserves a chance to make her own decision on the matter, don't you agree? Or does getting involved with you mean she'll be walking three paces behind at all times?"

Getting involved meant he'd be calling the shots, but only in bed. "I'm not that kind of asshole."

David snorted. "So, we have established you are *some* kind of asshole. Awesome. I wasn't completely positive."

There was no way he could stay pissed at his brother. Marcus shoved him in the shoulder and they jostled for a moment like kids.

"Go ahead and ask her." Marcus caved, but only partway. "But if you show up at training, I'll make you climb, and then everyone will know what a pansy ass you've become."

"Ooh, I'm scared."

"You should be. Devon attached a new Drop of Doom from the ceiling and set the rope to lock less than a foot from the floor. You'd scream like a girl. Again."

David shuddered. "Ass. Stop reminding me about that."

Marcus poked again. "If I can't tease my little brother, who can I tease? Now get the hell out. I have things to do."

Only he didn't, not really. Watching David drive off meant Marcus had plenty of spare time to go over more plans for the team. More plans of how to fill his day until it wouldn't be ridiculous to head back to the dorms and see if Becki was free.

More time to figure out how he was going to convince her she wanted him as much as he wanted her.

CHAPTER 9

''''''''''''''''''''''''''''''''

"So, thank you. For helping rescue me, and for being understanding." Becki smiled across the short distance between them on the climbing mat.

Alisha nodded. "It's not an issue. Really."

She looked so sincere Becki wanted to apologize all over again. Tearing down people's idols was tough, but they couldn't move forward until they'd discussed the situation.

"You're okay working with me?" Becki asked softly.

Alisha's head snapped up. "Don't you want to? I mean, if you don't feel comfortable, I don't want to push you or anything, but if you're worried about me worrying . . ." She laughed. "And now I'm blathering."

"Seems to be a bit of that happening this afternoon," Becki said. "I'd love to keep working with you. Just not sure what other surprises might come our way."

"Doesn't change anything for me," Alisha insisted. "You're still you."

Becki forced a smile. "That I am." All the confused, memory-missing, sexually frustrated parts of her.

The door opened behind them, and the other team members strolled in, conversation and laughter following them. Becki had read through the files Marcus had given her the previous day, and already the crew seemed more familiar, their individual quirks coming forward.

Anders stopped to tap his fingers on Alisha's head. "Hey, you. You never showed up at the pool after this morning's blood-and-guts session. Teacher's pet, or what?"

Alisha scrambled to her feet, Becki following suit.

"I was checking ropes and organizing the staff room. You should thank me that you don't have to deal with Devon's stinky equipment anymore."

Tripp snorted as he stepped into his climbing harness and secured it around his hips. "You were dealing with Devon's tackle? Nice. How come I didn't get offered the chance?"

"You wanted to deal with his junk?" Alisha raised a brow. "Now, Tripp, I didn't know you swung that way."

Anders snorted. "Devon swings any way he wants, from what I hear."

"Notice I said nothing, and still they attack?" Devon tugged on Becki's sleeve. "I'm a sweet, innocent boy. Really."

"How did I get in the middle of this?" Becki asked.

"Impartial witness?" Devon's baby-faced grin didn't do anything for her, not with images of Marcus's mature good looks filling her mind, but she saw why the young man was considered a bit of a heartbreaker.

She patted his cheek. "The only thing I want to witness is your skill on the wall. I don't care how legendary you are anywhere else, Mr. Leblanc."

The door opened again and Marcus strode in, and suddenly all the physical reactions she hadn't had with Devon whipped right on through her. She nodded curtly, then turned to the team to hide from him the flush heating her skin.

Her memory might be gone, her climbing skills broken, but her libido was just fine, thank you.

Becki got their attention, putting the wisecracks to a stop.

"Thanks for the opportunity to train you. Hope you get something out of it. I'll work you hard, but the goal is to sharpen you in the areas you need it most. Any questions?"

Lots of foot shuffling, no comments, not even smart-ass ones. Becki was impressed—the team was on their best behavior, at least so far. She looked forward to seeing how they liked what she had in mind.

"We're going to work on dynamics. When I watched you climb yesterday, I saw some good moves, but not consistently. We'll do more rope work in the coming weeks, but getting into position takes climbing skills. And sometimes there's nothing to be climbed. Then what do you do? Suggestions?"

"Hope like hell Erin can lower us in," Anders offered.

Becki nodded.

"Go from the top. Descend to the rescue." Devon snapped out the answer, all trace of teasing gone as he moved into position beside Alisha.

The young woman poked him. "That's the point of the question, idiot. What if you can't make a vertical approach?"

"You can always go from the top," he insisted. "If you've got enough rope."

"Not always," Alisha rejoined. "You're going to belay from the top of Mount Rundle to a rescue?"

"Children," Becki snapped, stepping between the two of them. "Enough."

"Same old, same old for us," Tripp pointed out. "Keeps us awake on long missions, listening to these two."

"Great. So I know just who to partner up, then."

"Really?" Alisha groaned. "But Anders and I climb together."

Becki shook her head and pointed across the gym. "Not today, you don't. Alisha and Tripp, get in position for belaying. Everyone else is on the wall climbing. Marcus and I set up pitch four with your workout."

Devon flashed Alisha a smile. She spun on her heel and ignored him.

Becki stifled her amusement. The lesson was going to hit harder than she'd expected.

"Holy shit, this is a route?" Anders stared upward. "Becki? Did someone remove a few of the holds?"

Marcus stepped beside her. "Told you they'd be pleased to meet your challenge."

"No, you told me they'd freak out," Becki corrected him. She turned to the group who were now all staring her direction. "Dynamics. Explosive moves from one position to another. You need a good starting point, a good target—"

"And a set of wings," Anders broke in. "Again, *holy shit* that's a reach."

"Good thing you've got a spotter, then. Okay guys, figure out how to make the route and get awarded honorary wings."

Marcus tipped his head. "You want me to belay Xavier? You can observe the entire team, then."

She nodded her thanks, trying to focus harder on the task at hand and less on being aware of *him*.

Anders and Tripp were already working together well, trying to solve the puzzle she'd presented them. Marcus moved into position with Xavier. Becki turned her attention down the line, making sure all the pairs were working.

Devon and Alisha seemed involved in some strange dance. He moved forward, Alisha retreated. The ropes attached to them both hindered her from withdrawing too far.

"Alisha, you having any troubles?" Becki called.

The young woman shook her head, then poked Devon in the chest, pushing him toward the wall.

Suddenly Marcus was there, bent in close to whisper in Becki's ear. "Glutton for punishment, pairing those two up. Oil and water."

"They're a team. Getting along is important. If they don't trust each other, they're a potential for disaster. I'm surprised you let them get away with being stupid."

"Oh, they trust each other's skills. They just constantly try to outdo each other as well. Keeps the entire team on their toes watching the battles."

Becki nodded slowly. "A challenge isn't always a bad thing."

"That's what I imagined you'd say." He stepped away to rope up with Xavier, his body brushing Becki's as he left.

She watched him go, figuring his words and actions were a direct challenge to her. Being ready to accept it was another matter entirely.

Instead, she concentrated on the team. Devon leapt across the wide expanse between the lower section and where she'd placed the next set.

He caught a hold on his first attempt, grinning in delight as he clung by one hand. "That wasn't so bad."

Becki folded her arms and moved beside Alisha, who held his still-slack safety rope. "You're not at the roof yet, Mr. Leblanc. Clip in, please—I don't want to scrape you off the floor more than necessary today."

He rotated back, clinging by his fingertips. Devon passed the rope attached to his belt through the carabiner hooked to the wall, guaranteeing he would fall only a few feet if he slipped. He tipped his head back and looked for another hold. "Alisha? Suggestions?"

"Umm, can you swing to the left and grab that blue pincher? Okay, I see why Anders was swearing. Becki, that one hold is bombproof, but there's nothing around it for miles."

"Have fun, kids." Becki glanced over the other team members. "Anders. More thrust with your legs. You can't reach the hold if you don't use full force."

"Got it."

She stepped farther to the right. Marcus had his gaze firmly on the climber in front of him. She was the one who had troubles moving her gaze to the proper person.

Man, she had it bad.

"Xavier. Nicely done," Becki complimented as he hung in the same position Devon had achieved. "Now what?"

"I use the jet pack we're all going to be issued?" Even as they laughed, Xavier brought both hands together and jerked his torso upward, snatching for the next nearest hold. Marcus cheered loudly when Xavier managed to get a piece of it.

A second before he fell.

"Good effort. Try again." Becki observed for another fifteen minutes, giving them plenty of time to attempt different variations. All the while she kicked her own butt for being far too interested in watching the one person in the room on whom she wasn't supposed to be fixated.

Alisha was having a hell of a time. Becki had called for a changeover of climbers, much to Devon's disgust, since no one had managed to complete the challenging move.

Marcus sent Xavier to work with the other pair before moving to Becki's side to view Alisha and Devon more closely.

"More power, Alisha. You're nearly—"

"Shut up, Devon. I'm powering all I can," Alisha snapped.

Devon lifted his brows at Marcus as if to say, *What can I do?*

Becki shook her head as Alisha dropped to the floor and shook out her arms. "I get that you're frustrated, but you can do this."

"I'm six inches shorter than Tripp and Devon, more than that for the other two guys. My overall reach is smaller, and even with their height advantage they never succeeded before you had us switch." Alisha dragged her hand through her hair and readjusted her ponytail holder, snapping it tight. "I'm not trying to be disagreeable, but it seems the point of this exercise is to prove there are some things we can't climb. Is that it?"

Becki shook her head. "Success will take two things. First, you need to use more core body—you're holding back from hitting your full extension. Come on, I'll show you." She stepped in behind Alisha. "Permission to touch you?"

"Of course. I want to do this." The young woman's frustration was clear.

Becki placed her hands on Alisha's stomach. "Scrunch up a little. That's it. Now when you press, you're using your legs, arms all the way out, but you're not elongating your abdominal muscles enough." She curled herself over Alisha, holding on tight. "Slow motion, extend up, yeah, that's it. Now finish the stretch, right here." Becki slid her hands apart, stopping just shy of covering Alisha's breasts and crotch.

Alisha finished in a vertical stance, still obviously confused. "Nope. I thought I was doing that."

"Okay, try this."

Becki peeled off her shirt, and Marcus swallowed hard at the instant rush of chemicals that shot through him. She wore a sports bra underneath, but damn . . .

"Put your hands on my stomach so you can feel it." Becki pulled Alisha in behind her and placed the other woman's hands on her flat abdomen. She bent over, and Alisha pressed against her back to keep her hands in position as Becki took her through the move a couple of times.

Devon shuffled his feet uneasily, and Marcus glanced at him.

"I'm getting a fucking boner watching this," Devon confessed quietly.

Marcus, too, but he wasn't about to admit it.

"Okay, maybe I felt something different. I'm still going to get stuck where the guys got hung up." Alisha moved away from Becki to stare up the expanse of the wall. "Unless you have a magic pill for me?"

"I have something better." Becki shook her head, turning to take in the team one by one. "You've all worked under Marcus for a while, and you still can't figure out what I'm looking for in this exercise?"

They blinked at each other sheepishly.

"Or do I blame Marcus?" Becki inquired.

"Me?" Marcus stepped forward. "How did I get called into this mess?"

"Just double-checking something. You still as fond of lists these days as"—Becki paused for such a split second, he was probably the only one who caught it—"as before? You teach these guys your four rules for surviving and thriving?"

"Of course he taught us. They're plastered on the staff room walls," Xavier said. "Be patient, move decisively—"

"Oh, God . . ." Alisha dropped her head into her hands. "Rule Three. Trust your team? Is that all you were going for?"

"All?" Becki barked out the word. "Do you have any idea how quickly you could have gotten this task over and done with if *all* you'd done is worked as a team with your partner? And I don't mean looking for pretty holds for him to grab. I mean brainstorming and thinking outside the box."

Marcus's admiration grew as Becki stepped forward and pointed at individuals in turn.

"Right off the bat Xavier attempted an innovative move. But because the distance was impossible for individual success, he gave up instead of sharing it with the rest of you. His idea could have triggered others.

"Tripp—you've got more sheer upper body strength than anyone else here. Devon, your agility set you into a starting position fast and easy. Alisha—you will be able to hit that hold, and once you're there you've got the flexibility for moves these guys can only dream of. Since you're the lightest, you also have other advantages."

"So we can't complete this challenge on our own?" Tripp asked.

Becki shrugged. "Maybe you could, but as a team *maybe* goes all the way up to *yes*. And if that's the difference between saving someone's life or not, which is more important? Getting to crow as an individual, or sharing the celebration among the team?"

She moved to face them all, her back toward the climbing wall. "I'm going to make some wild assumptions right now, but I doubt I'm wrong. When you heard that Marcus had asked me to come train you, I bet what instantly came to mind were things like Devon mentioned that night at the pub. *Becki James's* reputation as a climber extraordinaire. My solo records here at the school, my famous single-handed rescue last year. Am I wrong?"

Tripp shook his head. "Can you blame us?"

"Not for it being the first thing you thought of, but I'll be damned if it should have been the last thing you focused on." Becki planted her fists on her hips. "This isn't school boot camp. You're not trying to win a job placement; you have one. You're no longer six individuals, but a team. Every single training exercise should be done with that in mind, even if your instructors fail to emphasize the fact.

"Don't try to be me. I got lucky. You guys are the ones who got attention for your joint skills, your teamwork. You're all incredible individuals, but as Lifeline, you're a whole lot more. Don't forget that. You fought for that honor. You deserve that honor. Now don't let yourselves slack off— don't let your teammates take the easy way out—fight to keep making *the team* stronger."

Alisha's chin had lifted. Devon grinned. Someone clapped and the entire team joined in, the staccato sound echoing off the walls and ringing in his ears. Becki's cheeks flushed red, but she smiled.

Marcus wanted to give her more than a standing ovation.

"Go on." Becki waved them off. "You're done, at least with me. Check your schedule for the rest of the day, and I'll see you tomorrow."

Marcus waited until the gym was empty, the gear put away as the crew left one by one. "I'm still applauding. That was damn impressive."

Becki blew a sigh of relief. "That . . . is reassuring. I'm a little lost right now, feeling my way, and I don't want to mess this up."

"Training my team?"

"That, and the teaching gig in a month for David. Just— starting a new life in a way." She laughed, bitterness in the sound. "A new life because there's still so damn many holes in the old one, I can't walk forward without falling out the bottom."

"Hey." Marcus caught her by the arm. "You go on and listen to your own lecture. You don't have to do this alone. I said I'd help you. The team will help you."

She paused. Nodded. "You're right. You're right, and I said I was going to face the future and move on. Damn yo-yo emotions."

"Girl stuff. Can't help you there."

Another laugh escaped her. "Don't be an ass."

"What?" He slapped her on the shoulder lightly, guiding her toward the offices. "In the interest of teamwork, I have a suggestion. We talked yesterday about the schedule for training Lifeline. How about we do the same for our training sessions, so you have that in place?"

Becki looked him over with a wide-eyed wonder, as if she were surprised he hadn't also spouted off some sexual innuendo, as he'd done at every other opportunity up to now.

"If you're serious, that would be wonderful. Occasionally doing things last minute is fun, but I like being organized. Thank you."

He ignored the sexual side of the equation for a moment. Taking advantage of the attraction between them seemed a very . . . selfish . . . thing. After her sermon on the matter, perhaps focusing on the teamwork they needed was the right thing to do.

At least for now. He still planned on getting them back into bed. On trapping all her wild energy and excitement, and soaking in it. But not today.

Agendas didn't have to be abandoned. Sometimes they could simply be delayed.

CHAPTER 10

The phone rang.

Marcus ignored it.

His cell phone rang, and he let it go to messages.

The curtains were drawn, the room was dark, and he wanted to crawl under something and hide.

The fact that he had heard the ring was probably a good sign. Only probably, because along with awareness of the pain came the realization that while it was dark in the room, there was light sneaking around the edges of the curtains. Daytime—no interior lights on—and together that could only mean one thing.

His ghosts had taken over. Now the question was, how long had he been gone this time?

The landline rang again. He reached over the edge of the couch to the side table, picked up the receiver, thumbed the mute button, and slammed the phone back on the table.

The pounding in his head was nothing new. He dimly remembered that searing pain in his left hand had woken him in the middle of the night—and wasn't that just fucking great? That something that wasn't even there anymore could still hurt that damn much.

Marcus grabbed a drink from the fridge and dropped back onto the couch, stared at the shadows on the walls, and waited for the darkness inside to go away.

He wasn't sure how long he sat there. Minutes? Hours? The front door opened.

He moved instinctively. The crash of the bottle hitting the door frame sang out the same moment his brother swore.

"Shit, stop. It's me. David. What the hell?"

God. He didn't want to explain ever again. Didn't want to talk. Marcus grabbed the arm of the couch and held on for dear life. "Get out."

David was already stooping to pick up the broken glass from the floor. "No can do. You've been MIA for three full days. According to our agreement, I'm allowed to come kick your butt at this point."

Shit. Three days meant Thursday. Still, he wasn't ready to move. "I can throw something else at you if you want. I'm changing the goddamn rules. Get out. Now."

David laughed, the glass echoing as it hit the sides of the metal garbage can, sending shards of pain through Marcus's temples. "Nice try. I'm not listening."

He came and sat on the coffee table directly in front of Marcus.

Marcus's jaw ached from grinding his teeth. He glared at David, hoping his expression alone would be enough to persuade his brother to turn and walk away.

David raised a brow. "Interesting. Does the caveman-slash-madman look work well on women?"

"Fuck. You." Marcus dragged his hand through his hair, then changed his mind, pointing at the door instead. "I'm not ready for an intervention. Tomorrow."

David's cocky smile faded, replaced with sympathy. "Look, normally I'd leave you alone. I understand you have . . . issues. But this time is different. No extensions. Deal with it."

"Dammit, David."

"She's threatening to come over here."

Marcus stopped cold. "Who?"

"Becki. When you didn't show up at training a couple days back, I covered for you. Hoped you'd be out of your funk quicker than usual. This time you have to choose to drag yourself back to the real world, bro. Once I assured her you weren't deathly sick or something, she got royally pissed. She's ready to kick my ass, your ass. Hell, she's been kicking your team's ass—you might want to consider pulling yourself together for their sake."

"What the hell has she been doing with the team?" He slid forward in his seat.

David hesitated, then spat it out. "She's kind of taken them over. You had all the rest of their training organized, but when you didn't show up, she stepped in and has been running the show. She thinks you jammed out on her. Something about missing training plans, and ignorant assholes . . . and there was more, but I was trying to keep far enough away from her that she couldn't hit me, so I might have missed a few of the more choice swear words."

Marcus laughed before he realized what he was doing. Her actions were twisted enough to break through the pain. Only Becki.

David nodded. "I thought that might get your attention. Come on. I get it that you need time, but grab a shower. I'll make you some food. You need to get moving or don't blame me when Genghis Khan shows up here to haul you out to the training centre."

The idea of anyone calling sweet Becki terrible names was funny as shit. "In spite of the fact I still feel like crap, fine. I'll be there."

His brother stood and pulled him off the couch, shoving him toward the back of the house. "Shower. You're currently the nearest thing Canada's got to a nuclear meltdown situation."

"Get the fuck out. I can wash my own ass." Marcus paused in the doorway to his bedroom to confirm that his brother hadn't followed him or did something stupid. Fortunately, David had headed to the kitchen and was ignoring him. "You're a bloody pain, you know that?"

"Dickhead," David shouted back easily. "God, what died in your fridge?"

Marcus retreated to the shower. His head still throbbed, but his curiosity was high enough to drag himself out of the house. After he'd shoveled in whatever David managed to drop before him.

He hadn't tasted a thing, too intent on discovering what kind of punishment he would have to take for disappearing without an explanation. Because he had a feeling Becki hadn't liked it one bit.

There was no sign of anyone in the gym, even though he recognized the cars in the parking lot. Marcus checked the pool, the weight room, the boardroom. No one. Frustrated, he pulled out his phone and called her.

"Marcus. How nice. Where the hell have you been?"

The chill in her voice shouldn't have made his dick harden. "Taking a vacation. The palm trees were calling my name. Where are you, and what's this bullshit I hear about you taking over my team?"

"Well, you weren't there. Someone had to do it. And if you have any more ideas of talking smack to me, shut up now, because I won't take it. You left without a word. I did my job and you weren't there, which means I'm not the one who's a bastard. Also? I don't care about excuses. You're three days behind on the training you and I specifically sat down and planned, and if you think I'm going to let you fuck with my head anymore in terms of spouting off about teamwork and shit? Dream on."

The violent sexual attraction he felt as she called him out wasn't right. His urge to track her down and fold her over the nearest flat object so he could fuck the hell out of her wasn't normal.

But he was honest enough to admit he wanted to. "Issues of you and my training aside, you didn't answer the question. Where are you?"

"Outside."

"Oh, that's helpful. We're in the middle of a one-and-a-half-million-acre national park. It's damn big outside, Becki. How about a more specific clue?"

"You're the goddamn search-and-rescue ace, so search."

The line went dead, and he swore. Stomped out the gym doors to start a calculated hunt.

He found them at the far end of the building. Or more accurately, he found them *on* the far end of the building. Running across the roof. Marcus bit back the shout that wanted to escape, ordering them all to the ground.

Couldn't interrupt like that, not only because it wasn't safe. Frightening one of them into a wrong move could send them tipping toward the earth—no crash mats, no protective gear.

He was going to find Becki and rip her a new one for whatever the hell game she was playing with his team.

He was spotted before he took more than two paces into their line of sight. Tripp's call was followed by brief waves from the squad before they ignored him and continued moving forward, the entire group bunched up and hanging on to each other.

Marcus hurried his step, trying not to stomp like some pissed-off juvenile. He got to the edge of the parking lot in time to observe them forming a human chain, lowering Tripp from the top of the two-story building to the narrow flat-topped roof over the entrance doors to the gym. With him acting as anchor, one by one the team crawled their way to the ground. Alisha was the last to be lowered, dropping from his hands into the outstretched reach of Devon.

She settled against him for a second, face to face, before they flew apart like two positive magnetic charges. They jerked around to gaze intently back at Tripp, last man on the building.

He made as if to jump, and Becki sang out, "Forget it. You want to start all over? Don't be impatient and blow it now."

Marcus hadn't seen her, leaning against the smooth wood of a birch as she stared at Tripp, glancing at her stopwatch.

Xavier and Anders rushed forward and formed a cradle with their arms. Alisha stepped into it and stood, instantly lifted high enough to catch hold of Tripp's fingers as the man reached down from his sitting position.

Somehow they pulled him off the roof and caught them both, Tripp changing places with Alisha, Devon there to help them both to the ground, like some intricate cheerleading routine. The five of them rushed forward to tag the tree Becki leaned on.

She clicked off the stopwatch and sighed heavily, totally ignoring Marcus as he stomped over to join their circle.

"No. Please, no—tell me we did it faster this time," Xavier groaned.

The others added their pleas, Anders dropping to sit next to Devon in a heap. "If we messed up again, I'd like to suggest something easy instead. Like a five-mile run."

Becki spun the stopwatch around, and they all leaned forward to peer at it.

Their shrieks of delight nearly drowned out her words.

"Good job. You're done. Showers, stretch, and tomorrow I'll let you play with ropes."

"Thanks, Becki," Alisha called, already racing toward the change room doors. "Hi, Marcus. We missed you."

Sure they had. The team scattered quickly enough he managed to contain his anger until the last one was gone.

Becki grabbed her bag from her feet, turning without a word toward the building.

"Oh no, you don't walk away from me without telling me what the hell you were doing with my team."

"Training them," Becki shouted over her shoulder as she kept going.

"They were on the fucking roof with no gear."

Becki planted a hand on the door handle and tossed him an evil glare. "They were never allowed to be more than two feet from another team member any time they moved.

They were each other's protective gear. They were being a team, which, if you had been here at the start, you would have known was the goal of the session." She bolted through the door before he could stop her.

He was going to go out of his goddamn mind.

Marcus jerked the handle to discover she'd locked it. By the time he'd dug in his pocket and found the correct key to open the stupid thing, she'd disappeared. The gym was completely empty.

He marched across to the women's change room and stormed in.

Becki turned from the lockers and dropped her fists to her hips. "Excuse me? Get out. Alisha is showering."

"Climbing the outside of buildings is illegal and dangerous. I thought you'd gotten that kind of immature stunt out of your system years ago."

She stared him down. "Well, if you don't like my teaching methods, you can take over. Or you can show up on time so we can discuss things first, and we'll all be much happier."

She spun on her heel and headed toward the showers.

"We're not done," Marcus snapped. "I'm supposed to train you. Help you work yourself back up to being safe on the wall."

Her pace slowed before she rotated on one heel, arms crossed in front of her chest. "I don't feel like climbing right now, thank you."

"I don't fucking care what you feel like. Gear up." His roar echoed off the walls, made even louder by the fact that the shower had cut off.

Alisha stuck her head cautiously around the corner, water dripping from her hair. She glanced between the two of them. "Umm, everything okay?"

"Just a discussion of training methods." Becki's voice came out rational and calm. Light-years away from the maniacal asshole he must have sounded like. "Marcus. Wait for me in the gym, please."

Great. He slammed out the door and paced the floor,

fighting to bring his temper back under control. Slowing his breathing, making the effort to look around and consider what training he could possibly do with Becki that didn't involve him tying her up and either spanking her ass or fucking her blind.

This wasn't what he needed. Not today, not with pain still pulsing through his brain and his arm aching. Although, to be honest, usually after he'd experienced an episode, or whatever he wanted to call them, he'd be exhausted and pissed for days.

Now he was pissed, but strangely energized. He had enough in him to want to take Becki over his knees and—

"Bye, Marcus." Alisha again, sneaking out of the change room with a towel still wrapped around her head, basically racing for the exit.

Now his team thought he was a raving lunatic. Awesome.

Marcus rubbed his temples, looking for some sort of miracle to give him enough strength to get through the next hour without throttling Becki. He went to where he'd dropped his gym bag, grabbed his prosthesis, and shoved it on, gritting his teeth at the sensation of the sleeve squeezing his stump. Doing up straps distracted him for long enough to realize she was taking a bloody long time getting ready.

He pushed open the change room door. "You coming out this century?"

No answer.

If she'd decided to blow him off and take a shower, he had no objections to taking his hand to her bare ass. He threw open the door and entered, looking around for where she'd hidden. Not in the change area. Not in the showers.

He felt like an idiot bending over in the bathroom to see if he could spot her feet in one of the toilet stalls. "Becki? You okay?"

The teeny wisp of concern that had started to weave its way into his anger evaporated as he noticed something by the open change room window blowing in the wind.

She'd left him a goddamned note taped to the wall.

Training today starts with a run. If you're not too hungover/lazy/whatever the hell happened to you, run the Tunnel Mountain trail. Otherwise, call me tonight if you still want me to train your team.

Becki

Frustration still boiled. Pain hovered. But . . .

Marcus closed the window and bolted it. Then he went and exchanged his prosthesis for his running shoes.

CHAPTER 11

''''''''''''''''''''''''''''''''

Running took away the anger. It was difficult to hold on to fury when every ounce of focus was directed toward gasping for air and moving one leg after another. Smacking her feet into the ground was incredibly gratifying even though she knew she'd regret it later, her overenthusiastic clomps burning up energy she'd crave on the downward journey.

The trail zigzagged again and she turned the corner, lactic acid scorching her thighs as she pumped out another sprint of a dozen steps.

Marcus had the gall to show up after vanishing for three days, then give *her* shit for her training methods?

Screw him.

Okay, maybe she hadn't gotten rid of all her frustrations yet, but after three days she'd built up a fine head of steam, and it was going to take a bit to let this go.

The climb was steep enough that she could push thinking out of her head. Concentrate on the trail. On the blood pumping through her veins. In her ears, a rhythm pulsated—her feet like drumbeats, her pulse a living accompaniment. Each intake of breath timed to settle between the thumps.

When she reached the first lookout she slowed to a walk, sucking in air and pacing slowly to settle her breathing. She wondered if Marcus would come after her.

She wondered if she'd be able to resist kicking him if he did.

Becki grabbed onto the railing and stretched, looking over the valley. The pine forests of the foothills created a carpet of green to contrast with the gray and black of the towering Rockies, snow still clinging to their peaks. The thin line of the Bow River cut through the distance, a sliver of shining silver winding back and forth like a ribbon. She couldn't see the falls or the main parts of the town site. Far enough up and far enough away to feel as if she were alone in the bush.

The wilderness closing in around her.

A shiver of fear whispered over her skin that annoyed her far more than Marcus's desertion over the past days.

She was not going to be defeated. And if Marcus couldn't be trusted to come through and help her train, she'd find someone who could. Climbing had been such an important part of her life—yeah, she'd told Marcus she was trying to find new ways to be happy, but that was partly a lie.

She wanted to do new things, but she didn't want to give up the old. Having everything she was renowned for torn from her grasp hurt. Everything that had meant something in her life—her position, her future . . .

Dane.

Another flash of pain struck her, and she actually hissed, twisting away from the railing and preparing to run the next section of trail. Ready to run to escape the hurt.

Marcus crested the hill and slowed to a walk, approaching cautiously. His gaze fixed on her, his face blank.

At least he didn't look ready to commit murder anymore, as he had in the change room.

She stood her ground as she waited for him. He came all

the way to a stop directly in front of her. Her arms crossed involuntarily. A barrier between them less formidable than their recent emotional confrontation.

Marcus looked her over, his chest moving heavily as he caught his breath. He'd left the prosthesis off, his long-sleeved shirt dampened with sweat in spite of the cooler temperatures. His hair had gone wild from the wind, or more probably from him dragging his hand through it as she'd seen him do a number of times.

There were dark shadows under his eyes, a thick layer of scruff on his chin and upper lip, and no matter how upset she was, she couldn't help wonder what really had happened over the past days. David had been noncommittal other than giving assurances that Marcus was fine.

"You climbed out the window," Marcus noted blandly.

"You were being a jerk," she rejoined.

He snorted. "Yah, well, there's nothing new in that. Not sure why you were surprised."

"Because it was now," she snapped, her concern flickering and ready to die away. "That's not the man I signed up to spend time with. So if there's a change in situation, let me know."

She planned to turn, to hit the trail, when he caught her arm. "Becki. I'm sorry."

Becki wavered. Part of her didn't want to be generous and listen. "If I call *bullshit* right now, I suppose I'm not being very forgiving. But you want to tell me a little more specifically what you're sorry for?"

"I shouldn't have shouted at you," he admitted. "I'm still mad, and we need to talk, because I get you're upset as well. But I shouldn't have raised my voice."

She nodded slowly, fighting to resist sharing the internal dry commentary that noted the shouting was the least offensive part of the entire situation. Still, he was a man. That "sorry" would have cost him. She caved a little—the only area she was willing to accept he had a smidgen of a right to bitch about. "I wasn't being careless with your team's safety. I clearly went over the parameters of how and where they were allowed to move. And climbing a building is illegal only if you do it without permission."

His lips twitched. "Or if it's a world heritage site."

"You're never going to let me forget that incident, are you?"

His gaze heated, the staid, controlled man melting away as if memories of their nights of passion snapped to his mind as quickly as they did to hers.

Good grief. Maybe she should haul him back to her dorm room and get this out between them. The urge to strip naked was as bad as it had been seven years earlier, a pile of kindling ready to burst into an inferno.

Then thoughts of what she'd lost intruded, and the far more bitter memories of fear and terror wiped away all sexual lusts.

Dane was dead. Her memory was gone—except for the haunting dreams that had begun the night after she'd frozen on the wall. Nightmares that made her want to start running again and not stop until she was exhausted.

"Why are you looking like that?" Marcus asked, his fingers soft on her shoulder. "Becki? Are you okay?"

She took a deep breath, focusing on the ridge of clouds sneaking over the mountain range. The answer to that question was far too big a topic to break open on the side of a trail. "We should finish our workout before the weather changes."

He withdrew his touch, staring at her silently. Becki twisted away under the guise of stretching to avoid having to meet his too-perceptive gaze any longer.

At least they weren't ready to strangle each other anymore.

"Come on." Becki tilted her head toward the trail. "Let's burn off the rest of the gunk in our brains."

Without a word, Marcus joined her.

Sharing the hard physical pain of a demanding workout was far easier than sharing the emotional turmoil inside.

He knew he should say something. Explain where he'd been, why he'd blown off training the past three days, but by the end of the run he was hurting so badly he could barely think. The entire time-delayed backlash from his episode hit at once, and he stumbled into the gym after Becki, all his concentration on putting one foot in front of the other.

Stars floated in front of his eyes as he lurched for the mats, hoping to get to them before he collapsed on the hard wooden flooring.

A cool cloth pressed against his face. Something rigid into his palm.

"Marcus. Drink." Becki's voice prodded him. She didn't sound pissed anymore. That was good. He didn't want her pissed at him.

The cool water slipped down his throat, easing the pain. Loosening the numbness until he could blink and glance around the room.

Becki squatted beside him, one hand resting on his shoulder. "You with me?"

Damn. "We taking turns blacking out now?"

"I don't think you went anywhere, but you were a touch dazed." She squeezed her fingers. "Now I'm the one who needs to apologize. I exploded like a crazy woman and assumed you blew off training for no good reason. That was wrong of me."

He struggled to get the words out. He'd held them for so long it was difficult to actually come out and let someone other than David know. And why the urgent need to say anything now, to Becki, drove him, he wasn't sure.

But he *had* to say something. "I have these . . . episodes every now and then. No warning, no idea how long they will last. They're getting less frequent, though. That much is good."

Her eyes widened. "Damn."

Marcus shrugged. He took another few swallows before he cleared his throat. "So much for my superpowers."

She settled back, stretching her legs in front of her. "Yeah, well. Looks like neither of us is quite who we used to be."

He hadn't been for a long, long time.

Marcus glanced over. There were shadows under her eyes and faint lines at the corners, but the signs of her sheer enthusiasm were also unmistakable. Her hopes of getting back into the world that had been torn from her. He couldn't destroy that hope. Even though he'd discovered for himself there were some things you never recovered from, that didn't mean *she* never could. And as long as there was hope, he would goddamn not let himself become a barrier to her dreams.

He deliberately pushed aside his personal frustrations and reached out with every bit of acting skill he had. "You'll get there. We'll train you. Get you back into the swing of it. You're good, Becki. Good with the team." *Good for me.* "Thanks for stepping in when I bailed."

She nodded. "They were—something positive to focus on."

"Were they tough days? Not just the filling-in-for-me part."

She stared at the ceiling, biting her lip. When she turned to face him, the corners of her mouth had turned down. "Nightmares. Since I froze on the wall, I haven't been sleeping very well."

His skin crawled, but he kept his response to himself. "The accident?"

Becki sighed. "Yeah, but you don't need me dumping on you."

He caught her by the wrist when she stood. "It's not dumping. Sounds as if you've been dealing with fallout from the accident for a while, and maybe the whole wall thing will finally let you move past it."

"Still don't need to take it out on you."

"You want the name of a good shrink here in town?"

She pulled a face. "I'd prefer to dump on you."

He laughed, then regretted it as his temples throbbed. "I hear you, but they can help." Not always, but again he kept his opinion to himself. His situation was not hers.

They were both standing now. Marcus forced his feet to remain steady.

Becki folded her arms around her body. "I'll take you up on your offer if the nightmares get worse. Maybe having mentioned them out loud will be enough to make them go away. I'm going to shower, and you look like you need to crash as well. You going to be okay?"

"I'm fine."

If he hadn't felt like a wet rope, he would have insisted on doing more for her. He was a short time away from a crash. Still—"Becki?"

"Yeah?"

A spark of an idea flew, triggered by David's conversation. "You interested in grabbing some dinner tonight? Taste of Banff is happening in town. We can enjoy a few samples. You can see how the restaurants have changed. A chance to talk—about whatever."

It was an olive branch, the best he could manage with the anvil resting on his brain.

She smiled. "I've got to remember this trick. Shout at a guy, and get offered a dinner date. Awesome."

"You game?"

"After a nap." She covered her mouth as she yawned, but he still caught it and the two of them grinned sheepishly at each other when they were done. "Like I said, we're a matching set of zombies right now."

"Just what Banff needs. The Zombie Apocalypse. Typical Thursday." He grabbed his things. "If you want to shower here, go ahead. Pull the gym door shut behind you when you leave."

Becki nodded. "What time shall I meet you?"

"Can you be ready by six?"

"No problem."

They stared at each other for a minute, neither of them willing to leave. Neither of them willing to make any further move forward, either.

Marcus twitched. "Zombie is right. I'll catch you in a few."

Walking away from her was tough, but the numbness needed to be answered before he totally fell apart. Hopefully after a couple solid hours of sleep he'd be able to figure out what was the next step. What he could do to help her avoid the trap he'd fallen into.

If he could push her to the light, maybe it would make his darkness a little more bearable.

CHAPTER 12

''''''''''''''''''''''''''''''''''

She'd been cold to start, and now that the wind picked up, the moisture in the air soaked her completely. The least pleasurable part of climbing was made all the worse by the fact that he was being an idiot. Just as he'd been for over a month.

"You ready? Sometime today . . . would be great."

His hesitancy was clear. Probably figured she was going to freak out and give him hell again. "Bastard."

He sighed heavily. "I heard that."

"Bastard with Superman hearing. Good for you." She didn't care how rude she was being. Maybe if he heard it a few more times he'd stop being one. "Dane, I can't see a bloody thing. I could be exactly on route, or hanging over a thousand-foot free fall for all I know."

"You want me to go first?" His instant response was so puppy-dog eager she felt a second's twinge for being snarky.

Only a second, though. She snapped out, "You couldn't have said something fifteen minutes ago? Jerk."

"Yeah, but I'm your jerk, right?" Begging for approval.

*Stroking her like he longed to have her forgive him and
move on. After the weekend they'd spent together she'd had
enough. It only highlighted the way he'd been acting over
the past weeks.*

*Something had changed, and she hated what had become
of their relationship. And once they got off the bloody mountain, there was no way this was going to continue. Still,
humouring him for the moment was the only logical decision. "Yes, Dane, you're my jerk."*

*Because taunting the person holding your safety line?
Monumentally stupid.*

"Bec? Love you."

*She leaned back, staring up the hillside. What the hell
was the matter with him? "Dane?"*

All hell broke loose. . . .

She curled into a ball as she waited for her heart to stop
pounding. Sweat covered her skin, and her scream of terror
echoed in her ears. It was a good thing the dorms were still
empty, or she would have had people pounding at her door
to see who'd been murdered.

Her brilliant idea of a nap had backfired.

By the time she'd managed to unroll herself, Becki was
more pissed off than frightened. The nightmares were
becoming worse—having mentioned it to Marcus hadn't
helped at all. If anything, it was more terrifying now than
it had been the night before.

If only they didn't keep changing. Maybe a recurring
nightmare she could take, but one that every time made her
think something was about to happen, and then it didn't . . . ?

She'd been able to redirect her dreams before, but these
were going to drive her mad.

It took a second shower to clean the stench of the nightmare from her body. She rubbed cream all over herself, got
dressed.

Realizing that she now wore her prettiest bra and undies

was another kick in the gut. She wasn't intending to let anyone see her in them. There was no reason to take extra care with her makeup and hair.

No reason other than the fact that concentrating on Marcus and sex was far preferable to panicking about what mysteries remained hidden in her brain.

When he picked her up, she was more tongue-tied than ever. His black jeans and grey sweater made his eyes look darker, the stubble on his chin emphasizing his strong jaw. He stood beside the door and helped her in, his fingers warm against her cold ones.

"You keeping the beard?" she teased.

"Shaver wasn't charged, and I slept too late to mess with a razor one-handed." He glanced over her, approval on his face. "You look great."

She'd never been a blusher. Not even when she was young, but right then and there, blood rushed to her cheeks. "Thanks."

He found them a parking spot, escorted her to the door. Together they moved through the line of people exchanging ticket stubs for tiny portions of different local menu samples. Buffalo steak. West Coast wild salmon. Marcus balanced his plate on his left elbow, using his right hand to point out items for her to try. He'd given her control of the coupons, and in the end he carried both their full plates to the table while she passed over the correct stubs to the woman at the end of the lineup.

Becki eased into the chair opposite him, suddenly glad she'd accepted the invitation to Banff. No matter how far she had to go, being there was right.

Small talk and comparisons of the various foods followed. Becki lifted a forkful of her venison for Marcus to try, and he licked the utensil clean, his gaze riveted on her. The meal was comfortable, and yet not.

Anticipation hovered between them.

Unanswered questions.

Their after-dinner coffees had already been poured

before she decided to stop being a wuss and talk to him about something more important than climbing shoes or gasket selections.

"I had another dream this afternoon." She sipped her drink, watching him over the brim.

His shoulders tightened, focus narrowing. "You okay? Why didn't you mention—"

"—it earlier?" Becki cut in. "Because I'm tired. And being tired is getting old. I can't let this get the better of me."

"Not sleeping makes it worse."

He had that right. "I keep thinking I'm about to find out the next thing that happens. But then the dream folds over and repeats. Like some twisted *Groundhog Day* movie in my brain. I see the same scene over and over again."

"The accident?" he asked. She nodded. "Frustrating. It would be better if it moved forward."

She snorted. "Part of me thinks it would be better if the dreams went away altogether, but you're right. Maybe then I could actually know what happened. But even the stupid loop is mucked up."

Marcus rested his elbows on the table and leaned in closer. "Mucked up how?"

"It changes. It's still the same scene, it's always me and Dane, but we're different. We act differently, show different emotions. One time he was such an ass to me, I woke up wanting to punch him. Well, after I got back to breathing normally. And the next time, oh my God, I could have thrown myself off the cliff. I was such a bitch. Completely out of control and irresponsible."

She took a deep breath, shook her head in frustration. "I don't know which of these is the truth. Maybe I did cause the accident. Maybe I was out of line and did something horrible that ended up getting him killed."

He grabbed her hand. "Trust me. The scenario where you were a bitch? That's not the one that's true."

Yeah, right. "After I ragged on you for no reason this afternoon? I don't think you're considering all your facts."

"Actually, our little debate today is exactly why I don't

think you did anything belligerent when you were out there."
He released her fingers. "Even when you were rightly furious with me you still behaved in a professional manner—
well, except for the climbing-out-the-window part, but that's
in character as well."

Her cheeks twitched with the urge to smile. "I swear I
haven't done anything like that for years. You bring out the
devil in me."

His eyes flashed. Something dark and lust-filled stared
back at her. She felt her body heating up. Responding to him
as always.

"Talk about bringing out the devil in a person." Marcus
spoke softly. "You had all your medical work done up for
the school?"

"Of course. You think there's something in there that
would explain why I can't remember details?"

He stared at her lips before slowly rolling his gaze down
her body. "No. Just making sure your record is as clean as
mine."

Shit. A direct hit of desire to her core burst upward as if
he'd aimed a bomb between her thighs. She squeezed her
legs together to fight the urge to slip her hand into her lap.
"Are you trying to distract me from talking about nightmares?"

"It's your fault. I'm being distracted by your perfume.
Suddenly I don't want anything more for dessert but you.
Any way I can have you."

Her mouth went dry. "Marcus—"

"You on birth control? Because while I'd prefer to go
without, we can use condoms. They're a little tougher to
deal with one-handed. You'll have to help me put them on."

"What are you doing?" Becki whispered, glancing
around the room to make sure they weren't being overheard.
Their nearest dinner partners seemed oblivious, but Becki
wasn't sure if she should slap him or jump him.

Damn stupid body for mixing reactions.

Then he leaned back and relaxed, his body language
shifting from sexual predator to casual friendship. "See, if

you were prone to doing something irrational and wild? You would have at least thrown something at me for being a jerk just now, even though we're in a public place. Only you're not like that, Becki. You're a good person. Whatever is hidden in your brain and pushing your buttons, it's not that you were a crazed lunatic, okay?"

Her pulse was still going a million miles an hour. She was torn between laughing and punching him in the gut, but however twisted his method had been, it had worked. He had a valid point. While she might be impulsive, she had never done anything cruel or malicious, nothing to indicate the whack-job dreams were real.

His method of making his argument, however, had been over the top and outrageous. She smiled. Kind of in character for him as well. Good thing she was bent, but not broken.

One good—*deed*—deserved another.

"Yes." She took a deep breath, filling her lungs and forcing her breasts against the fabric of her top. His gaze dropped from her face, involuntarily tracing the edge of her scoop-necked blouse as she arched slightly to make the swells ease upward even farther.

His breathing skipped a notch. "Yes, what? You agree you're not a crazy woman?"

"Definitely not crazy. Good point." She dragged a finger through the leftover chocolate on the plate before them, lifted it to her mouth, and slipped the gooey sauce between her lips. Sucking lightly and *humming* as she stared at him from under her lashes. "Also, yes. I'm on birth control. I far prefer being skin on skin during sex, but I'm picky about who I allow the privilege of partnering with me bare. Although the idea of putting a condom on you does sound . . . intriguing. I think I remember how."

"Fuck." Marcus breathed the word on a moan. His gaze lifted to meet hers, heat and desire widening his pupils. His nostrils flared. He adjusted position in his seat uneasily.

They stared at each other, Becki fighting to maintain her sultry smile without letting it turn into the real *take me now* expression that wanted to escape. Then he broke, amusement brightening his dark visage as he realized what she'd done. "Troublemaker."

"You deserved that," she insisted, hiding her real desires.

"Maybe. Probably."

"Try definitely." Becki smiled. "But as inappropriate and outrageous as we both were, you're right. I don't think I did anything wrong in September. I wish I could know for sure."

"Hopefully someday. In the meantime, are we back on for training tomorrow? I have an idea to try. I think it should work."

She shivered but straightened. "I'll be there."

It wasn't the notion of hitting the wall the next day that followed her for the rest of the evening. Wasn't the dread of going to sleep and once again experiencing a horrifying reenactment of Dane falling from the mountainside.

Something else made her blood hum the entire trip home as Marcus helped her in and out of the truck, walked her to the door of the dorms. Tipped an imaginary hat before strolling off whistling.

Sexual desire pulsed through her veins and heated her skin.

She'd never been one to leave herself hanging, and if she didn't want to be on the phone and begging him to come crawl into her bed, something needed to be done now. Becki slipped her clothes off and shook her head at the waste of her pretty underwear not getting to be admired.

Then again, the expression on Marcus's face when she'd mentioned going skin on skin? Fixing that image in her mind was more than enough to make her limbs tremble.

She grabbed her vibrator from the dresser, and slid into bed. The cool of the sheets brushing her torso as she squirmed into a more comfortable position didn't do much to lower her temperature. She leaned back on the pillows and dropped the toy aside for a moment as she raised her hands to her breasts and cupped them, picturing Marcus across from her, his gaze never leaving her body.

Breasts gone heavy and needy, her sex already wet, she

wasn't interested in a long, drawn-out event. Not tonight, not when foreplay started after dinner. And while Marcus had taught her the value of patience, rule two was *move decisively*.

She lifted the vibrator and pressed it to her clit, keeping the motor on low, knowing that anything more would make her break far too soon for satisfaction.

It was the thought of his touch—tongue, fingers, cock—that she wanted to send her over. That wasn't her pinching her sensitive nipples; it was Marcus using his teeth, his bite taking her to the edge where pleasure and pain blurred. His hand trailing between her legs to make her clit vibrate with need. His cock sliding deep into her, stretching as he thrust again and again. Faster, harder. Becki pulled her knees wide to the sides and felt him move over her, trapping her in position as he released the wildness she'd seen in his eyes. The need.

For her.

Her orgasm took hold and shook her hard, making her gasp as her core pulsed around a cock that wasn't there. She breathed out and let the sensation roll through her, wishing for more.

Aching for more.

She dropped the vibrator to the side and curled up, trying to imagine him at her back. Surrounding her to keep the nightmares at bay.

CHAPTER 13

''''''''''''''''''''''''''''''''

She moved smoothly across the floor, body-hugging work-out gear covering her, thin-soled climbing shoes on her feet. Marcus wondered if she was thinking about the previous climb, worried how her mind might respond to the challenge today, but her restraint was incredible. He could have asked her to join him for a cup of tea, she was so controlled as she paced to the equipment cubicles and pulled out her harness, then buckled and tightened without a word before turning to face him.

"Yes, sir. Where do you want me?"

Naked, in my bed shouldn't have been the first thought in his brain. "Pitch three. Nice and easy. You're going to use only the red route. We'll see if having a focus will distract you enough to finish the climb with no troubles."

Becki snorted. "You don't think much of my skills if you think sticking to the red holds is enough to sidetrack me."

He remained quiet as they both roped up. She lifted her chin to examine the route, and he saw it. A shiver as she reached to grasp the wall.

Shivered, but still went forward. Marcus admired her a whole hell of a lot in that moment.

"Wait. Put this on."

He held out the fabric he'd brought with him, and a crease appeared between her brows. "What's that? A flag to wave when I've had enough?"

"It's a blindfold. Put it on. Now."

She swallowed. "But—"

"I'll be your eyes. You have to trust me. And you'll have to concentrate, because once I tell you where a hold is? I'm not telling you again. You have to keep the location and shape in mind for when you'll need it for your feet."

"You expect me to climb blind?" She wiggled the cloth. "You're insane."

"You're just mad you didn't think of it first."

A snort of amusement escaped her. She glanced at him, and for the first time real fear showed in her eyes. "Marcus, what if . . ."

He shook his head. "No. Don't question. Yourself, or me. Do it. Put on the blindfold, Becki, and put yourself into my hands."

Her tongue snuck out for a second, and he fought the urge to go catch her against him and slip his own tongue along her lips. To taste her. To take. The headache that had haunted him over the past days was gone, replaced with lust like he'd not experienced in a long time.

He'd never had a cure like her around before.

Becki lifted her hands and pressed the dark material over her face, knotting the fabric behind her head. "I'm not going to ask where you found the blindfold."

He ignored the temptation to list the other toys he planned to use on her someday. "Turn, right shoulder back."

She straightened and took a deep breath, her chest moving too rapidly. "Marcus . . . I—"

"My voice. Listen to it. Nothing else. I'm your anchor, and I won't let anything happen to you. Do you trust me?"

Her chin dipped briefly.

"Right shoulder back," he repeated.

She obeyed, moving slowly, hands rising to shoulder height. "If I make it through this unscathed, you should win some kind of award."

He planned to be rewarded, all right. Just hadn't decided exactly how much he was going to take. "Stop. Right hand out. Finger hook hold at two o'clock."

She caught it, then slipped her fingers all the way into the solid U-shaped hold. "On belay?"

A mixture of pride and respect washed through him. Even changing up the rules, she slipped back into climbing mode without hesitation. He could believe she'd done a rescue on autopilot. "Belay on. Left hand, eleven o'clock. Shaped like a tennis ball."

His voice echoed slightly in the wide-open space of the gym, her breathing creating a systematic pulse under his words. He took her up the wall far slower than she'd probably climbed for years, but she didn't waver. Didn't complain, either, thank God. He made her pause at each position, adjust her weight.

Made her work her body and her brain, all the while hoping like hell she wasn't about to freeze again.

"Don't rush. Right leg, extend another inch and you'll have the hold. That's it. Weight transfer. Lift your other thigh. Picture where you left the sloper—it's got a nice flat surface for your foot."

He talked her through a dozen more holds before she interrupted him. "Marcus. Can . . . Can I just climb?"

"Without the blindfold?" He wasn't sure about that. Success to fifteen feet wasn't full-out success.

"No, with. Only, no route. Talk me through if I can't find a hold, but I like how this feels. I'm itching to go faster."

A stroke of adrenaline hit him: pride at her courage, familiar need in his own gut. "Who am I to hold you back if you're ready to fly?"

She twisted toward him and smiled, her mouth and chin the only parts visible under the wide blindfold. Then she faced the wall and moved.

Marcus worked the rope silently, his voice silenced but

ready to help if required. Ready to coax or rant, depending on her need.

She didn't need anything. Becki reached overhead, sliding her hands blindly. She skimmed her fingers over each hold as she found them, testing the surfaces before moving to the next. When she selected one she liked, she caught hold, adjusted her grip, and rose. Her feet found new positions, the edges of her climbing shoes pressing against the smallest of protrusions without a thought.

She was three-quarters of the way to the ceiling before he spoke. "Nicely done. You have lovely technique."

"Take," she ordered.

He pulled up the slack and secured her in position. "Got. How you doing? Ready to come down?"

Becki held the wall with one hand, the other wrapped easily around the rope as she sat back and allowed him to support her weight. "Yeah. I guess."

"Feels good?"

"Feels . . . weird." Her lips twitched. "I can feel the air around me, but the only clue I have of the height is your voice. And honest? I'm not ready to take the blindfold off."

"Then don't. You achieved one goal. Accept it, celebrate it. Get in position and I'll bring you to earth."

She faced the wall, legs spread, feet firmly in position. "Lower."

He let the rope through the clamp slowly, easily, twisting to release it an inch at a time. Becki walked her way to the floor and lay back on the mat, arms limp to the sides. Blindfold still in place.

"Why do I feel as if I finished climbing a 5.11?"

"Good analogy. Until you get over this bump, everything is a freaking win. Got that?"

Marcus had the rope free from his harness in record time, stepping beside her, his heart pumping with excitement. "Give me your hand."

She raised her fingers in the air, and he caught her wrist. He lifted her to her feet easily. When she would have pulled the blindfold away, he spoke.

"Stop."

Becki paused, her hands on the fabric. "Umm, why?"

Because he was more than ready for the next stage. "Celebrating your successful climb. You said if it worked, I got an award."

He curled his hand around her neck and brought her mouth to his.

She'd known this was coming. Expected it. Not this instant, but soon. The fever between them burned too hot to be ignored. After yesterday and the myriad of emotions they'd gone through—anger, frustration, lust—she wanted this. Needed it.

Something to combat the terrors she'd experienced when he'd gone missing. The nightmares and the fears that had swept in and threatened to overwhelm her. She shoved everything aside for now. Inflamed by her success in overcoming at least one ghost, she pressed against him eagerly.

The kiss started softly, just a meeting of lips, but like fire trickling along the edge of a paper, heat and desire grew. Spread. He stroked her mouth with his tongue, dipping in softly, testing her willingness.

His chest against hers was solid and hard, a barrier she couldn't get around, and one she didn't want to avoid. When she parted her lips and let him in, a rush of adrenaline made her light-headed. With the blindfold in place there was nothing to see, only sensations. Nothing but their own ragged breathing to hear. The taste of his lips, the feel of him under her touch.

She slipped her hands across his chest, savouring the way his muscles tightened as she explored. The way he groaned and caught her around the waist with his left arm. His tight grip brought their torsos into contact and the rising hardness of his erection was clear, no matter how many layers of webbing there were between them.

He kissed her harder. Consumed her, pulsed his groin against hers and let his excitement show in the way he took her mouth. Made her ache.

He tore his lips away only to press them to her throat, her neck, biting and nipping his way along her body. His right hand slipped upward until he cupped her breast, holding her intimately.

She arched into him. Needing. Aching. Wanting more, to take the rush of endorphins from her climb and put them into stripping him and fucking him right there, damn the consequences.

He tugged her shirt free, heated fingers skimming over her waist, coming back to jerk her sports bra out of the way so he could take possession of her naked breast.

It was too much, and not enough. She twisted against him, rubbing until the webbing of her harness caught his, and they were both trapped.

His fingers pinched her nipple and she moaned out her pleasure. Marcus dragged his teeth up her neck, returning to capture her mouth yet again. Becki breathed him in. Breathed in the scent of chalk dust in the air, the sweat of the climb, her lingering fear.

God, she wanted him.

When he slowed she whimpered in protest, the sound escaping louder than expected as his lips left hers. He adjusted her bra, straightened her shirt, smoothed a touch over her waist.

And stepped away, leaving her panting and wavering on her feet.

"Take off the blindfold." The order whispered out, nonetheless commanding for the volume.

She lifted her hands to undo the knot, knowing that she was flushed. Wondering what she'd see on his face.

What she found made her breath shake as she fought to fill her lungs.

Pride.

Admiration.

Craving.

She was still reeling from his kiss. From the euphoria of the climb. From the way following his every order had made her tingle with nearly forgotten satisfaction.

Seven years ago while he'd played her body like a fine instrument, he'd shared his philosophy regarding climbing. No—more than that. It had been his attitude concerning *living*, and she'd grasped hold of those beliefs with two hands and not let go.

Not until the accident had torn her world from her.

Every reminder of who she *had* been helped keep alive the hope that she could get herself back.

Marcus forced her to remember that life was more than the ability to climb. That her passions ran deeper than the job she did and the people she rescued. Made her wonder if perhaps fate had put this man in her path, again, for more than one reason.

Now she needed the courage to accept and take the next step.

CHAPTER 14

Becki stuck around after Lifeline's Saturday morning training was complete, hanging over the deck railing to observe Erin hover the team over the drop site as they rappelled to targets Marcus placed on the ground.

No matter how enjoyable staring after the man and admiring him from a distance was, it didn't make her next decision any easier.

They'd left the gym the day before without speaking of the kiss. Without Marcus making any more demands or requests of her, which was good, because if he had suggested they go back to his house and spend the night locked together, she would have agreed in an instant.

Then regretted it in the morning.

"Tripp. Haul ass up and try again," Marcus shouted. Tripp waved before hooking his hands onto the swinging rope and moved hand over hand toward the chopper. A safety rope dangled from his harness, but he did the work himself, rising to the level of the open side door, where hands reached to drag him into the cargo bay.

Alisha stepped out, rappelling downward efficiently, stopping five feet from the ground and gesturing toward the field. Anders could be seen in the opening as he adjusted tensions, Erin shifting the entire chopper to the south.

Smooth and serene, as if she were walking down the sidewalk of Banff Avenue, Alisha used the momentum of the rope to launch herself the final distance to land directly on a target, both feet squarely in the center.

Marcus gave her a high five, the young woman's face beaming with delight as he motioned his approval to the aircraft with a thumbs-up.

Becki applauded as Alisha unclipped and headed toward the building, a wide grin on her face.

Yes, Marcus knew how to time things, whether deliberate praise as to Alisha, or the perfect moment and method he'd used the previous day to coax a climb out of her.

To coax a climb, a kiss, and a grope—oh, the man had no issues with timing whatsoever. Becki still wasn't sure what to think about it.

Passion was a good thing. Enjoying sex was fine—she wouldn't even consider it an indulgence. But she was old enough to want everything she did to be for more reasons than it felt good at the time.

She needed her mind engaged as well as her hormones.

Becki was still pondering her current dilemma an hour later when the exercise was done and everyone had turned to relaxing. The guys took off without a word, leaving Becki with Erin and Alisha at the staff headquarters.

"Lunch?" Becki asked.

"Boys are bringing food back. You can pour me a juice," Erin requested as she made her way to the couch. She threw herself down and propped her feet on the coffee table. "I'd ask for something with a kick, but I swore off the rotgut until boot camp is completed."

"Nothing for me," Alisha called. "I want to finish this chapter before lunch arrives."

She grabbed a book from her backpack. Becki filled two

glasses with orange juice and brought them over to where Erin was sprawled. "Keeping yourself on your toes?"

"Damn right. Plus now I don't trust Marcus not to call and get me out of bed five minutes after I collapse from a binge."

"He would, too." She sat across from Erin and shook her head. "Tough session?"

"Wind kept shifting. Flying March to May around here is a whole lot more exciting than the rest of the year put together. Did you hear it's supposed to snow tonight? The mountains and the changing temperatures make me doubly glad there's not a lot of people on the trails this time of year." Erin closed her eyes, head back against the couch. "Still, wouldn't trade it for anything. The adrenaline rush is like crack."

If anyone would understand the thrills she missed, and her continuing confusion, it was another SAR member. The one extra component was what added to the intricacy of this situation. Becki swirled the last of her drink against the ice and considered whether discussing her uncertainty with Erin would be totally out of line.

She stuck with a safer query. "You like working for Lifeline?"

Erin sat up slowly, as if considering as she pulled her hair into order, the thick black mass of it barely contained in her ponytail. "Lifeline rocks. The team is great. They don't drive me totally mad, only partially. I get to fly and usually have enough spare time to indulge my bad habits. What's not to love?"

"Bad habits, huh?" She looked Erin over with curiosity. Becki bet it would be interesting to discover what Erin, so poised and confident, considered an indulgence. After reading the team files Becki knew they were nearly the same age, and having someone she could talk to about more than work was definitely on the list of things needed in her life.

She didn't realize how long she'd been silently pondering when Erin laughed. "You're twitching like you've got something on your mind. Ask or don't. No skin off my back. But if you want to talk, I've seen more than the little blonde girl in the corner."

Becki smiled, glancing over at where the young woman in question was curled up on one of the couches on the far side of the room. Alisha was totally engrossed in her book, eyes going wide every now and then as she read. "She is sweet, isn't she?"

"Like honey on an ice cream cone. Gets everything around her sticky and messy as well." Erin shuddered. Becki laughed. "Well, it's true. She talked me into going to see some Disney release the other day."

"Hey, they aren't all bad."

Erin sniffed. "I know, and I won't even lie—I had to break out the tissues at one point. God, I hate that."

Alisha stood with a jerk, slipped her finger between the pages to hold her spot, and left the room without a backward glance.

"And . . . countdown to Devon entering our view in three, two, one . . . On schedule." Erin mock-bowed as the blond young man crossed into their line of vision. He stared after Alisha's retreating back as he dropped to the couch, his expression clearly one of frustration. "You know, I can hardly wait until those two get this twisted foreplay out of their system and just fuck each other stupid. It's getting old putting up with their weird dance."

"Really?" Becki looked Devon over again, this time armed with Erin's suggestion, and thought through all the interactions she'd seen between Alisha and Devon. "I suppose that makes sense, in some weird way."

"See? Twisted."

Becki smiled. "Well, I might be nearly as twisted. What do you think of Marcus?"

"My Marcus? Like the guy who pays my salary so he's allowed to shout at me and demand all sorts of insane things from me? Like making me stand on a platform in the dark and practice recognizing which direction the wind is coming from?"

Becki couldn't stop her laughter. "Where does he get these ideas from?"

"You should talk." Erin grimaced. "Are games some kind of obsession with you? Because the next time you set up orienteering, I'm calling in sick."

"What are you complaining about? You did great."

Erin shook her head, "Oh no, you're not distracting me anymore. What's got your knickers in a twist? We already established the *who* as Marcus, which, hello, no surprise there since you've been working with him for a week now. Some guys just have a way of getting under your skin like nobody's business."

"Yeah." Becki considered carefully, making sure Devon was still out of earshot on the far side of the room. At what point was she sharing too much? "We had a fling once."

"Oh really?" Erin raised her glass in salute. "Nice. Not that I want details, but I always imagined he's the type to know what to do under the sheets."

And against the wall. On the floor. Becki smiled. "Decisive is . . . an understatement."

Erin nodded. Waited. Finally made a face and laughed. "So, let me guess. You're considering another round?"

"Considering, then thinking *no*. Considering, then thinking *yes*. I'm like some weird sexual yo-yo, and it's driving me crazy."

"Is it because you're working together?" Erin shrugged. "Because I don't think what you've got going is a big deal. It's not as if you'll be running rescues together. That's the time when relationships get freaky."

"I was sleeping with my climbing partner," Becki confessed.

Erin twisted her mouth to the side. "But you worked search and rescue in Yellowstone, and he didn't, right?"

"No, but . . ." Yeah, she saw the point. "It's still Dane I'm thinking about."

The other woman sat quietly for a moment. "How long ago is it again? Eight months or so?"

Becki nodded.

"Oh hon, you're tying the knots tighter and faster than you can untie them. You miss him?"

Guilt and confusion made lousy analytical tools. "Maybe? We were comfortable. We weren't in love."

Erin sat back and sipped her drink for a minute. "I had a guy once. We were close, same kind of thing—good together in bed, enjoyed each other's company to a point. It wasn't perfect, but it was . . . there. A constant. Like you said, comfortable."

Becki gazed over at Erin curiously. "What happened to him?"

"It got uncomfortable. Not sure if it was him or me that changed. I decided I had to move on. Did I miss him for a while? Hell, yeah. There's nothing like a guy you've trained to know what you like in bed."

She wanted to laugh at Erin's blunt comments, but Becki's mind was racing. "I do miss Dane. Miss the company. I feel guilty, like there was something more I could have done, and I'm not talking about the missing pieces of what happened that day."

"Like you should have loved him more? If only you had . . . Oh, girl, don't do that to yourself. And more importantly, don't go thinking what you *had* means you can't ever have again."

Becki paused. "What does that mean?"

Erin sat forward, fully focused. She lifted a finger at Becki. "What if you had been in love with Dane? Head over heels, rings on fingers, bells on toes, all of it. And he died. Don't think how, just think—he's gone. Would you really put on sackcloth and sit in the ashes for the rest of your life?"

"Of course not."

"Would you ever think about getting involved with another person?"

"You're making this sound simple."

"It *is* simple." Erin shook her head. "If you're not ready to fool around, then you're not ready. Get a fresh set of batteries, or invest in a movable showerhead, whatever turns your crank. But if you are interested and you've got a guy who's pawing at your door, don't go tacking some self-imposed timeline to the grieving process. You can miss the hell out of one guy while you're boning the hell out of another."

Becki lost it. She laughed so hard she ended up gasping for air. Erin sat and silently observed, one brow raised high, a smirk on her face. "Glad to be of service. I'll be here all week, try the veal."

CHAPTER 15

''''''''''''''''''''''''''''''''

Something had changed. Marcus eyed Becki closely, but he just couldn't put his finger on it.

She'd run the team through the most creative exercise that morning that required them to climb the peaks beside the hoodoos and lower the "bodies" they'd found. The light layer of snow that remained from last night's fall had turned everything to sheer mud by the time the sun had come out to bake them for a couple of hours.

Still, even grubby the squad had worked together amazingly, and the dirt and grime seemed to pull them together even more than a good clean session in the gym.

Becki clapped loudly. "Great job, guys. Amazing."

Tripp took a bow. "Nice exercise. Where did you get the bodies?"

Devon stepped closer, a mud-coated mannequin under each arm. "And do we have to return them?"

"Why, you looking for a date?" Alisha taunted. A unified chorus of *oooh*s rose as she curtsied. "Thank you, thank you. Although yes, totally wicked exercise, Becki. Thanks for training us today."

"Brownnoser," Devon whispered.

Becki laughed. "Drop the bodies in the back of Marcus's truck, then you're free to go. Enjoy your Monday off."

"But don't even think of being late on Tuesday. You start at oh five hundred with flash first-aid scenarios." Marcus accepted their groans with a nod. "Go on. I'll make it oh six hundred if you're all out of here in under five minutes."

Their screeches of joy were deafening, people scattering in a rush.

Becki leaned on the side of the truck bed, her arms crossed in front of her, a smile on her face. "Softie."

"What? Can't let you be the only good guy around here."

She laughed. "Right, like you're worried about competing with me. They totally look up to you. I can see why Lifeline's done so well over the years."

Okay, there it was again. "Compliments now. I'd think you were looking for something from me, but I'm not ordering you to get out of bed at the ass-crack of dawn."

"Just calling it like I see it."

He leaned over and adjusted one of the mannequins the crew had tossed haphazardly in the back of his truck. "What do you want to do with the girls? And the team was right, inspired training session, by the way."

Becki jumped up on the edge of the truck box, twisting to sit beside where he rested his elbows. "Thanks. It's always more fun to have to rescue a real body, but breathing, flesh-and-blood types tend to complain when you bury them in the mud for too long."

Her arms were bare, and streaks of dirt coated her, not as badly as the rest of the fake bodies beside her, but still. He touched her arm delicately, smearing a blob down her bicep. "You need a shower nearly as bad as they do."

"Hmm."

Marcus looked up, and the heat in her eyes made him twitch. He'd been dreaming about her looking at him like that, seeing *yes* written all over her face—he wasn't sure if maybe he was imagining it. "You want to help me clean them?"

"I don't suppose we can lash them down and run through the automatic car wash?" Her voice had gone silky. Stroking him and flipping every damn one of his switches past *on*, all the way to *high*.

"Someone would call the RCMP and suggest we'd done mass murder. What about the shower room at the school?" *Where we both can get naked after the props are clean, and get dirty all over again?*

Becki licked her lips slowly, her gaze trailing over him like she was one second away from consuming something delicious. "I think that's a marvelous idea."

Hot. Fucking. Damn.

He stepped to the side, between her legs, and leaned against her.

She lifted her hands into the air. "Marcus, I'm covered in mud."

"You think I care?"

He reached for her, but she caught hold of his wrist in midair, blocking his left forearm against hers. "I'm not saying no. I'm saying I don't want to coat the inside as well as the outside of your precious truck with mud."

"I don't give a shit about the mud." He dropped his forehead to hers. "But since you're not saying no, I'll be patient and wait. Only, kiss me first."

"Just a kiss?"

"Down payment. Appetizer. Something to hold me off from ravishing you right here against the side of my truck."

Becki swallowed hard. Interesting reaction. Marcus filed that idea under *future places to fuck Becki mindless*.

Then he wasn't thinking anything because she lifted her chin and touched their mouths together. Lips open, breaths mingling. Her tongue reaching out to tease his.

He wanted to eat her alive. He was going to at some point. But now? He soaked her into his system and learned her all over again. The softness as she moved her lips over his. The sharp snap along his spine as she closed her teeth over his lip and nipped. The gentle caress as she broke contact, then stroked their cheeks together.

"How fast can you get to the school?" The words whispered past his ear.

He lifted her off the box, down his body, groaning at the pressure as she rubbed against his full cock. They scrambled in different directions, settling into the cab. She was still buckling up as he put the truck into gear and spun out the tires.

"Do you have to return the girls?" he asked again. Never had discovered whether the mannequins she'd had the team doing cliff rescue with were loaners.

"No, they now belong to the school. Is this another exercise-in-patience thing? Talking about the muddy plastic models instead of ravishment?"

"Yes." Marcus snapped his teeth together to stop from wanting to dirt-talk a little more. He was so close to exploding at the thought of being with Becki, it was stupid.

Going slow would be impossible.

He pulled up beside the access doors and was out of the vehicle and headed to meet her in seconds flat.

Becki had already dragged one mannequin free from the truck bed.

"What are you doing?" he demanded.

She tossed the bald, life-sized form at him. "Cleaning up the girls. Easier to do it now than after they completely dry."

Had he totally misunderstood? He was sure the plan was to fuck each other senseless as soon as possible. Frustration and confusion warred in his brain. Becki propped the door open and carried in two more, following him into the men's shower area.

She laid the mannequins in a row on the floor and turned on three taps, adjusting the showerheads to the proper angles. "I'll grab the rest, you start washing."

Marcus eyed the mud-caked plastic bodies with less and less enthusiasm. "I'll trade you. You wash, I'll carry."

Becki laughed. "What, you have issues rubbing your hands all over naked women?"

He stopped and stared her in the eye. Deliberately let his gaze drop over her body, pausing on her breasts, the V between her legs. "Get naked, and I'll show you how few issues I have."

Becki moved in closer. Her fingers explored his waist, trickled up his torso. Tantalizing, addictive. "Getting naked with you is one of my favourite memories."

Her palms pressed flat to his chest. His mind filled with the image of her pressed against the wall in that decadent suite, him fucking her from behind as the water poured over them in the enormous shower enclosure—his control was on the edge and he hadn't so much as touched her.

"Start washing before I change the plan." His voice edgy, uneven. He was going to flash off into spontaneous combustion.

"Patience, remember?" She turned it into more than a question. Her whole body softened, the invitation there in her eyes. Everything about her screamed *come and get me.*

His body vibrated with need. He stripped his shirt off over his head and threw it to the side of the room.

Her eyes lit up as she took a leisurely trip down his chest. "I guess I should get scrubbing the girls. Once they're out of the way, we can move to other things."

Their bodies were only inches from each other, the heat from her skin coiling around him like a spider's web. "Maybe we should consider *other things* first."

Something clicked. As if she could no longer resist, Becki crowded against him and tilted her head back. "Fine. I knew you were bossy. If you're volunteering to wash me, go for it. I'm feeling a little . . . filthy."

She skimmed her hands over his hips, using her nails to trace the waistline of his running pants. The only thing stopping her from being able to grasp his cock was how tightly their bodies were pressed together.

He growled and pinned her in place, dragging their

mouths together. He'd seen her time and time again over the years, the images from their nights together flashing through his brain as his hands jerked a response from his dick.

Those experiences had been black and white—pale, blurry images on a faraway screen. This was high-def, high-resolution—real scents, real tastes. He took her mouth, the scent of their skin rising raw and passionate around them.

Becki offered and he took, a nearly violent kiss, border-line in control. Their noses bumped, tongues dueled. He slid his fingers around her torso and down to cup her ass. She was tall enough that he didn't need to lift her far to bring everything into perfect alignment, the hard and ready line of his cock behind the thin fabric of his cotton pants meet-ing the soft warmth of her sex. The fine-weave material of her climbing gear offered a scant barrier between them as he ground them together.

She hooked her right leg over his hip and squeezed. He gasped into her mouth, a growl following hard after as he twisted to bring her against the nearest wall, the firm surface giving him something to support them as he worked his cock over her clit. The coals that had flickered ever since he'd laid eyes on her roared to full-fledged flames covering him inside and out.

"Oh God, Marcus." She bit his shoulder and jerked a shout from his lips.

Fighting his need to rut on her like some kind of wild animal, Marcus chose the only solution he could think of. He had to get her off quick before sating himself because it was going to take all of three seconds to come, he was so fucking primed.

He tugged at her shirt and she helped him, slipping out of both T-shirt and bra in a flash, pivoting slowly as she peeled down her khakis to present her naked ass to him.

Stripping off his pants and briefs one-handed had never been more frustrating. He might have ripped something in his hurry to hit the next stage.

Marcus turned on another shower, catching Becki against him and tugging her under the spray.

He rested her body against his chest, capturing one breast. Something hard brushed his palm and he glanced over her shoulder. "Sweet mother of God, you did pierce them. I thought I felt a ring."

"First summer break. I told you I was going to."

She had, and wondering if she'd ever done it had played a part in his memories during the time he'd been stuck in no-man's-land. At least until he had decided that torturing himself that way wasn't healthy.

He fondled the ring in her nipple, tugging the tiny circle, and Becki dropped her head back and moaned her assent. He slid his hand down her body, over her belly to part her curls, and he swore again. "A clit bar? *Jesus*, Becki, I'm going to fucking explode."

He was one second away from coming all over the small of her back, his dick rubbing as she writhed under his touch.

"More, Marcus. Harder."

He closed his eyes and fought the pressure in his body. One adjustment and instead of sliding his cock in the valley between her ass cheeks, he could be fucking her. But not until she came.

He worked her, teased her, the steam from the shower billowing around them like some kind of sci-fi stage setting. Becki panted, little moans rising in volume as she spread her legs wide and thrust her sex against his hand. He slipped two fingers into her core and flicked the clit bar with his thumb, and she melted, body jerking as he supported her, all the weight of her torso held cradled.

His arm still trapped Becki against his body as she drew herself to vertical.

Marcus didn't give her time to go anywhere. He squatted slightly, centered his dick against her heat, and thrust in from behind. Her welcoming gasp rang off the walls, but it was the tight clasp of her body that overwhelmed his senses.

They stumbled a step to the side and Becki pressed both palms to the wall, thrusting her ass back toward him and offering herself. He stared at where they joined, mesmerized by his cock disappearing into her.

"You going to stand there all day?" she teased, the words uneven and yet happy. He tore his gaze up to see her smiling over her shoulder at him. "Go on, fuck me hard."

Permission granted—there wasn't much else he was capable of. Slowing down, certainly not. The only thing in control was his cock, balls as a backup, both demanding he drive into her warmth. His grip on her hip anchored him and allowed enough purchase so he could do as she'd demanded. One thrust after another, fucking, hard and dirty. Yet her sounds of pleasure continued, increasing his desire. He was so close, so close to the edge that one more move could shove him over. Bending over her, he thrust his right hand between her legs and found the clit bar.

She screamed and shuddered. The tight squeeze around his shaft broke him, tore him apart, and his cock emptied, his brain fleeing into the wilderness.

They stood locked together for the longest time, the heated water streaming over their skin. When his cock finally softened and slipped from her body, he pulled her upright and rotated her to rest against his chest.

It might have been fucking, but it was also fucking good.

He dragged his fingers through her hair, brushing the strands off her face and over her shoulders. He'd been right. One taste wasn't enough. Their mad rush had done nothing but confirm he wanted her. Again and again.

CHAPTER 16

Sex in a shower room had definite benefits. Warmth flowed over her shoulders as Marcus adjusted their stance, their naked bodies still sealed together. Under her ear his heart rate slowly settled. Her breathing relaxed to something closer to normal.

Becki stroked her fingers over his back as they relaxed silently, loving the feel of rock-solid muscles under the slick surface of his skin. She took her hands in circles—higher, lower. Cupping his ass briefly before repeating the move all over again.

After a long dry spell, hard, fast, and dirty as all get-out had been a most spectacular sexual homecoming.

"You keep touching me and we'll be starting all over in three seconds flat," Marcus warned.

"You say that like it's a bad thing."

His chuckle rumbled in his chest. "I'm taking you home, Becki. Feeding you. Then we can move to the next round."

Hmm, her earlier thought about how bossy he could be struck again. Not just domineering, but overlord-like. Parts of her loved having him order her around. Parts had no intention of giving up control so fast.

Becki tilted her head back to take him in. She'd decided what she wanted—as per Erin's excellent advice—so she'd taken. He enjoyed their time together as well, if that satisfied expression she was staring at meant anything, the interest in his gaze still keen.

They hadn't promised each other more than physical pleasure.

She slipped away and stretched lazily, deliberately arching her back to display her breasts. Spread her legs wide and let loose a contented moan as a trickle of moisture escaped her core.

A few porn style moves could be exactly what she needed to keep him off balance. "Well. I don't know. What if I already had other plans for the day?"

"You don't, so let's not play stupid games. You and I both respect the truth too much for that." Marcus grabbed the soap from the wall dish and motioned in front of him. "Get back here so I can clean you up."

Definitely bossy. "I can wash myself."

"Becki."

She shivered as his tone tugged deep like a siren's call. She lifted her gaze to his, and a pulse of desire struck her core, an echo of her recent orgasm. There was something about his expression. About the way he held his torso, all barely contained passion and tightly held control.

Something inside warned her that following his commands would feel very, very good. Something inside was afraid of wanting that too much. She scrambled for a response other than the one her feet were only seconds from making for her. Of carrying her to his side and letting him . . .

Anything.

Hiding from urges that she didn't want to accept. "The mannequins need to be cleaned, Marcus. There's no use in us washing up twice."

He crossed his arms over his firm chest, and her mouth

watered. Prime naked male, biceps glistening with water. A trail of dark hair led to where his semihard cock and heavy sac hung between muscular thighs. She was crazy to resist.

"You start washing then. I'll find us towels." He dropped the soap back in the dish and rinsed his hand clean.

His suddenly caving in to her request shouldn't have left her so befuddled. His ass muscles taunted her as he walked away, each flex showing off the taut curves and making her fingers twitch with the memory of caressing said ass only moments earlier.

She grabbed the first of the girls and scrubbed with more vigor than needed. Punishment for having denied herself another piece of the fine man she'd chased away.

He returned a little later, dry towels tucked under his left arm, the two final mannequins under his right. Seemingly completely unconcerned that he was pulling a full frontal as she dragged away the mud-coated props.

She didn't stare, but oh, she wanted to. Wanted to ask for a chance to change her mind and have him soap her from head to toe. Because then? Then she could do the same for him. Touch him and drive him mad.

"Once they're clean we'll leave them stacked in the corner. I'll let David know and he can figure out which storage room he'd like them in," Marcus offered.

Becki blinked, pulling her thoughts into order. Switching from doing wicked things to Marcus to the ordinary and mundane.

Your own damn fault, that dry internal voice taunted.

"Sure. Sounds great."

What did she want to follow their frantic sex? She'd decided to take, true, but she hadn't been so stupid as to think once would be enough, right?

Suddenly the situation wasn't nearly as difficult as she'd been making it. She'd do what she needed to do, and have a good time as well. And in the middle of carrying on, maybe either the missing portion of her life would show up or she'd learn to do without it.

"I need some time to plan next week's training. I would love to bring supper over, though. If you're interested."

Marcus laughed, grabbing a mannequin and putting it into position as he'd suggested. "I already said I was. Yes, I want you to come to my house, and I won't argue whether it's now or three hours from now as long as it's today. If you want to bring food, fine."

He was being far too agreeable. The expression on his face as Becki glanced up was nowhere near as relaxed as his tone seemed to imply. He refused to let her go, holding her with his sharp gaze. Heat and desire flooded her system as he spoke.

"Make no mistakes, Becki, I want you in my bed. But it's not just about giving pleasure, getting to enjoy more sex. I like you. We could be good for each other."

A rush of emotion swooped in. Sexual tension danced through her, strangely muted. Delight struck at his final few statements.

He likes me.

She laughed out loud, the setting so impossible. They had continued to work as they spoke, the showers a steady drip in the background, steam filling the corners. They were still stark naked and he was being wonderfully honest.

"I'd rag you about showing your girly and emotional side, but you said *sex* a few too many times."

He shrugged. "I'll say it again a few more if it makes you haul ass faster."

"What about training?" She was teasing now, and they both knew it. They knew where this was going to end up. His bed, as he'd pointed out.

If they made it that far.

Marcus swung past her as she held another mannequin under the shower for a final rinse. His hand smacked on her ass, and she gasped at the sting.

"Training can wait until tomorrow. The team's off all day. We can do anything we want in terms of climbing then."

Streaks of heat radiated from her butt cheek. "Between sessions of sex?" she asked.

"You're saying *sex* a lot," he noted. "Which is not a complaint, mind you."

"I've kind of missed it, to be honest."

"Honest is best." Marcus tilted his head toward an empty shower. "Go on, get cleaned up. I'll finish dealing with the girls."

He didn't want to wash her anymore?

Becki stepped back and let her gaze trickle over him. It seemed as if he ignored her, working to clear away the rest of the mud, but his cock told a different story. The long hard length was back to full force, bobbing as he walked. Jutting upward from the dark curls at his groin to as good as shout that he wanted her again.

She pivoted under a steady stream of water and lathered up. Asking why he'd changed his mind was stupid when she'd been the one to tell him to stop in the first place.

Going forward, she was going to be careful what she asked for, because at times like this?

Getting her way sucked.

Marcus took his time mopping the last of the mud from the floor. Becki dried off, dressed, and was out of the gym with a teasing smile before he lost control and dragged her under him again.

She wasn't twenty-three, both of them looking for nothing more than three days of all-out sex. They were going to work together as well as fuck, and he had to make sure he didn't push too damn hard.

Even though he'd wanted to. He'd wanted nothing more than to get her to stop running and trot herself over to his feet. He would have washed every inch of her delectable body before tasting her.

Memories of their past time together meshed with what he planned to do with her in the coming days, and damn if he didn't need to jerk off before he could dress and head home.

Staying in control was his norm. This time it looked as

if he'd have to stay in control of his urge to master her. It wasn't what he wanted. Not in the long run, but for now? She'd lost her lover, lost her memory. He would not be the jackass David had called him, and he would let the woman call a few of the shots. No matter how much it burned his ass.

At home he tidied up. Stared at the clouds that had turned the sky grey and threatened to dump more moisture on the town.

Pulled clean sheets onto the bed.

When the phone rang he'd just popped the cap off a bottle of beer, dropping into the leather recliner and flipping up the footrest. "What?"

David's sharp laugh made him smile. "Butt face."

"Yeah? What do you want?"

"Heads up—the paper is sending someone around on Tuesday to talk to the team in prep for next Saturday's event."

Great. Some of his favourite people were bloodsucking news reporters. "Can't they call instead?"

"Just passing on the message. You don't have to be there. Alisha already said she's willing to talk."

"Which means Devon will be there as well." Becki was right. The competitions between those two grew borderline disruptive, but at least at times like this, it meant they were predictable. "I'll deal with it. Thanks for the shout."

"No problem. You want to get together tonight and watch a movie or something?"

Oh, no. "Already have plans."

What were the chances that simple announcement would be enough, and David would drop the topic?

"Bullshit. You never have plans. You feeling okay after the incident earlier this week?"

"I'm fine. Just . . ." Yeah, his chances were obviously slim to none of keeping his and Becki's involvement under wraps from his brother for longer than twelve hours. "I invited Becki over for dinner."

"Hey, that's an awesome idea. I'll pick up dessert. What time is she getting there?"

This was not happening. "It *is* awesome. But nowhere in there did I mention your name."

"I hadn't even thought of it, but it's a great idea. I know you met her for drinks with the team, but I haven't had a chance to—"

"David, you're not invited. Period. Got it? You show up, and I'll throw you out on your fucking ass." Silence echoed for a moment before he heard his brother's laughter. *Oh jeez.* "You're such a shit."

David chuckled around his words. "Yeah, and you deserve a few pokes every now and then for the asshole you can so wonderfully turn into when I least expect it. Fine. I will not show up at your place with ice cream cake and shooters. You need anything else?"

There was one thing to be thankful for. "You're not going to lecture me and ask what the hell I'm doing with an employee of yours?"

"Why? You don't work for me. You're both adults. Besides, I'm pretty damn sure she can kick your ass all on her own if you get out of line."

Marcus sat up, the footrest closing with a snap as the recliner shot to vertical. "You don't need to sound so absolutely thrilled about that option."

"You shouldn't assume it's not a distinct possibility. She's not going to take any guff. Not from you, not from anyone. But at the same time . . ." David trailed off.

Marcus checked his watch "She'll be here in a minute. You got anything else to say?"

"Just that while I think you're adults and all that, don't go too fast, okay?"

"Relationship advice from my younger brother who is, oh that's right, currently not seeing anyone. Like I should listen to you about how to treat a woman?"

"I think you know how to treat her. I'm not worried about that. I'm worried about you."

Twisted. And confusing. "You're not making this easy, bro."

David sighed. "You've been through a lot. The other day

when I said I wanted my brother back? I meant it. I don't want to see you crash any harder."

His brother was concerned about him, not Becki? "I'll be fine."

The doorbell chimed and Marcus ditched David, happy to have avoided any further emotional bonding. He was still grinning when he opened the door to let Becki in.

She wore a dress. Her long legs showed all the way to midthigh, where the pale blue fabric stopped. Firm calves, lean but powerful quads. She had heels on—low heels, but heels nonetheless—and his jaw must have dropped a notch.

She wriggled a little as she stood there, holding her coat over her arms. "Umm, is something wrong?"

"You're beautiful."

Becki tilted back her head and laughed, the sound bursting out and making him realize he'd been staring instead of moving out of the way.

She held up her coat. "If you grab this, I'll get the food. I didn't want to try to balance it all at one time."

"I can get it—"

"No worries. You hold the door."

Marcus stared mesmerized as her hips swayed when she walked away from him, the bottom edge of the short skirt flaring around her thighs and flashing him glimpses of the skin beneath. When she opened the car door and bent over to grab something, the material rode even higher. Miles of smooth soft skin that was on his menu plan, no matter what she had in the box she pulled from the backseat.

He intended to taste each and every inch of her before the night was out.

Marcus stepped clear as she moved through the door, the scent of something meaty and rich wafting past his nose. Becki placed the box on the table and turned toward him.

"You have anything else in the car you need?" he asked.

She hesitated for a moment. "There's a bag I can get later."

She had brought things intending to stay the night. Marcus copied her nonchalance instead of grinning like a maniac. "I'll grab it now so you don't have to worry about it. You spread out dinner."

Becki tossed him her keys, and he slipped into the cool evening air with a whole lot of amazing thoughts warming him. As incredible as the sex earlier that day had been, having Becki James in his home and knowing she wanted to be with him for more than a mad screw changed something.

Made him eager to see what new lessons they could discover together.

CHAPTER 17

The low-grade fever burning through her simply wouldn't fade. Dinner had been consumed, the dishes put away. The visit up to now had been relaxed and easy. Small talk and lots of laughter.

No blatant innuendo or sexual caresses, but he was right there all the time. Becki couldn't move around the table without bumping hips or knocking elbows. She wasn't sure if it was all his fault, either, as she caught herself standing one pace too close to him so that as he turned, there was nowhere for him to go but past her. Brushing torsos, flirting glances.

He grinned as he held out his hand. "Come on."

Becki slipped her fingers into his and allowed him to lead her. "Where are we going?"

"Taking a tour."

She wandered through the house at his side, admiring the dark furniture, the solid wood side tables, and the stone accents around the fireplace. The heat of his thumb as he caressed it back and forth over hers made tiny shivers run up her forearm.

"I love the bold colours in here," Becki said, pulling him to a stop by the couch and running a hand over the soft leather. "It's all so grown up."

Marcus laughed. "Well, thank you, I guess."

She stepped in front of him and wrapped her free arm around his waist. "Grown up is a good thing, Marcus. I had mostly thrift shop furniture and cinder-block bookcases at my old place. I'd never gotten to the point of settling in and making a home. Good for you."

"I like my comforts," he drawled.

They stared at each other for a moment, silence stretching and drawing out the anticipation. Then he broke the spell and drew her down the hall, past a guest bath and a small office. All the way to the master bedroom. No dark wood in here, only a bed big enough for all kinds of acrobatics plus a full line of floor-to-ceiling windows facing the mountain range. The deck outside the French doors supported a hot tub and sturdy wrought-iron furniture.

Becki swallowed hard as Marcus stepped behind her and leaned over to kiss the exposed nape of her neck.

"This room is also grown up, don't you think?"

"Very." No frilly decorations like candles or silk pillows, but the room screamed comfort. Seduction. A world apart from the IKEA bed she'd been bunking on in the dorms. His tongue teased her skin, tasting her, making all sorts of lovely after-dinner entertainments come to mind.

He trailed his fingers up her arm, his left forearm wrapped around her waist to pull her against him. There was no denying he desired her as the hard length of his cock made contact with her back. "Hot tub?"

"Lovely." Becki twisted in his arms. "I hope you don't mind me skinny dipping. I forgot my swimsuit."

Marcus leaned over and brushed their lips together, only for a second before pulling back to speak against her mouth. "Why does that not surprise me?"

"Tell me you're disappointed," she whispered.

"I am." She must have made a face because he grinned. "Don't look so surprised. I was looking forward to ordering you to go without, and now you've stolen my thunder."

Oh really? "Well, perhaps you'll have to find something else to order me to do, then."

He released her and stepped back, his expression tightening as he looked her over. "Now there's an idea. What kind of commands would you enjoy, Becki? Shall we play that game in the bedroom as well as on the wall?"

What was he doing? "On the wall?"

He stepped to the high dresser to his right and held out a familiar dark swatch of fabric. The blindfold from the other day's climb.

Suddenly all her fantasies of this evening were wiped clean. She had memories of all kinds of games with him, but they'd never used a blindfold during the wild romp so long ago. "Marcus . . ."

He shrugged. "Your choice."

But he didn't withdraw the blindfold.

She stepped forward, ignoring his offering for a moment, pressing herself tight to his body as she caught hold of his face and kissed him hard. She was the aggressor this time, and he let her explore. Let her stroke her tongue over his teeth, allowed her to nibble on his lower lip, her fingers slipping into his hair as she took what she wanted. Snatching a few seconds of control before she softened her touch. Eased back, their lips separating with a quiet sigh.

As she stepped away, observing the fire in his eyes, she slid her fingers along his forearm to his wrist, to his palm. She tugged the fabric free from his grasp.

Covering her eyes meant all her other senses kicked into higher gear. She listened for any indication of what might come next. She waited, shifting her balance onto the balls of her feet as she wondered exactly what he had planned. Because she was ready for anything he wanted to dish out.

It wasn't that she heard him, but she felt him. Standing right beside her mere seconds before he stroked her arm again. Back of the knuckles? Fingertips? She wasn't sure, only he teased from her wrist all the way to her shoulder, finishing with his lips.

"Very nice. Your nipples have hardened. Can you feel them pressing against your dress?"

She nodded, unable to speak past the knot of rising lust. If she could have said something, she would have told him she was also wet, an aching sensation growing between her thighs.

"As much as I loved this afternoon, I want you a whole different way this time. I find myself wanting to anticipate. To prolong coming together until we're both ready to burst."

"Try five minutes ago, then," Becki managed to say, steadying herself more solidly on her feet in the hopes she wouldn't melt into a puddle.

Her zipper released. One tooth at a time, the rasping loud in her ears as the fabric peeled back to allow a brush of cooler air over her heated skin. His hand landed on her shoulder and pushed off one strap, letting it fall to the side and expose the upper swell of her right breast.

This time she heard when he drew in a breath of air. Controlling himself, perhaps? Not that she cared if he lost control and threw her on the bed this moment. She was more than ready for him.

But the going slow was very nice as well. If *nice* was anywhere near the correct word.

"No bra." Marcus slid his hand down her waist and over her ass. "No panties as well, or will I find a thong to explain why you have no lines?"

"Thong." A very wet one by now, if she guessed right.

"Hmm." The sound rumbled from some point below her, and she was the one to gasp when he touched the inside of her thigh, edging the bottom of her skirt up slightly as he reached underneath and caught hold of the fabric.

Without the ability to see, she found that her skin was far more sensitive, the rub of the material as he tugged it down her limbs sending out small tingles, all of which seemed to rebound back and hit her in the core. She caught his head in her hands. She brushed her fingers through his hair, leaning one hand on his shoulder as he indicated for her to lift her foot.

One breast was exposed, nothing else on under the flimsy layer of her sundress. Becki arched her back and waited, longing for him to touch her again.

When he wrapped his lips around her nipple, she gasped in delight. The other shoulder strap fell away, and the dress slipped down, catching momentarily on her hips before Marcus brushed it to the floor.

He kissed the other nipple, laving his tongue around the tip to moisten it before pulling off with a light popping sound.

She swayed on her feet as he withdrew. Naked, unable to see what he was doing. But she figured she knew pretty well he wasn't disappointed.

"You're grinning like a cat that's got the cream," Marcus pointed out.

"Nice analogy. I'm enjoying this blindfold thing. What are you planning next?"

What he planned apparently involved dropping to his knees again and covering her sex with his mouth. No further warning, just a single clasp around her butt to hold her in place, then a determined assault to drive her mad. He licked along her labia, using his fingers to open her curls. Tongue tip teasing the sensitive spot at the apex of her slit until her legs quivered.

A finger slid into her core and she widened her stance, thrusting her hips against him to try for more. The little extra she needed to get the detonation building inside her to trigger. He added another finger, pumping lazily while his tongue and teeth worked her to the brink.

"Touch your breasts," Marcus commanded. "Grab those rings and tug them the way you like."

Becki didn't hesitate, raising her hands and cupping herself, thumb and forefingers rolling the tiny loops she'd placed in before getting dressed. The small bite of pain shook her hard, and she gasped.

"Oh yeah, that's it. I knew the instant you tugged—your

body squeezed so tight. I want to be in you again, Becki. Wrap your sweet cunt around my cock and let you squeeze me like that as you go off."

She was going to suggest he should stop talking and use his lips on her a little more, but the deep timbre of his voice stroked her as hard as his tongue.

"Do it," she begged. "I want you."

"Oh no, this time is for you." Marcus slid his fingers in, rubbing over a spot deep inside that made her head spin. "You're going to come for me. Standing, your legs ready to give out, but you won't fall because I've got you."

He did. He had her tangled into a throbbing heap, and when he touched her with his mouth, it was too much. Fingers thrusting, pushing her as he moved again and again. His tongue hard on her clit, satisfied sounds rising as he greedily ate her pussy. She pinched her nipples as he'd told her to, and the wave slammed into her. Sharp. Hard. Her sex constricting, breath catching in her throat. It wasn't enough—not nearly enough.

"Marcus, oh God."

He slowed, fingers easing from her before slipping in one last time. Once more. Every brush set off another wave, and he held her upright with his left forearm and bicep, her hands clinging to his head and shoulders.

A tender kiss landed on her belly. He stood, gently helping her find her balance. He kissed her and she tasted herself on his tongue. The taste of sex and desire, and longing for more tangled with satisfaction.

Her curiosity rose. "Can I take off the blindfold?"

"No." He caught her hand in his and brought it to his chest. "Undress me."

"While I'm blindfolded?"

He didn't answer.

Becki started on his buttons, moving until their hips were touching and he had to hold on to her. The texture of his shirt was slightly rough, a brushed cotton that dragged over her skin like sensual sandpaper—impossible to ignore, impossibly erotic.

The first button popped through the hole, and she swore she heard it. Felt the teasing rub of the dusting of hair on his chest. When she pulled the shirt from him, she took every advantage of the chance to study him with her fingertips.

"This is nice," Becki mused.

"Nice?" The tension in his voice made it clear her touch was getting to him as much as he had gotten to her.

"I loved our shower sex, but there's something to be said for a long, slow seduction."

She leaned over to press a kiss to his firm abdomen, soft curls tickling her nose, urging her to follow the treasure trail as it vanished into his slacks, and he sucked in a gasp.

"Only who is seducing who?" he asked.

"Does it matter?"

"Not really. Not this time."

She was too preoccupied to think that through. Popping open his button, easing the zipper over his rigid cock—those things were on her mind now. She wasn't willing to be distracted from the wonderful task at hand.

Getting Marcus naked.

She tugged the jeans off his hips, reaching impatiently to see what he was wearing. Her fingers met boxer briefs, wetness marking the spot where the rounded head of his cock pressed the fabric. "Hmm, someone else is ready to go off soon."

She moved blindly, but with her hands to guide her she leaned forward and found his shaft, dragging her teeth lightly along the length, wetting him even more.

"Becki. Take them off."

Guttural. Harsh. She was swamped by the power in his command and hurried to obey, dragging the material down and helping him step out from where it bunched around his ankles. Then she was up and reaching for him, finding his hard shaft and fisting her fingers around him. She pumped slowly, firmly. Listening for a sound from his lips.

A groan, a swear.

A command.

When it came, she shivered with delight.

"Suck me. Get me wet, and cover me with your mouth."

She obeyed eagerly, reaching forward with her tongue to catch the first taste of him, the salty essence spreading through her system like ambrosia. His taste thrilled her, his long low moan of satisfaction making her smile as she opened her mouth and sank over him.

Working his cock with her tongue and lips shouldn't turn her on this much. There was nothing against her body, no smooth caress of her skin, and yet she felt as if a million butterflies glided over her, teasing and edging her closer to another orgasm, all without a touch.

Marcus stroked her cheek and she slowed. Opened as wide as she could to accept the thick cock stretching her lips.

"So beautiful. But there's one thing missing." Marcus tugged the blindfold from her and dropped it to the floor. He smoothed her hair from her face, his cock balanced on her lower lip. "I want to see your eyes."

Looking up his body—he'd said she was beautiful, and maybe that word didn't apply to guys, but *damn*. The edges of his abs, the tight six-pack of his belly as he slipped his hips forward. Perfectly sculpted chest, muscular shoulders. He'd cupped his right hand behind her, fingers holding the long strands back to keep them from getting in their way. The bonus was that she saw him clearly.

His jaw was set tight, but he had that smile, the one that almost wasn't there but still managed to turn her insides to jelly. He gazed down, watching closely as slow motions of his hips pulled his cock nearly all the way from her before feeding it back in again oh so carefully.

She caught hold of his ass, curling her fingers around his smooth skin. Stroking the muscles that flexed under her touch. Anchoring herself to allow him to go harder. Faster.

The entire time she stared up, a slow simmer of lust driving her to give at least as much pleasure as he'd given her, if not more.

Marcus rocked again and again, the taste of pre-come growing as he groaned.

"Becki . . ."

She pulled back, lips tight, sucking hard, and he shouted her name again, this time throwing back his head as the climax hit. Bursts of heat hit the back of her throat, semen filling her mouth. Satisfaction at having caused him to lose control filled her at the same time. He pressed forward again, and some liquid escaped her lips, slipping down the side of her face.

Marcus shuddered, dragging his eyes open to smile down at her as she licked and sucked, enjoying every last moment.

"Clean me up, sweet Becki."

She caught his softening length and pulled it as far into her mouth as possible, licking him clean, glancing to see his approval. He skimmed his thumb over her cheek and caught the spill, pressing it toward her lips. She licked the pad, biting the surface lightly, and heat flared in his face.

He helped her to her feet, pulling her tightly to his body as they kissed, limbs wrapping close, rubbing again and again.

"I can't get enough of touching you," Becki confessed.

"I'm not complaining," Marcus rejoined, reaching under her and lifting her into the air. She threw her arms around his neck and held on, her hip bumping his abdomen as he paced across the room. "Get the door."

She twisted the knob and pushed the glass door open. He carried her to the edge of the tub and carefully lowered her, her feet slipping into the heated water, skin tingling from his earlier attentions and the snap of the near-icy evening air on her naked body.

He turned away to shut the door, and she sighed happily.

Naked man, hot tub, incredible mountain views. She'd already given and received an orgasm.

The night was young. She could hardly wait to see what else they could come up with.

CHAPTER 18
''''''''''''''''''''''''''''''''''

Marcus grabbed a couple of water bottles from a box beside the door, handing them to Becki before joining her in the water. She twisted one open and passed it back, relaxing on the bench facing the view.

She hummed. "You scored big-time."

His laugh interrupted his drink. "I did. Thank you."

"You nut. I meant the deck. How did you manage to find a place like this? So lucky."

"Took a while." Marcus put his bottle aside and turned to face her. She had knelt on the submerged seat, the water level bouncing along her nipple line distracting him. "David had been looking around for a place for me off and on. By the time I ended up coming home, he had something waiting."

"He's a great guy."

Marcus shrugged. "He's my brother. He's great *and* an ass in turns."

Becki nodded. "My family's like that. My sisters and I get along fine, long-distance stuff since most of them are settled on the prairies with their families. But my little brother? He's too much like me. One minute we get along gangbusters, and the next we're ready to kill each other."

"I can't remember. Big family?" He tugged her closer and she came willingly, straddling his legs and settling herself in his lap.

"Five kids. Colin is the youngest; I'm second from the top. One of the middles—you know, the type that always wants to do what's right."

"Ha. In what dream world are you living?"

"So speaks an oldest son, correct?"

"Oldest and wisest. Of course."

She snorted. "Oh please."

Marcus enjoyed the banter, but most of his attention was on touching her. Stroking his hand up her waist, cupping one breast at a time so he could caress her nipples to tight points. There were times not having two hands made a difference, but only because he was greedy to have more.

She finished taking a long drink, stretching her throat back and giving him a flash of déjà vu to her sucking him earlier, and his cock flared to full rigidity, snapping tight to his belly. Then she leaned against him to put her water bottle beside his, breasts compressed to his chest, hips rising as she rocked over his dick.

"Hmm, that feels good." She undulated over him, her sex wrapping around the ridge of his erection. The motion brought the tip of his cock closer and closer to slipping between the soft folds of her body. It felt damn amazing, but he wanted more.

"You don't think we've had enough wet sex for one day?"

Becki rose until her breasts were level with his mouth. "I suppose we could try the bed. It was looking very lonely."

"You're not a very good hot tub soaker. We've been in for what? All of ten minutes?"

"Better things to do with life than sit."

He could agree with that, especially with the bounty of distraction before him. She sighed happily as he took one nipple into his mouth, playing with the other side, his tongue and fingers working to flick the tiny loops rhythmically. It still blew his mind that she was pierced.

She pressed her mound against his torso harder, rubbing and pulsing back and forth, and he smiled.

"You haven't gotten any shyer over the years," he noted.

"You disappointed?"

"Hell, no. I loved how you were so eager to try everything back then. How you have no troubles telling me what you need right now."

He slid his fingers down her belly and through her folds, keeping going until he could press a finger deep into her core.

"Oh God, yes. That feels wonderful. Sex is fun—it feels good. Why should I be quiet about what I need?" She shuddered as he pinched her clit, shaking the clit bar with his thumb even as he kept rubbing.

He watched her face, checking to see when she needed more, what she needed. Harder, softer. When he added a finger and she melted around him, he nodded with approval.

"No reason at all. Ask for what you want, but what I want is to give you what you need before you even get a chance to ask."

He lifted her on his hand until he could catch hold of her breast in his teeth. When he bit down and nipped, she cried out, another orgasm taking her as she writhed over his fingers, hips thrusting as if to keep him where he was.

He wasn't going anywhere. At least, not anywhere that didn't involve her coming along.

She'd never been carried so often in her life. There was the rescue the other day, and a couple of times this evening, including now as Marcus plucked her from the water while she was still boneless from her climax. Becki was used to hauling herself everywhere, but this luxury, if she was honest, was kind of nice. It was so very decadent to be carefully laid on the bed, helpless to do anything but accept his touch as he proceeded to dry every inch of her.

She was in heaven. It took him a long time as he inter-mingled the caress of the tufted cotton with kisses and small intimate touches. Tiny bites to her inner thighs as he smoothed the towel over her legs. He rubbed her breasts delicately, then kept on rubbing, alternating with soft wet suckles until her nipples were tingling and tight.

One caress after another followed until she was squirming on the mattress, needing more. Needing something other than to lie there and allow him to drive her higher and higher without a safety rope.

When he moved over her, his hard muscular body forming a cage around her, she had to gasp for air before she could speak. "You want me to dry you off now?"

He bumped her thighs with his knees, his weight on his elbows. "I want you to get me wetter."

The fat head of his cock nudged her sex, slipping through her folds as he rocked his hips. He paused, the tip spreading her, bare skin to bare skin.

Becki dragged her legs wider apart even as she teased, "You are insatiable."

"Yes?"

Becki opened her mouth to answer, but her face must have already given the go-ahead. Marcus pressed in all the way to the root in one shot, his cock filling her deep.

She rolled her hips under him, adjusting to his girth. "Oh God, yes."

He didn't move, just stayed in one place, and with every second that passed he seemed to grow larger. Thicker. Becki squeezed her internal muscles, lifting her legs to wrap them around his waist. The adjustment in position changed the angle of his entry, and she moaned.

Still he didn't move. Just stared at her, that wicked expression making all sorts of additional pleasures race over her skin.

She rocked upward, using her legs to try to work herself on his cock.

"Frustrated?" he asked.

"Yes," she snapped. "Move, dammit. I thought you were going to anticipate what I wanted."

"I am."

Marcus lowered himself until not only his cock spearing into her sex held her pinned in place, but his torso as well. His body wasn't heavy enough to make her uncomfortable, but it effectively stopped her from moving anything.

Except her internal muscles, which she used as unmercifully as possible. Squeezing, clenching tight around his cock. Doing everything she could to get him to react.

The only response seemed to be the gathering storm in her core. God, she was going to come like this—nothing touching her clit, no outside stimulation but that thick unmoving pressure and the wicked knowledge that it was his cock filling her.

Words whispered past her ear, chocolaty smooth, dark and even. "Grab the headboard."

Anything to get him to actually move. Becki reached overhead, tilting back to look for something to clasp. Perfect vertical bars waited—the solid sections of tree limbs that made up the headboard the right size to wrap her fingers around and hold on tight.

He took advantage of her slightly arched position, wetness closing over her breast as he sucked hard on one nipple. The sensitive tip stung as he tugged, electric pulses zinging through to her sex.

"Marcus, please," she begged.

"Please what?" He caught her earlobe in his teeth and bit lightly seconds before licking the sensitive spot behind her ear, still not moving from his position as he put his lips to her skin.

She wasn't sure what she wanted. For him to go fast and drive her over quickly as he had in the shower, or to keep torturing her. Her mind had turned into a pile of mush, and sensory overload strummed along her nerves.

"Let your legs down, Becki. Open yourself to me."

Releasing her grip and pulling her knees farther to the

side made his cock all the more apparent. He pulled back, and she felt every single inch, as if her insides had grown hypersensitive while waiting for him to move. The flared head of his shaft slipped free of her pussy so gradually she had ample time to enjoy the tease.

Hands wrapped into wood-filled fists, she stretched under him and anticipated.

Slowly again he filled her, exquisitely slow. Stretching, running over sensitive nerves, driving her upward. Less of a powering forward, more a deliberate joining together, followed by a retreat. There was nowhere for her to go, nothing for her to do but accept his cock possessing her body again and again.

She closed her eyes as he paused, the tip of his cock taunting her. Rocking in and out until she gasped, so hair-triggered she was ready to break with one more surge.

"Becki." A whisper-soft kiss pressed against her lips. "Is it good?"

"Oh, yes."

"You ready?"

She squeezed tight, holding on to what little control she still had. Stretched out, nothing but him over her, and she was ready to explode.

He thrust. Hard. Fully burying himself in one motion. Her breath escaped in a gasp, forced from her lungs. She had no time to inhale before he pulled out and plunged in again. One after another his thrusts possessed her. Pushing into her like he was claiming her. Becki clung to the headboard for dear life, her body rocking with the power of his drives. He wasn't delicate as he took her to the limit. Thrusting again. Again. Until everything tightened and she screamed, her pussy wrapping around him and trying to hold him in place as her orgasm raged.

He pressed her thigh to the side and changed the angle, completing three more strokes, each one as urgent as the ones that had come before. He froze deep in her body as he came. Shoulders tight, muscles clenched as his cock jerked within her.

Becki lay there and savoured it all—the rush of blood through her veins, the lingering aftershocks as her sex reacted to the slightest change in his position, the slick of sweat on both their bodies as he moved over her, his breath fanning past her cheek.

He kissed her. "Sleep. I don't want to move yet, so tell me you'll sleep and let me take care of you."

His cock still stretched her, the sensation strangely comforting. To have him touching her so intimately was like an anchor. After her long sexual hiatus she should have felt sorer, but there was nothing filtering through her but deep contentment. Adding all the orgasms she'd experienced that day to the fatigue caused by the past night's restlessness, exhaustion hovered.

"I could sleep. You don't mind if I snore, do you?" The words trickled out like a slumberous yawn.

The soft rumble of his laughter wrapped her as tightly as his body. "Sleep. I've got you."

I've got you. The words echoed in her mind. How many times had she heard that phrase? How often had she said it herself? At the climbing wall. During years of working ropes. A simple expression, but one that meant so much more than it seemed on the surface. There had to be trust involved—complete trust. *I've got you* wasn't just a nice sentiment, it was life and death in her world.

The fact that she trusted Marcus to the full extent of the meaning made something inside her glow a little warmer.

CHAPTER 19

‖‖‖‖‖‖‖‖‖‖‖‖‖‖‖‖‖‖‖‖‖‖‖‖‖‖‖‖‖‖‖

Icy cold fingers trickled along the back of her neck. She opened her eyes to see the cliff face slowly rotate past a few feet away from her as she dangled on the end of a rope. Everything else remained shrouded behind a veil of cloud. She stretched out a hand to stop herself from spinning, bloody knuckles shaking as she tried to touch the rock. It remained out of reach. Too far for her arms to span.

How long had she hung there?

She clutched the rope and peered below her, still revolving in circles as the wind caught her. Zero visibility. Two feet below her to safety, or a death drop?

Becki sat up with a gasp, heart pumping wildly.

Marcus pressed his arm around her farther as he sat as well, naked chest warming her back. He surrounded her as he made soft shushing noises, rubbing his chin against her shoulder. "It's okay. I've got you."

She rotated in his arms, not caring that she was being a

total wimp. Every inch of her was cold with dread, and she buried her face against his neck, hiding in his arms.

He wiggled upright and pulled her into his lap, leaning them both on the headboard as he stroked her hair. "I got you," he repeated. "You're safe."

She drew a shaky breath. "Nightmare."

"I figured. No worries."

He kept touching her, dragging his hand through her hair, his left arm wrapped around her as far as it would go. She was plastered skin to skin with him, and it was barely enough. His heat remained a faint whisper—barely making a cut into the frigid stench of her fear.

Take back control. Refuse to give up. I am the master of my soul. . . .

She forced out the words, fighting to find something to focus on other than her fright. "If I shake much harder, you can pretend this is one of those vibrating beds they show in cheap B movie hotel rooms."

Marcus tucked his fingers under her chin, tilting her head back far enough so he could press a kiss to her forehead. "Do those things exist anymore?"

He knew what she was doing, or he was at least willing to play along. "I don't know why. Can't imagine they add anything to the experience more than what you bring."

"Flattery will get you everything," he promised. "You want a drink?"

She nodded. Staying in bed was out. She itched to run. To do something to wear herself out until the nightmares stayed away.

They separated, crawling off the mattress. Marcus handed her a robe, his dark gaze meeting hers until she looked away, too ashamed of bringing her fears into their situation. It was too soon for this to be considered a relationship, and she'd already tossed a great big enormous wrench into the works.

Go her.

He dragged on a pair of sweatpants, then held out his hand. It might have been pathetic, but she accepted his clasp like a lifeline, linking her fingers with his and holding on as they walked back through the dimly lit rooms to the kitchen.

"Tea? Something stronger?"

She shook her head. "Tea is enough."

She sat on one of the tall bar stools at the breakfast counter while he filled the kettle, a thought nagging her.

"It was different."

He turned back to her. "What's that?"

"The dream. It wasn't the same one that's been kicking my butt all week."

"That's . . . good. I suppose. Still sounds as if it wasn't pleasant."

"It wasn't, but at least maybe the skipping memories will stop. They might move ahead now." She could handle being terrified if she got to the truth.

Marcus leaned forward, resting on his elbows as he faced her. The counter separated them, but with him staring so intently, his presence still held her surrounded. "You'll get there. It will come back. In the meantime, you need to sleep. You can't keep going on an empty tank."

"I don't want to take drugs." She shivered and wrapped the soft fabric closer around her shoulders. "I did eight weeks of treatment after the accident, and I hated the side effects."

Marcus nodded. He squeezed her fingers for a second before turning to the cupboards, looking for something. "I hear you. I cut out of my therapies well before they said I was supposed to. Typical of our kind of minds—too stubborn to simply accept the traditional therapies."

Watching him move around the kitchen was distracting if nothing else, his naked upper body highlighted in the dim lights he'd clicked on in the hall. The resulting shadows and faint glow only highlighted his muscles as he dropped loose leaf tea into a pot, reaching back into the upper shelves to bring out cups. His sweatpants sat low on his hips. Bands of muscle wrapped around his waist, his abdomen flexing as he moved.

He used his left arm as much as his right, comfortably

holding items to his body, or clasping the tea jar in the crook of his elbow. For the fiddly work he used his right hand, but other than that, he seemed unaware of the missing portion of his arm.

She'd been oblivious last night. Never once during sex had it registered.

"You're staring," he noted. "Do I have something stuck on me I can't see?"

"I was looking at your arm," she confessed.

Marcus pushed the teapot to the side and walked around the counter. "Took you long enough."

He lifted his arm toward her, as he had when she'd checked out his climbing prosthesis. Only now there was his arm and the stump end, nothing covering it. Becki looked up at his face as she laid her hand on his elbow and pressed it down. "I was just noticing you don't allow it to stop you."

"Oh God, don't start that." He lifted his arm again, nudging her with it until she grabbed on. "I don't have fingers. I can't reach out the same way I used to. It's a royal pain in the ass at times, but mostly it just is. There's nothing to be admired. I'd prefer you were drooling over my sexual prowess or something I have more control over."

Becki touched him, wrapping her fingers around his bicep even as she smiled. "Well, there is that as well. Yes, on a scale of one to ten, I admire your cock a whole lot more than your arm."

He laughed.

She ran her fingers over the four inches or so that remained of his forearm. The dusting of hair was dark against his light tan, the skin smooth. Muscles and tendons flexed under her touch as she worked her way lower until she cupped the end. There the skin was rougher, slightly rumpled in spots.

Marcus shivered.

She jerked her hand away. "Does it hurt?"

"You're tickling me," he teased. "Let me grab our tea."

Becki let him go. He might not want to be admired, but she still did because he had done what she wanted to do. Gone on living. Put his energies into a new direction.

Marcus pressed a cup against her fingers before jerking his head toward the living room. "Come on, curl up on the couch and we'll get cozy until the tea kicks in."

"You giving me some patented home remedy?"

"Herbal. Yeah, it's one of those 'calms you down, makes you drowsy' natural Chinese blends."

He sat first, and she unashamedly crawled right back into his lap as she'd done when she'd woken up. Marcus didn't say anything at first, just sipped his tea and held her close.

Marcus spoke quietly. "I think it freaks people out."

"Your arm?"

He paused. "You know, it's more like they can't understand why I'm not making a bigger deal of it. Like I'm supposed to be all emo and pissed that I lost a limb. Fuck it—I'd take my life over my hand any day, and that's about what it came down to. People don't know the big picture, though. They see what they see, and expectations and assumptions creep in."

"If you're handicapped you're supposed to be a victim, you know."

"Right," he drawled, "or admired for doing what simply isn't a big deal. People need to get real. If we're honest, everyone deals with physical limitations of some sort, whether they're too short to reach into high cupboards, or too out of shape to run for the bus. It's the mental stuff that takes more effort. Takes incredible bravery."

She fought to keep from whimpering. "I don't feel very brave at the moment."

"Oh, Becki. I know." He put down his drink, rubbing her back gently as she clung to him. His voice carried to her ears, a low whisper, yet full of conviction. "Listen to me. Trust me. You have more than enough courage to face this valley and, in time, climb out the other side."

She took a deep breath as she let his reassurances settle over her.

Being with him helped. Marcus could truly understand the haunting pain she fought. He still struggled with his own demons—she was sure of it. The days he'd gone missing, his *episodes* as he called them, had to have a cause. The caress of his hand said this was more than a standard show of sympathy.

Somehow, without another word, she knew he understood her battle. And while the war still raged for him as well, he hadn't given up. His determination motivated her beyond belief.

The heat of his chest lulled her, as did the warmth of the tea. She finished the mug and he took it from her fingers, nestling in tighter as she wrapped her arms around his torso. It was quiet except for the sound of their breathing, the faint pulse of his heart under her ear.

If the nightmares came, he'd chase them away.

Marcus waited until her breathing calmed to a smooth rhythm. Too many emotions waged inside for a simple answer to his current state of mind. He'd given her tea, supported her. Done what he could to ease her fears, all the while not letting her catch a glimpse of what was hiding inside.

When she screamed, he'd been the one frozen in terror.

Memories rushed in, the unanswerable cries that haunted him. The unspeakable pain of being unable to help. But Becki was flesh and blood, and his drive to soothe her had forced his personal demons into retreat.

They returned now to poke him as he lifted her and carried her back to bed. All the while as he slipped off her robe and arranged her limbs on the mattress, his mind raced with unsolvable scenarios.

Becki curled up so sweetly, her fingers clinging to his arm as he touched her. He tugged himself free to strip off his sweatpants then rejoined her. She pressed her body against his, reaching back to pull his arm over her. Her fingers lingered on his stump, running lightly over the sensitive skin on the inside of his elbow. Then she fell fully asleep again, leaving him with his tortured thoughts.

Seeing her struggle with her fears only emphasized his

faults. Not his hand—he'd told her the truth when he said he could live without a goddamn hand. It was the pain of what he couldn't fix that preoccupied his nightmares.

What if he couldn't do for her? What if somewhere along the road he failed her? He should leave her alone, but he was too damn selfish to want that as an option.

He was still no closer to an answer when they woke the next morning, pissing rain smacking against the windowpane.

She twirled in his arms and kissed him, squirming away before he could do anything more than blink drowsily. "Sleepyhead. I've been awake for an hour."

"Why didn't you take advantage of me then?" He leaned on his elbow as she strode naked to the window, hands pressed to the glass. She wrinkled her nose and pouted at the weather.

"Stupid rain." She turned again, arms crossing over her breasts. "Ravishment was not on the list for this morning."

"It *is* on the list, though. Good to know."

She grinned and plopped back on the edge of the mattress, far enough away that he'd have to lunge to grab her. "I feel wonderful. Your miracle tea and the rest of the night's sleep did wonders. Thank you."

"You're welcome." Good thing one of them had gotten some rest. "Plans for the day. You have anything you need to do?"

She shook her head. "I've got the week organized, so if we want to train this morning, I'm game."

"Breakfast first?"

"God, yes, I'm starving." Becki stood and went to her bag, pulling out clothing before swinging away from him toward the bathroom. "I'll shower, then you can tell me what to make, okay?"

Being around her was comfortable. Relaxed.

Maybe too relaxed. Marcus lay back for a moment and debated the wisdom of getting into the shower with her and starting all over again. He hadn't had nearly enough of her yet.

She was right, though. Getting out for a while wasn't a bad idea. Burn off a little energy, then they'd come back and see what other mischief they could get into. So he ignored his morning wood and slipped to the kitchen to see what he had in the house. Something with a lot of calories to make sure they had enough to keep going for a long, long time.

CHAPTER 20

¡¡¡¡¡¡¡¡¡¡¡¡¡¡¡¡¡¡¡¡¡¡¡¡¡¡¡¡¡¡

The first hour of training was a complete and utter failure. Becki collapsed onto the mat beside him and cursed wildly.

Marcus waited for her to finish letting off steam. He rested his hand on her thigh, rubbing lightly as she lay with her arms crossed over her face.

She'd warmed up, roped in, and attempted to climb. Each time she'd been no higher than the five-foot marker before she'd call for a stop and he'd lower her to safety. He'd suggested other routes, other things she could do to train, but she'd insisted.

She might be willing, but her fear was having nothing to do with it. She was like a clipped bird, stuck on the ground.

Her chest heaved as she dragged in a huge breath and released it slowly.

"What am I going to do, Marcus? I can't wrap a blindfold around my head and expect you to follow me everywhere, talking me through routes."

Frustration and anger—at herself—screamed out no matter how softly she'd spoken.

"Why are you pushing so hard to go vertical?" he asked. "You need to get into shape again, and there's no reason why you can't do that while staying close to the floor."

She cranked her elbow out of the way to deliver a scathing glare. "Baby steps."

"I'll join you," Marcus offered. "Come on, it's way more fun to have someone else to work over and laugh at when they fall off a section you aced than worrying about what you can't change right now."

Becki flipped to her stomach and crawled toward him. "Stop being reasonable. I was getting ready for a good pout, and you had to go and ruin it for me."

He caught her around the waist and pulled her close. Becki rested her hands on his shoulders while his fingers teased the line of skin at the edge of her shorts. "Sorry, but tell me that *reasonable* isn't what you'd have suggested if our positions were reversed."

"Hmm, reversed positions. Now you're onto something." She made contact with his chest and pushed. The move came quickly enough that he lost his balance, landing on his back to discover he was looking up at her. She'd straddled him, a shining grin exchanged for the anger she'd shown only a moment before.

"Don't get too comfortable," he warned. "I just suggested wall circuits. I'm not going to fool around until you've done at least two."

"Oh, really?" Becki undulated her hips, and he gave his dick hell for reacting.

She leaned down, the swoop of her climbing top low enough to reveal the rounded line of her cleavage. He looked forward to exploring her all over again very shortly, but first? Self-control was demanded. "You know you want to climb."

Becki planted her hands on either side of his head and sighed lustily. "I want to climb *you*, but fine. Work first. Play later."

She kissed him. Lips soft and warm. Eager tongue slipping to tangle with his. The position put her full-out over the top of him, and he was seriously considering throwing the workout aside for at least an hour when there was a loud slam, and a rush of cooler air filled the room.

She sprang back, scrambling to her feet. Marcus joined her as three people walked through the door, their loud joking echoing in the gym.

"I still don't believe you did that." Tripp poked Devon in the chest. "Alisha is going to kill you."

"She's got to catch me first." Devon stopped a few feet away from them, his bright grin innocently shining out. "Hey, Marcus. Becki. What's up?"

Marcus looked over his team. Devon, Tripp, Xavier. "What're you doing here on a day off?"

"Interview for the paper. The reporter wants shots to accompany the article, and we figured David wouldn't mind if we used the gym."

Devon seemed oblivious, but Tripp was giving Becki and him some pointed looks. Xavier had already wandered off to the change room, no doubt to grab harness and climbing shoes.

"Umm, you don't think David will mind, do you?" Devon fidgeted, finally picking up on some of the tension in the room.

Marcus wanted to say yes, but he couldn't lie, no matter how much he regretted losing their privacy. Of course, now the likelihood of getting their workout completed increased exponentially. "Not a problem at all. We'll stay out of your way."

He joined Becki in the corner where she'd retreated. "Sorry about that. You still game to continue?"

She leered at him dramatically, then laughed. "Well, sure. Why not?"

He glanced around quickly, and when he realized they were alone for a moment, he leaned in, caging her with his body. "You know what you started earlier?"

A slight wiggle was enough to rub them together intimately. "Yeah?"

"We're finishing later. Deal?"

"Deal."

Becki rotated slowly, rubbing her butt against him as she got into position on two small holds barely off the ground.

He wanted to lean over and bite her, but the guys burst from the change room at that moment.

Plans postponed, not cancelled.

She settled into a routine. Stepped to a new hold, joined her feet or crossed them over. All the time as she traversed, she never picked any hold higher than her arm's length up.

She might have called this exercise baby steps, but it was still valuable conditioning, and they both knew it.

"Hey, stop staring at my ass and get moving," Becki taunted, too softly for the boys to hear on the far side of the gym.

"It's a nice ass."

She laughed, and something inside him rejoiced at seeing her making the best of it.

He switched attachments on his prosthetic, leaving the claw behind for a small ax-shaped device instead. One side a point, the other flat, he could use it pretty much like a hand without worrying about it coming apart or getting stuck on him.

He paced past Becki, supposedly to check her positioning, but really to take advantage of the position she was in. He caught hold of her ankle and adjusted it, lightly stroking her inner thigh until he paused with his hand cupped over her sex. He kept his body between her and the team, blocking his movements.

"You know, whatever you do I'm doing back to you first chance I get." Becki pumped her hips over his fingers.

Marcus glanced over his shoulder to ensure that his team was otherwise occupied. "You can grope me anytime you'd like."

"Game on," Becki whispered.

The exercise should have been called *sexual tension repeats*. She hopped off the wall and challenged him to try a section. The entire time he worked on placing his hand, hook, and feet, she was right behind him, touching him under the guise of "guiding him into position."

"There's a nice spot longing for you to fill it over here, Marcus. Slip your fingers in nice and slow. That's right. Oh, yeah, and now push with your hips. Another inch. Hmmm, come on, give it everything you've got."

He took smaller steps as his cock reacted. Fell off the wall to get a little relief. Then he'd turn around and taunt her in return, both of them working like the devil to keep their laughter and filthy comments low enough not to be overheard by the others.

When the knock sounded, Marcus had almost forgot about the reporter. He briefly debated ducking into the change room until the invader and his accompanying cameraman left. But the team seemed to have it under control. Becki watched for a moment with a wary expression, and Marcus leaned in close.

"You look thrilled to see them."

"Let's just say reporters aren't my favourite people."

Marcus paused. "You want to get out of here?"

Becki nodded. "If you don't mind. We can stretch in the dorms or something."

He bumped her to draw her attention from where she was staring across at the two men setting up camera equipment. "You're not trying to get out of spending the day with me, are you?"

Her eyes were tired, but she smiled. "Sorry. Distracted. No, we can go back to your place. I'm good with that."

He wanted to see that smile return that she'd worn only moments before.

Marcus motioned to her gym bag, then grabbed his own things, keeping Becki close by his side. They'd almost made it when he noticed the reporter waving.

Ignore the man and pretend he hadn't seen? They weren't close enough to the door to duck out without making it obvious that their departure was an escape.

"Heads up, Becki, company," he warned as the reporter jogged across the room.

"Hi, Marcus. Good to see you climbing again."

"Ted." Marcus acknowledged him with a brief nod.

"Wanted to say hello." Ted extended a hand to Becki. "Ted Martin. You're the new instructor?"

Becki smiled politely as she shook his hand. "Working with David and the instructors."

"Awesome. You'll be at the gala next weekend, I assume?"

She nodded. "I'll be there."

Ted stepped back with a smile. "That's great. Hope you're enjoying Banff. We'll see you around."

He spun on his heel and trotted back to the team. Marcus took advantage of the moment, and they escaped, not stopping until they were seated in his truck.

Becki twisted to face him. "That was . . ."

". . . really weird. Yeah. I wonder what he's up to?" Ted knew better than to try to get Marcus to do a real interview, but that meet-and-greet had been strange. Marcus drove in silence, both he and Becki deep in their own thoughts.

She followed him into the house. After the disappointment of the failed start of training, they'd fallen into so much fun teasing each other on the scramble. She'd lost sight of that while distracted by the reporter.

Damn her brain for doing a yo-yo anyway.

She dropped her bag by the door. "You have any chocolate?"

Marcus laughed. "Is this a trick question?"

"It's being asked by a frustrated female. I'd call it an important question to answer quickly."

He caught her by the shoulder, rubbing the tight muscles. "What if I can relax you another way?"

"I suppose that means you have no chocolate."

"Right. Guy pad. I have beer. . . ."

She twisted to face him, longing for something to change. "I enjoyed training. Sorry for being such a wet blanket at the end. I don't like reporters."

"Hey, I get it. Trust me." He cupped her chin in his hand and stroked his thumb over her cheek. "Offer still stands. You want me to help you relax?"

What did she want? She went for honest.

"I don't know. I don't want to decide. I don't want to have to think. I want to . . . not be in charge right now."

His eyes flashed hot, and she swallowed hard as the lusts inside that had faded roared to full strength.

He nodded. "If that's what you want, then I can definitely help you with that."

He led her down the hall, this time to the master bath. She'd been in there briefly to shower, glancing longingly at the oversized soaker tub.

Now he stopped beside it and reached for her.

She stood motionless as he stroked his hand down her body, the sensation sparking her senses and helping the anxiety to fall away. "You have such a decadent house. Hot tub outside, Jacuzzi in here. Shower big enough for two."

"I like my comforts. Take off your clothes."

She stripped as he twisted the taps and filled the tub, holding her hand and helping her step into the water. Becki sighed as heat enveloped her, cocooning her in soft pleasure. Marcus arranged her in the bath, laying her back and lifting her arms to rest along the ledges.

"Wait right here." He pressed a kiss to her temple, then paced away. She watched him go, admiration for his willingness to care for her overriding the lust she had for his ass.

She closed her eyes and luxuriated in the heat. At times it seemed she was always cold—a chill lingering in her body from the accident that clung to her soul like icicles. Here she felt safe, warmth trickling in not just from his actions and the sexual heat between them.

She didn't know everything about Marcus, but she trusted him. Completely.

A sweet rich scent filled her nostrils, and she glanced up to find he'd returned. He sprinkled something around her, kneeling to put the tin aside and stir the water's surface with his fingertips. A flowery aroma with tones of fruit surrounded her.

"What is that?"

Marcus leaned back, his hand still dangling over her. "Tea."

She laughed. "No way."

He shrugged. "The magic works on the outside as well as when you drink it. Now close your eyes and let me take care of you.

Maybe she was being selfish, but she totally loved every minute of what followed. He washed her, reaching into the water to touch and caress all of her. Slow, seductive motions. Thorough and yet brief. He didn't linger as he stroked her breasts, took as long to wash her arms as the folds of her labia. But by the time he was done, she was both boneless with relaxation and buzzing with desire.

He helped her stand and walked her to the shower to wash away the fine bits of tea that still clung to her skin.

He dried her. Brought her to his bed.

"It should be my turn to take care of you," she commented.

"You're not in charge." He flipped her to her belly and straddled her, covering her skin with oil, squeezing her muscles and loosening all the fatigue. For having done a gentle climb, she was amazingly tired. His fingers dug in deep, pulling and working until she was totally relaxed and warm from the inside out.

"This is lovely," she sighed happily. "Thank you."

Marcus kissed her shoulder, moving off and sitting next to her hip. "We're not done. You ready for more?"

More? Curiosity rose. "You're in charge."

"Exactly." He paused. "Becki, I do anything you don't like, tell me to stop."

She lifted herself on her elbows so she could meet his gaze. "Are you worried I won't enjoy what you're about to do?"

"Oh no, I think you'll enjoy it a lot, but I had to warn you. You have total control. Say *stop*, and I will."

"Go for it." Saying *stop* was the last thing on her mind.

CHAPTER 21

Marcus brought her to the middle of the room, standing her on the soft area carpet in front of the fireplace. She smiled, head tilted to the side. He couldn't resist pressing a kiss against her cheek before stepping away to flick on the gas control.

Becki laughed. "Did I say decadent? Spoiled rotten is more like it."

"You get to enjoy the results. Are you complaining?"

"Not so far." She stretched her fingers toward the flame. "I should move to a tropical island or something. Why am I here in the Rockies where it's still snowing in May?"

He pulled over the footstool, placing it the perfect distance from the heat. "Because it's the Rockies."

"Right."

She stared at him from under her lashes. Marcus waited long enough to make her squirm. "Sit."

Becki moved slowly, centering herself on the footrest. She sat with her legs slightly apart. She rolled her neck slowly, stretching the muscles lazily like a cat.

"Comfy?" he asked, moving forward to squat at her side. He stroked his hand down her back and caressed her ass, circling up to trail his fingertips along her spine.

Her words seemed to contradict the shiver that rolled over her. "The leather is soft and warm."

"Put your arms behind you," he commanded.

She caught her fingers together. The position brought her into a slight arch, firm breasts thrust out proudly. He stroked his forefinger up her body and between the smooth rounds, pausing to cradle one in the palm of his hand.

Becki wiggled against him, obviously looking for more. And he was so willing to give to her. But first . . .

He leaned in and kissed her again. Just a tease. Pulling away before more than a whisper of response escaped her. Marcus grabbed his gym bag and pulled out the soft hemp rope he had coiled inside.

When he returned to the footrest, she was watching intently. Her smile was gone, replaced with something else.

"Are you afraid?"

She shook her head. Didn't speak.

He dropped the rope to the floor, the mass hitting with a solid thump. Becki never broke eye contact. Focused on him and him alone. She'd played with ropes before, that much was obvious. As was the way she felt about them. "I can't surprise you, can I?"

"I figured you knew your way around a rope or two." She exhaled the words. Slow. Even. Already slipping into the mindset of being totally cocooned and protected.

Marcus bent and grabbed the rope about a foot from the end. Brought it up and draped it over Becki's shoulder. Dragging the weight forward so it stroked her skin.

Becki squirmed, her intake of air a little more jerky. She caught herself before he needed to talk her through it, deliberately breathing in through her nose and out through her mouth—a climber's refocusing trick, and Marcus smiled.

She knew what she needed. She trusted him to give it to her.

"Hold this," he ordered, laying the rope end in her palms.

She opened them wide for a second before closing her fingers over the cord. He pressed her shoulders down, making her shift into a more relaxed position, hands close to her ass.

Then he began. He held the extra rope away by hooking it over his left elbow, allowing his right hand to control the loose portion. Up over her right shoulder. Across her torso and between her breasts. One loop settling around her body. The rest just above it. Trapping her in an erotic spider's web.

Her breathing echoed softly, mingling with the crackle of the fireplace. Rain splashed outside the windows. A hushed noise from the rope as he manipulated it. His own laboured breathing as the sight of her turned him on more and more.

When he tucked the final loop into place so it wouldn't come undone, he was as hard as a spike. "Still with me?"

"Hmm, yeah."

Her eyes were closed as he knelt, her upper body swaying.

"I'm going to touch you. Take care of you. Let me take you where you need to go."

She nodded.

He gazed at his handiwork. The ropes crossed above and below her naked breasts, two strands running between them to frame and lift the tender mounds like a rope bra. The rest of it was coiled around her abdomen, locking her arms in position. He leaned in closer, stroking one breast, then the other. Smooth motions, avoiding her nipples. Paying attention to all the soft surfaces before moving in and caring for the tight tips. He covered one with his mouth, wetting it and sucking the tiny ring. Switching sides, listening to the changes in her breathing and sensing how she pressed forward looking for more.

She spread her thighs when he tapped the inside of her legs.

"God, you're wet," he praised, before drawing his fingers along her folds and finding the tight bundle of nerves at the top. Marcus played with the clit bar, stroking it gently even as he returned to tasting her breasts. He couldn't get enough of her.

She shuddered and came far quicker than he'd expected. Head thrown back, a groan of pleasure escaping her lips. He stood and adjusted her, guiding her to lie belly down over the footrest. Her ass bent over the edge, thighs spread wide.

He ran his hand over her wet cunt, dipping his fingers in. Enjoying the evidence of how turned on she was. Sitting on the floor, he covered her with his mouth.

"Oh yes." Becki wiggled under his attention, small noises sneaking from her, somewhere between moans and gasps as he licked from top to bottom, lapping at her. Playing with her clit before dragging all the way to the tight rosette of her ass. Her taste filled him. Drove him mad. He speared his tongue into her, fucking her with it. Eating greedily as she grew wetter for him. Because of him.

Then he rose over her and lined up his cock, dragging the fat crown up and down against her opening until she arched as hard as possible. Pressing her ass toward him, trying to get him to enter her.

He gave her what she wanted and angled in. Slowly, captivated by the sight of his cock vanishing into her warmth, relishing the sensation as her body wrapped around him like his rope was wrapped around her.

Tight heat. Slick wetness. He caught hold of the ropes and used them as an anchor. Becki called his name and her cunt squeezed him, catching him by surprise yet again.

"So beautiful." So responsive. He drove all the way in and paused, savouring the rippling of her body as her orgasm rocked on and on. Every time the pulses slowed, he dragged back and pressed in again, prolonging her pleasure like some hedonistic torture.

When she finally sighed lustily, he thrust. Pushing her to the limits. Pounding into her, the fronts of his thighs slapping against her legs, balls banging her clit on the end of every stroke.

His climax approached and he exploded, her tight passage tearing pleasure from him, ripping his seed loose and making his mind go blank for a moment.

He covered her with his body, surrounding her, holding her close, pushing away the hair that lay over her sweaty cheek. Still intimately connected, hearts racing. The presence of the rope between them barely registered, it was so soft and warm from her skin.

He withdrew, moisture following him as her cunt tightened in response, and Becki moaned. He lifted her. Untied her. Let the rope fall unminded to the floor as he carried her to the shower and held her in his arms, waiting for her to come back from the place she was.

His embrace replaced the rope. The warmth of the water replaced the fire. He waited patiently, wondering why thoughts of tying her up and never letting her leave him were so very strong.

Water hit her face. Protected and at peace, Becki didn't fight the euphoria still holding her in its grasp. Just accepted it. Went with the sensation.

She knew Marcus was caring for her. He'd known how to tease and control her body as he'd brought her to orgasm. He'd perfectly handled the rope that had held her so tight she didn't have to worry what came next.

As she leaned against his chest, part of her was aware she stood in the shower with him, but she could have been anywhere safe and warm. The reality of here and now fell away. The only things that remained were emotions. Driving into her like the pulse of his heart. One beat after another.

Safe.

Guarded.

I've got you.

Cherished.

The trees were gone. Before her was nothing but rock, the wide ledge on which she sat solid and flat as a table. Her head ached, and she climbed gingerly to her feet, muscles protesting. Hell, all of her was protesting. Her fingers stung as she used the cliff behind her to help haul herself upright—that hurtful moment when blood returns to too-cold digits making her swear. The weight of her pack dragged at her as she found her balance. She unhooked her helmet, tempted to let it fall to the ground. Habit forced her to stretch protesting muscles to reach around and clip it to an out-of-the-way strap.

Her fingers brushed past her harness, the . . .

. . . world blurred.

Becki stood motionless. Her heart raced as if she'd completed a sprint. She looked around, checking for signs of danger. The soft sounds of the wilderness greeted her. Nothing to indicate why she fought the rush of adrenaline panic flooding her veins. The weather had turned, full-out rain falling, and her face was wet. She adjusted her hood to guard herself from the full deluge as she examined the territory.

There was a clearly visible track leading off to the right. Not anything remotely like a maintained park trail or even a well-traveled climbing route. It was more likely an animal path, but it was something to follow nonetheless.

Walking along the narrow cliff gave her something to focus on. She had to concentrate to keep from slipping as the rocks underfoot grew rain-soaked and slick. She'd gone for a couple of hours at least, stopping and taking drinks, constantly making her way downward. She had to approach one of the high-traffic paths eventually.

Rounding a corner and coming face-to-face with two very pale-cheeked teens barely surprised her. What else could this mountain throw at her?

They were stuck, of course. On a ledge—one of those lovely looking pitches that were easy to get up and the devil to get down without training or a healthy dose of chutzpah. Becki stepped forward and waved.

Becki sucked for air, opening her eyes to discover that she had Marcus clutched around the neck with a death grip.

"Hey, *shhh*, you're okay. I'm here. You're good." He kissed her temple and squeezed her close.

She wasn't sure if she should laugh or cry. "Marcus, I remember. The accident."

He shut off the shower, all his attention focused tightly on her face. "Explain."

"Not everything, but I remember finding the girls. The rescue. And a few hours before that." She accepted the towel he wrapped around her shoulders, her insides buzzing with a strange mix of sexual hangover and giddy enthusiasm. "Holy *shit*, I remember."

Somehow Marcus had her sitting on the bed as he finished drying her off. "Well, not the normal reaction I get to tying up a woman, but if you're happy, I'll take it."

Becki threw her arms around his neck and squeezed him tight. When she let go, she caught his grinning face in her hands and kissed him solidly before pulling back far enough to allow their foreheads to rest together. "The sex was wonderful. Thank you."

He stared at her, the blue in his eyes shining bright like a summer day. "You okay to get dressed? We'll get something to eat and you can tell me about it."

She nodded. Caressed his face carefully. "I enjoyed myself completely."

"No complaints over here, either."

As they separated to find clothes, Becki sorted through all the images in her brain, including the new ones, the ones that had been hiding from her for so long. There were still things she didn't understand, but the fact that a bit of the missing information had chosen to come to light encouraged her a ton.

She pulled a clean shirt over her head and stared across the room at Marcus as he dressed.

The memories were awesome and thrilling, but the sensation of being completely and utterly cared for by him? It wasn't as if she could compare the issues, but she was so pleased she'd gotten to experience both.

She joined Marcus as soon as she was dressed. He had

leaned down and nabbed the end of the rope, coiling the long section in a smooth motion by wrapping it around his arm. Had it been too soon for them to be playing games? Not as far as she was concerned. Sex had always been fun, but Marcus took it up a level way past fun. There was no hiding the shiver that took her as she watched him handle the cord so expertly.

He'd seen it as well. Her response.

"If you don't stop grinning like that, I'm going to call you the Cheshire cat," she warned.

"Meow."

She smacked him on the shoulder as she slipped past toward the kitchen. Something bubbled inside, between her mental delight and physical satisfaction.

She'd remembered. Holy cow, so incredible.

Marcus came and directed traffic as they put together sandwiches and soup. A simple task, which was good because she was distracted sharing the bits she'd seen.

She'd barely finished when he pulled the pickle jar from her fingers and stole one. "Does everything you told me line up with what the rescue crew reported?"

"Pretty much. I don't think I'm remembering a told memory, though. There were too many details that weren't mentioned. Like the colour of the girls' jackets, and where we met the first team of searchers."

Marcus nodded. "It does sound promising."

Becki carried their plates to the table. "Doesn't tell me anything more about what happened to Dane."

"Give it time." He held her chair, then sat. He stared across at her for a moment.

"What?"

Marcus coughed. "Tell me honestly. Was that too soon to break out the ropes?"

She couldn't stop her smile. "We're climbers. I'm surprised we didn't start with ropes."

"I'm serious."

He looked so grave and solemn that she laid her hand on his arm. Was it too soon? She made herself pause. Pushed away the euphoria of the aftermath, concentrated instead on the actual sex. On being with Marcus.

Only a few days before she'd been unresolved about getting over Dane. Why had moving forward with Marcus felt so right?

She spoke slowly. "I think we're in a strange situation. Someone looking in might see things as going fast, but we didn't start this relationship at zero. We've got a history, even though it was a long time ago. And maybe some of the things we've got in common make us click."

Marcus stroked her arm, his strong fingers squeezing hers briefly. "Good. I'm not asking because I don't think it was right, but I want to make sure I wasn't off in left field."

"Baseball analogies now. Fine, then, you knocked it out of the park." His mouth twisted up into the smile that made her want to stop talking and start all over again with the sexing. "But thank you for checking. It's one of the reasons I trust you."

He leaned back in his chair, stretching his legs toward her and casually tangling their limbs together. "Plans for the rest of the day?"

"Want to go for a walk?"

Marcus glanced out the window and grimaced. "In the rain?"

She shrugged. "We won't melt. I should get back to the dorms afterward anyway."

He nodded, busying himself cleaning their dishes. Becki stared at the rain marks trickling down the window and wondered how long it would take before she learned everything that was missing. Wondered if as the memories returned she'd be able to face the wall again without having heart palpitations at the thought of doing an actual climb.

Marcus loaded her bag into her car, and they drove in separate vehicles to the trailhead of Lake Minnewanka.

It was only after they were thoroughly soaked and she was back in her dorm room alone that she realized he'd been strangely quiet all afternoon. They'd discussed local climbing routes and trips they'd enjoyed, but she'd probably done the lion's share of the talking.

Becki pulled a few sheets of paper from the desk and took notes about the new things she'd remembered about the accident, but writing the details down didn't give her as much satisfaction as she expected.

Frustrated, she collapsed onto the bed and stared at the ceiling, flipping through all the reasons for the sudden itch under her skin, and it hit her. What she wanted was to be seated in the same room as Marcus. They didn't have to be talking, or fooling around. Just there. She wanted to be able to look at him and have him smile back at her before he returned to whatever task he was working on.

The realization simultaneously pissed her off and made her wonder.

CHAPTER 22

ıııııııııııııııııııııııııııııı

The dreams returned that night, leaving her confused and bewildered. Small teasers into what might have happened plus the new play-by-play all mixed together and shook her until she once again woke in a cold sweat.

There wasn't enough coffee to deal with a morning like this. She stirred the dark liquid again and again, wondering where the line was between being pleased that her memories kept moving forward, and being scared to death.

Her phone rang—and the way she reacted to the tone she'd assigned to Marcus emphasized how much she'd appreciated having his comforting touch the previous time she'd had a nightmare.

Stupid reactions. She was a grown woman. He couldn't hold her hand all the time. Time to distract herself and redeem the rest of the day. "Morning, Marcus. What evil things have you devised for your team today?" she asked.

He sighed wearily. "I'm so misunderstood."

"Right." She could picture him leaning back in his chair,

long legs stretched out as he grinned at her. "I'm not feeling the sincerity in that."

"You should talk. I read your training plans for them for the coming week. I'm going to lose my Evil Lord title to you by Wednesday. Hey—you had self-rescue on the list for today. Interested in taking the crew to the Cliffs of Insanity for that exercise instead of using the wall?"

"Really? That would be perfect, only I wasn't going to make them hike that far since they're doing other conditioning already."

"We'll do a drop. Erin is flying patterns, and hovering in that area is good for her."

A rush of absolute terror stopped Becki from being able to answer right away. He expected her to rappel to the training area. She stared out the window and attempted to keep the little coffee she'd swallowed from coming up on her.

"Becki? You still there?"

"Just, I don't think I can do that, not yet, Marcus. The wall would be better."

His confusion was clear. "You can't do what?"

The words came out broken as she whispered, "Rappel from the chopper."

"Oh God, no, Becki. I didn't mean you." His deep voice soothed her even as her heart continued to race. "Erin will land the bird so you and I can hop out. Yes, you'd have to feel comfortable getting in the beast, but I thought you should be okay in the cargo bay. If you're game."

Becki took a deep breath. "Okay. Yes, I think I can handle that. Sorry for panicking."

"I should have been clearer," he apologized. "I'll come and pick you up in an hour to hit the shop. We'll gather equipment there."

She promised to be ready and hung up, the phone dangling from her fingertips as she leaned her head against the cold glass and looked over the grey day, wondering if this was a really bad move, or if it would end up simply being another step on her way to full recovery.

One thing was certain. There was nothing wrong with her hormones. Other than they were still trigger-happy anytime she got around Marcus. He pulled to the curb and hopped out, grabbing her gear bag and tossing it in the back. She wavered on her feet before choosing to ignore the urge to steal a kiss, instead yanking open the door and crawling into the passenger seat.

Marcus checked her out slowly before closing the door for her. She focused forward, fingers locked together, nervous about the upcoming chopper trip, confused by how awkward she felt being with him and not sure what stage of affection to show.

The ten-minute ride to the field was far quieter than she'd expected.

The silence that had surrounded them as he drove was only made more shocking when contrasted with the high volume of voices and shouting they discovered in the storage bay. Becki leaned against the wall out of the way of the action and simply observed as the team pulled together the equipment Tripp called out.

It was loud and wild and totally good-natured, and some of the edge eased from her soul. Maybe the sleeplessness of the night before had affected her more than she'd imagined.

She went through her own gear bag, double-checking that she had all the required equipment. Even if she wasn't able to climb, she wanted to be sure to have the supplies to make examples. Short lengths of lightweight cording, neatly coiled and tied off. Extra carabiners, tape. Her knife.

She slipped to the side where there was an open table and smiled at Devon, who was working in that area.

"Got room for me?"

"No problem." He indicated her gear. "By the way, let me know if you need anything—I'm cutting ropes this afternoon and can get you new lengths to order."

She nodded. "Thanks, I'll let you know."

Across the room, Xavier and Tripp continued to shout at each other. Erin wandered through the doorway, fully suited up, and waved at Becki. Marcus supervised and stepped in as needed.

The rush and excitement of the preparations made her ache to be back on active duty and stirred up the sense of loss all over again.

Alisha zipped a bag and tossed it to the pile of prepared gear. She wore a most indignant expression as she slapped her hands clean, her gaze focused on Devon. The sight of the small blonde stomping across the room toward them had to mean trouble. Becki poked Devon in the side, then tilted her head as a warning. Devon turned in time to discover Alisha glaring at him.

"Did you have a nice day yesterday?" she demanded.

"Um, yesterday? I guess so." Devon frowned. "Was pretty laid back."

"Good to hear it wasn't any trouble. I thought maybe it was too challenging, you know, keeping track of details. Little things like mentioning to all your teammates when you make a scheduling change."

Devon wrinkled his nose sheepishly. "Oh, that."

Alisha shoved up to Devon and got right in his face, which was pretty impressive considering she was a good foot shorter than him. "Yes, that. Imagine my surprise when I called the paper this morning to ask a simple question and discovered the interview already happened. Didn't want me around? Jerk."

Uh-oh. That was what the guys had been talking about the day before. Becki wondered how Devon was going to explain this one.

"Alisha." Devon patted her shoulder. "It's not like that—"

"Don't bother with the excuses." She twisted her way out from under his touch, crossing her arms and lifting her chin in defiance. "I wasn't interested in taking part anyway, but you're still a jerk."

Alisha spun on her heel and slipped away. Devon stared after her with something near hopeless adoration on his face. There was a good chance Erin had been right about Alisha and Devon being attracted to each other, at least on Devon's part.

"Your trick backfire?" Becki asked, stepping in closer so she could speak without being overheard.

He shook himself alert and glanced in her direction. "What's that? Oh, yeah. Well, it wasn't really a trick." Devon examined the area, but no one was looking their way. "Ted was shooting off his mouth the other day about what a hot bod Alisha had, and it was right after that when the idea of bringing a cameraman along became a part of the interview."

Good grief. "Where did you hear . . . ?" No. Lecturing Devon was not a part of her responsibilities. Only, it was, now that she'd been working with them. "Clearly, changing plans to protect Alisha from the big bad wolves without her knowledge isn't the way to earn brownie points."

Devon nodded slowly, watching Alisha as she carried the supplies out the door to the chopper. "Obviously. Only Ted didn't really do anything wrong, and it's not like I have the right to say anything."

God, it was like being back in middle school again. She wanted to fluff his hair, he was so damn cute. "Well, if you're going to get the girl, you're going to have to work a little harder now, aren't you?"

Devon blinked in surprise. "Get the girl? . . . Oh."

Becki snorted. "If you're trying to hide your interest in Alisha, you're doing it wrong."

Devon flashed his hundred-watt smile, and she wondered why Alisha seemed to be trying to avoid him. He was somewhat addictive, if you liked them sweet.

Marcus stepped back into the building, and the rush of hormones that hit clearly indicated her tastes ran much more to the savoury. The dark and dangerous. He didn't walk, he prowled, and every nerve tingled in response, which was both lovely and frightening.

He stopped by her side and looked her over carefully. "You ready for this?"

Another shudder of upset roiled through her stomach, and she fought to keep it under control. Maybe her current case of nerves had nothing to do with the sexual tension between them. "I think so."

Becki turned toward the chopper and took a deep breath.

She could have been climbing the gallows for how enthusiastically she moved. Marcus glanced around the passenger seats to double-check that all the team were ready before crawling into the back with Becki.

They found their places in the smaller jump seats, the space around them dark and windowless. It didn't do much good for his nerves, but this wasn't about him, but about Becki and helping her take the next step. She buckled in, and he managed his own straps, both of them reaching for the headsets hanging on the wall.

The solid hum of the props was blocked by the headset he slipped on, clicking the transceiver to channel two. He held up his fingers to indicate the number to Becki. She clicked her own button before catching hold of the chest straps and white-knuckling them.

"The rest of the team is on channel four. I told them to stay off this line. You need anything, let me know."

She nodded rapidly even as she attempted to slow her breathing through her nose, lips sealed into a thin line.

Marcus cursed the fates that had taken this woman and torn her apart so hard. The fear in her eyes and the tension in her body—she hadn't done anything to deserve the torment, and he wanted so badly to make it better. To take the fear from her.

All he could do was be there as much as she allowed him, and staying behind the limits she seemed to have built in the past day was killing him.

"Okay to go?" Marcus laid his hand on her thigh. He didn't know if she needed it, but he damn well did.

Becki's head snapped up, her gaze darting off whatever point on which she'd focused on the ground, and she nodded agreement, still without speaking.

Terror hovered in her eyes, and he nearly called the entire

trip off. She must have seen what he planned, or sensed it. Becki slapped at her speaker button and shakily answered him. "Ready for takeoff."

Maybe her voice was unsteady, but her expression dared him to do anything but let her try. He signaled Erin to go ahead, his gaze focused intently on Becki.

He'd abort the lift in a second if needed.

The buzz of the props increased even through the protective headset. Becki swallowed hard but otherwise didn't move as the pressure changed and the floor beneath them angled slightly as Erin took them skyward.

Becki's nostrils flared as she breathed in, eyes closing. Under his hand her leg quivered, and he squeezed lightly.

She caught hold of his fingers, and his heart leapt. Her firm grip remained for about a twenty count as he breathed with her. Willing her to be able to take the trip. Praying for her to be able to get back the control she so wanted.

It took five minutes before anything changed. Her eyes remained squeezed shut, but her death grip loosened. Marcus breathed easier. With every moment that passed, they got closer to the drop site. If they could get off the chopper without her having a panic attack, it would make the next time that much smoother.

At least that was what he'd found. Success bred success.

The helicopter shook briefly, probably caught in an eddy around one of the mountains, and Marcus cursed as Becki choked. She scrambled for the bag he'd discreetly tucked beside her and lost her breakfast.

The override broke through his headset as Erin spoke. "Sorry, boss, the cross turbulence caught me by surprise. How bad was it back there?"

Becki was white-faced and shaking, clinging to the arms of her chair with the bag propped between her legs. She looked miserable, but she wasn't screaming in terror.

"Estimated time to arrival?" he demanded.

"Ten minutes to hover site," Erin snapped back.

"Put us down first, then you can lift and do the drops for the crew."

"Shit. Affirmative." Erin clicked on briefly. "Sorry."

Marcus tapped Becki on the back of her hand with the hankie he'd stuck in his pocket in case of this event. She clutched it and, to his amazement, smiled slightly. She wiped her mouth, grimacing the entire time.

When she clicked the intercom, the disgust in her voice was clear. "You got any water?"

He pointed beside her seat. She leaned over warily and snatched up a bottle, rinsing and spitting the first couple of mouthfuls into the bag before gingerly rolling the top and tucking it aside.

She caught his eye and shook her head in derision.

Marcus raised his brow. "Is this a good time to mention that I threw up on the feet of the first nurse who tried to sweet-talk me after my operation?"

She blew out a long breath, balancing herself. "Classy."

"I thought so." He indicated her bottle, and she obediently sipped at it. "Nearly there. You're doing well."

Becki met his gaze and forced a smile. "I know. Although I hope you brought more bags, because I have a feeling the trip home might not go so smoothly."

"You can listen in on the crew line if you want to be distracted for a bit."

Her eyes widened. "Right. And take the chance one of them is talking about food? No thanks."

She'd caught his fingers in hers again, and he stroked her knuckles softly. "I didn't even ask—I assume this is the first chopper trip since?"

"First flight, period."

Anger and annoyance at himself slammed in. "What? I assumed you flew into Calgary."

She smiled now, more real. "I've got my car, Marcus. How did you think it got to Banff, rock gnomes?"

"I didn't think, period." He kicked his own ass for that fact. "I'm sorry—"

"Prepare for landing," Erin's announcement cut in. "Marcus, all clear?"

He adjusted channels to speak to his pilot. "Clear. Soft

as you can, or I'll make you do bump and grinds all afternoon."

"Got it, boss."

Becki raised a brow, and he realized she'd been listening. He clicked back to channel two. "What?"

"You're such an ass," she teased.

"What can I say? They love me."

She closed her eyes, blew out another breath, and hung on tight. Marcus watched with admiration. Whatever she was, courageous was certainly at the top of the list.

CHAPTER 23

Training was going well even though the entire time the thought hovered that there was still another flight to endure. Eventually Becki simply resigned herself to the fact that she would probably be ill on the return trip.

Still, preventive maintenance wasn't a stupid idea. When she turned down the granola bar Tripp offered her, Marcus didn't say a word.

He watched, though. His gaze fixed on her while she coaxed his team through the exercise, although skillwise there wasn't much she was able to actually teach them.

She stepped beside Marcus and stared at the narrow ledge Alisha had managed to ascend to without any trouble. "They are good. This is definitely just a refresher for them, having me around."

"I agree and yet, there's something to be said for trying to impress a hero—they're a lot sharper since you walked onto the scene. I don't see them goofing off as much in training because you're here."

"I think they're all a bunch of show-offs. They enjoy

having an audience to perform for." Becki pointed to the family that had stopped to picnic, observing the team train. Marcus casually slid his hand behind her back as she spoke, and she hesitated. "What are you doing?"

"Hmm?" Marcus glanced down. "What?"

"We're training." She caught his fingers and tugged until he let go. Then she ignored Marcus and shouted instructions to Tripp, focusing her attention back on the team.

His rumbling laugh snuck along her nerve endings like a low-grade electrical shock, tingling and making her that much more aware of him.

They stopped for a break, Devon and Tripp stretched out on the grass, Xavier and Alisha chatting with Anders as they rested in the shade. Erin sat in the open door of the cockpit reading a book, her dangling feet kicking like a kid.

Marcus stroked her arm and she instinctively jerked away, hiding the motion by grabbing her jacket and slipping it on.

He frowned. "What's wrong?"

"You keep touching me."

"And that's wrong?"

"It is while we're training." Becki pointed to the ropes that hung from the rock face. "I think the last thing today—"

"No, wait, back up." Marcus twisted until he was directly between her and the cliffs she'd been trying to discuss. "I'm a little confused here. Is there a specific reason why I'm not allowed to touch you in public?"

"While we're training," she corrected. "You touched me in public a few times, I seem to recall."

"But never while we were around my team." His face darkened. "Are you trying to keep our relationship a secret from them?"

Becki paused. "Our relationship?"

"Isn't that a typical guy line? Yes, our *relationship*. Are you planning to hide the fact that we're seeing each other for some reason? Because if you are, you neglected to inform me. Also? Forget it."

"But I'm not . . ."

She stopped and thought it through. She'd talked briefly to Erin about getting involved with Marcus, but was she trying to keep this under wraps? She didn't think so, but her reactions had said that pretty firmly.

"I don't know why I'm so antsy. Maybe it's because I'm tired. I'm not trying to hide anything." He lifted his brow, and she had to give him that. She was a basket case. "Maybe throwing up on top of too little sleep is making me stupid. I'm sorry if my actions came out wrong. I'm not ashamed to be seen with you. Far from it."

What he chose to focus on was unexpected. "Why didn't you sleep? More nightmares?"

Drat. "Yeah, but I'll be okay. It's bound to take a while—"

"Dammit, Becki." Marcus lowered his voice, but his anger screamed out loud and clear. "Why the hell did you go back to the dorms last night? You should have known that might happen."

"There was nothing you could do about it. If I'm going to have a nightmare, I'm going to have one, and it's not like you can stop them."

"I can be there to help you deal with them," he snarled. He glared over the rock face, his shoulders tight under his T-shirt. "That's it. When we get back to town we're grabbing your things from the dorm and you're moving in with me."

Something totally wild flashed in a series through her. The muted cheer of him wanting to care for her was rapidly swallowed over by a rush of indignation. "I'm moving in with you?"

"Yes." He stared her down. "You can't stay in the dorms for much longer anyway, so you may as well get settled where I can keep an eye on you."

Oh, he did not just go there. Becki was certain her jaw was on the ground. "Keep an eye on me?"

She didn't seem to be able to do anything but repeat his words, they were so incredulous. For a smart man he seemed rather oblivious to her unenthusiastic response. Becki wondered exactly how long he planned on digging this particular hole.

"There's no reason you have to suffer through sleep deprivation. I'll take care of you." Marcus stroked her cheek with his knuckles, and she just about lost it.

Her face flushed hot and all traces of exhaustion vanished completely in the rush of anger that filled her nicely. She rose to her feet and glared down, happy to be able to tower over him for once as he remained seated. "Excuse me, did you really just order me to move into your house? What alternate reality are you living in that makes you think bossing me around is a good thing? Especially when it comes to something major like where I live?"

He had the grace to look confused while he rose to his feet. "But I thought you enjoyed staying with me. I thought it helped that I was there the other night when you had the—"

"This discussion is not happening. Not now." Becki glanced at the team, who still seemed unaware that she was close to throttling their boss. "I appreciate many things about you. The fact you didn't freak when I lost my cookies during the flight—I appreciated that a lot. Doesn't mean I'm moving in with you."

"You like more about me than that." Marcus caught her arm and twisted her back to face him. "The conversation is good, the list of things we have in common is long, and the sex is more than spectacular."

"None of which are enough reasons for you to be able to order me around. Good grief." She yanked her arm free.

He glared daggers at her, opened his mouth to undoubtedly say something stupid—

An alarm rang out from the chopper, and they all jerked in reaction.

Erin was up in an instant. She vanished inside the cockpit as the entire team snatched their bags and gear from where it lay and began piling things into heaps. Marcus was gone, hitting the side of the chopper as the siren faded to a low echo in her ears.

Panic button—she should have known Marcus would have one working, even with the team on training. The props started the slow buildup to full liftoff, the sound of the blades cutting through the air still light as she prepared for the worst.

Becki raced to help Tripp stuff ropes as Alisha and Devon gathered the lines scattered on the hillside. "Emergency call?"

Tripp never stopped. "Guess they didn't get the memo we were on training this week. You coming with us?"

Her heart pounded harder than it should, and it wasn't just the thought of being in the chopper. Dealing with a rescue—not possible. Not yet.

"I'd only be in the way."

"Five-kilometer hike back to the highway. It's fairly level, though." He pulled out a cell phone and handed it to her. "If you hit number three when you're near the highway, my roommate will come and give you a ride to your place."

"Got it." She slipped the phone into a pocket and zipped it up. "I know the route back—done it a million times or so."

He grinned at her, and they both grabbed handfuls of gear and headed to the chopper at a dead run.

Marcus had the team already moving into position. "We're headed north. First roll call. Anyone want to bow out? Too fatigued from training? No penalty, no foul, but assess your abilities and let's get rolling. Erin can drop anyone who says no on the highway. Anders?"

"In."

"Alisha?"

"In." She twirled and clambered into position, full harness already in place. She and Anders set up to be able to winch her down as soon as they hit the rescue site.

Marcus continued rapidly through the list, but his gaze was on her. Becki scrambled past him to the cockpit and grabbed two of the water bottles from the cooler. She slipped them into her pack and checked that she had the rest of her gear and clothing.

If he argued with her, he was going to be flying the rescue with sore balls.

"Becki—crawl in the back and batten down."

"Negative. You don't want a civilian along. I've got an

exit plan, water and a ride. If Tripp has a couple granola bars for me, you can be off."

"Becki . . ." Marcus's jaw was so firmly set she was afraid he'd hurt himself. Still, she didn't waver.

And how he responded to her right now was going to set the direction for what happened next between them. Because while she might enjoy having him dominate her during sex, ordering her around in life decisions was the next wrong progression up from that macho *you will move in with me* bullshit he'd just tried to pull.

Maybe he knew that. His gaze stayed sharp, but he nodded briskly, glancing at his watch. "Sunset. I'm calling David. If you're not at the highway by sunset he'll come find you. You got numbers? Phone fully charged?"

Tripp leaned across him and tossed Becki a couple of granola bars. "Fully charged and all the numbers labeled. She's a go. We're ready to roll, boss."

Marcus took a deep breath. "If you're sure. Throwing up during a flight isn't the worst thing ever, Becki."

"Go. I'm a hundred percent to stay."

He shook his head but moved, climbing in and getting into a seat. The chopper was already lifting into the air as Becki tucked and ran from the revolving props.

Watched it rise and leave her behind.

Marcus ran on autopilot. His team worked efficiently, completing the rescue without a hitch as they pulled victims from the crevasse. He'd made sure his focus stayed on directing as needed, observing the talented group as they worked together. He really did have the finest team around.

The entire time, though, there was a part of his brain wondering where Becki was and how she was doing. His focus stayed sharp enough, so it wasn't a danger, but until his cell phone hummed and the text came through that she was home, something inside stayed tight with worry.

He'd fucked up big-time back during training.

Then again, so had she.

Having her twitch away from him had made him angrier than he expected. Although her explanation about being exhausted made sense—bad decisions were made while sleep deprived—he still wouldn't allow her to brush them off like that.

Only she was right as well. Ordering her around wasn't his brightest move ever. Her fire and determination were part of why he admired the hell out of her. Why would he want her to cave in?

Convince? Cajole? One of those would be far better, considering their personalities.

By the time they were headed home, he had his plan of attack figured out. Debrief first—a formality since the team had worked like a well-oiled cog this time. Next up would be a non-emotional call to Becki offering his company.

A strong drink if she turned him down. Maybe two.

Erin landed them back at the pad, the clock ticking over to nearly ten P.M. David stepped from the hangar doors to greet them, a group of four local students rushing forward to take gear from his weary team.

David slapped him on the shoulder. "I thought you'd like a little help unloading."

"Thank you." Marcus pointed at the showers. "Lifeline, you've got a fifteen-minute reprieve. Soak your brains, then regroup. David's students are cleaning up your mess."

"Yeah, David." Tripp high-fived him as he passed by.

Alisha stopped and gave David a kiss on the cheek. "You have a heart of gold."

"Don't expect this all the time," he warned. "I felt sorry for you doing both training and pulling bodies." David glanced at Marcus as activity wove around them. "You okay?"

Marcus nodded. "You heard from Becki?"

"She's fine. Hiked out with the group of tourists who had been watching your team train and got a ride with them. She called me, and she said she'd contact you as well."

"Texted. Is she okay, though?"

David held out his phone. "Call her if you're so worried."

Marcus shook his head. He wasn't going to make his call in public. "I should give her a little room."

"Uh-oh." His brother leaned in closer. "What did you do now?"

Fuckhead. Marcus ignored him and sat on the couch to wait for the crew to return. "Remind me why I like her?"

David laughed and slapped him on the shoulder before heading over to guide the volunteers through their tasks.

By the time all the team had gathered and they'd completed analyzing the rescue, Marcus's shoulders were aching with tension. It seemed to take forever until the staff room was finally empty, the last of the squad headed yawning for the door.

He hit autodial before he could think it through.

She picked up on the second ring. "Rescue went well?"

"All safe, team intact." All the things he knew she'd want to know. "Alisha did this three-point twirl that was sheer poetry. Fastened rescue lines and clamped belayers into position all with blood rushing to her brain. How the hell that girl can keep oriented is damn freaky."

Becki laughed. "When you like climbing, it's not that difficult to know right side up even when you're upside down."

Marcus was silent for a minute. "Sorry for abandoning you. I . . ." *No.* Telling her she should have come with them, at least to the highway, was out of line. She'd been safe; she'd made her own decision. It wasn't what he wanted, but he'd have to suck it up. "How are you?"

"Good."

She wasn't going to make this easy. "Do you want some company?"

Becki sighed, the telltale sounds of the creaky student bed complaining in the background as she wiggled. "Marcus, I need to think. And the walk out wasn't long enough. So, thank you for offering, but not tonight."

Marcus pinched the bridge of his nose and held on to the words that wanted to burst out. Instead, he spoke slowly and tried for *reasonable* instead of *asshole*. "If you change your mind, let me know."

"Sure." Noncommittal. The word clipped and tight.

Screw that. Holding on to *reasonable* got a whole lot harder. "Becki, I mean it. I'll back off now because you've asked me to. But you call me even in the middle of the goddamn night if you need something. Got it?"

"No problem." Becki couldn't seem to get out of the conversation fast enough. "I'd better let you go. I'll see you at training tomorrow."

He stared at the phone and wondered how bad he had it that his first reaction to that crap was to head over to the dorms and use a little rope on her until she came to her senses.

Anger rushed through him, blazing out of nowhere. Having to leave her behind had nearly ripped him in two. The nausea and fear that had earlier numbed him flipped into fury and he roared, the sound echoing in the empty staff room.

A sharp pulse of pain struck, and he cursed as the demons in his memory swooped in. It was as if they knew he was susceptible—the sight of her wide eyes and her fear bringing in a flood of guilt and regrets.

You can't help her. You can't save yourself . . . you can't save anyone.

He fought the rising violence. Fought the urge to tear apart the room in his frustration. Ignored the aching call that followed that demanded he lie down and disappear into the mindless state that an episode would reduce him to.

Instead, he focused on Becki and clung to the hope she'd brought him. He pictured her green eyes, not fear filled, but full of passion and life. The memory anchored him, and he caught hold as if she'd personally extended a safety line. Remembering her vivid expressions soothed his raw nerves—all of her moods, whether passion, stubbornness, or righteous anger.

Imagining the caress of her hand on his skin held him back from the precipice.

He forced himself to head home, determined to keep from falling into the darkness again. For Becki's sake.

The night was cold and shadow-filled, and he wondered if part of the reason he'd wanted so badly for her to accept his offer was for his own sake.

All the rest of the week she kept that barrier between them. He avoided being around while she worked Lifeline, only showing up for their agreed-upon personal training times. Becki hit the wall and fought it as if she were grappling with her own demons instead of handholds. She didn't argue with him but didn't have any kind of breakthrough in terms of going vertical.

When it was her turn to take the lead, she was demon-possessed there as well, putting him through workouts that left him drenched in sweat and almost too tired to be annoyed that things were moving in the wrong direction.

Restraining his temper and holding his tongue without insisting that she listen to him and let them get back to where they had been headed was damn hard. It seemed it was going to take something big to get her to listen, and the only big thing that came to mind made *him* nauseated. Being patient was no longer working—that was clear from the dark circles under both their eyes. It was time he stopped letting her call the shots.

If he had to dress in a tux and face a formal event to make nice, he'd grit his teeth and do it.

CHAPTER 24

''''''''''''''''''''''''''''''''''

"I could get used to this far too easily." Becki ran a hand over the leather seat between her and Alisha. There were water bottles in the drink tray, and soft music played over the limousine's speakers.

Alisha lifted a brow. "It's just a car. With champagne and a driver."

They grinned at each other.

Becki leaned back in the seat. "David set this up? I mean, it's nice and all, but I didn't need to be impressed by being brought to the event in a stretch limo."

"Last year we had the same thing. I think it's part of the package deal they get from the Banff Springs when they book the room. Just enjoy." Alisha cracked open one of the bottles and took a long drink before leaning forward and peering out the window. "It's too short a drive. We should have asked him to loop through town a few times."

"Long enough to enjoy." Becki relaxed as the vehicle turned down a residential street and pulled to a stop outside a tidy house. Erin stepped out and made her way to meet them, her silver skirt flashing against her dark skin as she moved. Becki shifted her legs out of the way as the third woman settled into the open space.

"Ahh, a night of total luxury and pampering. How will we ever put up with it?" Erin lifted her water in the air. "To the Banff SAR School. May there be plenty of wide-open pockets tonight."

They clicked plastic together.

Becki turned to Alisha. "David mentioned you're speaking tonight?"

"For a few minutes. Alumni in the area means the sponsors are always keen. David and Marcus have done so much for me over the years, I figure it's only fair that I do a little to help support them." Alisha's eyes widened. "Not that you aren't supporting them. I mean, I understand completely why you don't want to talk. I mean . . ."

"Stop while you have only one foot in your mouth," Erin suggested dryly.

"Oh drat, I'm so embarrassed." Alisha pressed her hands to her cheeks. "Sorry, Becki, I didn't mean to be stupid."

"It's okay," Becki reassured her. "It's not the same thing, either. Yes, I went to the school, but I'm barely back. I think it's far more important that you tell them about what you're doing. I'm not actively in SAR anymore."

"Not right now, but you'll get there," Erin pointed out.

Becki ignored the blushing Alisha and concentrated on how wonderful the thought of getting back into working full time made her feel. "I'd like to think so, but teaching isn't going to be a hardship. Working with Lifeline over the past couple weeks has been good for me."

"You've been good for us, as well," Alisha insisted. "My foot-in-mouth disease aside. And good for our boss—if you don't mind me mentioning that."

Becki glanced at the young woman. "Because me testing his blood pressure on a regular basis is just what he needed?"

Alisha smiled. "Whatever. All I know is that Marcus is planning on coming tonight, and he *never* comes to these events. The only reason he's doing it is for you."

"Where do you hear these things?" Erin demanded.

An innocent shrug lifted Alisha's shoulders. "If you sit quietly and pretend you're a mouse, all sorts of interesting information falls into your lap.

The limo crossed the bridge, closing in on the hotel, and Erin frowned. "I thought we were picking up Devon?"

Alisha shook her head. "He'll meet us there."

Only she grew redder in the face than before, and Becki wondered what was going on. Especially when Alisha suddenly took a great interest in her nails.

"Oh, you naughty girl." Erin lowered her voice to a whisper and leaned forward across the distance between the seats. "Did you just leave Devon stranded?"

Alisha pulled out a mirror and checked her makeup. "Well, I might have mentioned something to the driver about only needing to make two stops."

"Alisha . . ."

Blonde curls swung as Alisha flipped her hair over her shoulder. "Payback is a bitch. He dropped me from the interview and photo shoot. He can take his bicycle to the gala."

Becki hid her grin as best she could. "I thought you said you didn't care about the interview."

"I didn't, especially after I overheard the guys talking about what a dog the reporter is and his possible plans to simply play up the fact that I'm female. I'm definitely not interested in being exploited as the sex symbol of Lifeline."

Erin frowned. "Then why the revenge on Devon?"

Alisha raised a brow. "It should have been my decision, not his. If he'd told me about what he'd learned, we could have discussed it. Taking the upper hand and tricking me out of being there? Jerk. That's why he can find his own way to the fund-raiser."

"Bossy guys suck," Erin agreed. "Here's to making our own decisions and being in charge."

Even as Becki joined in the toast, there was a part inside her that had to qualify the toast. When it came to her life, definitely, she wanted control. Maybe she was a little twisted, but she didn't mind having Marcus take charge in the bedroom. At least at times.

More often than she wanted to admit.

She stared at the hotel as it came into view, the fairy-tale castlelike structure looming large even against the backdrop of the mountains. She had a vast amount of memories tied up in the place. "So gorgeous."

"All that rockwork makes my fingers inch," Alisha admitted. "I get the urge to pick a corner and see how far I can climb."

Becki swallowed her urge to answer *Pretty far.* If they hadn't already heard about it, these two didn't need to know about her foray into illegal excursions. "Do you know where we're going inside?"

Erin nodded. "Same as last year. The ballroom is easy to get to."

The limo door opened, and Alisha stepped out far more gracefully than Becki was able to. There was no long skirt to get in her way, but she hadn't expected Marcus to be right there waiting for her, and the sight of him in a formal tux made her jerk to a stop. One leg out of the vehicle, one still in, she stared in surprise.

The creamy white of his collar only highlighted his dark good looks, a faint hint of shadow already colouring his freshly shaved jawline.

"Wow." It was the only word in her mind that seemed safe to say. She didn't think *delicious* would go over as well.

His gaze trailed over her as she managed to at least bring her feet together and accept his extended hand. "You look pretty nice yourself."

He steadied her as she balanced on her unfamiliar heels, his left arm coming around her body as he kept hold of her hand. The other women waited on the platform for them to cross, cars coming up behind and dropping off passengers.

"Take the side entrance," Marcus instructed Alisha. "We don't need to traipse across the hotel lobby to get there."

"Got it. Come on, Erin, race you to the finger foods."

Erin gave Becki and Marcus a sly grin before grabbing Alisha's hand and turning her toward the doors. "You want to make me crazy again. I am not eating jalapeño poppers all night like last year."

Becki watched the other women hurry off. "How can Alisha move so fast in those heels?" she wondered. "They've got to be four, five inches. I'd break my bloody neck."

Marcus shrugged. "Don't ask me how she does it, but she's got a gift, that's for sure. Someone dared her to climb in a pair once and it barely slowed her down."

Incredible. "Give me climbing soles any day. The two inches I've got on are enough of a challenge."

Marcus squeezed her, and she realized she'd naturally cuddled in under his arm as he led her not toward the doors where Alisha and Erin had disappeared, but in the direction of the lookout. Mount Rundle filled most of their view, Tunnel Mountain occupying the left. The narrow valley between the two peaks filled with the green of spruce forest and the shimmering waters of the Bow River.

She drew in a deep breath, enjoying the peace and quiet before the noise of the evening began. "I can hear the wind in the trees. That's always such a huge part of what makes me feel as if I'm in the right place—the sounds."

"What's the sound associated with this place?" he asked. "With the Banff Springs?"

She turned and smiled. "Lots and lots of panting moans and gasps."

Marcus chuckled, losing his hold on her waist and leaning his hip on the stonework of the railing. "You're not planning on climbing the outside of her again to get to the gala, are you?"

She turned to look at the wall where she'd managed to make it to the three-quarter point before crawling over a balcony. "It was a crazy thing I did back then."

"On a dare, right?"

Becki nodded. "First year at the school, and there was nothing I wouldn't try. Still, I'm not sorry I did it."

Marcus raised a brow. "You're not sorry you free-climbed the outside of the hotel? Because you didn't get caught?"

"But I did—*you* caught me," Becki pointed out. "And I

know it was a long time ago, but I don't know that I ever thanked you."

This time he outright laughed, a big hearty sound that filled her with happiness. He lifted her chin with his fingers. "Thanking me for the three days that followed where we holed up in one of the rooms and fooled around sounds kinky."

"Thanks for sharing your philosophies with me. The sex? Was bonus."

"Bonus is good. . . ." Marcus leaned forward slowly, giving her plenty of time to say no.

She didn't want him to stop. Their lips met, and all the sights and sounds vanished while her senses became totally occupied by the man before her. The way he touched her so perfectly. Soft at times, rougher at others.

She wasn't sure why, but every time she was around him she became nothing but a big bundle of emotions. He brought out the most in her. Made her feel fully alive again.

They broke the kiss but stayed wrapped around each other for a moment.

"I enjoy spending time with you," she admitted. "I'm sorry if it seemed as if I were pulling away."

Marcus stared in silence. Looking her over carefully. "I'm afraid I'm pretty obsessive about things when I get an idea into my head."

That wasn't a bad thing. "I'm used to taking care of myself. It seems odd to have someone who wants to do more for me than I expect."

"Nice. Now I'm being called odd." They smiled at each other. "I'm trying to give you space, Becki, but it's a part of who I am. You've become important to me, and while I don't want to smother you, caring means you don't have to do things on your own."

"I know. I mean, I know in my head." She squeezed him. "I'm still figuring out what that looks like on a practical level."

Fighting to keep from saying *You could start by moving in with me* was amazingly difficult. Even after reading himself the riot act, the urge to take over was nearly stronger than he could control.

"How has it been lately? Sleeping, I mean."

Becki stared over the view. "The sleeping part is fine, it's the waking up bits that are driving me crazy."

"Still?" He swore lightly when she confirmed it. "New things?"

Becki twisted. "I don't want to talk about it now. We should go in."

Damn this fighting against doing what he needed to do. "Later, though?"

She nodded slowly. "I would like that. In the meantime, distract me?"

He kissed her again because he'd missed it so damn much the past few days, then tucked her fingers over his arm and led her into the building.

The room was filled with black and white attire and the soft sounds of sophisticated music, and the entire place smelled like money.

Marcus had to admit that David knew his way around organizing a fund-raiser.

He sauntered in with Becki on his elbow, smiling and nodding as needed but itching under the collar for the night to be over. The only reason he was there was the woman at his side. His own memories of black-tie affairs were far too twisted to be pleasant.

David turned from where he was chatting with a couple and caught sight of Marcus and Becki. He excused himself, grin growing as he headed across the room toward them.

Great. Marcus leaned over and grabbed Becki a glass from the tray going past. "Here, you'll want one of these as a bracer before things get going."

She met his gaze as she lifted the delicate flute in a salute. "To bossy, forceful people, and the ones who care."

"Now are we going to argue about which one of us is which?"

"No arguing. Not tonight."

They touched glasses just before David stepped to their

side. "If it isn't my favourite brother and the most talented instructor in the school."

"Lay it on a little thicker," Marcus muttered. "The answer is still no."

David widened his eyes. "Whatever do you think I'm going to ask you to do? I'm in shock that you actually showed up."

Becki glanced around the room. "Nice turnout. Typical?"

"About. There're a few new people I hope to amaze, but don't you worry about schmoozing with them. Alisha will be impressive enough."

"Good, then we'll talk later." Marcus tugged Becki away, heading to the side of the room where they could see everyone but have some space.

"You don't usually come to these events, do you?" Becki asked, her lips close to his ear as she leaned in.

"Never."

Her lips brushed his cheek lightly. "Thank you for coming to be here with me."

"Who said it was for your sake?" he grumbled.

She snuck her hand under his dress jacket, tucking her strong fingers into the waistline of his slacks. "A little birdie told me."

"Little birdies need to keep their mouths shut." She tugged at his shirt until it came loose, and her palm rested against his bare back. "What are you doing?"

Other than making his body react like crazy.

She twisted, turning her back on the room and slipping in front of him. Her light blue dress was soft under his fingers, and he wanted very badly to stroke every inch of her. Becki gazed over his face, his torso. Examining him. The heat in her eyes making him hopeful and making him insane.

When she licked her lips, he was a goner. "Becki?"

"You know, there's a great view of this room from up high. I'd love to see how it looks from there."

Mischief and heat mingled in her expression as she tugged him toward the side exit door. He went willingly enough. He was no fool.

CHAPTER 25

'''''''''''''''''''''''''''''''''''

She held his arm as they paced along the main corridor. "Not that I want to change your plans, but what are your plans?"

Becki glanced up and down the hall, then pushed open an EMPLOYEES ONLY door. "I told you. I want a pretty view of the room."

"Brilliant woman." It was the most logical explanation for trespassing possible.

She'd found the correct door. The stairwell rose and she laughed softly, racing the stairs in her high heels with a lot less difficulty than she'd claimed.

They exited into a narrow corridor with doors off the right-hand wall.

"You have any idea where we're going?" Marcus asked.

Becki paused. "I thought I did, but now . . ."

"Good." Because he knew just the spot. "Follow me."

The third door revealed his target. What would probably be called a theater box anywhere else, but here, it was a damn fine view overlooking the main dance floor and the grand ballroom.

Becki slipped beside him, resting her hands lightly on the railing as she peered down. "Whoa, that's sweet."

Shit. "No problem with the height?" Because having her freeze would totally make all the other plans winging through his brain impossible.

Becki looked again, then shook her head. "Not sure why, but this is okay."

"Solid footing beneath you might make a difference."

Then she stood and faced him. The powdery blue of her dress glistened with the fine threads of silver shot through the fabric. She'd twisted her hair into a fancy do, small bits hanging beside her face to frame her smile. A faint blush coloured her cheeks, her eyes outlined with thin blue that made her pupils look bigger. Or maybe that was because of the way she was looking him over, like he was on the menu.

He sure the hell hoped so.

"You have something else in mind other than checking out the fancy event from the heavens?" Because if she didn't, he most certainly did.

She leaned toward him, and the fine silver chain around her neck swung forward, the tiny heart locket popping free from the neckline and flashing for a second in the light. "I've missed you," she breathed quietly.

He waited. Damn if he didn't want to do more, but this was her time to take the lead. And lead she did.

She pressed her hands to her waistline and skimmed lower over her hips, bending slightly until her fingers reached the bottom edge of her skirt. She didn't have far to lean, not with the leading edge striking midway up her long limbs, but it was far enough to offer him a lovely view of the curve of her breasts, the creamy white shining against her dress like twin clouds in a blue sky.

"If you're trying to drive me insane, it's working. I think I just wrote a poem about your breasts."

Becki caught hold of the edge of the material and wiggled it upward. "Poetry. Limericks or puns?"

"Fuck." Marcus slammed his hand over his cock, need-ing something to ease how fast the damn thing had gotten hard. She wore stockings and a garter belt. Nothing else but her bare sex revealed as she held the dress to her waist. "Fuck, fuck, fuck."

"A bit repetitious for a poem, but kind of catchy. Yes. Let's," she commanded. He reached for her and she evaded him. "Not slow. Just hard and dirty. That's what I want."

Marcus had her pressed to the wall so fast she gasped. He pinned her in place with his body and ravished her mouth. Four days since they'd fought. Five days since he'd had her last, and he was an addict craving a hit.

Becki fumbled for his zipper as he touched her ass again and again. Hungry for her skin, wanting more than a fast fuck against the wall, but needing the fast first.

He slipped his hand between her legs, drawing moisture over her clit. Her head fell back as he thrust his fingers into her cunt and rubbed the clit bar with his thumb. Caught her neck and sucked. Bit down on the muscle of her shoulder as she creamed around his touch.

Frantic now, her breathing ragged. She'd managed to release his cock and somehow, both of them kissing, scrambling, she propped one leg up on the chair beside them and guided him into her heat.

It wasn't enough. Melting into her, surrounded by her. Marcus slammed in all the way and she keened out her pleasure.

Becki caught hold of his face and kissed him wildly, teeth and tongue taking control. He was so big inside her, plunging deep. There was no ignoring his presence, although she'd tried for the past days. Mentally, he was there even when he wasn't in the room, and she'd given up worrying about it.

Physically? *God.*

He filled her again, cock stretching her to the max. The solid wall cold behind her shoulders, his hot breath panting over her skin. He wasn't careful, his fingers on her ass squeezing tight enough to leave bruises. She didn't care, arching into his movements, helping him drive even harder.

She needed this. Wanted it. She'd missed him too damn much over the past few days, and taking charge and letting him know what she wanted made all the tension in her body finally ease.

He leaned his left elbow on the wall, steadying his torso over her. "You look like an angel in that dress."

Becki lifted her leg higher and her breath hitched as he slammed in again, their groins snapping together. "Dark suit. Dark hair." She pressed her hand against his cheek and the stubble. "Dangerous like a demon."

"I needed this. Need to feel you around me." Marcus slowed and leaned away slightly, peering down at where they joined. Her dress was scrunched around her waist, his cock sticking out from the fly of his suit pants wet with moisture, his belt done up and shirtfront still tucked in. "You fit me so perfectly."

He eased back a bit more, pulling his hips away until the broad head of his cock clung to her lips. The purple head contrasted against the lighter colour of her body, soft skin wrapping around him as he eased forward and her body accepted him in.

"Oh God, Marcus." Becki slipped her hand down and separated her labia, watching eagerly as he did it again. Deliberate. Thorough. The sight of him taking her made her limbs shake, combining vision with sensation that was powerful and edged her to the breaking point.

"I see your clit bar wiggle every time I fuck into you." He moved again and hummed in approval. "It's all wet and shiny with your juices. Makes me want to pull out and eat you alive."

"No." She clutched his shoulder with her left hand. "Don't stop."

"Play with yourself, sweet Becki. Let me see you come. Let me feel you on my cock."

"If I touch myself, it's all over," she warned. "You've got me so ready. Hell, I've been ready for days."

"Did you play with yourself when you were alone?" he asked.

When she didn't answer, he pulled all the way out. A

whimper of dismay escaped her. "Yes, but *please*. Finish me."

He thrust into her fingers where she'd caught at him. "This is better with another person, isn't it? Instead of cold toys, or your hand. That's nothing but physical release. Takes off the edge but it's missing something."

He bumped the head of his cock against her opening, and she tilted her hips to help guide him back in. Her sigh of happiness matched the shiver of satisfaction that shook her to her toes. "Fuck me. Please, don't stop."

He kissed her and plunged in, swallowing her groan of pleasure. Three or four more times, deep and hard, burying himself to the root and pausing before withdrawing slowly, teasing her already quivering nerves.

She slipped her fingers higher and flicked the tiny gold bar the way she knew was most effective, and that was it.

"Marcus . . ."

He covered her mouth with his and stopped her screams from echoing off the roof as her climax broke her apart. Her sheath constricted around his heavy shaft, tearing his response from him. Wetness and heat bathed her as he ground their hips together, moving the clit bar and prolonging the ecstasy flooding her system.

They clung to each other until the shaking stopped, their breathing uneven and ragged as they gasped to find control. The continuing clatter of the party below them rose to the balcony. Tinkling of glasses, the low murmur of masculine tones, the occasional higher-pitched female laugh.

Sophisticated and mature sounds. Miles away from the *hell, yeah* whispering past her lips.

Marcus caught her chin in his hands. "You are one in a million."

He kissed her again, less like a starving animal and more as if he were a good friend who'd missed her. Wetness trickled down the inside of her legs as he withdrew his cock.

Marcus stared. When she would have wiped herself clean, he pinned her arms back. "Wait. That is so fucking sexy."

His gaze locked between her thighs, he squatted and ran his fingers through his seed and her wetness, stroking her labia lightly.

She shivered. "I'm not going to be able to walk if you touch me again."

The intensity on his face should have scared her. She'd spent the past few days trying to figure out exactly what she wanted to work on over the next months. Making sure she was clear on her desires, her needs. Who was in charge of her life. All of it, not just her sex drive.

When he cupped her sex so delicately, pulled a handkerchief from his pocket and wiped her clean—

All her organized thoughts vanished in the continuing desire he stroked from her willing body. This man could turn her best plans to nothing with a single glance.

He cleaned her, straightened her stockings, planting kisses on the insides of her thighs as he smoothed them into position. Easing his palm down her skirt to help it lie neatly over her ass. All the while, wearing an expression of huge satisfaction.

"Since I plan on hanging on to you for the rest of the evening and even dancing, you might want to try to look a little less contented before we head back to the ballroom or there will be no doubt whatsoever we were up to something."

"They can all be jealous I've got the most beautiful girl in the room."

Marcus stood and pressed her to the wall, and she let him hold her there. She smoothed his hair with her fingers. "That was lovely. Thank you."

He nodded. "Would you accompany me home after the gala tonight?"

Asking, not ordering. Politely worded even. She beamed at him. "I'd like that very much."

Grinning like the conspirators they were, they slipped back down the stairs, pausing outside the party.

Becki tugged him to a stop, smoothing her hands over her hair. "How do I look?"

"Like you were ravished by a madman against a wall," he whispered.

A snort of laughter escaped before she could stop it.

Marcus pirouetted her, his gaze lingering on her legs before snapping back up to her breasts and finally her face. "You look gorgeous. I can't wait to show you off."

She twirled a finger and he obediently rotated for her inspection. All the long, lean length of him, moving at her command, and when he faced her again, she couldn't speak.

He lifted a brow. "That bad?"

"That good. I'm drowning in my drool over here."

He held out his hand and escorted her back into the frivolity. Small talk and music. Happy smiles, and the occasional questioning look. Marcus hadn't bothered to wear his prosthesis, and the gazes of people who didn't know him stuttered to a stop on his pinned-up jacket sleeve.

Becki pulled him toward the side of the stage, ignoring the curious. They were there; the event was going well. Inconsequential things could be ignored. And tonight she would go home with him. Even having one thing settled was a relief.

Happy endorphins still hummed through his bloodstream, making it far easier to give in to Becki's determined tug across the ballroom. Marcus would have been happy leaving now, but if he had to put in a little more face time, hiding with his team was as good a place as any.

The women held court over the Lifeline team, Devon shadowing Alisha.

"Did you speak yet?" Becki asked Alisha.

The blonde shook her long curls. "David said to wait until the top of the hour, so about fifteen minutes still."

"Marcus, you wash up pretty well," Erin teased. "So good to see you. Isn't it good to see him, Anders?"

"Shut up," Anders grumbled.

Marcus eyed them all. Erin's grin was far bigger than usual—normally it was Anders wearing the Cheshire grin while his pilot carried herself with far more control. "What did I miss?"

"Name the last time you showed up at one of these events," Anders complained. "Erin bet you'd be here, but I went with the odds. You cost me fifty bucks."

"Well, sorry for being unpredictable, but it's the best way to keep you on your toes." Anders stared rather pointedly at Becki on his arm, and Marcus laughed. "Also, can't help it if you aren't more observant of what's happening around you."

A flash went off to their right. Marcus blinked rapidly as he twisted to face the culprits. Ted and his cohort with the camera smiled politely, but their focus was on Becki and not the team, and all sorts of warning signals went off inside.

"There you are." Devon stepped forward, strategically plopping himself directly in front of Alisha and Erin. "We were talking about you. We thought a photo shoot by the windows would work if you'd like to wait until after Alisha's spoken."

"Sounds great," Ted agreed. "First, I wanted to get a few general questions answered."

Marcus squeezed Becki's fingers where they lay on his arm. He backed up, doing the same as Devon and blocking Ted from a clear shot at the ladies. "We'll leave you to them, then."

He turned and tucked an arm around Becki. Trying to make their departure look less like fleeing and more like a casual need to get somewhere else.

Ted didn't let them take more than a few steps before raising his voice loud enough to be overheard by the party-goers standing nearby. "Before you go, Becki, did you have anything you wanted to share regarding your accident?"

Goddamn reporters. Marcus was going to rip his head off. Becki pulled to a stop, patting Marcus's arm soothingly. "Don't worry, it's not an issue."

She smiled at the curious onlookers as she turned, facing Ted with a slight shake of her head. "Actually, no. I think you can find everything on file you need. If you don't mind . . ."

"I meant regarding the new developments," Ted interrupted. "Will you be going back to Yellowstone for the funeral now that they found your partner's body?"

It wasn't a gasp that escaped Becki, more like a total and complete cessation of breathing altogether. Marcus caught his arm around her as she wavered. Questions and confusion rose on the air as the news spread rapidly, as those who hadn't been aware of Becki's presence caught hold of the word and turned to see what was going on.

"Ted, not here—" Marcus's attempt to slow down the train was destroyed by the very insistent man.

"I have the news report from the team that found him earlier today. Seems there're some irregularities. Have you been contacted yet by the state police to find out if you can help answer their questions?"

"What irregularities? Where did you get this information?" Becki had Marcus's hand in a tight grip, but she was moving now, stepping across the room to Ted's side. Another flash went off, and Becki glared at the cameraman. "Call off your hound and let's go somewhere private to finish this."

Marcus tugged her back. "Don't talk to him. We can go. We can make the calls ourselves to find out what the ass is up to."

She pressed her lips close to his ear and whispered rapidly, "But if we get him out of the room, he can't continue to mess up David's event."

He didn't give a damn about the fund-raiser right then. All his energies were aimed in one direction—getting Ted away from Becki as soon as possible. "Let's take this outside, Ted."

Ted lifted his hands in protest, then pointed toward where the Lifeline crew had all risen to their feet, standing at attention. "Just wanted to get a reaction from the team as well. Since Becki's been training them." Ted checked a paper he pulled from his pocket. "How do you feel learning that Dane's safety line appears to have been cut?"

CHAPTER 26

‖‖‖‖‖‖‖‖‖‖‖‖‖‖‖‖‖‖‖‖‖‖‖‖‖‖‖‖‖

She'd gone numb. There was a faint ringing in her ears but beyond that, nothing.

Becki leaned her forehead against the window of Marcus's truck and stared at the lights flashing by, the water on the streets reflecting the streetlamps and creating a far too beautiful setting compared to the pain rippling inside.

Dane.

A soft touch landed on her shoulder as they paused at an intersection. Marcus squeezed her briefly before taking the wheel again. "We'll make some calls. Find out what happened."

She nodded. "I know."

"I should have shoved that damn reporter's notebook up his ass the first time I met him," Marcus growled lightly as the truck moved forward. The slick of water being spun from under the tires and the windshield wipers stroking back and forth merged into a rhythm and gave her something to cling to.

She wanted to smile, to tease back that she figured Ted was plenty afraid of Marcus now, after he'd hauled the man from the room and given him hell.

She couldn't. All that consumed her were images that stacked and fell apart, never creating the correct picture, teasing her with their incomplete story.

They'd found Dane's body. That alone would have been enough to give her pause. She might have shuddered briefly to a stop but made herself keep moving because that was what you did. People died on the mountain, and you kept on. She'd mourned Dane, stopped asking *why*, and over the past couple of months slowly accepted that she might never know the truth.

Hearing how they'd found him had been blunt and definitely announced to be hurtful.

Dane's safety line had been cut.

And now, the questions were all out there again. What had happened? Why couldn't she remember?

Oh God, had she done the unthinkable?

They stopped and she sat there, unable to move. All the while as Marcus guided her into the house and slipped her into a chair by the fire, she was only borderline aware of what was happening. She closed her eyes to shut out the pain, but it refused to leave her alone, haunting her.

"Becki." Marcus's voice cut through, but she didn't want to answer. What would he do? What would he think? Opening her eyes, would she discover that he had a look of sympathy on his face, or distrust, or . . . ?

She wasn't sure what emotion she expected from him, or which would be the worst.

Dane's rope had been cut. The one that had held the two of them together.

"Becki—you're in shock. I'm going to get you warmed up, and then we'll talk."

He undressed her—*when had they gone to his room?*— and helped her into sweatpants and one of his oversized sweaters. Something sweet and warm passed her lips, and she swallowed instinctively.

Tea. Marcus's magical blend.

Then she was nestled against a strong chest and being held. Protected. The phone rang and they ignored it, Marcus stroking her hair as she clung to him, holding on tight.

"Should we answer?" she asked, choking out the question through a tight throat.

"Tomorrow is soon enough. David and the team know how to reach me if there's a real emergency. This call isn't important."

"I'm not going to fall apart. I'm not," Becki insisted, knowing even as she said the words they would seem ridiculous.

"You're going to be fine," Marcus agreed. "But you don't have to hide anything from me. Don't have to be strong 24/7. I won't judge."

"God, I wish I could *remember*."

"You will," he reassured her. "When you're ready. In the meantime, whatever you need, take."

She didn't know what she needed. To scream her frustrations at having huge, vital gaps in her past? To punch and hit Ted for deliberately choosing the worst possible time and place? Part of her was even tempted to curl into a ball and pretend none of it had happened. Not the news announcement that night, not the accident eight months ago. Never learned to climb, never left the farm . . .

A sense of the ridiculousness of that last thought struck her, and a snort of derision escaped. Okay, maybe not that far back.

A wave of mental exhaustion was settling in and turning everything darker than it should be. The one thing she was sure of in the middle of all the other doubts was that she trusted Marcus.

Maybe more than she should, but trusting him was the only thing left solid and firm.

"I don't want to feel. I don't want to think," she admitted. "And having this reaction almost pisses me off more than not knowing what happened."

Marcus shifted under her and cupped his strong fingers around her chin. "I get it. But right now? If you want to pop a couple of pills and sleep, no one will judge you for it. We'll make calls tomorrow when you're fresh."

She searched his face, but there was nothing there accusing her or judging her. "I can't go back to the dorms. . . ."

"I never expected you to. You'd already promised to spend the night with me."

Their passionate interlude seemed a million miles away, hazy and more like a dream than reality. "Well, I thought I should double-check. The game changed tonight."

Marcus shook his head. "A new hand got dealt, but we're still in the same game. I want you here with me."

She nodded. "Thank you."

Becki grabbed her cup and sipped the tea, soaking in the warmth, her fingers icy cold on the ceramic. "Marcus? You have anything to help me sleep tonight? I hate taking shit, but . . ."

He rose and led her into the bathroom. "Again, there's nothing you can ask for that will make me judge you as lacking." He held out the box to her, retaining his grasp until she looked into his eyes. "I've been there. Needing to be cared for. Let me help you."

The fact that his life hadn't been picture-perfect, that he knew how the world could change in an instant, made him perfect for her right then and there. She took a pill and swallowed it with a bit of water, staring at the face of a stranger in the mirror.

Marcus took down her hair, trailed his fingers through the strands. Handed her a face cloth to wash away the fancy makeup she'd taken such pains to apply. All the while Becki floated in a haze. The sleeping pill slowly overpowered even the numbing confusion in her brain.

She tugged him after her as she crawled into his bed without caring how it might look, clinging to his hand and refusing to let him go.

Sleep would release him. Until then, she needed to know she wasn't alone.

Marcus slipped away when her breathing finally relaxed, the fierce tightness in her body fading as the drug took effect and forced her to relax. He moved quickly, wanting to be back if she stirred. Needing to be there.

Damn Ted and all his kind. Marcus snatched up his phone and called his brother.

"You guys okay?" David asked. "Oh, first. Thank you for not killing the man in the middle of the room."

"It was close," Marcus admitted. "What'd you find out?"

"Ted contacted someone over in Yellowstone only days after I arranged to hire Becki. He's been in constant communication—was probably digging for shit to try to make some kind of story when the report came in regarding the discovery of Dane's body. There's not even an official write-up yet, for God's sake."

"Damn leeches."

"I know, it's not news, but it is. The timing sucks, and by tomorrow I expect Yellowstone SAR will have someone making contact with Becki, but it's a moot point. She's already sat through one investigation. It's been closed."

"What are you saying?"

David sighed. "I looked into the legalities, Marcus. I had to when I asked her to come teach at the school. The criminal investigation was as thorough as it could be, and she was cleared of wrongdoing. Even if she did cut his rope, she won't be charged."

"I never thought she would be."

"Just making sure so you can reassure Becki on that point. Criminal intent is required, or criminal negligence. Neither applies in this case."

Marcus dragged his hand through his hair. "You're sounding awfully legal-minded there, bro. But thank you, that's good to know. Did Ted's showboating screw up the rest of the event?"

Unexpected laughter rippled from the phone. "Are you kidding? Total solidarity from your team, and I'm buying Alisha the biggest damn bouquet of flowers I can get her. She's a miracle worker on the podium. I've never seen anything like it."

"Alisha?" Marcus locked the house and closed all the curtains, speaking softly as he passed the master bedroom. "What did she do?"

"Off the cuff, adjusted her entire presentation and charmed the money from their wallets. Took the idea of team and trust, and how her time at Banff SAR taught her how being part of something that was bigger than yourself meant knowing what to do in life-and-death situations. That saving lives wasn't an emotional response, but a trained instinct. I should have taken notes on her, but I was too mesmerized by the reaction of the audience. When that girl leaves Lifeline down the road, she's got a bright future in politics."

"I'll make sure she knows you were impressed." He had stopped in the doorway and stared at Becki's still form for a moment as David had spoken. The next days were going to be tough, no matter what truths came out. "Thanks for looking into things for me."

"No problem. And Marcus? Hell of a thing to happen your first foray back into high society, but I have to say it. I was impressed to see you there."

"Shut up."

David paused. "Shutting. Except—damn it all, you can shout at me later for being an interfering asshole, but I have to say it. You two are good together. You and Becki."

Well. That was weird. "Any particular reason you're sharing this right now?"

"Because it's important. You've changed, even in the past couple of weeks, and the only difference in your life is Becki. So I'm calling it as I see it. Whether it's her dragging you back or I don't know the hell what else, I'm glad you two hooked up."

The urge to snap out some sarcastic response was strangely lacking, mainly because he agreed one hundred percent with David's assessment. "Thanks for that."

"Call me if you need anything else."

Marcus tossed his phone onto the table beside the couch. He debated briefly hitting the liquor cabinet for something to take the edge off his nerves but decided what he really needed was a long warm shot of something else.

He stripped and joined Becki in the bed, wrapping himself like a barrier between her and the world. She shivered, her arm that had escaped the covers cold against his. He threaded their fingers together and lay there waiting for his brain to slow.

The words—the accusation—that Ted had thrown at Becki repeated in his mind. Had Becki cut the rope on her partner?

If she had, did he care?

It was an unanswerable question in a way, because it wasn't a logical question to ask in the first place. Tying yourself to another person was a signal of ultimate trust. You handed control over to them and believed they'd make the decisions that had to be made.

There were times during rescues he'd worked on when things had gone wrong, but he'd never once doubted that every choice he and his team made were based on reaching the best possible outcome.

Becki had shown herself to be that same kind of person.

She'd been reckless years ago. He liked to imagine that it was partly his hauling her aside way back when she'd been a student that had been the catalyst that set her on a better path.

Now, as David had said, she'd been the catalyst to pull him back from the darkness that he could have easily gotten lost in. From the moment she'd arrived in town he'd felt the difference, as if she'd begun to anchor him by her mere presence. The difference she'd made the other night was undeniable as well.

All he knew for certain was that when it came to climbing, he'd let her control his ropes—let her make the decision if it had to be made to cut the line. On the mountainside he had no doubts at all in her instantaneous decision-making skills.

Yet in their relationship he wasn't willing to give up that kind of trust. He wasn't willing to let her cut him free.

The contrast in thoughts was enough to keep him awake for hours.

CHAPTER 27

''''''''''''''''''''''''''''''''''''

*The ground swept away before her, the heavy weight of
Dane's body at the other end of the rope dragging her downward. Becki fought for a handhold, scrambling backward
crablike. Heels digging in, fighting for purchase. She caught
a boot against a firm protrusion and leaned back to stop
her momentum. Her harness lifted her hips from the ground
as the rope insistently tugged her toward the cliff edge.*

*She would have sworn, would have called for help.
Would have begged if there were the slightest possibility
anyone could hear her.*

*The root beneath her foot wiggled. The stump crumbled,
the soil around the rotting wood coming free. Becki kicked
her other heel into the hillside, trying to form a divot, desperate to hollow out a place to hold herself steady.*

*The rope groaned, twisting with the weight on the other
end. She was losing the battle. Another rock worked
loose, the wind howling past her and forcing her to turn her
head to the side. The scent of fresh earth and loose rock
dust mingled together and filled her nostrils. She peeked*

longingly at the trees behind her, so close and yet totally out of reach.

Her vision blurred as she fought to focus. Looking ahead for anything that would provide an anchor for a safety loop.

Nothing. An inch at a time she lost ground. She'd slowed her approach to the cliff edge, but it looked inevitable. It wasn't a matter of if, but when.

She was going to be dragged over the edge by the weight of her partner.

Becki scrambled at her leg pocket, bruised and battered fingers protesting as she tore up the Velcro and yanked out her knife. She'd lost little bits of fingernails on her right hand, and sharp pains stabbed her as she frantically pressed the safety catch to release the protective covering. The casing fell away to expose the serrated knife edge. Becki longed for a nice fixed blade, something with an extended reach and more than a three-inch cutting surface. She slipped her forefinger into the holding loop and stabbed at the ground behind her, working to find a spot firm enough to allow her to Just. Stop. Sliding.

She swung again and again, each time the ricochet when blade met rocks bounced through her hand and arm to grip her with pain. For a moment, she thought she had it. The blade sank in deep and she clung tight, gasping for air. Biceps flexed hard, muscles shaking as her descent slowed. Praying for a moment to recover her position. If she could find something to brace against.

The blade quivered.

"No. No, no, no. Stay in place, oh please please, stay in place," she begged. Kicking frantically. Fingertips of her free hand scratching for purchase.

She was almost at the point where she'd warned herself she had to give up. Three more feet before she'd have to turn her back on everything she'd worked toward for so many years. But if she crossed that imaginary line, if she couldn't stop herself from slipping past it, she would go off the cliff, and she and Dane would both die.

That invisible boundary was the last possible moment she had to save herself.

And while every bit of her protested dying, she wondered how she'd ever deal with knowing she'd as good as killed her partner.

Her instinct to jerk upright was stopped by something heavy across her body. Becki held her breath and tried to pull herself together, ordering her heart to slow enough so that it wasn't about to pound its way out of her chest.

Warm lips touched her cheek, heated air caressing her as a firm grip caught her arm. "I'm here. You're not alone."

Becki nodded and curled under him, burying in tight like a kitten looking for protection. The scent of his skin soothed her and she inhaled deeply, attempting to find the balance that had been torn away the previous night.

Dreams shouldn't be able to do things like this. "What time is it?"

Marcus lifted his head slightly, glancing over her at the clock on the nightstand. "Nearly eight A.M."

"Good drugs. I never sleep this late."

"You needed it. Don't fuss. You want to get up, or shall I let you hog the covers without me?"

Becki wiggled far enough away to look into his face. "Lots on the agenda for today?"

Dark eyes stared back, searching her carefully. "Nothing but you."

She wanted to protest that he didn't need to, but that would be the opposite of what she wanted. Especially with the dream lingering in her brain. "I need your help, Marcus. I need to have someone there to help me deal with the next few days."

He brushed his fingers over her cheek and into her hair, cupping the back of her head tenderly. "Thank you for asking."

Becki gave a wry smile. "Well, I figured you were planning

on taking charge anyway, and this way I can't complain because it's my own damn fault."

"You know me too well already."

"I know how your brain works, yes. I think I have a bit of the bossy gene in me as well. Makes us clash."

He grinned. "Fighting sucks, but the makeup sex is pretty hot."

The memories made her body warm and tingle in spite of everything crowding her brain. Or maybe because of the things that had gone wrong. Sex was easier to concentrate on than anything else. Natural, easy, with the added bonus that in the end you forgot everything except pleasure, at least for a little while.

She was suddenly very aware that they were both naked. Becki stroked a hand over his chest, watching closely as she played with the curves of the muscles. Spreading her fingers wide as she pressed on his chest and rolled him to his back.

There was no way she could have made him go unless he was willing. When she lifted her knee over his hips to straddle him, Marcus pulled off the blankets, then folded his arms behind his head.

"I'm not even going to pretend to wonder what you're doing," he said.

"Is it wrong?" Becki asked, slipping herself backward far enough to grasp his erection and stroke it carefully. "I need you. This way as well."

He didn't answer, just thrust against her grip, the skin over his shaft so soft compared to the hardness beneath it. She pumped him unhurriedly, bringing him to full rigidity before lifting herself over him.

One hand on his chest as she braced herself, the other guiding him in. That sense of fullness and pleasure distracting her. Helping her concentrate on nothing but the here and now. Marcus reached up and stroked her breasts, one, then the other. Trailed his fingers down her body softly, like the brush of wings teasing and making her more sensitive.

All the while she rose and fell over him, undulating slowly and savouring having him fill her.

He touched between her legs, bringing up moisture from where they met and lifting it to her clit. He rubbed firmly, tilting his hips and adding a small thrust every time she dropped, and suddenly the sex wasn't as calm as it had been a moment before.

She closed her eyes and just felt. Relished the sensations, the caring in his every touch. The climax that was fast approaching.

"Fuck." Marcus rolled her and scrambled from the bed, jerking the discarded blanket from the floor and tossing it over her. He stormed to the French doors and snapped one open, buck naked and still aroused. "Get the hell off my deck."

Becki clutched the sheets to her chest like some old-time romance heroine and stared at the windows. "Marcus?"

One movement and the door slammed shut. Two steps and he had the narrow gap in the curtains snapped closed. He rotated toward her, anger in his eyes, body gone tight with tension. "We had a visitor. I'm calling Ted to inform him that next time, the cops get involved."

Her stomach fell. "You think it was reporters?"

Marcus grimaced, pacing back to sit on the bed, the mattress dipping slightly under his hips. "I don't usually have neighbours coming over on a Saturday morning to borrow cups of sugar, if that's what you're suggesting."

"No, I understand how they get." She had far-too-clear memories of being hounded by reporters. "I'm sorry."

"Don't be. Nothing you did." Marcus stroked her leg under the sheet, looking her over carefully. She tried not to show how out of whack she was, but it must have been apparent because he sighed. With a pat to her thigh, he changed topics. "Come on, I'll get breakfast."

Her nerves still tingled with her almost-orgasm, but he was right. Slipping back into sex wasn't going to work. "Frustration is not my cup of tea. Just to be clear."

Marcus's smile twitched. "Mine, either, but we can finish this later. Hit the shower."

By the time she stepped back into the bedroom, wrapped

in a towel, clean clothes were waiting for her on the bed. She dressed quickly, the comfortable familiar clothing helping to set her a little more at ease.

Whatever was going to happen today, she would survive it. She was strong, capable. No matter how confused, she could do this. Having Marcus to help her . . . Maybe she shouldn't have felt as much comfort at the thought that he'd promised to be there for her, but right now she wasn't about to wonder why.

He had breakfast laid on the table, the curtains opened to the view. Becki walked to the glass and peered out on the grey and cold.

"There's snow again," she complained. "Haven't we had enough?"

On the deck a clear line of footprints led to the windows, then disappeared around the corner toward the bedroom.

Marcus stepped beside her and hugged her briefly. "Our Peeping Tom. I made a few calls."

Becki nodded, then deliberately turned her back on the mountains, choosing a chair at the table where the only thing she saw was Marcus seated across from her.

Which wasn't a bad view, to be honest.

Fighting the numbness inside, Becki pushed herself forward. She'd been here before, ready to fall apart, and sheer determination had rescued her. One day at a time.

She had to get through this day, and that meant getting through this hour. "Tell me what you've already done, and what's next."

Marcus went through the list of people he'd been in contact with while she'd been showering and dressing. It was short but made it clear he wasn't messing around. The newspaper and the RCMP were both on the list. Every point he mentioned, she nodded, eating her breakfast with more appetite than he'd have been able to muster in the same conditions.

When he reached the end, he leaned back in his chair and examined her carefully. "Good so far?"

"About what I'd have done, although you have all the contacts here in Banff to do it quicker. Thank you." Becki pulled over the notepad she'd been jotting down notes on. "I need to call Alisha and thank the team for their support. The news must have been a terrible shock for them as well—I'm grateful they stood up for me."

"You've made a good impression on them, Becki," Marcus assured her. "You're not just Rebecca James, some unknown superstar, anymore. You're obviously considered part of the team."

That conjured her first full smile of the day. "Thanks. Still, I want to let them know it means the world."

"Monday will be soon enough—there's no training this weekend." Something occurred to him. "Hmm, the fact that it's the weekend might make it more difficult to reach anyone in Yellowstone. I assume you have contacts?"

She nodded.

"If the authorities need to get hold of you, they will, e-mail or phone. If you want to make contact first, that's fine as well." Marcus hesitated, but had to ask. "Did you want to return to Yellowstone for Dane? A memorial or something?"

She clutched her fork a little tighter but shook her head. "We already had a funeral, and there's not anyone who wants to do it all over."

And after more than eight months, he didn't want Becki to have to deal with the body. "Family who might want him buried somewhere in particular?"

"No. It's too bad they found him, in a way." Becki lifted her gaze to his. "And I know I can say this to you, because you'll get it. I'm not talking about the trouble this means to me—them finding his body. It's just, things were done, and now they're not. Even your question about a memorial. Dane wasn't close with his adoptive parents. He'd gotten in contact with his birth mother for the first time a couple of months earlier, but nothing more seemed to come of it. It's sad he's gone, but being buried on the mountainside was what he would have wanted if he'd had the choice."

She shivered, and her eyes grew wide.

"Becki?"

"Thought I'd remembered something." She stared across the table and sighed. "It's gone. I'm not sure what it was, but you need to know—last night I dreamed about the accident again."

"Figured you would."

"I remembered the next part after that scene when things repeated all the time. Dane fell and I got yanked upward. I rigged new lines to haul him up, but they failed. I got dragged nearly off the cliff—" Becki shivered hard enough her body shook. She lifted her tired gaze to meet his, sorrow and fear overwhelming her. "And that's where it ended. I had my knife ready, Marcus. And I was being pulled toward the ledge."

He didn't snap out the first thing that came to mind, because if he did, she'd probably wave his assurances away. Instead, he took a step back. "For the record? I understand what you meant about Dane and the mountain."

She nodded, small jerky motions. "Thanks."

The doorbell rang, and she shot to her feet.

Marcus waved her down. "I'll get it."

He cautiously opened the door a crack. What he found on his doorstep made his temper flare. "You're not welcome here, Ted."

The other man shrugged. "Had to try. I'm not the only one looking for information. Of course, if I get a story then the others will probably back off a little more. No promises, but it might work. If Ms. James wants to talk?" The reporter raised his voice at the end.

Marcus crowded forward. "Get off my property."

The man stared over Marcus's shoulder. "Sure. No problem."

Marcus didn't believe that for a second. This intrusion was only the first attempt. He knew it. Ted knew it.

When he turned to face Becki, he could tell from her expression she knew it as well.

"They won't go away because you told them to," she warned. "They never did when I was in Yellowstone."

He paced to her side. "We'll do what we can to help. All of us will. Maybe there will be some huge political scandal in the next few days, and they'll all scurry off to bother someone else."

Becki folded her arms over her chest, fingers cupping her upper arms as she rubbed. "I hate this. I hate not knowing. I hate being poked." She stared into his eyes, concern creasing her face. "If they go by rote, we'll be trapped in your house or swarmed every time we leave. I'm sorry."

Marcus slipped his fingers around her neck and pulled her against his chest. "Now that's one of those 'Don't be stupid and apologize for things you didn't cause' statements."

"I asked to spend the night with you."

"And it would have been so much better for you to be alone in the dorm rooms this morning. Where Ted and everyone else would have complete access to you. Bullshit."

Marcus had thought this through a dozen times, setting aside his conclusions because she'd asked him not to make decisions for her, but the solution rose again. It was the only decision that made any sense.

Only he had to phrase this correctly. He'd learned that much.

"Get in touch with your Yellowstone contacts. Once you know what they need, I have a foolproof solution to get the media off your back."

Becki backed away, taking a moment before looking at him. Standing strong, but with that edge of lost in her eyes. "Are you rescuing me, Marcus?"

"That's what a team does. Do you trust me?" he shot back.

Becki paced to the window and looked out. There was a small break in the clouds, allowing a bit of brightness to light the view of the town. It also showcased the footprints just starting to melt on the deck

She shivered.

Turning to face him, she lifted her chin high. "I trust you one hundred percent."

Rule three. Trust your team. The fact that she'd put him into that role—acknowledged there was a connection beyond casual between them—was enough to make something inside him very content in spite of the circumstances that brought them there.

Marcus nodded. "Let's get organized."

CHAPTER 28

On the seat behind them lay gym bags packed with clothing. Food-stuffed boxes rested in the truck bed—David met them at the off-ramp to the highway to transfer a load. He gave Becki a brief hug, slapped Marcus on the back, then sent them on their way.

The three-hour drive that followed was more than enough time to let her relax. Becki had taken to staring at Marcus since the rain coating the windows and the clouds around them continued to obscure the view.

He handled the truck with impressive competence. They'd left the main highway behind more than an hour ago. The less-traveled path they currently followed required four-wheel drive, the section steep enough to make her heart race, but he maneuvered the massive vehicle along the narrow rocky road without a qualm. His sure and controlled motions mesmerized her, along with the complete comfort he displayed driving in the foul weather.

His jaw remained tight—although she was pretty sure

that was because he was still furious at the reasons that had sent them into retreat.

She wasn't in the clear yet.

"How much farther?" she asked. Again.

His solemn expression broke. "I swear, you're as bad as the kids in the commercials. 'Are we there yet? Are we?' Still thirty minutes if the road doesn't get blocked by another tree."

Becki curled her legs under her and twisted until she was facing him, seat belt still tucked around her body. "I'm *bored*. There's nothing to do."

His snort of laughter made her smile.

"You do that far too well," Marcus noted. "Although I'm not surprised. Adrenaline junkies don't make the best travelers."

"Actually, that was me channeling my kid brother. He's eight years younger than me, so the last couple vacations I did with the family he was young enough to be an annoying brat. He got way better in his teens, but he sucks at sitting still."

Marcus nodded. "You mentioned you were a lot alike. You haven't stopped squirming since you got in the truck."

"I feel guilty for running away," Becki admitted. "And pissed off that I've allowed myself to be chased from Banff by stupid people."

"Consider yourself kidnapped then, if it makes it better," Marcus offered. "Don't beat yourself up over doing what's right for you. We'll have the radio to stay in contact with the real authorities if they need you for anything. The rest of the people trying to track you down are not worth worrying about."

She knew that. And she and Marcus had already discussed the team not needing more training from her at the moment—areas other than ropes would fill the final week of boot camp. Now she had to adjust her brain and accept this time was for her. To make the most of it.

The edge of fear stealing back over her soul infuriated her even as it scared her. She'd been breaking free of her worries a little at a time, and now they all seemed to be crowding her again. Depression and darkness—running away from Banff was no guarantee she could escape from anxiety.

Becki leaned her head on the seat back and watched a drop of water edge backward on Marcus's window, pushed by the wind outside.

"You think I'll keep remembering details?"

Marcus nodded. "It's likely. From what I've heard, there's usually an emotional reason for a memory block like yours. Now that more of the story has come forward, you might figure out exactly what happened."

She dreaded and longed for that to happen, the conflicting emotions also making her crazy. "I'm running hot and cold at the idea."

He didn't say anything for a moment, just adjusted his fingers on the wheel. "You're strong enough to handle whatever the truth is."

The absolute conviction in his voice made her throat tighten. "Thank you."

Marcus glanced at her briefly, nodded, then focused back on the road.

Time to change the topic. "Tell me more about the cabin."

"The lap of luxury." He slowed to maneuver past a fallen tree. "Four walls, a roof, and the best view ever. The place is actually David's. He bought it back when I was still gallivanting around the globe and was too stupid to go halves with him. Now he refuses to let me buy him out."

She peered out the front window. "It's got the privacy thing down pat."

He laughed. "Don't worry, there really is everything we need. Consider this your holiday before heading to start teaching."

"Right." Ahead of them the road leveled, the trees clearing to low brush as they rounded the edge of the mountain. To the left the clouds were lifting, revealing a long line of peaks loaded with fresh snow. They were far enough down to stay below the snow line, the gravel road wet with moisture but not covered with fresh snow. "Tell me there's a fireplace and I'll be happy."

"Airtight stove, not open fire, but the effect is still the same. The light shining through the glass window will look beautiful on your naked skin."

Well, now. "There's a change of topic."

"You're really surprised that I'm bringing up sex? We'll have a bit of time on our hands. I thought you might as well know up front how I plan to occupy some of it."

"Some?" Becki teased. "Marcus, the last time we were holed up together for three days we did little more than have sex. Oh, wait. When we had to take a breather, we occasionally ate."

"We have a bit of food with us. Only for emergencies."

The laughter that escaped felt good. This was what she needed. Maybe he was distracting her on purpose, but suddenly the notion of completing what they'd started that morning seemed a very good idea. "I can handle sex in front of the fireplace. I wonder if there's a sturdy table in the kitchen area. Or a big bed? David strikes me as a king-size kind of guy."

Marcus choked for a moment, glaring briefly in her direction. "Stop thinking about my brother and beds, if you don't mind."

Oh, really? Becki leaned back in her chair and decided the tormenting-slash-distracting could go both ways. Although the idea of fooling around with David didn't turn her on. He'd been her teacher for too many years.

"It's not David I wanted to get tangled up with. Just wondering if he's got the same furniture designer you have. You know, the headboard with the convenient handholds. The couch at the perfect height that if I lean over the back you can fuck me from behind."

Marcus growled softly, a rumble in the back of his throat. He adjusted position in his seat and sure enough, the front of his jeans was more crowded than before.

Becki wiggled impatiently, snapping open the button on her pants and unzipping. "I won't expect the type of bathroom you have in your house—that kind of opulence would be pushing it, but then a tiny shower has advantages as well. No room to move without rubbing skin against skin."

"Are you trying to make us go off the road?" he asked.

"You've got better control than that." Becki stretched her legs out to the floorboards and eased her hand into her pants. "Hmm, thinking about all the things we can try over the next few days—you don't mind if I start early, do you?"

She slicked her fingers over her clit and gasped, not worrying about staying quiet. Okay, maybe even making more noise than she usually would.

Marcus peeked at her once or twice, but he managed to keep his focus forward in the most impressive way. She ignored him for a moment, slowly stroking herself, planning what she'd do when they got to the cabin to reward him for everything she was currently putting him through, the sexual teasing the least of it.

"Becki. Pull your hand out of your pants now."

"Why? *Ohhh . . .*" She moaned the word softly, dragging it out to taunt him. "Feels so good."

"You know I'm going to get my revenge at some point. I think what you're doing right now is usually referred to as poking the bear."

"I hope the bear plans to poke back." She pulled her hand free reluctantly. "But if you insist—"

"Let me taste," he demanded.

She lifted her hand to his mouth and he sucked her fingers, licking them clean. Circling with his tongue as he teased, pulsing his lips around the digits lightly as she pulled her hand free.

The tingling between her legs had nothing to do with her provoking him anymore.

"Slip off your pants." Marcus's voice dropped a notch. Deeper. Darker.

He stared straight ahead, but somehow she knew he watched her. Becki didn't hesitate. She wiggled out of her khakis and abandoned them on the floor with her shoes. The leather under her butt was soft and warm, the bare skin pressed against the material because there wasn't much back there between her and the seat.

"Thong as well?" she asked.

"Yes."

She slipped them down her legs and dropped them on top of the pile on the floorboards.

"Put your feet on the dashboard. I love how flexible you are." He leaned forward and adjusted the air vents. "Now touch yourself. Tell me what you're doing."

A quiver raced up her spine. It was one thing when she was the one in control, trying to drive him mad. Now, having him turn the tables on her, she felt everything that much more intensely. Becki adjusted herself so she reclined a little more, widened her knees, and crept her fingers over her belly. Let the anticipation build.

"Talk to me," Marcus reminded her, maneuvering them over a bumpy section of road. The swaying vehicle made her shake slightly in her seat, and she pressed her entire hand over her sex to try to ease the rising fires.

"I want to take it slow. Pretend you're the one touching me. There's an ache inside, like a ghostly memory of being filled with your cock this morning. I want to have that back, to remember what it feels like to be stretched by you."

She dipped her fingers in, sliding over skin that had gone wetter as she thought about what they were doing. Her touch felt good but lacked so much. "It's not enough. My hand. I can tease, but there's no comparison between this and having you inside me."

"Rub your clit. Get yourself off fast." Marcus whispered the words.

She slid her fingers higher, moisture coating her labia. Becki used both hands, opening herself with one and using the other to rub in tiny circles over the sensitive spot at the apex of her sex.

Marcus flipped a switch on the dashboard. A rush of sound filled her ears, the strong current of air from the heaters rushing out and striking her sex dead on.

"Oh my." She increased the speed, pressing harder as the

tingling pulses rose, beckoning on her climax as the strange sensation of wind blowing over her wet body added to the tension. It wasn't as good as a vibrator, but it was enough to make her tremble on the edge.

"Come for me, Becki. Let me hear you lose control. Let me hear you."

His words stroked as hard as her fingers, and together they were enough to make pleasure bloom inside. Body squeezing down, a soft barely there climax.

She wanted him, not her hand, to be taking her over.

She twisted her head to look at him, finally aware they had reached the end of the journey. Ahead of them a small cabin was neatly set into the trees. When she would have sat up and put herself in order, though, Marcus interrupted.

"The only thing you need to do is get ready to deal with me."

Oh my. Becki squeezed her legs together, squirming upright in her seat as the lust in his voice wrapped around her like vocal seduction.

They pulled to a stop outside the cabin, but they could have been anywhere for how much attention she paid to their location. It was all about him, about Marcus as he put the vehicle into park and flipped the steering wheel out of the way. One more move slipped the seat back a foot, then he turned all his focus on her, and Becki nearly stopped breathing.

He smiled. The sinful smile she was addicted to. "Take my cock out, sweet Becki. Take it out and get me wet."

Delight trickled over her and she moved, opening his button, unzipping his jeans carefully. His cock strained against the fabric, the thick ridge making her eager to obey him and give him what he'd asked for. She reached through the fly of his briefs and his cock snapped into her palm, hot and heavy as she fisted him.

She'd barely had time to stroke him twice before he growled at her. "Use your mouth. Cover me and take me deep."

Becki knelt on the seat, tugging her hair out of the way

with one hand and using the other to hold him upright. She licked the tip where a drop of creamy liquid had gathered, his masculine flavour racing through her system. Then she stopped teasing and moved forward readily, opening wide and lowering her head until his cock nudged the back of her throat.

She closed her eyes and repeated the motion, pulling her lips tight around him as she lifted, leaning her head to the side to let him see what she was doing.

He hummed with pleasure, his fingers threading through her hair. Then he tightened his grasp and tugged. A sharp motion, short and controlling, and the buzz of passion in her veins heightened.

"You like that, do you? Interesting." Marcus smoothed his fingers over her cheek. She moved slower. Let the slickness of her saliva ease the motion, his cock glistening in the light. He stroked his fingertips along the corner of her mouth, and she shivered.

Marcus ran his hand down her back toward where her butt was raised high as she knelt over him. His fingers glided over her ass, then back up as she continued to work his cock.

"I'm going to take care of you, Becki. All the ways you need caring for."

Becki smiled and sucked hard as she popped off, holding him vertical like a treat. "Who's taking care of who?"

He smiled. "I'm smart enough to know the answer to that is more complicated than it looks. Crawl on over and ride me. Finish what we started this morning. I want to feel you on my cock. I want to feel you wet and needy as you come."

Becki bit back the whimper that wanted to escape. She might be a strong individual, she might own her sexuality, but right now she was so damn eager for him she could barely see straight. She knelt on either side of his hips and rocked over his wet cock, gliding the hard length through her folds without letting him in.

He let her repeat the move a half dozen times before he grabbed her by the ass and held her in place. "Now, Becki. Fuck me. Fuck me until you can't stand it anymore."

She wasn't going to fight that kind of order. She tilted her pelvis and the broad head pierced her folds. Before she could lower herself, Marcus pushed her hips, thrusting up and burying himself to the root.

"So *so* good." Becki let her head fall back as she rested her hands on Marcus's shoulders and began a determined rise and fall over him. Every motion took him deep, her passage squeezing around his shaft as he filled her, as their movements caused all her sensitive nerve endings to be rubbed again and again.

He twisted his hips and held her ass tighter. Every touch of his increased her pleasure. Made her all the more aware of his possession. Of their heavy breathing as they strained toward release, of his hold on her body that made it seem he would refuse to let her go.

Passion and pleasure rising fast, mindless of everything else. Just the forceful connection between them. His willingness to give, her need to feel alive.

"Touch yourself," Marcus ordered. "Make yourself come on my cock."

His words strained out through barely parted lips, as if he fought to hold back. Resisting release until she joined him. Becki raced to follow his directions. She slipped her fingers over her clit, rubbing where they joined together, and he groaned in approval.

His shoulder was tight under her other hand, entire body poised and ready to go. She increased her tempo, felt the wave approaching.

"Now, oh now. Oh yes." She stared into his face as she came. A second later she witnessed the shock hit him as well. The flicker in his eyes, the tightening of his lips as his cock jerked with her. Pleasure taking her body with total abandon.

There were spots before her eyes, her head spinning as the climax stole through her body. Limbs slowly relaxing, Becki leaned forward and rested their torsos together, waiting for her heart to slow.

Marcus stroked her back, the thick length of his cock

buried in her core. "Welcome to the Landers Retreat House. Would you like valet service?"

"I'll answer when I can move again." She twisted her head to kiss his cheek.

He smiled indulgently. "Take your time. I've got nowhere I'd rather be."

Becki waited a moment, soaking in the last moments of pleasure from their romp. As a source of distraction, Marcus had all the moves.

CHAPTER 29

A tiny flash of something moving past the window made her push upright to stare in disgust. "Snow? It's really going to snow now?"

Marcus nodded. "Welcome back to Canada in May. Look at the good side. We could get trapped for a week."

"That's a good side?" She wiggled off his lap and grinned at his expression. "Well, yes, it could be fun, so you can stop leering. Another plus—I doubt we'll have visitors if there's any kind of accumulation."

She pulled her clothes back on while he adjusted and zipped, both of them opening the doors at the same time. The rush of fresh air and the scent of the spruce trees slammed into her with a powerful hit, memories of years spent in these mountain ranges settling her soul.

"This is a good place," Becki decided, glancing around with delight at the gorgeous setting. Peace settled a little harder—there was no way she could avoid it. The Rocky Mountains were as close to heaven on earth for her as it got.

It had always been that way. Paradise, the occasional touch of hell, but mostly a healing balm for her spirit.

They worked easily together, carrying in supplies. Marcus stopped her in the middle of one trip to wrap his arm around her and kiss her thoroughly.

She touched her fingers to her lips, still buzzing from the attack. "Well, that was unexpected. Nice, but out of the blue."

"We have no agenda, Becki," he pointed out. "No rush. No need to be settled in under five minutes. Slow down and take your time."

"Practice a little patience? Is that what you're telling me?" she teased.

"Of course." Marcus tweaked her nose, then twirled her toward the kitchen. "Take a peek and see how things look. I'll turn on the propane and the pumps."

He vanished out the front door, and she caught herself staring at his ass. Unnumbered days alone with him, and she couldn't wait. Forget going slow, this was the unexpected opportunity of a lifetime.

The weekend they'd shared so many years ago had changed her life. She'd been headstrong. Impulsive. Probably bound for an early grave if he hadn't talked her through her wild impulses and proved she could still have a good time while staying alive.

Her future at the time had seemed wide open, and he'd helped her see the real possibilities. Now her options were closing in, but surely out of all the people to be able to help her find her way, he was the one.

Her memory would come back. Marcus was right—she fully expected, sometime during the next days, to be overwhelmed with whatever it was that remained buried. Remembering was going to hurt, and potentially destroy all the plans she'd made.

It wasn't going to destroy her. She vowed it wouldn't.

She snatched up the broom leaning against the corner and used it like a weapon, taking out her frustrations on the small dust bunnies and leaves that had drifted in the door to lie tucked along the edges of the floorboards.

If she'd cut the line on Dane, there was no way she could go back to work on any rescue squad. Even if there'd been no alternative—it might have been her last choice, but that truth would also mean a lot of jobs would be off her list.

Like teaching. The team hadn't freaked out, but for everyone who took the time to get to know her, there would be those who judged her strictly on the past situation. She couldn't do that to David and the Banff SAR school.

She scooped the debris into the dustpan and carried it outside. Who was she kidding? Taking teaching off the list wasn't about being compassionate to David. She wouldn't want to go through life starting every semester with suspicion, reliving the hurt and the doubt all over again, and that was what teaching would end up doing.

Only a masochist would ask for that kind of punishment. She might like her sex a little rough at times, but daily life shouldn't involve pain.

Becki stepped inside and took a closer look around, distancing herself from her morbid thoughts. There was a sturdy table with four chairs, and a small kitchen counter and island across from it that separated the cooking area from the living room. A wood-frame couch and two chairs, thick cushions on both.

The infamous wood-burning stove in the corner of the room with a thick rug in front of it.

Cozy, but not in a smothering sense, more like compact and orderly. Another place of peace.

The first of the two doors in the back wall opened onto a tiny bathroom and she grinned. Indoor plumbing for the win. Rustic was good—outhouses, not so good.

"You see, your prediction about lots of skin rubbing together in the shower is one hundred percent correct." Marcus spoke quietly right over her shoulder, his arm catching her before she could turn. His right hand slipped around her belly and he tugged her back tightly against his torso. "I turned on the pump and the rapid-fire heater. We can shower in that thing until the stream runs dry and never lose our hot water."

Warm lips met her cheek and Becki stretched, leaning into him. Accepting his caress. "Did I say thank you for bringing me here?"

"You did. A few times. You can stop. I want to be here with you."

His sincerity was clear.

She turned and stared into his face, searching for understanding. "Why? Why are you doing this? I know what I want, I know why I'm here—"

"Or you think you do," he interrupted.

Becki poked him in the gut with an extended forefinger. He grunted in pain as he released her. "Stop with the assuming. I'm grateful you brought me away from the vultures, and I said I trusted you. Doesn't mean I want you putting words into my mouth and meanings to my actions before you hear what I have to say."

Marcus leaned on the wall beside her, trapping her in the bathroom space. "Or maybe you should accept that you're saying loud and clear what's in your head without having to open your mouth."

Oh really. "Mind reader now, are you?"

"If you want to call it that." Marcus caught her hand in his, tugging her after him. He moved slowly, like she was a wary animal. Maybe she was. . . . Becki kept her footing steady as Marcus smoothed his knuckles over her cheek, his perceptive gaze darting over her face. "I won't push. Not yet. But I'm here for you—one hundred percent, just like you asked."

She sighed, letting go of her tension. "Sorry for snapping at you."

"It's understandable. Come on, let's burn off a little of your aggression before we dig to find out what David gave us for supplies."

She dressed warmly, with sturdy hiking boots and thin but comfortable gloves. Gore-Tex jacket and a toque in her pocket, just in case. A nice long walk after sitting would feel good.

They were outside and pacing easily down a game trail

before she realized he'd avoided her question—the one where she asked for his reasons. In spite of his teasing, she knew why she was hiding in the wilderness.

What had made him willing to drop everything?

Marcus stirred the chili one last time, then turned to watch Becki pace the cabin.

Although she wasn't marching back and forth in the strictest sense of the word. It was as if all the unused energy she'd had to contain during their drive was still escaping, even after their walk and the impromptu workout she'd forced him to do that involved jumping jacks and torturous abdominal moves.

She'd found a box of candles in the box of groceries and had gathered all the possible candleholders from everywhere in the room. An eclectic collection of old bottles to antique brass. She'd filled them one at a time, carrying each back to a select spot. Now she systematically lit them one after another, leaving tiny beads of glowing yellow in her wake.

He dimmed the propane lantern on the wall behind him to allow her handiwork to shine brighter.

Becki turned slowly, pulling off her sweater and draping it over the back of the couch. "This cabin is beautiful. Although that stove is going to cook me out of here if we're not careful."

"I turned down the damper already," Marcus said. "I agree—it gets going and it's like the middle of summer in here."

She stood and stared at the flame, the dancing flickers from the stove meshing with the smaller torches she'd created to fill the space with luxurious warmth. The soft light caressed her skin. Turned the entire room unearthly.

He could barely speak. Intruding seemed sacrilegious.

Her hands reached for the ceiling as she stretched, lowering her arms and twisting to face him, a contented smile on her face. "Supper nearly ready? I'm starving."

"I love a woman with a good appetite."

She moved to his side and helped arrange things on the table. "Which should mean you cooked enough for both of us. Worst thing ever—first dinner dates that the pots are scraped clean and my stomach is still grumbling."

Marcus guided her to a chair, leaning in close to take a long inhale of her scent. "I promise to feed you well. I think David packed for three, so we're good."

She scooped chili into both their bowls, licking a drop from her finger as she passed his serving over. "David was a bit of a miracle worker to get all that together so quickly."

"Typical David," Marcus admitted. "I sort of suspect he figured out before we did that we'd head for the hills. He's good that way. Part of what's always made him do so well with the school. He knows when to step in, when to let things slide. Who's the right person for the right job. When to kick my butt and when to leave me alone."

She nodded slowly, staring at her bowl. "I hope I don't have to disappoint him."

Miracle of miracles. Would she actually talk about what she was really running from without him having to drag it from her? "In what way?"

She dipped her spoon into the chili, then lifted it, licking the bowl of the spoon as she clearly debated what to say. "Just thinking out loud. This is tasty, Marcus."

She set to eating as if she were starving, and he let the comment pass. He'd said he would give her space, and that was what he would do. As much space as a twelve-by-twelve cabin would allow.

But even if she wasn't willing to share right now what she was afraid of, he wasn't going to let her deal with it alone. He wasn't going to wait until she called for help before he did something to help her through the hurting.

Small talk. Dishes. They'd shifted to the couch, and she curled up at his side without being asked. It was natural and comfortable, which meant it was totally time to shake things up.

Time to move decisively.

"I think we should play a game," he proposed.

Becki snorted softly, stopping where she'd been drawing circles on his forearm with her finger. "If you suggest Truth or Dare, I'm going to make you sleep on the couch."

Marcus shifted her to the side so he could see her face more clearly. "Hate that game or something?"

"Hello—what do you think triggered that stupid assault on the exterior of the Banff Springs so long ago? Although there were shots of tequila involved as well."

"I was sure there had to be alcohol involved in that somehow," Marcus taunted. "No, nothing so childish as Truth or Dare."

"Strip poker?"

"I cheat."

Becki smiled. "Risk? Monopoly?"

Marcus shook his head. "As if you could sit for an entire board game. You'd have it upset with all your wiggling before I got to bankrupt you."

A log cracked, and they both glanced at the tiny fire he had going. "Twenty Questions? That's what it seems like."

"No. Let me help you. It's like Simon Says, but simpler. All it involves is you doing whatever I tell you."

He heard her quick intake of breath. "That might be fun."

"Well, you did mention you expected lots of sex over the next few days. I'd hate to disappoint."

"Ohhh . . ." she drawled, "It's going to be *that* kind of ordering me around. And here I thought you'd have me tap-dancing or something like that to entertain you."

"Trust me, I plan to be very entertained." Marcus waited, gazing into her eyes. Looking for a clue of what she needed right now that would get her past the coming confusion.

Her smile twitched, but she sat straighter, leaning toward him. She planted a hand on his chest, then brought their mouths together for a slow, sweet kiss. Languid tongues and easy pressure. Just enjoying each other as if they had all the time in the world. No deadlines, nothing hanging over them.

God, he wanted that to be the reality for her.

When she pulled away he'd nearly decided to forgo the

games and take her to bed. Nothing needed but the slow steady feed of the passion between them. Only her expression as she found her feet before him?

Longing, and yet fear. Not of him, he was sure of that. Of the future. Of what closing her eyes might reveal.

Marcus stretched out his legs, deliberately taking his time to settle into a comfortable position. Making it about him and his wants. Taking the focus off her. She was strong enough to call him out if he'd guessed wrong, but he didn't think he was.

"You ready for this?" he asked.

She shuffled from side to side slightly, getting her balance. Even breathing. In through the nose, out through her mouth. Every trick in the book to find her center.

"Game on," she whispered. Gaze straight at his. Eyes focused on him.

How could a woman who was so strong be so willing to offer it all up? Marcus took control of himself and vowed he'd do whatever it took. Whatever it cost.

Because it was going to cost him—that much he knew for sure.

He glanced the length of her body. Assessing, weighing. When he met her gaze again, he spoke softly. "Undo your hair."

Becki eased off the elastic she'd used to pull her hair back into a functional ponytail. She slipped the band into her pocket, then lifted her hands again, smoothing her fingers through the strands and fluffing it over her shoulders. The long tresses rested over her shoulders, slightly tousled, a lock falling over her forehead and into her eyes.

"Your top. Take it off. Slowly."

Her laughter rippled across the room. "I'm not a very good dancer, Marcus. If you want me to swing my hips and give you a show, you're going to be sorely disappointed."

"Oh, I doubt that very much," he said. "No dancing required. Undo your buttons, sweet Becki. One at a time. That's it." He followed her fingers with his gaze as she slipped the tiny pearl-white circles through the slits. "Every one you open reveals a little more of your skin. All the

candlelight in the room reflects off you and makes it glow.
I can see the edges of your bra cups now. Your breasts. It's
like a present being unwrapped before me."

She was silent as she finished the final buttons, the front
of her shirt gaping open so the light shone on her solid belly.

Her breathing wasn't as even as it had been a few
moments before.

Becki shrugged her shoulders and the gap widened.
When the fabric finally came loose she let it fall to the floor
at her feet.

Marcus stared hungrily at her, sure that what was in his
gut showed on his face. Hoping it did. This was more than
temporary desire, this was a need for her that was going to
last his entire life.

"You're beautiful. So strong, so powerful." Becki undid
the button on her pants as she smiled in response to his
comment. He jerked her to a stop with a single word. "Wait."

One brow rose. "I assumed you wanted me naked."

"Don't assume." He stood and stepped in close enough
that she could touch him without leaving her space on the
floor. "My turn. Take off my shirt."

She'd undressed him before, days earlier. That time she'd
been blindfolded and he'd watched her fingers tremble as
she moved. As she touched.

Now she stroked him with her gaze as well as her touch,
and he hadn't been prepared for how powerful the effect
would be. Becki undid his belt, popped his button. Lowered
the top notches of his zipper. That freed room for her to slip
her hands under his T-shirt, fingertips cool against his
heated skin. She stared into his eyes as she passed over his
chest, thumbs skimming his nipples. When she pressed
closer so she could reach behind him he took a deep breath,
the seductive scent of her body lotion teasing his senses.

This playtime might be about what she needed, but damn
if he wasn't going to enjoy it as well.

CHAPTER 30

It was like being drugged. The edge blurred between reality and fantasy, and Becki embraced the sensation fully, planning to savour every second.

She caught hold of the bottom of his shirt in the back and tugged it upward. "Lean over," she ordered, and he went willingly, bending and extending his arms over his head so she could drag the fabric all the way off.

Then she wasn't sure where to look as he straightened. He'd mentioned the candlelight, and wow—he wasn't kidding how the flickering glow made a huge impact on her senses. It was better than examining Greek statues in a museum. Every muscle was showcased in bold relief. The firm cuts defining his chest; the rigid lines that separated his lower abdomen into neatly packaged squares.

Becki peeked upward to discover that his eyes were still fixated on hers. Something about his complete attention made her cheeks flush with heat even as a deep need throbbed inside. Between her legs she grew wet, longing for more than glances and slow seduction.

She lifted his shirt, watching to see if he'd change his focus. The shirt slipped from her fingers to land on top of her abandoned clothes.

His gaze never flickered off her face, and the delicious sense of being totally enveloped by him increased. Becki eased back on her heels and allowed her hands to fall by her sides. Whatever was happening tonight, she would embrace it fully. If he wanted her to move, she'd assume he'd tell her so.

Marcus cupped her chin in his fingers and nodded. "Yes. Oh, yes, now you have it. Take off your pants, and when you're done I'll tell you what to do next."

His declaration stroked her like a physical brush. She wanted to rush, to give in to the urgency to strip everything off and fall to the next task, but his voice beguiled her. Eased her. She slipped open the button and the zipper on her slacks and pushed them off her hips. They bunched around her ankles, and she was surprised when he held out his arm to her. She clutched his elbow tightly and, instead of bending to free herself, stepped forward out of the material.

The move brought them skin to skin, the thin fabric of her bra the only barrier between them.

"My jeans now, and everything else. Strip me, sweet Becki."

His endearment made a shiver race up her spine. "I love how you say my name. Like I'm delicious, and you can't get enough of me."

She put her hands to his zipper and finished the task of lowering it. The clicking of the teeth separating echoed loudly in the hushed room. Smoothing her hands over his hips, pushing the material down, she knelt, keeping in contact with his body at all times. It would have been a moment's work to remove his socks along with the jeans, but she hesitated. Drew out the motion. Let him balance on one foot then the other with her shoulder as an anchor as she removed every stitch of clothing from him.

She deliberately stayed on her knees as she tugged his briefs off, his erection snapping up between them as soon as she'd freed it from the confines of the fabric. The hard length rose from the dark curls at his groin, and she wanted to touch, to taste, but first, she waited.

The heat from the airtight stove draped around her like a blanket, the soft rug cushioning her from the hardwood floorboards. She rested on her heels and stared at his naked magnificence.

Waiting.

Marcus hadn't once looked away. Every time she'd lowered her gaze to concentrate on her task, she'd returned to his face and discovered him watching. Tenderness in his expression. Hunger.

His call. His command. Tonight was his game, and she was eager to play it. All worries, concerns, dread had vanished to be replaced with nothing but rising passion and full concentration on this man.

"Touch me." The words rasped out, barely audible. "Touch me, everywhere. At your pleasure. How you want. No demands, no agenda."

His order wasn't what she'd expected. She sat dumbfounded for a moment, recalibrating her brain.

He smiled, that corner teasing upward. The familiar expression gave her something to cling to as she switched gears. He shifted slightly on his feet, muscles flexing as he moved, and Becki stared mesmerized.

Well, now. Anything she wanted—his demand might not be expected, but wasn't it exactly what she'd been wanting?

She got to one knee, moving upright to rest her palms against the outside of his thighs. She explored, stroked. Brushed the wiry hair on his solid thighs and skimmed past his hips. Moved into position to plant a kiss on that band of muscle that wrapped along the sides of his torso—the Adonis line. A perfect place to press her lips and tease with her tongue. Small circles over his skin, breathing deeply to take in the scent of him—masculine, addictive.

She moved around his cock. The neglect not intended to torment him, but because he'd said to touch him everywhere. If she gave in already to her desire to adore his cock, she'd stop without tending to everything else she wanted to enjoy. His chest beckoned, and she rose higher to stroke and smooth the firm skin, his dusting of hair tickling her palms.

Becki gazed into his face, her hands cupping his cheeks briefly before threading her fingers through his hair. He smiled but didn't speak.

"I like this game," she whispered.

His eyes flashed, but he stayed in one spot, allowing her control. She strolled behind him, impatient for more muscles to caress, his firm butt cheeks to admire with her fingertips. She was surprised her thorough examination wasn't driving him crazy as she worked him over, reading every inch like Braille.

No agenda—that was what he'd said—but suddenly there was one.

She wanted to give to him. Needed to share what she was feeling with him. It took a split second to peel off her panties and bra and toss them behind her. She stepped against his body, sighing as the warmth of his back connected with her torso. Her breasts pressed tight to him, she eased her fingers around his waist, stroking that wonderful band of muscle again, this time from behind.

When she curled her finger over his erection it was the first time since she'd begun she felt a reaction. Only because they were so close together did she know that her touch caused him to take a deep shaky breath.

She fisted him, pumping slowly, moving with caution. Cupping her hand over the head to find the moisture gathered there and spread it on her palm. His seed acted as a lubricant, but it wasn't enough. She licked her fingers, saliva coating her in exchange for the burst of his taste that came as her tongue made contact with his seed.

Then she returned to the task at hand. Slow, even pumps, a pause to run her fingers over his sac, fingertips rolling his balls delicately. When she grasped him the next time, he countered, pushing into her hand, increasing her tempo. Becki laid her cheek against his back and worked as directed until he quivered in her embrace, torso shuddering as he came, liquid spurting over her fingers as she caught what she could.

She felt strangely satisfied. Without a climax, without a touch, but endorphins were floating through her veins all the same.

Marcus knelt briefly and scooped up his shirt, using the fabric to wipe her hand dry. Then he turned.

She wasn't sure what her expression would reveal. Contentment? Hopefully not *gloating*, but she was far too satisfied by what she'd accomplished to be able to easily explain herself. Marcus pushed her hair back, his gaze darting over her face. Then he nodded. Once.

As he breathed slowly, his gaze finally moved down to trace over her body. The fire was nearly out, the candles around the room flickering with their last gasps. Still, enough of the pale yellow light remained to highlight her nakedness.

"My turn," he declared. "My turn to touch you everywhere. With my fingers, my tongue. My cock. Until I've pushed you past the brink again and again."

Her body quivered in response. To his words? Or to the thought of what was about to happen?

He offered his hand and she took it, surprised again when he brought her around the room and they extinguished the candles one at a time. When he escorted her through the bedroom door, the only light remaining was the pale flicker of red and gold through the glass of the stove.

Darkness filled the space. She might have been blindfolded again for how little she could see. Marcus didn't seem to have any troubles guiding her to the end of the bed and pushing her back until she sat.

"Stay here," he ordered.

This room wasn't as warm as the living area, the heat from the fire lingering in the outside room and leaving a chill in the air. A match snapped, the instant flash of light bouncing off the cabin wall where Marcus brought the stick to the candlewick. The faint scent of sulfur carried back to

her as Becki waited, curling up on the soft quilt covering
the mattress.

Two candles—three. Once he had a light source on every
wall, he turned back to face her and her heart skipped.

So beautiful. His rugged masculinity showcased in the
shadows dancing over him. He held a casual stance for a
moment as he looked her over as well, giving her time to
admire him.

Time to ache for him to move and do as he'd promised
in the other room.

She wiggled to her knees and smoothed her hands up her
body, cupping her breasts as she stared at him. His cock
jerked, the semi-aroused length hardening again.

"I never told you to touch yourself," Marcus warned.

"I'm being innovative and trying to anticipate." She
twirled the tiny rings and moaned happily. "Of course, if
there's something else you'd like me to do . . ."

Marcus stalked to the bed, and suddenly she was on her
back with him over her, pinned in place with his weight, his
mouth ravishing hers. She lifted her arms around his neck
and held on for the ride, loving the near frantic thrusts of
his tongue, the way his breathing skipped as he hauled their
mouths apart to plant kisses down the length of her throat.

When he caught hold of her breast with his right hand,
Becki sighed, widening her legs to allow his hips to fall to
the mattress. He licked and sucked, playing with the ring,
using his teeth just to the edge of pain. One side, the other,
desperate hunger in his moves.

That he was reduced to such passion for her—priceless.
She could only wonder and take it in. The way he made
every inch of her tingle, sharp bolts of pleasure from his
mouth connecting through her nipples to tug at her core.
She was so wet between her legs, so wanting to have him
touch her.

Yet when he moved lower, she regretted he'd gone.
"No . . ."

Marcus laughed softly. "Stop complaining. Touch your

breasts how you like it—I have something else to deal with right now."

Oh God. She'd thought she was wet before? Marcus pushed her thighs wider and covered her with his mouth. No slow approach. No more warning than shifting his position and he was driving her mad. Tongue connecting with her clit, driving into her deep as he rolled one thigh up and out to give himself more room to work.

She'd been primed before. Aching from teasing him and his breast play. The first climax hit her suddenly—shocking. Hard. Made her shake and gasp for air. When he didn't slow, she ignored her tingling breasts and drove her fingers into his hair.

To hold him in place or drag him away as she grew more sensitive, she wasn't sure.

He was having none of it. He picked up her hips and pressed his mouth tighter, not stopping until the slow curl was building again. When his fingers pierced her body, she cried out.

So good. So what she needed. Somehow she got her feet to the mattress to find purchase, and she pulsed her hips against him, demanding what he so willingly gave. Her core stretched around a third finger as he slowed, brushing the front of her passage just right, and sparks flew in front of her eyes as another climax tore her apart.

His name was still on her lips when he rolled her, pulled her hips into the air, and drove his cock into her from behind.

She'd never been so full. So possessed. He went deep, his torso bending over her as his cock pounded in. Pulsing over sensitive nerves, refusing to let her move. A layer of sweat formed between them, the loud slaps of his thighs slamming into hers carrying to her ears. Panting breaths filled the air—hers? His? Nothing but pleasure rolling through her body, all because of him.

Then he stopped. Completely. She gasped, body trembling on the edge, as she wondered and wanted.

He lifted off her, the cold air skating over the sweat clinging to her torso.

"Everything," Marcus growled. Dangerously soft. "Give me everything."

Becki took a shaky breath, wondering what else she had to give.

He stroked his fingers along her hip, playing so softly with her skin. Such a contrast between this tenderness and the wild ride of a moment before. She was still trying to catch her breath when his finger slipped between her butt cheeks and skimmed over the tiny hole there.

Oh God. That was what he'd meant. She wriggled, not trying to escape, but not sure what he required.

He caressed again, rubbing for a second before moving away. His cock still filled her, the pulse of blood through her veins going to take her into an orgasm without him doing anything other than possess her.

Liquid slicked over her opening and he worked it in slowly. As if waiting for her to tell him no, but she'd already said yes to everything. She wanted, needed. Instead of words, she gave him actions, lowering her head and shoulders to the mattress and pressing her hips higher against him. Begging for him to continue.

"Becki . . ." He slicked her up, moving quicker, as if his control was nearly gone. She arched her back and squeezed her sex around his cock in time with his finger pressing into her ass. "Yes, God, yes. That's it. I'm going to take you here as well. Make you know every single . . ."

His words faded away, but the meaning seemed clear enough to her. He was in charge and she was going to take him. However he wanted.

An edge quivered through her. Need now like the blade of a knife just waiting to happen dragged against her nerves. When he pressed the top of the lube to her ass and squeezed she shivered. The coldness in the room forgotten—her skin was on fire.

He tossed the container aside. She expected he would

pull free of her body, but instead he moved slowly. Dragging his cock back then thrusting in. All the nerves that had slowed to a nice even tingle flared to life as he stroked them, drove his cock over them again and again until she was ready to burst.

That was when he finally switched. Withdrew, pressed his cock to her anus and pushed forward. Becki bit her lip against the pressure. The pain opening her as she stretched radiated out and mixed with the still-frantic pleasure in her sex. It wasn't enough. None of it was enough anymore, and she leaned back into him to try to hurry him up.

Marcus caught her by the hip and stopped them, the fat crown of his cock popping through her tight muscle. "My speed. My pace."

"Oh God, please. More. Give me your cock. Fuck me now." She was sure she kept talking, but she no longer knew what she said, because gloriously, he listened to her and drove in all the way. The sensation rippled through her entire body. Oh it hurt, but it hurt like the most indescribable plea-sure. He pulled back and it wasn't just his cock in her, it was him inside her entire body. Making her squirm, making her need.

He planted his hand in the middle of her shoulders, rose slightly, and thrust forward. Driving her into the mattress as his cock reamed her. Opening her ass, taking everything she was willing to give. It was as if he were taking complete possession, working his cock in and out of her body, her ass slowly giving up resistance. Nothing but pleasure now as he buried himself deep and held himself there.

Torso curled over her, bodies connected so intimately. She wanted to sing out her delight, but damn if she could say a thing.

He kissed between her shoulders before lifting off and pulling his hips back until his cock popped free. He stroked her opening, and her anal muscles fluttered against his fin-gertip. Marcus caressed her hip for a second before placing his cock in position again. He pushed in slowly, her hole stretching wide with the faintest resistance around his hard length.

He did it again. And again, the sensation making her tremble as he waited just long enough for her to fully feel him enter her body each time. So intimate. Such complete abandon.

Trust.

When he leaned over to kiss her once more, she was ready for the next step. Ready for him to grab hold of her and turn up the speed. He thrust in and dragged out hard now, torsos locked together, her ass burning as he plunged in again and again.

When he reached between her legs and touched her clit, she buried her face in the mattress and screamed. Ass clutching him as her orgasm broke her down and tore her into ribbons of pleasure. Inside her sex the muscles pulsed, her breasts tingled—her entire body being taken along for the ride.

"Becki." He buried himself as deep as possible a second before his cock jerked, a flood of warmth filling her as his seed rushed out.

They collapsed together, his cock still a part of her, their legs tangled, both of them sweaty and panting for breath.

She'd never felt so alive in her life.

CHAPTER 31

''''''''''''''''''''''''''''''''

Her cheek rested on something cold and solid, flakes of dirt and grit under her palms where they were pressed to the ground. Becki pushed to a sitting position with the caution born of a thousand climbs—testing each hold before trusting her life on it.

She'd expected the spruce forest, but it had vanished, leaving nothing but the grey of cloud and granite. The rock she sat on was bombproof. Flat, solid. The perfect place to take a nap.

Right—as if.

Taking to her feet used more energy than she wanted, every muscle at the point of quivering in agony. Legs, head, torso—all a mass of aches and pains. Cold as well, as if she'd been motionless for a long time. She staggered under the pack's weight, pulled off her helmet, and rubbed her aching temples. Whatever had happened, she was still standing. Still breathing. It wasn't the end of the world. She stretched one arm back and clipped her helmet in place, the move more instinctual than planned.

Even her fingertips hurt. She shook out her hands gingerly, trying to get them to warm up, and she brushed her harness. Another habitual move kicked into gear and she reached forward, grabbing the figure-eight knot she found anchored tight. She slid her fingers upward to gather her rope and coil it neatly. When her hand slipped off far too soon, a rush of adrenaline shot through her. Sickening bile rose as her mind registered what was wrong.

The rope ended barely a hand's grasp from her harness.

She stared down at the cut rope, the ends of the twist already coming unraveled. The moisture on her face — she wasn't sure if it was the rain that had chosen that moment to become full out, or if it was tears.

What had she done?

Becki woke first, sadness sinking into her brain like a heavy blanket as her dream slipped from the distant place of the night to the here and now. Understanding brought so much sorrow. She rolled slowly, taking herself from under Marcus's left arm, which lay draped over her stomach.

Recovering the memory was strangely anticlimactic.

Maybe she'd been ready for it. Maybe that was why her heart wasn't pounding like crazy. While the truth hurt, and finally knowing changed everything, at least she could go on from here. Do what needed to be done.

That was at least something to be grateful for.

She stopped beside the bed, her vision caught by Marcus. The blankets in disarray around him, his naked chest exposed, his head tilted to the side with his right hand near his temple. His left arm, the one that had held her to him, lay across his chest, the shortened section of his forearm ending abruptly. Maybe it should have shocked her how seldom she noticed his missing hand.

He wasn't lacking, though. In any way. Strong and determined. Giving and powerful. Since the moment she'd met him so many years ago up to now, the only word she had for him was *extraordinary*.

Now she was going to have to leave him, and the realization hurt far more than she'd expected. The pain she anticipated taking control after her memory returned finally arrived. Only it was because having to say good-bye to Banff would mean leaving Marcus again.

The first time, after their fling, she'd missed him, but with the ease of youth she'd moved on.

She wasn't sure she'd be able to do that this time.

And last night? *God*. Last night had been so exactly what she'd needed. Having this man take control of her and drive her to new heights of passion . . .

Marcus scowled, his face tightening in a grimace. He twitched in his sleep. Head jerking as something rolled through his body. Becki stepped closer, concern washing away her own sorrows.

"Marcus?" she whispered. "You're dreaming. It's okay. Wake up."

He moved uneasily, beads of sweat forming on his brow. Moans broke free from his lips, words forming. "No, no . . . Don't give up."

Oh no. Whatever nightmares he fought, this could get ugly fast.

"Hang on. I'm coming. I'll be there."

"Marcus. Wake up," she insisted louder. Becki placed one knee on the bed and reached for his leg. He shot upright, arms flailing, and she jerked back to avoid being hit. "You're good, you're safe. It's me, Becki, and we're in David's cabin. There's nothing wrong."

His body continued to shake for a moment before his eyes slowly focused, and he collapsed back. "God, I'm sorry. I'm so sorry."

She crawled next to him, fingers light on his shoulder. "Nothing to be sorry for. You okay? Can I get you anything?"

He stared at the ceiling and shook his head. "I'm glad I didn't come out of that swinging and hurt you."

Becki laid her head on his chest, stroking him gently. Trying to ease his panic. His heart pounded like crazy, and

she deliberately breathed slower. Willing him to find peace.
She didn't want to have him hurting.

God, the list of what she didn't want was growing by the
minute.

Marcus rolled and surrounded her, cradling her carefully
against him. He pressed a kiss to the top of her hair. "How
long was I out?" he asked.

"Not long. You seemed to be having a bad dream."

He sighed. "Well, at least it was a short episode. Thanks
for being there to pull me out."

She wanted to tell him it was no problem. Wanted to say
that she hated that he had nightmares — to ask if they were
because of his accident, and was there anything she could
do to help.

But those were questions she would ask if she were staying. If this relationship was going to become more than what
they currently had. And she couldn't force him to stay with
her when she was about to blow their connection and the
entire SAR team apart. When she was going to have to go
back and change her life for good.

Instead, she gave him a partial truth. "Glad I could help."

Neither of them spoke much as they found their way out
of bed. Gathered breakfast cereal from the box. Marcus
brewed some of the strongest coffee Becki had ever had,
and the bitter taste barely registered on her tongue. Only the
heat. The bitterness seemed too appropriate for the day.

They bundled up in their thickest coats and sat in the chairs
outside the cabin door that let them look out over the Bow
Valley mountain range. Becki debated how long she wanted
to stay silent, but it was inevitable. They'd come to hide from
the media. With her memories intact, or at least the one that
was most important, there was no reason to remain hidden
anymore.

The scent of the breeze after it had passed over fresh
snow hit her face—adding another acidic, sharp flavour to
the day. The truth was going to burn for a long time. Why
prolong the pain?

"Marcus?" She kept staring over the beautiful panorama, but even that didn't provide any hope. "I . . . I cut the line."

He was next to her chair in an instant, kneeling at her side. "What do you remember?"

Turning to look into his face was possibly more heart-breaking than actually knowing what she'd done. Because now? She was going to sever the line between them and kill all hopes of a relationship. Of a forever between them.

She'd gone and done the worst thing possible. She'd fallen in love just in time to have to cut him free.

His eyes were dark—focused. Totally and completely concentrating on her alone.

Losing his confidence in her was going to be the second worst part.

"I did it, Marcus. I've been so certain all this time that I would never ever do that to a partner, but I saw it. The rope attached to my harness was cut, exactly the distance it would have been if I took a knife to it. I saved myself, and Dane died. We can go back—set up an announcement. I should let David know—"

"Bullshit."

His grip on her thigh had tightened as she spoke, but the sheer violence in his tone shocked her. She frowned in confusion. "What are you talking about? It's the truth. I can't deny it. We came here to avoid the reporters, but now that I know—"

"Stop it. You're jumping to conclusions. Stop rolling yourself forward so fast and tell me what you remember."

Becki bit back a sob. "Why are you doing this? It's hard enough to have to say it once, but this is cruel. I killed him, okay? I killed my climbing partner to save myself."

Marcus caught her and pulled her forward, and she allowed his embrace, her body still stiff, but her face pressed into the crook of his shoulder. Tears escaped no matter how hard she tried to stop them.

He held her tight and managed to switch their positions so she was cradled in his lap, his fingers stroking through her hair as he soothed her. When she managed to stop from shaking so hard, each breath dragging in raggedly, he let her go a bit, far enough that his caress moved to her cheek.

"I know what you've remembered seems shocking, and you're rightly upset. But I need you to tell me all the details, okay? Don't assume."

A flash of anger intruded. "You think I'm too stupid to know what I saw?"

"I think you're too upset to think rationally. Share, let me help you. I'm here for you."

Becki breathed out her fears and frustrations. This wasn't going to be settled in a minute, or a day. This was something that would haunt her forever. She might as well start the torture with someone she loved who would at least be honest and not vindictive. Because those responses were sure to be coming down the road.

"I saw the rope, Marcus. I was on my feet, gathering my gear after down climbing a rock face. It must have been after I'd cut Dane free, and I must have slipped and knocked myself out briefly. I had a cut rope attached to my harness. Right after that I found the descent trail I followed that led me past where the girls were trapped—the memory that returned earlier."

Becki sighed, staring at the mountains. "The two memories line up. I took that short length off and used it as part of the halter I tied to help the girls off the ledge. That's why I didn't see it before, why no one noticed."

Marcus continued to stroke her cheek with his thumb. "So you remember finding the cut rope, and discovering the girls?"

"The entire rescue of the girls—it's completely back." She twisted to face him. "Whenever you're ready, we can return to Banff."

He shook his head. "I'm not finished asking questions. You don't remember the actual moment, do you?"

Pain laced through her and she wiggled free, pressing to her feet so she could stand alone. "Not really wanting that memory to return, if I'm honest. Don't you think what I have to deal with is enough?"

"I think you're jumping to some conclusions," Marcus stated. "I think you've had a shock, and you need to slow down and be patient."

"Fuck being patient," she shouted. The anger that flared seemed unreasonable, but the knot in her chest was more than she could bear. "This isn't some training exercise, Marcus. This isn't about a weekend of us getting our kicks with each other. Someone died, and it was my fault."

She stomped into the cabin, slamming the door behind her, feeling childish at the same time that the rush of her anger covered some of the pain. Stuffing the few bits of clothing she'd unpacked back into her gym bag gave her a task to concentrate on for a moment. Something other than the fact that her world was falling apart.

She'd known he wouldn't leave her to brood. His warm body pressed behind her a second before he turned her to face him, his strong embrace tangling around her like a cocoon.

"I'm sorry." His chest rose as he took a deep breath. "I'm sorry for how much this hurts you. For what it's worth, I still trust you. Completely."

Another sob escaped at hearing the conviction in his statement.

Oh God. Out of everything he could have said—telling her it would be okay? That she'd make it through? She could have handled those.

His trust tore her apart.

Her fingers curled into a fist, and she pounded his chest in sheer frustration. "You suck, Marcus. I hate crying, and I'm going to bawl like a baby in a second because of you."

"You deserve the truth," he said. Simple words. Powerful words.

Becki tilted her head to stare at him. Maybe it wasn't rational, but knowing he still trusted her, or at least said he did?

She was going to cling to that like a lifeline even as her heart broke and she moved toward saying good-bye.

CHAPTER 32

''''''''''''''''''''''''''''''''''

Stubborn, hardheaded, fantastic woman. Marcus was torn between holding her or shaking sense into her.

Becki wiggled away and disappeared into the bathroom, the sound of running water spilling through the slightly open door. He peered in to see her press a washcloth to her face, bathing away her tears.

It was his turn to pace the room and stare at the walls, striving desperately to figure out what to do next, what to say, before she returned.

She seemed determined to ignore reason. Her fears were understandable, only she'd taken the tiniest scrap of memory, followed it with some assumptions, and believed the worst-case scenario as fact.

He got it—the wanting to move on. Accepting what you assumed to be true because the alternative was to stay frozen in one place. But he'd learned the hard way, though, that situations, even memories, weren't always what they seemed.

Alisha had shared that Becki wanted to go back to Yellowstone. If she'd been cleared to rejoin her rescue squad, he would have had to say good-bye. He would have, too. Would have lied his fucking ass off and pretended he was pleased for her, and enthusiastically sent her on her way.

He couldn't be a part of her world—not at the high-risk level she was capable of. Not with his arm, or the nightmares that still hovered. He might run a SAR, but he wasn't part of it.

And he loved her too much to hold her back.

Goddamn. It seemed he still had a heart after all. He'd given it away in spite of trying not to.

He'd fallen for her. Hard.

At times like this, his mandate of *move decisively* battled with *be patient*. Becki had asked him years ago how to know which of those two rules to act on.

All he knew for sure was he didn't want to lose her, and he didn't want to cause her any more pain. More than that, there were no easy answers, other than there was no way he could allow her to take the next steps alone.

She stepped out of the bathroom, chin held high, her face much brighter, if only from a vigorous scrubbing.

When you weren't positive what to do, you started at the beginning and proceeded step by step. He indicated the kitchen chairs behind them. "Come on. Let's make a list. Consider what needs to be done. There's no time frame for you to move. The authorities have waited for months. They can wait a couple more days if that's what it takes for you to be prepared. Understand?"

Becki nodded.

Before he could move, she was against him, hugging him tightly. "Marcus—thank you."

The thought of losing her was going to break him in two. "Nothing to thank me for. Come on."

She stood tall, pulling her shoulders back, that strength he'd always admired being dragged on like a protective coat. It made him admire her even more.

He found a pad of paper, then sat at the table. "Who do you need to contact in Yellowstone?"

Becki pulled out the chair beside him, staring into space before giving him names. "If you give me the sat phone, I can call them."

Marcus ignored her. "Who else?"

"David. I need to let him know. . . ." She cleared her throat. "You understand I won't be taking the position at Banff SAR now."

Her fingers shook, and he reached out to squeeze them. "I think you should talk to him before resigning, but let's put it on the page for now."

When she didn't argue, he breathed a sigh of relief. As far as he was concerned, David would be crazy to let her go, but he had to leave that decision up to his brother. He'd go along with the façade of pretending to agree with her on that one so they could keep talking. "What next? What are you thinking of doing for work, then?"

"Not sure." She picked at a gouge in the tabletop. "Nothing in SAR, that's for sure. I'll probably head home to the farm for a while. Doubt the media will want to make the trek into rural Saskatchewan, and if they do, my dad's got No Trespassing signs posted far enough back that I can at least be useful doing chores until the interest dies away."

Dammit. Her willingness to give up and move on so quickly pissed him off. Maybe being gentle wasn't the way to go. Honest. He'd promised to be honest, and here was his chance.

"You could do that. Or we could deal with the media, expect them to go away in a short while, and if David doesn't think your staying on at Banff SAR works, you can come and work for me."

Her sudden intake of breath and white face made him reach out to steady her, afraid she was going to collapse to the floor.

Words snapped out of her like a whip. "Are you *nuts*?"

"No."

"You *are*." She leapt to her feet and paced away, dragging her hands through her hair before twirling on him. "If I can't work at the school, how could it possibly be a good idea to join your team? No one will want me involved in rescues. No one will trust me."

"You're leaping to a lot of conclusions, but we'll cross them as they arrive. Don't you want to work in the mountaineering world anymore?"

"Stop this." She wrapped her arms around her. "Stop tormenting me with possibilities that are no longer within my reach."

It took everything he had not to rise and hold her again. But she needed to accept what he was saying. Needed to believe him.

"Answer the damn question, Becki."

"Yes," she shouted, utter despair on her face. "Yes, I want to work in the mountains. I want to climb and fly rescues. I want to experience the thrill and the adrenaline rush. I want to make a difference, and I can't. Don't you see? I can't do any of that anymore because it's—"

Her voice broke and her knees gave way. He was barely in time to catch her, holding her with his body as he guided her to the couch.

Becki attempted to shake off his help, but he held on. "Stop fighting me," he snapped. "Listen. For one goddamn time in your life, listen first. If I have to tie you up to make you stay put, I swear I will."

He sat her down and knelt in front of her again, catching hold of her chin in his fingers. Forcing her to look at him. She wasn't seeing the big picture, so he'd push her in the right direction until she came back to her senses. "This is not the end of your career in the mountains, and you're being ridiculous if you think it is. Yes, some people will avoid you. Yes, some people will say cruel and cutting things. Fuck them. Fuck them all."

Misery still stared back, but at least she was listening.

"Wouldn't that be your comment if years ago someone

had said you couldn't be on a squad because you were a woman? If you overheard someone taunting that there was no way a petite woman like Alisha could possibly be lead hand on an elite SAR team? You've always done what you've thought was right. You've let your actions show what you're capable of—let your skills prove that you're competent and strong. Since when have you cared what other people think when what *you* know—"

She held up a hand to interrupt, head shaking slightly as she blinked back tears. "But Marcus . . . what I *know* is I did it. That's what's killing me. That's what makes it impossible to join a team. Because when someone doubted me before, yeah, I did toss their opinion out the window. I knew I was qualified. Now? If someone looks at me and doubts? I can't throw it off. I can't say *fuck them* because . . . they could be right."

Her words had dropped to a whisper, but she kept going. Maintained eye contact as if willing him to understand.

Even in the middle of her confusion and sadness, she had no idea how strong she was. Something inside Marcus turned and settled. She would get past this, and he'd do anything to make sure she got that chance.

"Then take a hiatus until you feel you're back to speed. Train. Work in positions that build that trust again. I'm willing to take you on, Becki. I know it's not as glamorous a position, working the call centre, but your skills would be useful there. Don't give it all up when you don't have to."

Becki forced herself to look away and stare at the wall behind his shoulder, slowing her breathing. What he'd suggested made her ache—she wanted it so badly, but it wouldn't be right.

How could she deliberately allow her now-tarnished reputation to destroy what he'd worked so hard to build? She wouldn't dream of causing trouble to even a casual co-worker, let alone a compatriot she respected.

She definitely couldn't do it to the man she loved.

"I don't want to leave, but I can't stay. I can't ask you and Lifeline to make that kind of sacrifice for me."

Marcus caught her hand. "You've trusted me over the past couple of weeks. You put yourself into my hands on the wall and in my bed. Has that stopped? Do you not think you can depend on me anymore?"

Another shock raced through her as she shook her head in denial. "I trust you, but I don't see how that matters. My having faith in you doesn't change the facts."

"It matters because I don't think you need to leave, and if you trust me, you'll let me find a way to help you get through this temporary situation."

She collapsed into the cushions a little harder. It was useless. He wasn't giving up the fight, and she couldn't understand why he was being so stubborn. "And here's where we go back to fighting, because I doubt what I've got is a short-term issue."

"You're blinded by emotion right now. The situation will change. Don't leave me when a little time—"

He snapped to a stop.

The buzzing in her ears made her doubt she'd heard him correctly, but his shocked expression was a dead giveaway. Was that why he'd come away with her in the first place—the reason he'd refused to share? Was it possible he'd actually come to care for her as well?

"Marcus?"

He took a deep breath as he lifted her knuckles to his lips. "Don't leave *me*."

Her throat tightened and her heart raced, this time with a strange mixture of hope and lingering sadness. "I don't want to leave, either," she confessed.

"Then don't." He made it sound so simple. "I want you around. I want you in my house, and down at the gym, shouting at me to train harder. I want you working with my team, however you and they feel comfortable, because I'm one hundred percent sure there's a place for you."

Having a total change in her circumstances seemed

impossible. Becki stared at his eyes. Anchoring herself in what she saw there. It was the best of both worlds, if she was willing to take the chance.

Loud ringing tore them both from the moment, the metallic sound echoing strangely in the rustic setting.

"Sat phone." He rushed to the case that held it, snapped open the lid, and pulled it free. He lifted it to his ear.

"Marcus Landers." He frowned, and her stomach fell.

She wasn't ready to deal with a reporter yet. Becki wished she could crawl back into bed and hide for a while. The only thing keeping her from running in terror was the knowledge that Marcus wouldn't force her to handle this alone.

But he wasn't slamming down the receiver, either, which was what she'd have expected if it were something she could ignore. She stepped closer, a familiar masculine voice carrying over the line.

There was another short burst of words. Even at a distance she heard the fear. Marcus responded soothingly. "Hang on. She's right here. You're going to be fine. Just talk to Becki, and we'll come as quick as we can."

Marcus held out the phone. "It's your brother. He's in trouble."

CHAPTER 33

''''''''''''''''''''''''''''''''''

Her brother?

Becki snatched the phone from Marcus. "Colin?"

A slight static buzz echoed over the line. "Bec. I need help. I called Mr. Landers from the school and he put me through to you. He's sending a team to pick you up. We're trapped, and Rob's hurt."

Confusion rushed her. Last she'd heard, her brother was back home in Saskatchewan. "Where are you? Why are you calling me?"

"It was a surprise—I'm coming to SAR school this summer. My buddy and I figured we'd get in a climb before we have to settle in. It wasn't supposed to be a big deal, just a lark, but it's socked in so hard I can't see a thing. Rob slipped and fell—I think his leg is broken."

The confusion was still there, but Becki pulled herself back into routine. Somewhere in the background Marcus was moving, but all her focus was on the phone call and what they needed here and now. "Colin, I need you to give me short answers. Are you hurt?"

"No. Rob is."

"Where are you?" How he'd tracked her down didn't matter at this point.

"In the Needles. I told Mr. Landers that, and I gave him our GPS location. You brought me here, remember? The summer after you graduated?"

Oh God. That area was fabulous on a clear day, a hellish maze when the weather turned. Becki swallowed her fears, strode to the door, and jerked it open. Here in the cabin they were above the clouds, the peaks opposite them clearly visible, but everything below them was shrouded in thick cloud cover. It must have crept in over the past hour.

"Is Rob okay?"

"I made him as comfortable as I can, but I don't want to move him too much. We're on a narrow lip, Bec. He was heading out on second lead and slipped before he set his first anchor."

"Enough. Is your platform solid?"

He hesitated, and her heart tightened. "I think so."

If David was sending the chopper, the soonest it could arrive at the cabin was thirty minutes. Adding travel time to the drop site, and hiking in? "Colin, you've got at least a two-hour wait for us to come get you."

She didn't even mention the trouble they might have finding the boys. In the distance the wind stirred the clouds like some witches' brew and she shivered, terror creeping up her spine.

"We'll wait. Anything else I should do?"

Becki wanted to tell him something to reassure him, but she was losing control. Standard rescue responses—those she could do. Thinking this was her kid brother buried in the fog on the side of a mountain? That was enough to make her nauseated.

Focus on facts. "Set a couple of anchors. Rope both you and Rob up tight."

"I can try to lower him—"

"No," she shouted. *Oh my God, no.* She forced herself to dial her panic down a notch. "Don't try to climb up or down, just tie yourself to the rock right where you are. Got it?"

"Okay."

"Promise me."

"I promise. Becki? Thank you." All his usual cocky arrogance had vanished.

Sheer panic loomed, but she didn't let any of it sound in her voice. "You're so much trouble, brat. Now give me your number, then stay off the line. We'll call you when we get close enough that you can guide us in."

She hung up the phone and twirled to face Marcus. "How much did you catch?"

"Your brother is lost somewhere in the Palliser Range and David's contacted my team. They're on their way here."

Becki swallowed hard. "Erin won't be able to fly them directly to the site, not with these conditions. How well does the squad know the Needles?"

"Shit." He obviously knew the issues with the area, as his face tightened with concern. "Some. Not that well."

Family rescuing family was a recipe for disaster at the best of times, and this was far from an ideal situation. "Then I'm going to have to lead them in."

The minute the phone had gone off, Marcus had snapped into prepared mode. No one that keen to get in touch with them could possibly have a good reason. Out of all the possible people who could have phoned, though, her brother wasn't even on the radar. Now they had a situation going from bad to worse fast.

Because she was right. If she knew the climbing area, she had to go along—a guide would get his team there as quickly as possible. They could do the rescue without her, but if one of the climbers was hurt, time counted.

He stopped her for a moment, though, hand resting on her shoulder. "You can do this. I know you can."

Her face was still far paler than it should be, but she nodded. "I have no choice."

"Get dressed. I'll contact the team and check their ETA. Did you bring your harness?"

"Full gear. We were going to train, remember?" Becki glanced out the window, and her entire body quaked. "What if . . ."

"No 'what if.' You will do this. You are capable," Marcus insisted.

She shook her head. "I don't care if I get sick in the chopper. What if I freeze, though? What if I black out and end up doing something that endangers my brother, or your team?" Becki caught him by the arms, her fingers going white as she clutched him tight. "Please. Come with me. I . . . I need you."

As if he had ever intended to do anything else. Marcus dragged her against him and hugged her tightly. "I'll be there."

They met for a brief, desperate kiss before splitting apart and heading into their separate preparations. Marcus pulled on his prosthesis, going for the claw end—chances were the first thing they'd be doing would be going down, not up.

Fifteen minutes and he was dressed, call through to his team.

Erin answered. "Roger base. You ready for a splash and dash?"

"As ready as we can be. Who's on board?"

"Nearly full crew. We're missing Tripp."

Winch and paramedic, though, two less things to worry about. "What's the airspace look like on the satellite?"

"Choices are a kilometer up or three more on level. We'll do a flyby, but that's my best guess."

Becki was back at his side, pulling her coat over her long-sleeved shirt. Marcus flipped the phone to speaker. "Becki and I are on the line—we'll wait for pickup and discuss the rest on approach. Any questions right now?"

"It's Devon. No questions, but hey, Becki? It'll be okay. I met your bro a couple of nights ago. He's a great kid. Good head on his shoulders. We'll get him out."

She had her fingers over her mouth, nodding slowly as she pulled them away. "Thanks for that. Over and out."

The radio went silent and she blinked hard, reaching for

her pack that lay on the floor. Silently, as a team they gathered the rest of their things from the truck before walking a few meters down the road to the clearing in the trees. They turned to face the mountains.

He grabbed her hand with his. She didn't change her focus, but she held on, wrapping her fingers around his tightly.

"Give me the rundown," Becki breathed out slowly. "I'll have to lead on the ground once we hit the maze, but keep your team consistent until then."

"I'm along for the ride. I won't be in charge. Anders calls the shots in the bay." A faint rumble in the air warned that the chopper was approaching. "We'll see who's calling ground when we crawl in. Tripp usually does, and since he's not there, it's a potshot. They're all qualified."

"They're the best," she stated firmly.

"They are, and so are you."

She nodded, concentration focused forward.

Time slipped into that eerie blend between going far too quick and far too slow that was so common during a rescue.

The chopper was down, wind batting them as they ran with heads lowered across the field to the door. Hands reached to pull them in, Becki first, Marcus caught up behind. Both of them settled into the nearest seats. They hadn't even buckled in before Erin lifted off.

Becki fought with the top snap, all her concentration on the webbing. Ignoring the air passing the windows as the helicopter tilted, Erin pivoted tight to head over the Kananaskis Range into the second ridge of mountains and their destination.

Marcus checked his team. Alert faces stared back, waiting in expectation. He tugged on his headset, then paused until Becki had done the same.

"Good job. Ready for this?"

Four heads nodded. Becki's jaw was locked firmly shut as she stared at the floor. He ignored her for the moment. Everyone's coping strategies were different, and he wasn't about to tell her to try something new. Not when she was clinging to her control.

Devon clicked on. "Erin said she'd fly by the Needles, but with the cloud cover, chances are we'll be coming in from the north or the east. I vote for the north—it's a shorter land approach, only it calls for a long rappel to the trails. Becki, any idea where in the maze they might be?"

"If they went to where I brought Colin before, yes. About twenty minutes from the entrance to the canyon. Three short climbs—none more technical than a 5.7—will get us to the main wall."

"We can do those in our sleep," Xavier offered. "I want to know which way we're coming out. Any way to send someone on a climb and get a drop line from Erin to avoid the long haul with a stretcher?"

Becki shook her head, then squeezed her eyes shut as the chopper wiggled in the changing air currents. Marcus held his breath for her, but she managed to pull herself back under control. "In and out, the only possibility unless the clouds clear."

Marcus cut in. "Colin's got a phone. We can call him as we get into the canyon to get him making noise. He'll have a whistle or something, right, Becki?"

"If he doesn't, I'm going to kick his ass once we find it."

Grins appeared around him, tension settling into that peak range for an operation. Too much adrenaline and things went to hell fast. It was impossible to maintain a high for hours, especially when they needed to do the actual grunt work to get in and out.

Marcus checked his team one by one as the buzz over the headset went back to random discussion, just keeping loose as they moved closer to the drop point. He saved Becki for the last, even though he was completely aware of her the entire time.

She was staring past him wearing a do-or-die expression. Her lips moved, only he missed the words. He switched to channel two and her voice cut in.

". . . trust your team. Give one hundred percent. Be patient until it's time to move, then move decisively. Trust your team. . . ."

She was repeating it like a mantra.

He nodded and flipped his speaker on. "One hundred percent. Give it all you've got and even a little more."

Her focus changed off the wall and onto his face, and a tentative smile appeared. Her expression was still serious, still scared, but there was something extra she gave just for him. "Thank you. For everything."

They were surrounded by his team, dropping toward a rescue, and all he could think about was her. "Together. We'll do it together."

What he wanted to say was he never intended to let her go.

CHAPTER 34

A trickle of sweat ran between her breasts as Becki strode after Devon. The weight of the emergency supplies on her back was familiar, and the burn of lactic acid in her thighs as well. They'd already dropped into the clouds, and the trail was visible for maybe twenty feet before the thick grey masked everything from them.

Gear rattled behind her—probably Xavier and Anders with the portable stretcher. Ropes and carabiners clicked softly, the occasional heavier gasp for a breath. No one wasted energy talking right now. As socked in as they were, the path forward remained amazingly clear. Well worn, although most people who traveled this section were on their way upward before returning in a loop to their base camps.

Becki focused on her feet as she tried to avoid the wettest sections. She stepped over fallen limbs and the occasional lingering snowdrift. They were at a low enough elevation that the trail was down to mud and rotting leaves instead of the thigh-deep frozen mess they could have been slogging through.

What was Colin thinking, going for a climb so early in the season? Reckless, impulsive, stupid fool.

Kind of like you at that age, her mental voice taunted.

Still, planning to give her brother hell was a good distraction from the next challenge on the way there. The last time she'd been on a rope without freaking, she'd been blindfolded, letting Marcus talk her through the climb. Wasn't going to happen this time. This time she was on her own.

Only she wasn't. . . .

Marcus walked behind her. Far enough to avoid the branches that snapped back at him when she brushed past, close enough she knew he was there. Felt his presence. It comforted her in a way that might have bothered her if she didn't know he wanted only the best for her.

He'd said she was strong, and she was. She'd find the power needed to rescue Colin. When they got this mess of a day done with, she'd be strong for herself and face the media, and whatever else waited ahead.

And then she'd be strong enough to take Marcus up on his offer and see what they could build together. Doors might have closed, but the one that had opened seemed better than what she'd had before.

Devon held up his hand to signal a stop, slipping his pack off and reaching for a rope. "Gear up here. Anders, set your anchor. We'll drop one at a time."

The team gathered around, everyone moving with the skill of familiar experience. Becki avoided looking at the edge of the cliff only a few paces away to their right. Instead, she focused on the ropes being looped into a triangle at the base of the two nearest trees.

A hand touched her arm and she snapped her head up to discover Devon checking her over carefully.

He cleared his throat. "I might not be the most eloquent on the team, so if I say this wrong, take it the positive way I intend. We need you to lead once we hit the Needles. There's a chance you could freeze on this descent, and I want to avoid that. You need to be at one hundred percent at the canyon. There's no reason for you to do this drop alone. In fact, it's better if you don't, so I want to harness you to Anders. That way you don't have to look, you don't have to worry. Save your strength for when we need you on the next section."

She'd expected this idea to come up, only it was nice how he focused on what she could do for the team more than the fact that someone had to babysit her right now. "Damn, you're good."

Devon tossed her a grin.

Becki nodded. "I get it. Well advised. Only may I request one change?" Devon was already moving away, and she hated to be demanding things like a rookie, but even the sight of the ropes being prepped made her skin crawl.

Devon paused. "What's up?"

"I've done something like this before with Marcus." Marcus stood at the sound of his name, and she tilted her head toward him. "I know I can deal with the descent if he's my guide. Request to change partners."

"I should have thought of that." Devon called and waited for Marcus to join them before continuing. "Your decision, Marcus. Either you or Anders guides Becki. Whoever it is, she's going down third. Get ready."

She turned and found him standing there. The tall muscular length of him, addictive smile and all the rest. "You want me to anchor you?" he asked.

"I want you."

That was all she said, and yet it was everything.

It was like a flashback to being in the cabin before all this started, Marcus's expression a repeat of the one that had returned her hope. Connection, companionship. Understanding.

Maybe more.

The area became a flurry of activity. Ropes. Carabiners buckled and locked, packs in position. Alisha disappeared over the edge. Devon.

Then it was their turn, hers and Marcus's, Xavier holding their backup.

Marcus leaned away and, using the rope as a counterbalance, walked off the ledge. Becki stepped closer, trying desperately to stay vertical, but it was a useless attempt. Instead, she went to her knees and rotated until her butt hit the ground. Only then could she force herself to crawl backward off the flat surface of the mountaintop until she was nestled into his arms.

The thick fog masked just how far up they were, but the memories of climbing the ridge years ago told her all she needed to know. It was far.

It was far enough to kill them if anything went wrong.

"How are you doing?" Marcus asked.

Speaking and breathing at the same time shouldn't be this difficult. "I'll be fine."

"Ready?"

"Lower."

Marcus tucked his left arm around her, his right on the main line. She had her own rope to cling to as well, and the twisted fibers pulled through her fingertips, the harshness a blessing. The rough texture gave her something else to focus on as they descended the cliff face.

"Still good?" His breath fanned past her cheek, and she nodded. She was surrounded by him, but the rope setup allowed her to control herself, or at least gave the illusion of control.

Damn her breathing, though. She couldn't get it to calm down. "I'm not going to lie. If the angle changes and we end up dangling in midair, you'll have me in your lap for real."

Marcus chuckled. "As if I'd mind."

So normal, all their responses. Teasing about their attraction, laughing and panting with effort. Her brother was still out there, but if she could get past this point, past her heart in her throat, she could be ready to lead the team to him.

She had to trust that Colin would be in one piece when they arrived.

One foot caught on a rock. Becki stumbled, biting back a scream.

"Don't rush," Marcus warned. "We'll get down soon enough. Once we're on the trail again you can go as fast as you want, well, as long as we can keep up."

"My nerves are on edge. He's going to be okay, isn't he?"

"He's going to be fine," Marcus assured her. "Bonus? He'll get razzed all summer for being the first of the class that needed rescuing. I thought getting into trouble didn't start until they'd officially checked in."

"Colin always was precocious."

"He's following after his sister," Marcus teased. He squeezed her. "I mean it, I'm sure he's fine. You warned him to stay put. We need you to find him for us. I'll call him once we hit the canyon opening. It'll all work out."

Distraction. The entire conversation was nothing but distraction, but the diversion of the banter worked. The cliff wall in front of them passed by steadily as they walked their way down it. Ropes above fed smoothly. Marcus's warmth cradled her. "I feel stupid saying thank you so much, but it's needed. You've been a rock."

"That's not always a good thing," he pointed out. "But I get it. You're welcome. A little more and we're done. That wasn't so bad, was it?"

"I'm too freaked out over Colin to be worried about me," Becki admitted. "Although I don't know that I suggest this as a cure for everyone's acrophobia."

They finally hit bottom, and Becki's stomach unknotted from the tight ball it had formed while they'd descended. They stepped out of the way, but when Becki would have headed to prepare for the next part of the rescue, Marcus stopped her. Pulled her to him and crushed their lips together.

She kissed him back frantically. Feeling alive, feeling everything that they had between them in that moment. She trusted him with her life. With her brother's life. All the stolen moments up to now faded her fears.

She just needed him.

Someone wolf-whistled, and they separated reluctantly, Marcus cupping her face before he set her free. "You did wonderfully. You are an amazing woman."

Becki grinned back. "You help. You help so much."

"I can see why it's not good to date people on your squad.

Enough with the kissing business." Alisha pushed Becki away from Marcus. "And you." She gave him a dirty look. "You should know better. Focus."

"I was focusing," Marcus stated. "But yes, full steam ahead."

Alisha smiled at Becki as she handed over a pack. "Come on, let's go get your brother."

The entrance to the canyon stood like twin sentinels before her. The twisted myriad of paths beyond the gateway stretched gnarled fingers toward the sharp cliffs that should have been visible in the not-too-far distance. Becki didn't pause to admire the towering pillars, their heads hidden in the fog, just headed straight in, determined to find Colin as quickly as possible.

They were trails she hadn't seen for years, but the familiarity was there. Scrambling over sections where flash floods or new growth had changed the course was far simpler than she'd expected. Grey and washed out, the scenery gave her nothing to admire as she raced them all forward. Ten minutes brought them to another junction, and she chose the left path without a qualm.

"Becki, this trail backtracks," Devon pointed out.

"It's the right route," she insisted. "Trust me."

Saying the words made her heart quiver. What if she was wrong? What if she made a mistake and her brother was the one who would pay this time?

The vision of the cut rope in her fingers danced in front of her eyes, the strands rapidly unraveling, no longer a life-saving device, but one that stole life away.

She stepped faster, thighs burning as she pushed herself into a run in spite of the weight on her back. Ten more minutes. Five. There was no use in stopping before they'd gotten close enough to the rock face to hear a response.

When she finally figured they had to be near the cliffs even though the sky was no more visible than before, Becki pulled to a halt and waited for the team to catch up.

Devon leaned on a tree. Alisha paced slowly, hands on her hips as her chest moved rapidly. Anders dropped to one knee and shook his head as he gasped for breath. "Holy. Shit. You want to go a little faster next time, Becki? I don't need my lungs."

"Blistering. Pace. Awesome," Alisha managed to pant.

Marcus pulled out the satellite phone and put through the call.

"Colin. Still good?" Marcus made eye connection with her and nodded. "Right on. Okay, we're ready for you to signal us. Single blast to start."

He pulled the phone away from his ear at the same moment the shrill cry of a whistle rang from high and off to their left

Becki had to squat, her head between her knees to stop the spinning relief from knocking her completely to her back. *Thank God.*

"We're close," Alisha said, staring into the clouds.

Devon nodded. "Spread out in a line. Marcus, get him to signal again. Everyone raise your arm high for me and point. Let's see if we can use triangulation to narrow our choices."

The team moved into position smoothly, no questions, no hesitation.

"Colin, we heard you." The calmness in Marcus's voice as he spoke to her brother spread over Becki like balm. They were getting close, and everything was going to be okay. That was what his mannerisms said, that was what she'd believe. She closed her eyes to block out distractions, and when the next shrill whistle rang in response to Marcus's command, she pointed.

While she waited, she focused on her hand, bringing the tremor in her fingers under control. They were nearly there. Nearly there.

The thought echoed like a drumbeat.

Devon gave a shout. "Hold. One minute . . . and got it. Compass reading set for now. Marcus, have him signal every sixty count if he's able." Devon turned to the rest of the team and pointed. "Alisha, Xavier. You'll be climbing when we get there. Set back a little if you want, slow your heart rates. We'll get the gear in place for you. Just don't lose sight of us in the fog, got it?"

The two of them nodded, Alisha sipping from her water bottle, Xavier stooped over, hands resting on his knees as he caught his breath.

Becki stretched her legs and got herself ready for the final sprint. Marcus stepped beside her, and she checked him over in a glance, making sure he was okay.

She laughed when she realized he was doing the same thing in return.

His gaze snapped to hers. "Ready to go again?"

Becki nodded.

This was when the team walked the fine line between being primed or falling over the limit into enough adrenaline to make them crash. The hard labour of the run helped as Becki followed Devon this time. He had his compass out, all of them alert for the steady stream of whistles drawing them closer to the wall.

Suddenly they were there, the base of the cliffs appearing out of the grey like a curtain being pulled aside at a theater.

"Colin," Becki shouted.

Instant response. "Yes. God, you guys are fast."

Devon and Marcus had their packs off, ropes being arranged in loops, helmets snapped into position.

"You ordered the best," Becki answered. That was as much as she could get out before her throat closed.

Nearly there. Nearly safe. She removed her pack and placed it with the others, the sweat on her back cooling in the lower temperatures.

"Colin, I've got a climber coming up. How's Rob?" Devon asked.

"Stable."

"I hope you guys brought beer with you. I'm thirsty," a second voice joined in, far softer than Colin's robust shouts.

"Beer is for wimps. Xavier's got way better stuff once we get you in position." Devon motioned Alisha forward. She was into her harness and rigged in less than a minute.

"Tell us about your platform. Room for more up there, or cozy?"

"Cozy. I'll need to get out of the way for anyone else to visit Rob."

"Got it. Stay put for now, okay?" Devon ordered.

Becki tipped her head back and still couldn't see a thing much higher than she could reach. Marcus joined her, and she slipped her fingers into his hand. She didn't care who saw the motion. "How far up are they?" she asked.

"Far enough, I'd imagine. Guessing fifty feet from his volume."

She nodded. "That's about the right height for a second lead to start."

Marcus twisted her until he could stare into her face. "You did incredibly back there. Never a moment's hesitation. You were what got us here so fast."

"It's a relief to be done. I want Colin on his feet where I can hug him."

"Will I do for now?" Marcus asked, and she slipped into his embrace, turning to face the wall. Leaning back against his body and accepting his support. "I'm very glad I'm not going up this time, though." Alisha stepped to the rocks and began her ascent. It took an incredibly short time before the young woman had disappeared into the clouds, Devon working her safety line. "Damn, she is good."

"I don't often get to observe the team in action like this," Marcus said. "I'm back at base, or in the chopper. I'm proud of them—they've got the teamwork part down damn well."

"And the rest of your rules."

Xavier waited for his turn, assembling supplies and working efficiently with Anders. Devon had a steady stream of banter going back and forth between him and Alisha, the dialogue vital now that she was invisible to them.

Becki rested her head on Marcus's chest and worked to slow her breathing. There was nothing they could do at this point but wait.

Waiting. Story of her life lately.

"Take," Alisha ordered.

Devon responded, securing the rope as somewhere above them in the unseen grey, Alisha reached the ledge.

"Try not to hold your breath," Marcus warned. "You want to be able to hug your brother when he gets down, not be sitting on your backside with your head between your knees."

"Bastard," Becki muttered.

Marcus chuckled and adjusted her position, wrapping his arm around her until his mouth was directly by her ear. "This is what you were made to do. Nothing is going to stop you, understand? You will not have to give up doing rescues. Trust me."

His complete and utter conviction cocooned her and gave her the strength to wait as she peered upward and waited for Colin to appear.

CHAPTER 35

''''''''''''''''''''''''''''''''''

It was something Marcus thought he'd never get used to—a person suddenly appearing out of nowhere, parting the clouds. Colin twisted into sight, lowered on a fixed rope. Marcus intended to stay aside, out of the way of his team and the reunion about to take place. Becki had different ideas as she dragged him with her as she rushed forward, only letting his hand free when her brother's feet hit the ground.

"You stupid, stupid, stupid fool." Becki nearly leapt on Colin in her need to make sure he was okay. "I have no idea why you thought climbing out of season was a good idea."

Marcus grinned as Colin glanced around sheepishly, accepting his sister's clutch and her condemnation. "Well. The mountain was there. It had to be climbed, you know?"

"Sorry to intrude. I need your rope, dude." Xavier shouldered between the siblings without a qualm to work the safety knot from Colin's belt. "So, until hell broke loose, was it a good climb?"

"Awesome." Colin grinned, streaks of dirt and blood on his face, the hours of waiting in the cold forgotten. "I can't wait to come back and do it again. Well, without the Rob-hurting-himself part."

Xavier nodded. "Sounds like a plan. You let Becki look you over for a minute, okay? I think you're all right, though."

Marcus approved of it all as his team slipped easily into action around him. Alisha had dropped another rope from the anchor she'd set on the ledge. Anders worked to attach the stretcher and medical supplies. Devon was already belaying Xavier as he headed up to work his magic on the injured climber.

Becki had taken her brother aside and was assessing him, her training crystal clear in every move. This was what she was meant to do, and if she was willing to work with Marcus's team, he'd feel privileged.

He wasn't going to lie, either, and pretend her skills were the only reason he wanted her.

Becki waved him over, and he responded quickly. "What's up?"

"He's good, as far as I can tell. You have any heating pads in the supplies before I go digging through everything?"

"I don't need to be babied," Colin complained, glaring at his sister. He glanced at Marcus. "Tell her I don't need heating pads."

"You expect me to argue with your sister? Not likely," Marcus said, stepping aside to grab what she'd asked for out of the medic bag.

"She's not that scary," Colin insisted. "And she's a total wimp when it comes to ridge running."

Yeah, this kid was going to be interesting to watch. Marcus caught Becki's eye, doing his own assessment of her now that her brother was safely on the ground. Dark shadows under her eyes, weary body positioning. She was headed for a crash, the adrenaline rush wearing off, leaving room for everything else she'd been dealing with to surface. "Becki, grab some food and drink. You need a sit-down before we head out. I'll take over checking Colin."

"I don't need . . ." She snapped her mouth closed on the

near-mirror complaint to the one her brother had just uttered. After one final scruff of Colin's hair, she scrambled to her feet and marched past Marcus, bumping him with her shoulder and whispering as she went by. "Bastard. I'll get even with you for that one."

He chuckled. "I hope you try."

She stopped unexpectedly, cupping his face tenderly before moving to follow his directions.

Marcus wanted to grab hold of her and squeeze her tight. To pick her up and swing her around in celebration of all the successes she'd had that day. The quiet dignity she showed, though, was exactly right. Totally Becki.

Whatever life was going be like in the coming days, it was never going to be boring.

Becki found a spot to the side where she could lean on a rock, see everything and not be underfoot. The granola bar and drink she'd grabbed did help—Marcus had been right.

The setting remained otherworldly, people at the edges of the working space shifting in and out of her vision as the clouds rolled through. Sometimes higher, sometimes lower. A thick layer of condensation coated everything.

She tugged her jacket tighter against the cold. Colin moved to the right a couple of steps and vanished, and her heart jolted until she realized he was fine, just hidden in the mist.

The stretcher came into view, and she rose to her feet as Marcus rushed forward to help Devon guide the solid platform. The tired and pain-filled face of a young man barely out of his teens appeared as the flat surface lowered to the ground.

"You enjoy your roller-coaster ride?" Marcus asked.

Rob nodded. "You guys are like angels."

A snort escaped Marcus. "Well, that's a new one. I'm usually called the opposite."

"Relax, Rob. We've got a ways to go, but you shouldn't have to spend the night on the mountain." Devon squatted beside the stretcher, adjusting straps.

"Thanks to Colin. He was awesome." Rob's words slurred as he closed his eyes. "I thought I was fucked. Of course, the mountains wouldn't be a bad place to die. I wouldn't mind it, you know, being buried here, but not for another eighty years or so. . . ."

Xavier landed beside them, unknotting and moving back into position to check Rob. "You aren't dead, you aren't dying. Please, my artistry is so underrated."

He glanced at Becki and winked, lowering his voice. "He'll be either out in a few minutes or singing to the forest elves. I gave him a painkiller to take the edge off."

Becki nodded, stepping away as Anders and Xavier relocated the stretcher to the side of the clearing to rig a carrying system. She swayed, the euphoria of having made it this far making her light-headed.

Marcus brushed her cheek with his fingers. "I'm going to gather gear with Alisha and Devon. We'll be heading out in less than ten. Take a rest. You did great."

She smiled and nodded, but there was something not quite right with her legs as she returned to her place against the wall. The torn-up sections of her palms burned, and her fingertips were cold, so she sat and tucked her hands under her arms.

. . . wouldn't be a bad place to die.

Rob's words echoed in her head. Becki's heart gave a giant thump, and she jerked upright, searching the scene frantically. Anders and Xavier were barely visible now, hidden by the trees. The only thing visible in that direction looked like a body lying flat out on its back.

. . . the mountains wouldn't be a bad place to die.

Her breathing sped up. Blood rushed to her head. Becki pressed against the rock and fought to stay alert, but a rush of blackness swept over her and everything went dark.

She was nearing the edge. The point of no return. Becki clung to her knife blade even as she scrambled frantically to find a way to avoid sliding toward the cliff.

As suddenly as it started, everything stopped, the heavy weight of Dane's body at the other end of her rope no longer dragging her.

She wanted to scream in delight. To cry and laugh and celebrate that she'd survived. Only there was no way to know exactly why they were no longer moving. If Dane was tangled on an unsteady rock, their reprieve could be short-lived.

She scrambled to set a real anchor, using her hammer to pound in a long screw. She set a quick emergency rope before taking the time to make a bombproof one. Only then did she stop to breathe and rejoice a tiny bit.

"Dane," she shouted. "Can you hear me? We're going to be okay. We made it. I'm coming to get you."

A quick sip of water, a bite of an energy bar to get some strength into her shaking limbs. She sucked back a power gel, set a rappelling rope, and willingly went over the edge that had nearly killed her.

She was strong. It had been the most frightening experience yet in her climbing career, but they'd avoided fate. They were going to make it.

The clouds were still there. The wind, the moisture. A few drops of rain hit, and the idea of a downpour made her happy. It would make things miserably cold, but the cloud patterns would change.

They were going to make it.

Over her right shoulder she spotted him. "Dane, I'm coming."

He didn't move, his body a long line collapsed on the brink of the ledge. The platform was wide enough to be safe, and he was roped to her safety rope, so she wasn't worried about him rolling away before she reached him. Becki down-climbed cautiously, her fingers and arms protesting. She didn't give a damn how much she hurt. They were both alive.

She could put up with a few aches and pains.

Another base. Another anchor. Becki wasn't leaving anything to chance. She rearranged ropes to make sure she *was attached to the wall, Dane still attached to her, before she even moved to his side.*

She stroked Dane's hair from his face. "Hey, wake up. Nap later—it's your turn to carry me."

His eyes fluttered open, and he groaned. Pulled himself up on one elbow. "Crap, I thought I was dead."

"Rock fall." She wouldn't bother to tell him right now what else had nearly happened. That was a story to share over beers in a warm bar once they were completely off the mountain. "How you doing? Any injuries?"

He shook his head. "I'm fine. Fuck. How did that happen?"

She helped him up and stabilized him until he was no longer rocking on his feet. "This all happened because you were supposed to go first. I'm sure of it. Hey, where you going?"

He'd stepped to the edge to peer over. She joined him, a rush of nausea hitting at how close a call they'd had. If the three-foot-wide ledge hadn't been there, the steep cavern at their feet would have been their grave.

"It's so unfair," Dane whispered, turning back to her, staring at the wall behind her as if he weren't seeing anything. "People come out here all the time. To the mountains. They drive past in their cars, and they point up and say, 'Look how beautiful. I'm so glad we came.'"

Becki caught Dane by the arm, pulling him farther from the cliff edge. He sounded . . . confused. "We do get a better view from here, don't we? Although their cars seldom fall off cliffs."

"It wouldn't be a bad place to die." Dane breathed the words slowly, and Becki's gut tightened.

"Dane? What's wrong?"

He pulled off his helmet and tossed it aside, the streaks of dirt on his cheeks and his tangled hair making him look a little mad. "Nothing. Everything."

Shit. He'd gone into shock. "Come on, I'll make us something warm to drink; then we can—"

"I'm dying, Becki," Dane blurted out. "Some weird-ass

form of muscular dystrophy. A stupid genetic thing that isn't any fault of mine, but it's going to take me away from here. Put me in a car until all I can do is look up and say, 'Oh, aren't they beautiful' from there. Never climb again."

Nothing made sense. "You're dying?"

"Found out when I met my birth mom. Did some tests." He shook his head in frustration. "All my muscles will shrivel up. Until I can't breathe on my own. And it'll happen so slowly, I'll know what I'm losing."

"Oh God, Dane, I'm sorry." Becki caught him against her. The time for talking this through was once they were away from the mountain, but now she understood why he'd been acting strangely.

Dane held her tight, like he was never going to let go. When he finally released her it was to lift his fingers to gently stroke her cheek. "It sucks. Not your fault. You've been great."

"Let's go. Get out of these cold wet things. We'll talk, okay?" Something jerked her waist harness, and she glanced down to discover he'd taken his knife and cut the rope between them. "Dane? Let me untie you. You don't need to cut it."

He shook his head. "I don't want you rescuing me. I will choose where I die. And it won't be in some hospital bed after months or years of not really living."

Oh my God. A flash of understanding hit too late. Becki reached for him to drag him to safety, but he shoved her back violently. She staggered away, fighting to keep her balance.

Dane turned and stepped off the cliff.

Becki screamed.

The world went dark.

CHAPTER 36

''''''''''''''''''''''''''''''''''

Marcus had one rope halfway coiled when he paused. Stood. Glanced around quickly at the team, looking for whatever it was that was sending him warning signals. He turned back to Becki just in time to see her lean hard on the rock behind her, body shaking.

"Shit. Alisha—take over. Becki's in trouble."

His lead hand snatched the rope from him. "Shock?"

"Maybe." He was across to the wall and crouched at Becki's side in a moment, catching hold of her cold fingers with his. "Becki. Come on, what's happening?"

Her eyes were wide but unfocused, as if she were watching a screen he couldn't see.

Screw protocol. Marcus dropped to the ground beside her and scooped her into his arms, cradling her from the cold and protecting her from the rock. "Come on, Becki. Come back to me. You're okay, the rescue is going great. You made it this far. You're going to make it all the way."

She dragged in a shuddering breath and snapped her

hands free, arms jerking outward as if grabbing for something.

"Hush, come on." Marcus kicked his own ass. He should have been prepared for this possibility. Should have been there to stop her from going it alone. He put his lips next to her ear and spoke softly, rocking her carefully. "You're the strongest woman I know. Brave, committed. Talented. Damn, I have no idea why you were willing to put up with an ass like me, but I'm so glad you did. Now you need to come back to me, sweet Becki. You need to give me hell a few more times."

Her hands moved until her fingers clutched the fabric of his jacket. She gasped, then buried her face against his chest. "Oh God, no . . ."

The utter misery in her cry tore him apart.

A hand touched his shoulder, Xavier leaning in close. "Boss, you need help?"

As if the unfamiliar voice were a trigger, Becki's head snapped up, her green eyes sparkling bright with the tears that filled them. "Marcus—oh God, Marcus, I know. I know it all."

"What do you know, sweet Becki?" And more important, was she aware of what was going on, or did she need medical care herself? "Are you here with me again? Tell me where we are."

She sucked in a huge breath of air, shakily letting it escape as a tear trickled down her cheek. "We're in the Needles. We rescued Colin and Rob. We need to get them out for medical attention. I know where we are."

Marcus glanced at Xavier. "Gear up. We'll be okay."

"Three minutes to exit, if you can be ready," Xavier warned.

Becki responded before Marcus could. "I'm good. Sorry for making trouble. We'll be ready."

"Hell, you're not trouble," Xavier insisted. "FYI, clouds are clearing a little."

The paramedic left them, and Marcus lifted her chin so he could stare into her eyes. "What happened?"

"I think the rescue prompted it. The final missing part."
She sighed and shook her head. "But we have two minutes
and a rescue to finish. I'll tell you the rest at home."

Goddamn. "Becki . . ."

"Give one hundred percent, Marcus. We're not done."
She ran her hands up his arms until she could wrap around
his shoulders and squeeze him with her strong grip. "It looks
as if you were having to babysit me."

"I'll do it again in a minute." He was going to go crazy
on the hike out, not knowing the details, but she was right.
They weren't out of the mountains. Still, there was something he had to tell her before they went anywhere. Before
she told him anything, because whatever she said, he'd made
a decision.

The past few hours had only strengthened his resolve. It
wasn't a case anymore of wanting the best for her. That was
a priority, but it wasn't the only thing. No matter what it
took, he wasn't going to let her leave him behind.

He pulled them upright, keeping her in his arms for a
moment, his fingers skimming over her cheek until his palm
cradled the back of her head. He pressed their lips together
and kissed her. Gentle in pressure, but as possessively as he
knew how. A brand of ownership—only in reverse.

A declaration that he was totally hers.

There was a question in her eyes as he pulled away, and
he paused to rub his thumb lightly over her bottom lip. "I've
got your back," he promised.

Becki tilted her head to the side, wonder still on her face.
"One minute to get ready," she warned.

"We're ready." For anything. Convincing her of that was
now his number one objective. No matter what her memories
had brought, they were going to go forward together.

The trip out passed in a blur. The trail, the headwall. Marcus
never more than a pace away from her, his presence comforting, reassuring.

There wasn't as much to distract her on the outward journey. Colin walked in front with Devon, or Alisha, listening to school stories from them. Xavier and Anders carried the stretcher, the entire team moving smoothly on the steeper sections to ease the awkward object forward.

Even at the headwall there were no hesitations. Alisha and Devon swarmed up the rock and had the stretcher rising into the shrouded air in what seemed to be moments.

Marcus hugged her from behind as they waited their turn. His breath warm by her ear, his hand curled possessively around her hip as he cradled her between his thighs. He hadn't poked to be told what she'd seen, and she appreciated that. It was too big to spit out in a moment, too huge to simply blurt out in one sentence.

Only the truth changed everything. Beckl twisted her head to touch her lips to his cheek, needing to at least let him know that whatever was between them hadn't changed.

What she was going to do next was still up in the air.

A shiver struck as the first fixed rope for their ascent smacked the ground. "I'm so not ready for this," she confessed.

Marcus patted her butt and pushed her forward. "Don't be so hard on yourself. You can't expect to leave the past behind that fast."

Anders held her rope until she clutched it tight, knotting herself in, staring straight ahead and focusing until Marcus moved behind her.

If she closed her eyes for most of the time they were in the air, she figured Marcus wasn't going to blame her.

The final bit of trail vanished under their feet, the chopper dead ahead, Erin hanging out the door to help load the stretcher before giving Devon a fist bump and disappearing back into the cockpit.

Marcus boosted her into the chopper and took the seat next to her, grabbing hold of her fingers as soon as they were both buckled in.

She rested her temple on his shoulder and didn't bother to turn on the headset. She was officially done for the day—someone else could make the decisions from here on.

Only the lift and travel time gave opportunity for the images of Dane to repeat. She struggled against them, choosing instead to go back to the earlier days; to try to remember the moments that she'd thought were out of character for him.

Exhaustion took its toll, and even the memories faded, her eyelids heavy, sleep pulling her under.

CHAPTER 37

,,,,,,,,,,,,,,,,,,,,,,,,,,,,,,,

A brush over her cheek woke her

Everything had gone quiet. Shockingly quiet, with no helicopter or voices. Something soft cradled her head, and she glanced around to discover the familiar walls of Marcus's bedroom. He sat beside her, reaching out to stroke her hair behind her ear and down over her shoulder. "Sleeping Beauty wakes."

Curtains closed, no clue of the time of day. "Did I pass out?"

He shook his head. "Fell asleep. Like a rock. There was no need to wake you, and sleep was the best possible thing."

She rolled slightly and stretched, arms overhead, back arching. Aches and pains in muscles screamed that she'd gone from full out to full stop way too fast. "I won't even be embarrassed. Much. How are Colin and Rob?"

"Rob's in a cast and Colin spent the night at Devon's place. I think they're getting along well."

"It's morning? Wow." Although after crashing, sleeping

around the clock wasn't unexpected. She stared up at him and wondered what to say. "Your truck's at the cabin."

He smiled. "Anders and a friend are picking it up for me." Marcus shifted to his feet and offered his hand to her. "Grab a shower. Get dressed. I'll make you some food, and then we can talk."

The hot water washed away the rest of the cobwebs but didn't help her get any further in making a decision. Becki tiptoed into the living room and spotted him moving easily in the kitchen. Strong body, arms flexing as he worked, and something heated inside.

She didn't want to give him up. That was all she knew.

Slipping beside him, she ducked under his arm and planted herself against his body, wrapped her arms around his waist, and squeezed, her ear resting on his chest.

The steady pulse of his heart soothed her.

"You should eat," Marcus scolded, but he cuddled her in spite of his protests.

"I need to tell you what happened more than I need food."

She was recovered enough that if he'd argued, she would have stomped on his toes before dragging him to the living room.

"I want to know," Marcus confessed. He turned off the burner, then scooped her up as if she were a feather, coming to a stop by the couch.

When he sat and refused to let her out of his lap, Becki smiled. "I can sit by myself."

"I need to hold you."

Her heart skipped a beat. The emphasis had totally been on *need* in that phrase.

She caught his face in her hands. "You were right. I didn't do anything to cause the accident. We could have made it off the mountain in one piece, but Dane chose—"

She drew in a long breath through her nose and fought for control.

He waited for her to continue, his own tiredness and confusion showing in his expression, his concern for her in his touch as he stroked her arm.

"Dane chose to die. When I call the authorities, we'll ask them to check for preexisting medical conditions. Contact his birth mom."

"Who cut the rope?" Marcus asked.

"Dane." Becki shook her head. "It doesn't make sense to me. I don't understand why someone would choose to die before he had to."

"Are you saying he committed suicide?"

She nodded as she fought back the tears she'd refused to cry earlier on the trail. "He was so young. And smart. I just don't understand."

Silence answered. Marcus shifted position so they were still holding each other, but there was enough distance that she could look him squarely in the face. He examined her cautiously, as if checking to ensure she could handle more.

She fell a little more in love.

He cleared his throat and spoke quietly. "When I got hurt—the accident. It should never have happened."

"You were out of the country?" He'd never really told her what he did for work back then.

He paused, only for a moment, then let her have it all. "I worked for whoever hired me. Did a couple of military jobs, but those were few and far between. They like their own people in position, but the word got out in some circles that I could climb anything. So I got calls. Ones on the quiet side. Paramilitary, usually."

This wasn't what she'd expected. "You were military?"

"No. I was—well, anything they needed, except I never carried a gun. I did actual rescues. I snuck into bedrooms. Sometimes they needed recovery of some object, sometimes a door opened and access gained to a restricted part of a building. I'd climb whatever they pointed me at."

"Recovery. This is all sounding very James Bond."

Marcus nodded. "There were a few times I climbed in a tux after leaving a fancy party. Including the day it all went to hell."

Tension curled around him, and she adjusted position to rub his shoulders. She didn't understand, but she didn't want him to stop. "Why are you telling me this now?"

"Because people make choices, Becki. Not always the ones we'd make in the same situation. I slipped out of the party I'd been planted at and climbed the building until I got in an open window. One of the team was waiting for me, and once I'd turned off the alarm system, he joined me.

"Only the place got bombed. Friendly fire—or at least friendly to us. The military reports had said there wasn't supposed to be any action until the next day, and that's why we were in there, gathering information before it all got blown to hell."

Becki shuddered. "The building blew up on you?"

"Parts collapsed. Most of the partygoers survived—the offices were in a different section of the building. Only we got caught, my teammate and I. Trapped under the rubble." Marcus stared at the wall. "My hand was crushed. He got pinned under some concrete, his legs mangled under the mess."

"Oh God, Marcus." She didn't like where this was going. "How long were you there?"

"Four days, but it was enough. We tried everything to get free, and nothing worked. We passed in and out of consciousness at times from the pain. And then—" His nostrils flared as he swallowed hard. "He made a choice, Becki. One that I didn't want to make. He offered to shoot me."

She bolted upright, shocked. "Why the hell would he offer to do that?"

"Because he figured we were going to die, and he wanted to die on his terms. He gave me the same choice."

Her stomach rolled, and she was suddenly glad she hadn't eaten before this conversation.

"I tried. I tried so damn hard to talk him out of it. To persuade him to hang on, that there were options." Marcus closed his eyes, his face tight with sorrow. "In the end I couldn't save him."

"It was wrong. It was the wrong decision."

Marcus nodded, wrapping his hand around the back of her neck and pulling their foreheads together. "It would have been the wrong decision for me. I chose to fight on. To wait and see what else would happen, and deal with the consequences. I knew my arm would probably be gone, but I didn't think giving up my hand meant I should give up my life."

The idea of him not being there tore into her soul. "Marcus, oh God. Your hand doesn't matter. Not one bit."

"It still tears into me. That I couldn't stop him. That's my nightmare—that's what torments me."

She brought their mouths together and kissed him. Needing his touch, the beautiful connection that had built between them to brush away the images in her mind.

Marcus held her tenderly but refused to take the embrace further. He pulled them apart and resorted to stroking her back in the hopes of distracting her. Maybe it hadn't been the right time to share his story, but when would it be right?

"In the end, we all make our own choices, Becki. Dane made his. Right or wrong, we can only go forward." Marcus stilled the urge to curse at Dane, though, for taking his own interests into the forefront and not thinking of what his decision would do to Becki.

If he hated Dane for anything, it was for being selfish and hurting someone he'd said he loved.

Becki nodded. She slid her fingers down his shoulder, finishing by holding his forearm. Her clasp growing stronger by the moment. "So . . . where do we go forward *to*?"

Marcus wanted to shout an answer—that they'd stay together—but she needed to make her own decisions. Only, like *hell* would he give up without a fight.

"You have wide open doors again, Becki. Once the reports come back from medical to confirm what you've remembered, you can do anything. Teach here, go back to SAR in Yellowstone for the fall." She stiffened even as he spoke. Her mouth opened, but no words came out. Whatever was wrong, it was killing him. "Becki?"

She glared, all the softness of the previous moment gone. "You trying to get rid of me?"

Wait. "What?"

"You just told me to go back to Yellowstone. Nice." Becki released him so fast he thought she was going to fall backward off the couch, and he reached out to steady her. "What happened to the offer to work with Lifeline?" she snapped.

"That's still on the table, but—"

"That's not what it sounded like. Seemed like you said I'd go one way, and you go the other? Bullshit."

Maybe he hadn't gotten enough sleep last night, either. "What the hell are you talking about?"

Becki grabbed him by the front of his shirt. "Back in the cabin you said you needed me. How does that work if I go back to Yellowstone, Marcus? What kind of relationship you looking to have when we're miles away from each other?"

Laughter burst out of him unchecked, and her eyes went wide with surprise. He hurried to calm her. "You, woman, are one of the most fascinating people I have met in my entire life. The way you jump to conclusions sets records. Listen to me. I didn't tell you what I was going to do. I asked what *you* wanted to do."

"But—" She snapped her lips together and nodded her head once, her rage dampened. "I'm still too wrapped up in layers to be able to deal with anything but straight-up facts."

"What do you want, sweet Becki?" he soothed, bringing their bodies into contact, the heat between them rising. Her torso relaxed against him as he stroked her back. "Because if you want to work for the school here in Banff, or Lifeline, you can. If you want to go back to Yellowstone like you told Alisha, then you can go. But whatever you decide, I'm not leaving you."

She released the death grip she had on his shirt, instead pressing her palms to his chest. "You'd come to Yellowstone? But the team . . . Lifeline."

"I don't need to be here for the team to continue," Marcus pointed out. "The squad is important to me, but it's not who I am. Not anymore. Other things are far more important. Worth changing my life for."

"Oh, Marcus." Her hands slipped up to clutch his neck.

He lowered his voice, whispering the words. Trying to convince her how serious he was. "I'm going to stick tight until you give up and decide you want me around all the time. The good, and the bad. I want it all." Marcus smiled, loving the way she fit against him. The way she'd fought when she'd thought he was leaving her. "I told you I've been haunted by what I failed to do. Since you've come back into my life, the darkness is fading."

"It wasn't your fault," Becki nodded slowly. "Just like it wasn't mine."

"Our lives, our choices. My choice is I want to be with you. I love you, Ms. James, and no matter where we live, that's not going to change."

Becki stared in shock. Even quietly spoken the words had exploded out of him, and she could barely believe her ears. "You . . . love me?"

"Yes. Does that seem so terrible?"

She shook her head. "I expected it would take tying you to a chair and threatening to do horrible things before you'd admit it."

"Well, I'm not as stubborn as you thought." He brushed a kiss over her lips. Brief, mouths just touching, then away. "I'm waiting. . . ."

Joy bubbled up inside. *He loved her*—there wasn't anything that could have brought this rush of days to a more fitting conclusion. Except teasing him a little, because it felt like the right thing to do.

"Waiting for what?" She batted her lashes.

He rewarded her with a smile, the one that turned her insides to sheer mush. "You want me to tie you to a chair? Wouldn't be a hardship on my part."

This time Becki kissed him. Wet wonderful heat passing between them as she possessively wrapped her arms around him. Hell, wrapped herself around him. When they finally came up for air, contentment rolled off her in waves. "I do love you. And you're what I want—I don't care where we live."

"You'd said Yellowstone was home," Marcus reminded her.

"*You're* home," she insisted.

It was a long way from their beginnings to where they were now. An impulsive girl and adventure seeker, now grown up and tangled in something bigger than she'd ever thought possible.

When he rolled her under him on the couch and convinced her all over again that they belonged together, Becki knew she was right.

This was home.

Turn the page for
book two in the Adrenaline series

HIGH PASSION

Coming from Berkley Books!

Sweat slicked the curve of his biceps as his arms flexed above her. He hung there for a moment, beautifully suspended, before lowering an inch at a time, total control in his every move.

Alisha Bailey licked her suddenly dry lips. She attempted to tear her gaze away, but she'd been mesmerized. Spellbound by the pounding beat of the music surrounding them and the ambience—overwhelmingly masculine, perhaps, but as if she were going to complain. He exhaled, and she breathed with him. Unconsciously their bodies moved in sync.

A lock of his blond hair fell over his forehead, and she was tempted to reach out and push it away. To drag her fingers over his shoulders and caress the ridges of muscle. To tug him closer until he wrapped all that leashed power and passion around her.

A metallic crash rang from their left and broke her fixation on Devon's half-naked body.

Reality set in far too quickly. She was on the treadmill, the belt flying underfoot as she secretly ogled Devon hanging five feet in front of her while he cranked out pull-ups on the horizontal bar.

People interrupted their workouts to eye the bodybuilder who'd lost his grip. Devon dropped lightly to his feet, pulled a towel from the crossbar, and wiped sweat from his face and neck as the weight lifter in question shrugged sheepishly and replaced the plate.

The low-level testosterone hovering in the air of the hard-core gym, a mix of dust and perspiration, made Alisha wrinkle her nose. With every gasp she took, the odor flooded her senses, and those breaths were coming far quicker than usual.

She wanted to blame her accelerated panting on the steep incline of the treadmill and her rate of turnover, but it probably had more to do with the eye candy than she wanted to admit. No matter how annoying Devon Leblanc was, how exasperating he was to work with, the entire aggravating package was a mighty fine one.

Not that she'd ever let him know it. He had a big enough ego as it was. He didn't need her stroking it. As much fun as *stroking* might seem some days.

The machine under her beeped a warning before powering up yet another notch. Alisha focused on keeping her balance at the near all-out-sprint pace. After a full summer of climbing rescues and spending all her spare time off hiking in the Banff area, she was in peak condition. Working to stay that way was now a way of life.

When the treadmill finally shifted to a slower speed she gulped a mouthful of water, forcing herself to finish the run strong. Follow through, all the way. No shortcuts, no sympathy.

As the smallest person in her business, and often the only woman, Alisha didn't allow anyone to cut her slack, especially not herself. That attitude had gotten her through training that had left older and larger men puddles on the floor of the search-and-rescue school. Her work ethic had gotten her to the top of the list by graduation and gotten her an invitation to join the top SAR team in the Canadian Rockies.

Maddening how her gaze automatically darted to Devon, who'd been her only real competition back in the day. The fact that the two of them had been hired straight out of school onto Lifeline still made a few tongues wag and bitter comments fly.

As if she cared what the gossips said.

She cleaned the treadmill before dragging herself to the stretching mats. The noise in the oversized arena was a lovely distraction from the throbbing lactic acid in her limbs. One of the reasons she enjoyed using the local gym instead of the weight room at the Lifeline building or the school.

She enjoyed her job, but didn't need to live in her teammates' pockets 24/7.

Once again Devon came into view, and she debated throwing something at him. The one person she wouldn't mind getting away from, and yet he constantly showed up. Damn him for being her tagalong shadow.

Probably did it to piss her off.

"Alisha."

She scrambled to her feet, pulling her blonde hair back tighter into her ponytail in prep for hitting the weight room floor. The three guys headed in her direction might know her name, but she wasn't sure who they were. "You looking for me?"

The two slightly behind their leader smirked and made some low comments, and Alisha's heart fell.

Oh goody. Another muscle-bound Neanderthal looking to impress her. The signs were everywhere as the one in front swaggered his way into her personal space. "I hear you're pretty good at climbing things."

"You heard right." She tilted her head back to maintain eye contact, refusing to look away while he took a leisurely gawk at her body. It was like clockwork, in a way. The scum always came out this time of year as new people filled the resort town in prep for the seasonal winter work.

This? This was the reason working out at the public gym

wasn't fun. What was it with guys thinking she'd make a good trophy?

Mr. Annoying leered. "You want to have something of substance to climb?"

Good grief. This one was stupider than usual. Alisha's watch went off, reminding her she had two hours to make it to her staff meeting. "You know, it's been fun and all, but I really have things I need to do. So, if you'll excuse me."

She shifted her body to one side, but he leaned with her, blocking her path. "I was thinking we could get together. I want to find some of the tougher climbing routes in the area."

"Buy a book." Of all the things she hated, guys who acted as if they had some kind of privileged right to access her time and knowledge pissed her off the most.

He didn't take the hint, remaining in her path. "You're not being very friendly."

Fuck. This.

She glanced up to make sure she had the ceiling height to play with overhead. Other than that, Alisha didn't bother to see who was around. No way would any of the locals condemn her for what she was about to do. She bent her knees slightly to get some momentum, grabbed a handful of his shirt material and leapt upward.

He swore, scrambling backward as she basically walked over him. One foot landed on his thigh, one somewhere in his groin area—she didn't worry about exact placement. She pushed her hands down on his head to get the final height she needed to place one foot on his shoulder and dive for the chin-up bar Devon had been using moments earlier. A gentle swing turned her momentum and she landed on the path between the stretching area and the exercise machines, now on the opposite side of the guy who'd gotten in her way.

The asshole cursed at her, but she didn't care, simply strode forward like he wasn't there.

Devon eyed her from where he'd been holding up the wall, sipping from his water bottle as if watching a circus performance. He straightened to vertical, clapping softly as he gestured her into the main weight room.

"Having a good day, Alisha?"

"Bloody idiot." Wrapping her fingers around a set of barbells and heading for the mirrors gave her a physical outlet for her frustration.

Devon chuckled. "Him or me?"

She paused for a moment. If Devon was going to hang around and drive her crazy with unanswerable longings, maybe he could actually help her for once. She looked into his laughing eyes. "Do me a favour and keep him from bothering me?"

Devon raised a brow.

She paused, "Please?"

"This your boyfriend?"

Alisha tensed as she realized the brute squad had moved in behind Devon. Only he didn't seem concerned. He winked at her, in fact, before he turned to face the jerk who'd interrupted her.

Devon checked out the three men. "I'm her friend."

The ass in front shifted his weight. "So, you're gonna keep me from bothering her?"

The last thing she expected was for Devon to burst out laughing. Full-out laughing. When he stopped, he was still shaking his head.

"You think this is funny?" The asshole stepped in closer.

"You have no idea how hysterical it is." Devon moved aside, opening a path to Alisha. "You want to mess with her, you go right ahead. I have paramedics on speed dial. I'll deal with your two friends if need be. She doesn't need my help."

Whoa. That was a vote of confidence she'd never expected to hear from Devon. Ever.

It was enough to make her grin.

Maybe she looked scarier than she thought, because Mr. Annoying faded away, his buddies with him.

"That simple, huh?" Alisha caught Devon by the arm and

squeezed. "Wish they'd gone away the first time I told them to."

"Yeah." He glanced at his watch. "Finish your workout. We have a meeting to make."

He turned his back, once again becoming a barrier between her and the rest of the room. For a moment she stood motionless, wondering at the compliment Devon had paid her.

Wondering why exactly he was there, *again*, underfoot.

She sat and struggled to focus on the motions of her arm workout. It was far too tempting to use the mirrors to track the location of Devon and the creep she'd crawled on instead of checking her form on each lift.

Maybe her response to the newcomer had been, well, over the top, but she was tired of having to fight for every damn inch of respect she got. You'd think it would get easier over time, acting as if she didn't care. Pulling on a fuck-it-all attitude like armor.

She loved her job with something close to obsession. Why people couldn't recognize that and respect her for it was beyond her understanding.

The noise calmed as athletes settled back into their routines. The newcomers vanished, and Devon took an unobtrusive spot at the edge of her peripheral vision.

Alisha put her irritation aside and focused on her body. On making it strong enough to handle anything tossed her way.

If only she could train her heart and soul as easily.

Devon watched.

He'd been watching forever, it seemed.

Across the room from him, Alisha sipped from an oversized water bottle as she visited with the Lifeline pilot, Erin Tate. Alisha looked like a tiny blonde doll beside the powerfully built black woman, but he knew they were both forces of nature, and that made Devon smile more than the disparity in their sizes.

The team winch man, Anders, lay sprawled over two-thirds of the couch discussing the latest mountain film he'd seen with Xavier and Tripp, their paramedic and avalanche specialist, respectively. The three guys were about as far apart in physical appearance as possible, but together they were a hell of a team.

Together they saved lives.

Whatever things made them stand apart didn't matter to Devon, as long as they worked together when it counted.

The door opened and their boss entered the room. Marcus Landers was a legend in his own way. Not that Devon would ever say that to the man—Marcus would tie him up and leave him dangling from a rope for mentioning how much he'd inspired Devon early in his career. And working for the man?

His level of hero worship at first was a trifle embarrassing to remember. Only Devon had put that reverence into what he considered good use. He'd joined Lifeline and committed to making a difference.

Marcus glanced around the room. "Damn. You're all here."

"Ha." Erin raised her middle finger in salute. "You're late. We should make *you* do circuits of the training field to make up for keeping us waiting."

Marcus grinned. The man was notorious for his creative training methods. And his creative punishments. "Just keeping you all at the top of your game."

"You enjoy it too much," Tripp pointed out. "We know better than to be late without a note from the hospital or visible stitches."

Everyone shuffled into position around the massive boardroom table. Alisha curled herself in a chair across from Devon, ignoring him and speaking to Marcus. "This must be an important meeting. You didn't bring us any Tim Horton doughnuts."

"Doughnuts before lunch? Ugh." Erin leaned forward and picked up the roll of paper Marcus had dropped on the table. "But you brought us a treasure map."

Marcus folded himself into the chair at the head of the table. "Treasure beyond your wildest dreams, Erin."

She raised a brow. "I can dream pretty big."

"Hey," Anders interrupted. "Before you get started on the official part of the meeting, what's happening at the Banff training school? I bumped into your brother the other day, and he was grinning far too hard."

"Probably still gloating over having Becki James as a head coordinator," Devon said.

Marcus's smile deepened at the mention of his lover. "The school is damn lucky to have her on full time. The grin, though? He got a new sponsor who set the school up with a couple of scholarships plus enough cash to revamp the entire training centre."

Tripp whistled softly. "Sweet. Unnamed benefactor?"

"Some Toronto bigwig with more money than God. Said he wanted to help support *the ongoing development of excellence*."

"Should see if he wants to pour some cash this direction," Xavier suggested. "Because you know this place could use a little sprucing up, and we are excellent ourselves."

Across from Devon, Alisha had stiffened, watching the banter, but no longer participating. There was a tightness to her body that hadn't been there moments before.

Conversation continued around them about what they'd do to fix up the staff quarters of Lifeline if they had a spare million to play with. Devon ignored them and instead thought through all the reasons he could for Alisha's strange tension. She'd grown up in Toronto. That was the only connection he could come up with without doing more research.

Marcus tapped his hand on the table to get their attention. "Okay, speculation about the Banff SAR school aside. I have news."

"Raises?" Erin teased.

"Actually, yes." Marcus waited until the hoots and hollering died down. "You're a horde of wild animals this morning. What the hell did you have for breakfast?"

"I don't know what she ate, but Alisha went climbing

over a gym rat." Tripp held his hands up in surprise as Alisha whirled on him in exasperation. "Well, you did, right?"

"How is it my business is all over this town in less than an hour?" She glared across the table at Devon.

He hated how quickly she looked at him to be the cause of her troubles. He shook his head. "Don't blame me. I have better things to do than gossip about your choice of workout equipment."

"Nah, it wasn't Devon." Tripp held up his phone and showed Alisha the screen. Her face grew red as she stared.

Devon grabbed Tripp's wrist and pulled the phone to himself to look. Someone had taken a picture of Alisha and Photoshopped it so she appeared to be climbing over King Kong.

"Enough." Marcus shook his head. "Bunch of children, all of you. You want the news, or should I take you to the nearest playground for a while?"

Only, his grin remained firmly in place. Marcus knew the truth. The teasing and joking—it was all part of dealing with the stress of life-and-death decisions. They played hard, they worked even harder.

Marcus looked them over one by one as he spoke. "It's been a good summer, guys. I'm proud of you and the way you've operated. There have been a couple of nasty situations we had to deal with, and you pulled together and made it happen. Thank you."

Goofing aside, Tripp relaxed back in his chair, pride on his face. "Did you hear back from that rescue we did up at Takkakaw Falls? Did the dad pull through?"

"He did." Marcus gestured down the table. "And that's what I mean about good work. That man would be dead without you. All of you, working together. The family would have lost their dad, a woman her husband."

"It's what we signed up to do." Xavier shrugged.

"It's what we love to do," Alisha corrected.

"And it makes a difference. Don't ever forget it. You might have won awards last year. This year, you quietly did your job, and got it done. So again, thank you."

"Easier without the media in our bloody faces all the time, anyway," Erin muttered. She focused on the roll, giving it a poke. "I take it your secret news has something to do with this?"

Devon agreed. Curiosity was eating at him. "Enough cheerleading, Marcus. I want to see what's on the roll."

Marcus gestured. "Go for it."

Eager hands reached forward and unrolled the paper, securing the edges in place.

"A map of western Canada?" Alisha tilted her head. "Oh, cool. You've marked the locations of our rescues."

Everyone leaned in then, pointing to markers and commenting on the toughest parts of the rescue they remembered, or the most memorable.

"This is like some kind of scrapbook, Marcus." Erin eyed him. "Who knew you had it in you?"

He grinned. "Becki's idea."

"Go, Becki." Alisha dragged a finger over the mountain range to the east of Banff. "It's an awesome idea."

"And, what's more exciting? We're going to have markers in a much wider range over the coming months and years. This is my news." Marcus leaned over the table and laid his forearms on a section of the map, his prosthetic left hand on the divider line between Saskatchewan and Alberta, his right arm down the center of British Columbia. "This, to date, has been our corridor. Now?"

He opened his arms wider and settled his right hand off the coast of Vancouver Island.

"Holy shit." Erin leaned forward. "We're taking over coastal duties as well?"

"Pacific rescues have been added to our list. With cutbacks to the government, we're now on call for any extreme situation between here and Port Tofino. As far north as needed."

A thrill of excitement shot through Devon. "Does this mean I get to break out the scuba suit a bit more often?"

Marcus nodded. "Probably in coordination with naval SAR, but yes. Your reputation as a guppy is now official."

The grin stretching his cheeks felt awesome. Devon glanced at his teammates, pleased to see the same thrill on their faces that he felt at the news.

Erin waved a hand in Marcus's direction. "Does this mean you're getting me a bigger, better chopper? Because those are some long-ass hauls you're talking about."

Marcus tossed her an envelope. "Try a man in every port. You'll have a chopper on the island to access—we're adding a plane to the team here in Banff. And yes"—he caught her with her mouth still open—"you get a bigger bird to base here."

Erin danced in her chair as she pulled out a manual and paperwork.

Tripp and Xavier were arguing about which one of them would get to drop from the new chopper first. Devon laughed, then looked across at Alisha to see what her response was.

She stared at the map, a smile pasted on her face that was so fake he could have peeled it off and put it on the shelf. "Alisha?"

She blinked at him before shaking off the cloud. "You and your scuba suit. I thought you'd gotten over that fixation the time you got stuck in the kayak."

He laughed. "That was five years ago, and say what you will, it was a blast."

She raised a brow. "Oh, so much fun as we hauled the entire kayak out of the pool on a winch system. I think I still have the newspaper report. The one with you as front-page news."

"Hey, when you got it, flaunt it. *Banff Crag and Canyon* needed my extraordinary good looks to peak sales that week."

"So giving." Alisha made a face at him as she rose to her feet, taking her empty glass with her. "Marcus, I need a refill."

Their boss waved her off, busy arguing with Erin about exactly what upgrades the pilot was allowed to get on the larger, brighter, faster helicopter.

Devon . . .

He watched.

Like he always watched, especially Alisha.

In the last five minutes something had gone wrong. The tension in her body as she'd walked away? The lack of gushing at Marcus's big news? That wasn't the Alisha he'd been obsessing over for the past five years.

She should have been vibrating in her seat, asking a million questions. Usually her reactions would have made him crazy with need as she poked and teased in what he'd come to consider the longest foreplay session in the fucking universe.

Walking away quietly? Something was beyond wrong. All the little clues he'd been putting together over the past months were there, gathered in a heap. Now he had to find a way to sort them out. Make them into sense so he could know what the hell was wrong with Alisha.

So he could fix it.

She'd shot him down once, a long time ago. Probably didn't even remember that she'd told him to grow up and get a life. To stop goofing around and wasting his opportunities.

He'd done that, so well, in fact, that his life had changed, and whether she was ready for it or not, he was more than ready for her.

He was going to find out what had put that fear behind her eyes. Find out, and help her deal with it.

No turning back.

LOVE
ROMANCE
NOVELS?

For news on all your favorite romance authors,
sneak peeks into the newest releases, book
giveaways, and much more—

"Like" Love Always on Facebook!
 LoveAlwaysBooks

Discover Romance

berkleyjoveauthors.com

See what's coming up next from your
favorite romance authors and explore all
the latest Berkley, Jove, and Sensation
selections.

See what's new

~

Find author appearances

~

Win fantastic prizes

~

Get reading recommendations

~

Chat with authors and other fans

~

Read interviews with authors you love

M14G0610